ReSCued

RESCUED

JERRY B. JENKINS
TIM LaHAYE
with CHRIS FABRY

TYNDALE HOUSE PUBLISHERS, INC.
WHEATON, ILLINOIS

Visit Tyndale's exciting Web site at www.tyndale.com

Discover the latest Left Behind news at www.leftbehind.com

Rescued is a special edition compilation of the following Left Behind: The Kids titles:

#13: The Showdown copyright © 2001 by Jerry B. Jenkins and Tim LaHaye. All rights reserved.

#14: Judgment Day copyright © 2001 by Jerry B. Jenkins and Tim LaHaye. All rights reserved.

#15: Battling the Commander copyright © 2001 by Jerry B. Jenkins and Tim LaHaye. All rights reserved.

#16: Fire from Heaven copyright © 2001 by Jerry B. Jenkins and Tim LaHaye. All rights reserved.

Cover photo copyright © by Digital Vision. All rights reserved.

Left Behind is a registered trademark of Tyndale House Publishers, Inc.

Published in association with the literary agency of Alive Communications, Inc., 7680 Goddard Street, Suite 200, Colorado Springs, CO 80920.

Scripture quotations are taken from the *Holy Bible,* New Living Translation, copyright © 1996. Used by permission of Tyndale House Publishers, Inc., Wheaton, Illinois 60189. All rights reserved.

Some Scripture taken from the New King James Version. Copyright © 1979, 1980, 1982 by Thomas Nelson, Inc. Used by permission. All rights reserved.

Designed by Jenny Swanson

Library of Congress Cataloging-in-Publication Data

Jenkins, Jerry B.
   Rescued / Jerry B. Jenkins ; Tim LaHaye.
      p. cm — (Left behind—the kids) #4 Vol. 13-16
Special ed. compilation of four works, previously published separately in 2001.
      ISBN 0-8423-8354-9 (hc)
      1. Christian life—Juvenile fiction. [1. Christian life—Fiction.] I. LaHaye, Tim F. II. Title.
PZ7.J4138 Re 2004
[Fic]—dc22   2003016696

Printed in the United States of America

08   07   06   05   04
9   8   7   6   5   4   3   2   1

JUDD clung to a steel railing as the motorcycle disappeared into the river. He tried to climb the side but knocked more concrete from the edge. If Judd didn't hang on, it meant certain death. He cried for help.

The shaking stopped. Then came a splattering in the woods. *Tick, tick, tick.* He wondered if this was another judgment of God. Then something hit his head. Raindrops, slowly, then pouring.

Judd slipped and nearly let go. The rain beat fiercely. A steel support lay between him and the river. He didn't want to hit that on the way down.

His strength was giving out.

Judd tried once more and found something firm with his feet. He was almost to safety when the slab gave way and tumbled into the water. He fell back, his hands barely grasping the railing. Judd closed his eyes and gritted his teeth, but he couldn't hold on.

As he let go, someone grabbed his arm.

The room felt ice-cold. Everywhere Vicki saw sheet-draped bodies on tables. A hand stuck out from the body in front of her. She willed herself to pull the sheet back. The face was chalky white.

Ryan.

Dead.

Vicki screamed as she awoke. Darrion and Vicki sat up in the small tent.

"What's wrong?" Darrion said.

Through the flap Vicki watched men carrying bodies. The earthquake was over. Fires dotted the campsite, casting an eerie glow.

"Nightmare," Vicki said. "Where's Shelly?"

"Somebody came and asked for volunteers," Darrion said. "Shelly said to let you sleep."

Vicki scurried out of the tent, still wearing the same tattered clothes from the morning.

"Where are you going?"

"I have to find Ryan."

Shelly raced toward them. "Good news," she said. "A lady says they've opened a shelter a few blocks from here. It's the closest one to your house, so Ryan might be there."

"Let's go," Vicki said.

"We have to wait till dawn," Shelly said. "They're shooting looters."

"I don't care," Vicki said. "I have to find him."

"We don't need another death," Shelly said. "Get some sleep and we'll find him in the morning."

Vicki dragged herself back to the tent and tried to sleep, but she kept seeing the white, chalky face in her dream.

Lionel turned the gun over beside him on the bed. The GC insignia was engraved on the barrel of the pistol. He had signed papers that made him a Global Community Morale Monitor. He felt proud, but at the same time, things didn't seem right.

"I thought you'd be asleep by now," Conrad said, sitting next to Lionel's bed.

"Looks like you're going to be my partner," Lionel said.

"Guess so."

"You don't seem too excited," Lionel said.

"I don't know what I'm supposed to feel," Conrad said. "Everything's changing so fast. And that stuff in your luggage has me spooked."

"What stuff?" Lionel said.

"The Bible and your journal," Conrad said. "I can't wait to get on the Internet and see if this rabbi guy will answer me."

"Maybe when we get to Chicago, we'll figure it out," Lionel said.

The man Judd had talked with on the mountain pulled him to safety. His forearm was huge, and he easily lifted Judd over the side.

"Let's get out of here before another aftershock," he yelled over the rain.

Back in the cave the man handed Judd a blanket and sat him near a fire. "We watched you from up here. You almost made it over."

"I should have waited," Judd said.

Judd was exhausted. The frightened-looking people in the cave were lucky the rocks hadn't fallen on them.

The man introduced himself as Tim Vetter. His wife was a small woman named Marlene. Tim introduced Judd then asked, "Why were you out here? Trying to get to Chicago?"

Judd wasn't sure what he should tell them. If they were somehow linked with the Global Community, he should keep quiet.

"I was traveling with a friend," Judd stammered. "He didn't make it."

"That wasn't your bike, was it?" Tim said.

"I borrowed it," Judd said.

The other men laughed. "There's not much difference between stealing and borrowing during an earthquake," one man said.

"Tell the truth," Tim said.

"I helped a guy out, and he told me to take it," Judd said.

Was God preparing Vicki to face the death of one of the Young Trib Force? She tried to shake the idea but couldn't.

The birds were out again the next morning, singing in

the few trees left standing. It seemed strange that all the sounds were perfect when the sights were so awful. She and her friends passed smoldering craters and collapsed buildings. Car taillights stuck out of the ground. Moaning and crying still came from the rubble.

The shelter was an apartment complex where workers had cleared plants and furniture from the atrium. Vicki told a guard holding a clipboard that she was looking for her brother. The guard showed them a list of names. On another sheet was a list of numbers for those who had not yet been identified. Some numbers were crossed out and had the word "deceased" written beside them.

Shelly pointed to a description. "This could be him."

A nurse led them to a storage room filled with beds. In the corner lay someone staring at the wall, a white bandage covering his head.

Vicki looked at Darrion and Shelly.

"You can do it, Vick," Shelly said.

"He can't talk," the nurse said.

Vicki approached warily. The face was covered except for holes for his eyes, nose, and mouth. His left arm was bandaged as well, and Vicki realized he had been badly burned.

"Ryan?" Vicki said.

The kid stared at the wall.

Vicki knelt beside him. "Ryan, it's Vicki," she said.

The boy shook his head. He motioned for pen and paper. "Not Ryan," he wrote.

Vicki sat staring at him.

"Go away," the boy wrote.

Vicki wiped away a tear. "I'm sorry you were hurt," she said.

Vicki asked the nurse if there was anywhere else Ryan could have been taken.

"A furniture store somehow made it through," the woman said. "A couple hundred survivors are there. More than we can handle."

———————————————

People stirred in the cave as Judd awoke. The men huddled around the fire. Tim motioned for Judd to come and eat.

Judd was sore and had scratches from skidding on the bridge. He ate hungrily.

"Some of us are going back to look for food," Tim said. "There might be a relief site set up by the Global Community."

Judd flinched. "I wouldn't be surprised."

"Will you come with us?" Tim said.

"Think I'll try to keep going," Judd said.

Tim scratched at the embers with a stick. "There's something you're not telling us," he said. "It may be none of our business. But when you share our food and shelter, I think we deserve to know what's up."

"You've been very kind," Judd said. "I owe you my life."

Judd wondered if this was why he hadn't been able to complete the jump. Maybe God wanted him to tell his story, despite the risk.

"My name is Judd Thompson," he began.

Lionel took tests and signed more papers in the morning. Though the earthquake had knocked out communication and travel, the Global Community rolled on. A GC doctor declared Lionel fit and ready to continue his classes. Conrad stopped by as the doctor left.

"I don't understand," he said. "Thousands are dead or dying, but the GC has everything set up and ready to go. It's like they expected this."

"That's not possible," Lionel said.

"What if it is? Maybe they were waiting for some kind of disaster to put their next plan in motion. That would explain why they're so hot to get us out of here and on the job."

Conrad showed Lionel his gun, standard issue for Morale Monitors. "Why do they trust kids our age with guns?"

"Maybe when they see how you shoot this afternoon at the range, they won't," Lionel said, smiling.

The girls wound through neighborhoods, taking shortcuts through what had been backyards. They climbed over huge mounds of dirt and rocks, then went around craters. Smoke from the still-burning meteors made them choke.

The furniture store was on the way to the Edens Expressway, a few minutes' drive away. But with downed utility poles, flattened buildings, pavement that had disappeared, and the girls on foot, it took much longer.

7

Shelly pointed to a neon sign on the ground. "My mom and I used to eat at that place," she said.

Vicki knew the furniture store. She had been there with her family. The sales staff had eyed them suspiciously, as if they knew she lived in a trailer and had neither the money nor the room for the bedroom set she wanted.

Only the roof of the building was visible. The rest had been swallowed whole. Rescue crews filed in and out, but there was no hurry. Everyone taken from the building was in a body bag.

"This could be a wild-goose chase," Shelly said. "What if he's not there?"

"We're gonna find him and take him home with us," Vicki said.

"How?" Shelly said. "What if he can't walk? We gonna carry him?"

"I'll find a way," Vicki said.

The furniture store was still standing, but there were no roads around it. Emergency vehicles pulled as close to the front as they could, then unloaded more injured.

"Most look pretty healthy," Vicki said. "Maybe Ryan's not that bad."

"We've got another problem," Darrion said.

Vicki gasped when she saw Global Community guards at the entrance. Only the injured and those with clearance cards were getting through.

The girls split up, then met again a few minutes later.

"The back is guarded too," Shelly said.

"The side doors are locked," Darrion said. "There's a

lot of smashed windows, but they're too high to crawl through."

"We'll have to get in another way," Vicki said, smearing mud on her forehead. She tore off a piece of her shirt.

"What are you doing?" Shelly said.

Vicki lay on the ground. "Carry me," she said. "And I expect some tears from you two!"

Shelly smiled. She grabbed Vicki's arms, and Darrion took her legs.

Vicki moaned. Shelly and Darrion began crying as they neared the store.

A Global Community guard stopped them at the entrance. "You can't bring her here."

"You have to help," Shelly said. "We have to get her to a doctor."

Darrion kept her back to the guard so he wouldn't recognize her. Shelly wept bitterly. "Please help us," she cried.

"All right," the guard said. "Put her down."

Vicki rolled her eyes and winked at them.

VICKI closed her eyes when the men carried her inside. She wailed when they sat her in a line of injured people. A Global Community staff worker took information. When she turned her back, Vicki quickly slipped out of line and down the hall. She ran up a flight of stairs.

What had been a showroom now held cots. People were sleeping, some badly wounded.

Vicki didn't want to risk talking with anyone, so she stayed out of the way. The doctors and nurses were so busy, no one seemed to notice her.

She looked at faces, read names on charts, and darted into a bathroom when a GC guard passed.

A woman in one of the stalls was crying. Vicki found a clipboard on a sink. At the top of the chart were numbers. Under "T-1" she spotted "Ryan Daley."

What's T-1?

The woman came out of the stall. Vicki washed her face, then quickly walked out.

As she hurried down a narrow corridor, she heard someone behind her, then felt a hand just above her elbow.

"You are under arrest."

Judd watched the group as he told his story. They didn't react strongly but seemed interested in what he thought of the disappearances. He told them what had happened to his family, about meeting Bruce Barnes, and about watching the videotape the former pastor had made.

"Before, I thought church was a stuffy place that didn't want you to have fun. They told you everything you weren't supposed to do. Now I see it as a place of life. God wanted me to know him. If anyone wants what I found, I can help you."

Tim looked at the other men and nodded. "We know what we have to do," he said.

The men dragged Judd to a corner of the cave. He struggled but couldn't overcome them. They tied his hands behind him.

"We were warned about people like you," one man said. "People like you are against Nicolae Carpathia. You're against the Enigma Babylon Faith."

"I didn't say anything about Carpathia," Judd said.

"You didn't have to," the man said.

Judd shook his head. His gut reaction about the people had been right.

"We're taking you back to town," Tim said. "We'll turn you over to the GC."

"For telling you about God?" Judd said.

"You must be running from something," Tim said, "or you wouldn't have taken such a chance. If you're innocent, the GC will let you go."

The group walked Judd down the hillside with his hands tied. He would soon be back in the hands of the enemy of his soul.

The men left Judd near the Enigma Babylon church building under the watch of Tim's wife, Marlene.

"We'll be back with food and water and the GC," Tim said.

A chill ran down Vicki's spine and she turned, thinking she would see a Global Community guard. But a wild-eyed young man with stringy hair, eyes darting, said, "Scared you, didn't I? You thought I was the police. Not supposed to be in here, are you?"

Vicki took a breath. "Do you always ask that many questions?"

The young man smiled, still looking away.

"What's your name?" Vicki said.

"Charlie, Charles, Chuck, Charlie." He spoke quickly, and his body seemed out of control.

"You scared me, all right," Vicki said. "You like scaring people?"

Charlie giggled. His teeth were crooked and discolored. "I like when they jump. I used to make my sister jump. Real high. She don't jump no more. Big shake got her."

"The earthquake?" Vicki said.

"Yeah, yeah," Charlie said. "Earthshake. Lotsa things got broken at our house. Big crash. Boom!"

Charlie screamed and laughed, and Vicki jumped.

"Be quiet," Vicki said.

Charlie put a finger to his lips. "Shh. Quiet."

"Are you a patient here?" Vicki said.

"No, my sister worked here. They had big TVs downstairs. Used to let me watch them. All busted now. Want to see 'em?"

Vicki shook her head. "I'm looking for a friend who might be here."

"Friend. I had a friend. His mom said I was strange, and he couldn't come over anymore."

"I'll be your friend," Vicki said. "I just need your help."

"I can help," Charlie said. "I can lift and carry stuff and hold doors open and SCARE PEOPLE!"

"Stop screaming," Vicki said. "There are sick people in here. Now I'm trying to find room T-1, or something like that."

Charlie squinted and squeezed his chin. "Is a *T* the letter that looks like a snake?"

"That's an *S*," Vicki said. She drew a *T* in the dust on a window.

"I know what a *T* looks like," Charlie giggled. "Come on."

He hopped along, taking big leaps with his right leg and dragging his left behind him. When Vicki finally caught him, he was out of breath and excited.

"Right here," Charlie said.

The sign above the door said Trauma 1.

Charlie opened the door slowly. "There's really sick people here. Better not be too loud."

Bright children's furniture lined the wall. Vicki passed cribs and strollers.

"Stay close," Vicki said.

Judd sat in the rubble of the Enigma Babylon church, now both hands and feet tied. He could tell the church had once been beautiful, but its stained glass windows lay in pieces. After all his work to escape, Judd was almost back in the hands of the Global Community. He had hoped the GC would find the van destroyed and assume he was dead.

Marlene Vetter paced, looking at Judd, then glancing away.

Judd rubbed his ankles together, trying to loosen the rope. The rope around his wrists was already loosening.

"How long have you lived here?" Judd said.

The woman looked like she had a secret. "I'm not supposed to talk to you."

"Why?" Judd said. "I'm dangerous?"

"What you say is dangerous," Marlene said. "Look where it got you."

"The things I say are true. I don't care where it gets me."

The more Judd talked, the more Marlene looked away. That gave Judd a chance to work free of the ropes. Finally Marlene said, "You really believe all those things?"

Judd spoke carefully. "The vanishings, the earthquake, the meteors, all that was predicted in the Bible."

Marlene shook her head. "I'm talking about God forgiving you without you doing anything but admitting what you did. I always thought if your good outweighed your bad that God, whoever he was, would eventually accept you."

"Is that what Enigma Babylon teaches?" Judd said.

Marlene sat and pulled her knees to her chest. "They say God is within us. We don't need to be 'saved' from anything but our own low self-esteem."

"What do you think?" Judd said. "Does that make sense?"

"I'm not sure anymore."

Judd kept working at the ropes.

Someone yelled for Charlie.

"Oh," he said, "I'll stay with you."

"No," Vicki said. "Go so they don't suspect anything. Promise you won't tell them about me."

"I promise," he said, scampering off giggling.

Vicki strained to see the patients in the darkened room. Several had died, and sheets covered them.

Vicki heard the familiar beeps of monitors scattered throughout the room. Finally, toward the end of one row, she saw Ryan. She rushed to him and ran a hand through his hair. It was caked with mud. His eyes were closed, and a bruise showed on his forehead.

Vicki's tears fell on Ryan's face. She hugged him, but he felt cold. She stepped back in horror. Vicki felt for a pulse.

Someone took Vicki by the shoulder. "What are you doing in here?" a woman said.

Marlene looked at Judd. "I've tried to believe like I should, but it doesn't work."

"You want me to go through it again?" Judd said.

Marlene nodded.

Judd explained that even though people are sinners, Jesus had died for them. "The only way to God is through Jesus, not through doing good things or believing in yourself. He created us. Sin separates us from God. To become his child, we have to be adopted into his family."

"But only if you're perfect?"

"I'm not perfect by a long shot," Judd said. "Ask my friends. But when God forgives you, Jesus lives in you. God doesn't see me and my faults. He sees Jesus."

"So I don't have to do anything?"

"You accept what God gives," Judd said.

Marlene stared off and shook her head. "Tim would kill me if he knew I talked to you."

Judd finally freed his hands from the rope.

"What you say sounds good," Marlene said, "but I don't know if I can trust you."

"Trust me," Judd said, showing her his hands. "I could free my legs and be out of here in seconds."

"Why don't you?"

"God's working on you," Judd said. "I can't leave you now."

Judd heard footsteps and hid his hands behind his back.

———————————

Vicki jumped back, turning to face the woman dressed in white.

"Charlie told me you were looking for a friend," the woman said sternly. "Is that true?"

"His name's Ryan Daley," Vicki said.

"Are you Vicki?"

"How did you know that?"

The woman pulled a piece of paper from her pocket. "He wrote this for you."

Vicki couldn't open the letter. "I have to know if he's alive," Vicki said.

"Not for long, I'm afraid," the nurse said. "He's in a coma."

Vicki bit her lip and wiped her eyes.

"Stay a while," the nurse said.

Vicki thanked her and sat on the floor. She unfolded the letter.

I'm writing this to you, Vicki, but I'm hoping you'll be in touch with Judd and Lionel as well.

First, I shouldn't have been surprised at what happened because this was everything Bruce said. The wrath of the Lamb and all. We can be glad God keeps his promises, I guess. The nurse said I should write to you. I never was a letter writer, but she thought it was a good idea.

You've been like a big sister to me. I never had one. Judd was a big brother, and Lionel was a good friend. I hope I wasn't too much of a pain to have around.

I guess there's a chance I could get up and walk out of here, but it doesn't look good. So I want to tell you all to hang in there. God didn't let us survive this long without there being a reason. No matter where you go or what happens, I want you to remember how much you mean to me. I can't thank you enough.

Maybe somebody else will come and take my place at your house or in the Young Trib Force. I hope they do. If you care for them half as much as you cared for me, they'll be really happy.

Promise me you'll take care of Phoenix. Tell Chaya and Shelly and Mark and John that I was thinking of them. I hope you all made it through the earthquake. I'll never forget you.

Love,
Ryan

Vicki lay her head on the floor and wept.

God, please don't let him die.

3

VICKI sat up, clutching Ryan's note. The nurse helped her stand and took her by the shoulders to a chair in the next room.

"It's my fault," Vicki said. "I told him to stay inside! He would have been OK if I hadn't insisted—"

"Ryan was smart," the nurse said.

"Was?"

"Is," the nurse said. "You're right. There's still a chance. But either way, this is not your fault. Last night Ryan tried to tell me something but couldn't find the words."

Vicki squinted. "What did he say?"

"Something about God, but he was out of his head by then. He really got to me. He's about the same age as my son."

"Charlie?"

"No, my son disappeared in the vanishings," the nurse said.

Vicki straightened. "I know what Ryan was trying to tell you."

Tim Vetter and the other men carried bags of supplies and blankets. Judd kept his hands behind him.

"Enough provisions for a few days," Tim said. "No GC yet."

"Just leave the stuff here and I'll keep an eye on it," Marlene said.

Tim pursed his lips. "The GC has a station on the south side. We'll take him with us. You stay with the supplies."

Tim untied Judd's feet and helped him stand. Judd kept his hands tight against his back. The other men were big and burly. Tim was the only one who could catch him if Judd ran.

Judd saw his chance at the corner. With the others behind him, he took off toward a mound of earth in the center of town. Tim was a few yards behind when Judd hit the embankment.

Judd scrambled up but slipped. Tim grabbed Judd's pant leg, and the others came lumbering. Judd kicked free and struggled to the top. Tim was close behind but slipping. The other men split into two groups, working their way around the pile.

Judd slid down the other side and raced toward a road by the river. He looked for a place to hide, but the quake had flattened houses and trees. He kept running.

"My son was a good boy," the nurse told Vicki as they walked the hallway between wards. "Never got into much trouble. Loved his video games. I was working the late shift the night it happened. It was crazy. We had pregnant women lose their unborn babies just before they were delivered. A friend of mine vanished from an operating room. It was awful.

"Then I came home to check on Chad. All that was left were his clothes. I blamed my husband at first. I guess that was wrong."

"What do you think happened?" Vicki said.

"I've read all the explanations," the nurse said. "An energy force, alien abduction, some kind of social cleansing. Whatever it was doesn't really matter. Chad's gone. When I saw Ryan, it made me think of him again."

"Did your son ever go to church?"

"As a matter of fact, he did. We went as a family only at Christmas and Easter. But Chad got involved in a youth group with one of his friends. They met during the week for some kind of study."

Vicki took a breath. "This is going to sound weird, but I know what really happened to your son," she said. Vicki told the nurse about meeting Ryan and how Pastor Bruce Barnes had shown them a videotape that explained the vanishings. Vicki knew then that what her parents had tried to tell her had come true.

"My mom and dad tried to get me to listen," Vicki said. "They told me Jesus Christ was going to come back

23

for his true followers. When I found their clothes, I knew I had been left behind.

"Your son was a Christian," Vicki said. "A true believer."

The nurse turned away as Charlie entered the room.

"I'm sorry that boy in there made you sad," Charlie said to Vicki.

"It's OK; he's a friend of mine," Vicki said.

The nurse gave a wary glance to Vicki and said, "I'll get in trouble if you're found in here. You need to go."

"But I want to tell you more about this," Vicki said. "And I don't want to leave Ryan."

"Come back late tonight," the nurse said. "I'm back here around ten. I'll meet you at the back door and let you in."

"I'll bring a friend," Vicki said.

Judd doubled back on his pursuers. He crouched behind the rubble of a house while the men passed. Several others had joined the search.

"I know where some GC guards are," one of them said.

"Go find them!" Tim yelled.

When the men were a safe distance past, Judd took off. He climbed the huge mound of earth, then stopped and peered around the corner to see if Marlene was alone.

"What are you doing here?" Marlene said as Judd rushed to her.

"They'll never think of looking for me here," Judd said, out of breath.

Marlene motioned Judd to the end of the street so they could watch for the others. "You should get out of here," she said. "I don't know what they'll do to you if they catch you. But now they know something's up."

"I'm OK," Judd said. "I couldn't leave and not finish our discussion."

Marlene took a breath. "I'm interested in what you're talking about," she said, "but I can't believe like you. It's too easy. If you're right, I basically don't have to do anything."

"You got it," Judd said. "You just accept what God's done."

"I'd feel a lot better if you told me I had to do something," Marlene said.

"That's the point," Judd said. "We're helpless. That's why Jesus lived a perfect life and died for us."

Marlene stared off. "Why would God . . . ?"

"In the Bible it says God is love," Judd said. "God doesn't want anyone to die without knowing him. But it's up to you."

Marlene got a wild look on her face. "If what you're saying is true, that changes everything," she said. "The Enigma Babylon Faith is a big lie."

"Exactly," Judd said. "That's why I want you to—"

Marlene jumped back from the corner. "Here they come!"

"I'm not leaving until you—"

"You have to," she said.

"All right, but ask God to forgive you," Judd said. "Tell him you're sorry. Tell him you accept his gift."

"Go!"

"Will you do it?" Judd said.

"I'll think about it."

Judd peeked around the corner. Tim and the others moved slowly toward them, no doubt dejected that Judd had escaped. Beside them was a GC guard.

Judd picked up the ropes he had been tied with and tied Marlene's hands and feet. He tied a rag tightly over her mouth.

"I overpowered you," Judd said. "I stole food, and you couldn't scream because I put this in your mouth. Got it?"

Marlene nodded and jerked her head, telling him to leave.

"God, thank you for letting me talk with Marlene," Judd prayed out loud. "I pray she will become your child. Keep her safe, and may she be able to tell others about you in the days ahead."

Judd heard footsteps. He ran the other way and grabbed some bread from the stash of provisions. He waited until the group turned the corner, then ducked into a brick-strewn alley.

Judd figured they had told the GC his identity, but with communication lines down, he doubted they would know he was supposed to be in a reeducation camp. They would expect him to cross the river and head toward Chicago. Instead, Judd ran the other way. Away from his home. Away from his friends.

The nurse showed Vicki the rear entrance that wasn't guarded by the GC. Vicki promised she would return late that night. "I want to talk to you more about what Ryan said," Vicki said.

"Just go," the nurse said.

Vicki circled the building and found Darrion and Shelly still waiting.

"What happened?" Shelly said.

Vicki tried to be strong, but she broke down as she told them about Ryan. Darrion took the news hard.

"What are we going to do now?" Darrion said.

"I'm coming back tonight to check on him," Vicki said.

"I'm in," Shelly said.

Darrion shook her head. "My mom. I've waited too long. I have to find her, and—"

"Don't do this," Shelly said. "The GC will be all over you. Your face has been plastered all over the news."

"I can wear a disguise," Darrion said.

"They'll lock you up like they did your mother," Shelly said.

"I don't care! She'd do the same for me. I have to find her."

Vicki led the girls back the way they came.

Shelly tried to talk Darrion out of leaving. "We need to stick together," she said. "If you leave, that's just another person we'll have to find. And if the GC gets you, you'll wind up like Judd."

Vicki looked hard at Shelly.

"Sorry," Shelly said. "I just don't want to lose anyone else."

"This is my mother," Darrion said. She looked away. "I can't expect you to understand."

"Why? Because my mom was trailer trash? Because I know she's dead?"

"I didn't mean it that way," Darrion said.

"Enough," Vicki said. "Shel, you're right, we ought to stick together. But Darrion needs to find her mom too."

"I'm really sorry about Ryan," Darrion said. "I wish I could do something to help."

Vicki said she understood. "You and Shelly should leave this afternoon and go—"

"No way," Shelly said.

"I can do this myself," Darrion said.

"I know you can," Vicki said. "That's not the point. I'll go back tonight and monitor Ryan. You've got a few hours of daylight left to find your mom. If you get into trouble, Shelly can help."

Darrion frowned and looked at Shelly. "I didn't mean to knock your mom."

Shelly looked away.

"Would you come with me?"

"I think it's the best idea, Shel," Vicki said.

Shelly sighed. "I guess if that's what Vick thinks I should do."

"We're almost to the end of the expressway," Darrion said. "The GC holding place was a few miles from here."

"I know where it is," Shelly said. "There's no way we can make it there and back before nightfall."

"Find a shelter nearby and stay till morning," Vicki said. "I'll meet you back at the tent tomorrow afternoon."

"Wait," Shelly said. "How are you going to get to Ryan after curfew? If you're out, you'll get shot."

"I've got a plan," Vicki said.

Judd ran south along the interstate, backtracking until he came to the bridge where he had helped the motorcycle rider, Pete. He hopped on the back of a four-wheel drive pickup that was transporting more bodies to the morgue.

When they arrived, Judd was surprised to see the injured lying outside on the ground. "Did they spend the night out here?" Judd asked a volunteer.

"The nearest hospital's flat," the man said. "Other buildings aren't safe. You got a better idea?"

Judd located a list of injured and looked for Pete's name. He was afraid the man had died but was relieved when he flipped the page over. Pete's name was on the back.

Judd didn't want to upset the man, but he knew he had to tell him the bad news about Pete's girlfriend. Judd found him sitting up and groggy.

"Didn't expect to see you for a long time," Pete said. "Couldn't make it to Chicago?"

"Ran into a little problem and had to leave your bike at the bottom of the river; sorry, man. How are you?"

"Doc says I have some temporary nerve damage," Pete said. "I feel pretty tingly right now, but I'm OK. It'll take more than that to do me in. You find my place?"

"Yeah," Judd said. "You left your bike outside the shed. It was a good thing, because everything else was destroyed."

Pete grimaced. "Same for the house?"

"I'm afraid so," Judd said.

Judd knelt beside the big man. The day before Judd had explained the forgiveness offered in Christ, and Pete had prayed. Pete's one concern was that his girlfriend hear what Judd had said.

"I managed to get inside the house," Judd said. "I couldn't find your friend for a long time and thought she might have gotten out. Then . . ."

"Oh, no," Pete said.

"She was in the laundry room when the quake hit. She didn't suffer."

Pete shook his head and wept. Judd felt embarrassed seeing such a big man cry. Judd put his hand on Pete's shoulder.

"What you said yesterday changed me," Pete said. "It really did. All I could think about was telling Rosie. Now she's gone."

Night fell. Pete cried. Judd slept on the ground beside him.

4

VICKI waited until dark, then made her way back to the hospital. She encountered Global Community guards and police several times. She dropped to the ground and waited until they passed.

Vicki crouched low when she came near the furniture store. Huge spotlights lit the receiving area. Vicki stole to the back and waited for the nurse. There was no way she was getting inside the front of the building with what she had planned. Finally, the back door opened.

"You have to come quickly," the nurse said.

"Is Ryan still alive?"

"Yes. Barely."

"You go ahead," Vicki said. "I don't want to get you in trouble."

The nurse left the door ajar. Vicki moved into the shadows, grabbed Phoenix's collar, and walked him inside. The dog panted and followed obediently.

"You have to be really quiet," Vicki said, hoping Phoenix would understand.

Vicki led Phoenix up the back stairs to the third floor. She reached for the door but heard footsteps and scampered back down the steps. A GC guard opened the door. The beam of the flashlight narrowly missed her. After a few moments, the man closed the door and walked away. Vicki headed for Ryan's room.

Phoenix shook, as if he were scared of the makeshift hospital. The strong medicine smell and all the bodies seemed to spook him. When he reached Ryan's side, the dog sniffed at the boy and licked his hand.

"I brought your best friend," Vicki whispered in Ryan's ear.

Phoenix put his paws on the bed and licked Ryan's face.

"What in the world?" the nurse said as she walked into the room. "Get that animal out of here! I could lose my job!"

"You don't understand," Vicki pleaded. "This is his best friend. They've been together—"

Vicki stopped when she saw the look on the nurse's face. The nurse pointed to the bed.

Ryan's hand twitched, and his eyes fluttered. Vicki's heart raced as she watched.

"Ryan, it's me, Vicki!"

Ryan tried to open his eyes but couldn't.

"It's OK," Vicki said. "I'll do the talking."

Vicki told Ryan where he was and that he had been hurt in the earthquake. Ryan nodded, and with each sentence he seemed to stir a little more.

Phoenix wagged his tail and whimpered.

"Lamb," Ryan finally said.

"That's right," Vicki said, "the wrath of the Lamb!"

"Water," Ryan said with a raspy voice.

Vicki grabbed a plastic pitcher and poured him a glass. Ryan's lips were chapped. She put the cup to his lips and helped him drink slowly.

"How did you find me?" Ryan said.

Vicki wiped away a tear. She was so overjoyed to talk with Ryan she choked as she spoke. "I had some help," was all she could say.

"What about the others?"

"Darrion and Shelly are OK. Judd was still in GC custody when the quake hit."

"Lionel?"

"Haven't heard," Vicki said.

Ryan looked toward his nightstand. "The letter."

"I got it," Vicki said. "Now listen to me. You're going to be OK. You'll pull out of this."

"No," Ryan said. He reached out and weakly patted Phoenix on the head. The dog licked him. Ryan's hand fell to the bed. "I'm ready."

"I know you are," Vicki said. "You have to get better; then we'll get you out of here."

Ryan shook his head. "Going home."

Vicki took his hand. "I can't move you right now or I would, you know that," she said.

Ryan smiled. "You don't get it."

"What don't I get?"

Ryan tried to raise his arm. He pointed a finger to the ceiling. Vicki bent closer as he said, "Home in heaven."

Vicki felt a chill go through her. "No. You've been through a lot, but you're still here. There's a lot the doctors can do."

He tried to sit up but couldn't. "When I went to the hospital the day of the bombings, Bruce couldn't talk much," Ryan said. "I think he knew he was going to die."

"That was different. We've lost too much as it is. You can't go."

"Friends," Ryan said. "They're waiting. I want to see Bruce. Raymie. Mrs. Steele."

"You'll get to see them soon enough," Vicki said. "You have to hang on."

The nurse touched Vicki's shoulder. "Can I talk to you a minute?" she said.

"I'll be right back," Vicki said to Ryan.

"As a nurse, you see things," the woman whispered. "I think he hung on because he thought you'd come. He's doing this for you."

"Then why won't he fight it?" Vicki said. "He can't die. I won't let him."

"It's not your fight," the nurse said. "You talked about believing in God. You must think Ryan's going to a better place."

"Yes, but not now. Not yet."

The nurse took Vicki's face in her hands. "He needs you to be strong. He needs you to tell him you'll be OK."

Vicki wiped her tears and nodded. "I just don't know if I will be."

Vicki returned to Ryan. His eyes were closed, his face pale. His hair was a mess. White beads formed at the corner of his mouth. Suddenly, Ryan's eyes fluttered. His face flushed with color. He smiled.

"They're coming," Ryan said.

"Who's coming?" Vicki said. "Who is it?"

Ryan opened his eyes and stared at Vicki. "I have to go now," he said. "I'm sorry."

Vicki wanted to scream. She wanted to run from the room. But she knew God had allowed her to be with Ryan in the final moments of his life. She had to think of Ryan, not herself. But it was so hard. She couldn't imagine what life would be like without him.

"I'll be OK," Vicki said.

"You have to stay safe," Ryan said. "Who will take care of Phoenix?"

Vicki smiled. "Hey, I was the one who talked Judd into letting you keep him."

Ryan closed his eyes again. "Can you hear them?" he said.

"Who?" Vicki said, but Ryan didn't answer.

Vicki buried her head in her hands. She and Ryan had been through so many scrapes together.

The nurse touched her shoulder. "It's time," she said.

Vicki summoned all her strength and took her friend's hand. "Ryan," she whispered, "you've been like a little brother to me. And you've been so brave."

Ryan smiled. A tear escaped one eye and rolled the length of his cheek.

"You have to trust me on this, OK?"

Ryan squeezed her hand.

"I don't want you to go. I want you to live and see the

Glorious Appearing of Jesus like Bruce talked about. But if you have to go now, I understand. It won't be the same without you."

Vicki turned and wiped her eyes.

"I feel like I'm letting you down," Ryan said.

"No," Vicki said, "don't ever think that. You've never let me down."

"You'll be OK?" Ryan said.

"Yeah. But you have to do me a favor."

"Anything."

Vicki closed her eyes and put her head next to Ryan's. "When you get home, will you tell Bruce I said hello?"

Ryan raised his head a few inches and opened his eyes. He looked straight at Vicki. "I'll tell him you were the best big sister anybody ever had."

He smiled again, then rested his head on the pillow and closed his eyes.

"So don't worry, OK?" Vicki said. "I'll take care of Phoenix. He'll take care of me."

A few minutes passed. Vicki watched as Ryan faded. His breathing became erratic. Phoenix whimpered.

Vicki came close to Ryan and whispered in his ear, "I love you."

"Love you," Ryan whispered.

Then his chest fell with a final breath, and he was gone.

Judd heard someone scream and awoke. Pete thrashed about yelling his girlfriend's name. Judd subdued the big man.

"Too late," the man cried. "We were too late to save Rosie."

"Just hold still," Judd said. Then he realized the man was moving his lower body.

"Pete," Judd said, "your legs!"

Pete looked startled, then gingerly sat up. "Help me," he said.

Judd helped him stand, wobbly at first, then Pete stood straight. "Look at me,"
he said. "Bet you didn't know I was this tall."

In a few minutes, Pete was walking. A few patients roused and clapped softly.

"You've got a little limp," Judd said.

"I'll take it," Pete said. "Come on, let's get out of here."

"You can't just walk away," Judd said.

"Watch me," Pete said. "I have work to do."

Vicki sat with Ryan a few minutes longer. The nurse felt for his pulse, then said, "He's gone." She knelt in front of Vicki and put a hand on her shoulder.

"You did a good thing here today. You made his last moments easier. I'm glad you came."

Vicki cried. She felt an emptiness she'd never felt before. When she lost her parents and family, she hadn't been able to say good-bye. She woke up the next morning, and they were gone. But this was different. Ryan's body was right next to her. She knew he wasn't there any longer, and her heart ached.

"What happens now?" Vicki said.

"With so many bodies, they aren't doing many burials. A lot of them are being burned."

"I don't want that for him."

"There's no way around it."

"Can you give me a few hours?" Vicki said. "I could find someone to help me carry him."

"It's out of the question. As soon as I report him deceased, they'll take him away."

"Can't you hold off till morning?" Vicki said.

"I don't know—"

"Please," Vicki said.

"I can try," the nurse said.

Phoenix jumped onto Ryan's bed and whimpered.

"Get down!" the nurse said.

Phoenix barked. A few patients stirred.

"You have to get him out of here!"

Phoenix barked again. Vicki grabbed him by the collar and headed for the stairs. She heard someone running up and looked through the window.

"GC guard!" Vicki said.

"In here!"

Vicki ducked into a closet with Phoenix as the door to the stairwell opened. Phoenix panted. Vicki clamped his mouth shut. She heard the muffled sounds of the guard and the nurse.

"I heard a dog bark," the guard said.

"Up here?" the nurse said. "You've gotta be kidding."

Another bark. Phoenix perked up his ears.

The guard shouted something. A door closed. A moment later, the nurse ushered Vicki and Phoenix out. Charlie was standing by the exit sign.

"I got chewed out, chewed out good," Charlie said with a grin. "I was watchin' you guys. Hope that was OK."

The nurse frowned. "I have to go on rounds. Get out fast before they find you."

"Yes, ma'am," Vicki said.

"I can do really good dog sounds," Charlie said. "I saw the guy come looking for your dog, so I made it sound like him, and the guy thought I was the dog. Pretty neat, huh?"

"Yeah," Vicki said, heading for the door.

"I can do a squirrel too. You wanna hear?"

"Not right now," Vicki said.

Charlie came close and whispered, "I can help you."

"You can help me do what?"

"Carry your friend," Charlie said. "I'm a real good carrier. One time I helped my sister carry a piano all the way from her apartment—"

"You want to help me carry Ryan?"

"Carry Ryan," Charlie repeated. "Carry him anywhere you want. Actually, I didn't carry the piano from her apartment, I dragged it—"

"OK," Vicki said, "I'd like your help, but we have to hurry."

———————————

Pete led Judd out of the camp. They found a man asleep in his truck, and Pete convinced him to give them a ride.

A few minutes later, Judd and Pete were in front of Pete's demolished house.

"We should wait until morning," Judd said.

"I can't let her stay in there another minute," Pete said.

Pete found an old lantern, and the two tore wood from the house until they reached Rosie's body. The sun was nearly up when Pete carefully carried her from the rubble. He dug a grave by the creek that passed his property and gently placed her in the ground.

"I don't know what to say," Pete said. "Shouldn't we read something or pray?"

"Whatever's in your heart," Judd said.

Pete sighed and bowed his head. He looked like a mountain. "God, I don't think Rosie knew about you. I'd give anything to talk to her now.

"I know I don't deserve you forgiving me after all I've done, but I believe you have. Help me to live right and follow you and make you proud. Thank you for my new friend. Amen."

Pete looked at Judd. "How was that?"

"Straight from the heart," Judd said. "You can't get better than that."

Pete threw his shovel at the demolished shed. "Now we gotta get you back to Chicago."

Vicki led Phoenix out. Charlie carried Ryan's lifeless body. As they slipped into the night, Charlie huffed and puffed. Vicki could tell it wasn't going to be an easy trip.

40

They rested as often as Charlie needed. At times, Vicki helped, but mostly Charlie carried Ryan alone.

A flood of memories came over her as they walked. Ryan had grown taller since they first met. She remembered their trips searching for Bibles. She had been there when Ryan found Phoenix. She had seen Ryan stand at Bruce's memorial service and say he was willing to give his life for the sake of the gospel.

By morning, they were near Vicki's house. Construction crews were busy clearing rubble and collapsed roadways. Vicki took Charlie near the spot where New Hope Village Church once stood.

While Charlie scampered off to find a shovel, Vicki pawed through the loose stones that led to Ryan's secret chamber. There was no sign of life at the church. Vicki moved enough dirt and bricks to crawl through. She grabbed a Bible and crawled out.

When Charlie was finished digging the grave, Vicki helped him lift Ryan. She unfolded the sheet from around him and placed the Bible in his hands.

"Is that for luck?" Charlie said.

"No," Vicki said. "The Bible was really important to him. He studied it just about every day."

"I had a Bible once," Charlie said. "Somebody took it."

Vicki reached into the grave and took the book from Ryan's body.

"What are you doing?" Charlie said.

"He wouldn't have wanted to be buried with it," Vicki said. "He'd want you to have it."

As the sun rose, Vicki knelt on the cold ground. She

looked at Ryan, and the tears came. Charlie stood back, his head bowed.

Softly, Vicki sang the words to one of Ryan's favorite hymns.

> *Amazing grace! how sweet the sound—*
> *That saved a wretch like me!*
> *I once was lost but now am found,*
> *Was blind but now I see.*

———————————

She made a crude cross and stuck it in the ground at the head of the grave. She wondered how many more crosses she would have to make in the days ahead.

5

VICKI awoke near Ryan's grave. Phoenix was sprawled out on top. When Vicki moved, Phoenix whimpered and pawed at the loose dirt. Charlie was gone.

Vicki shivered from the cold. She wished she could see Judd and talk with him about Ryan. If this was what it would be like for the rest of the Tribulation, she didn't know if she could go on.

God, why did you have to take him? Vicki prayed.

Vicki returned to the shelter but couldn't find Shelly or Darrion. A man asked for volunteers. "We need help with the injured."

Vicki raised a hand and followed him.

Lionel took the gun instructions seriously. He watched carefully as the instructor taught them how to clean it and use it safely. At the shooting range Lionel scored the highest. The instructor patted him on the shoulder. "Watch this guy and you'll learn how to shoot," the man told a girl beside Lionel.

"I'm not that good," Lionel said when the instructor left.

"Better than me," the girl said. She held out a hand. "I'm Felicia."

Lionel introduced himself, then headed to the morning session. "Once you've blended in with the communities you'll be sent to," the instructor said, "you'll listen for specific things. No one in their right mind is going to come out and say they're against the Global Community."

A computer generated images and phrases on a screen in front of the class. The words *Antichrist* and *Tribulation* flashed before Lionel.

"Anyone who talks about there being an Antichrist is someone you want to watch closely. If the person believes we are experiencing what they call the 'Tribulation,' these may be enemies of the Global Community."

The instructor stopped and looked over his glasses. "There are actually people who believe Nicolae Carpathia is an evil man." The class responded with groans and laughter.

A Global Community chopper landed in a nearby field, interrupting the class. The sound of the rotor blades was deafening.

"You are witnessing the arrival of your new boss," the instructor said. "Terrel Blancka. Never—I repeat—never call him by his first name. You'll want to call him Commander Blancka or simply Commander."

Lionel watched as a man with a barrel chest and a graying mustache strode to the practice area. He wore a GC field uniform with a beret. He carried a clipboard and spoke gruffly to the instructor.

"What do you make of him?" Conrad asked Lionel.

"Looks like he means business," Lionel whispered.

The instructor formally introduced Commander Blancka, and the burly man stood ramrod straight, his hands behind his back.

"Boys and girls," Commander Blancka said, "and you are boys and girls until we get through with you." He scanned the group for any response. When there was none, he continued. "I've made it no secret that I didn't want this assignment. I don't have time to baby-sit. But when the most powerful man in the world calls and gives an order, I follow it.

"Now listen carefully. You are part of an elite group, chosen for a specific purpose. You are the first of the Global Community's Morale Monitors.

"There's no question you're young. But that doesn't have to be a drawback. We think it's an asset. We'll send you into hot spots, places where we feel there may be resistance to the purposes of the Global Community. I can't emphasize enough the importance of this job. Let me tell you about my conversation with the potentate."

Lionel caught a glance from Conrad. Commander Blancka's message made Lionel feel important.

"Nicolae Carpathia came to me and asked that I put this program together," the commander continued. "The success or failure of it depends on you. And that means

my success or failure depends on you. So I'll be watching."

Commander Blancka looked steely eyed at the crowd.
"That means you will succeed. The potentate made it
clear. The secret to the success of the Global Community
is UNITY!" The kids jumped as the commander shouted.

"Those who want to divide us will be exposed. People
who want to live in peace and harmony will enjoy exactly
that. But those who want to cause trouble will be dealt
with. Swiftly."

A boy near Conrad timidly raised a hand.

"What!" Commander Blancka barked.

"Is the potentate safe, sir?" the boy said.

"Good question," Commander Blancka said. "Nicolae
Carpathia was prepared for this. He's in a safe place,
getting ready to have his ten international ambassadors
join him. Any more questions?"

Felicia raised a hand. "Sir, from what you've said,
we're in kind of a war, aren't we?"

"You bet we are," Commander Blancka said. "But not
with bombs and artillery. We're in a war of thought. We
can enforce laws on people's actions, but we want to go
beyond that. The potentate said he wanted a group of
elite enforcers of pure thought. Healthy young men and
women like yourselves. Strong people who are devoted to
the cause of the Global Community. So devoted that they
would be willing to train and build themselves. We want
people eager to make sure everyone is in line with the
potentate."

The commander scanned the crowd. It seemed to

Lionel that the man looked in each person's eyes. "Are you that group?" he said.

"Yes, sir," the kids said.

"You call that eager?" Commander Blancka barked.

"Yes, sir!" the kids said louder.

"That's better," Commander Blancka said. "You will not wear uniforms. We want you to blend in with the rest of society. You will, at all times, carry your weapon and a communication device. If you find yourself in mortal danger, or if you discover a situation to report, contact the base immediately. The communicator also works as a homing device so we can find you if we need to.

"One of the hallmarks of the society you've grown up in is free speech." Commander Blancka bowed his head and shook it. "Sadly, we can't afford that luxury. That's why we've trained you. You will root out those who by word or action oppose the purposes of our cause.

"A good soldier knows his or her enemy," the commander said, pacing now. "Who is the enemy? If you're smart, you're asking that question. I'll tell you. The enemy is anyone who seeks to divide. Anyone who says *they* know what's right and not the potentate. One of our main targets will be those fundamentalists who say their religion is the only true religion."

Lionel raised a hand. "What power are we given, sir?" he said.

"A Global Community Morale Monitor has no limit to his or her powers," the commander said. "We find the enemy. We subdue the enemy. By any means necessary."

"That means using a gun?" Lionel said.

"That means using whatever we must. If you do your job well, we'll have no need for you within a few years. The enemy will vanish."

———————————————

After a few hours of sleep, Judd and Pete set out to locate another motorcycle. They found a large one at Pete's friend's house. The man had also been killed by the earthquake. Before they left, Judd located an old laptop computer in an office near the front of the house.

"I could use this to make contact with some friends," Judd said. "You think we can take it?"

"My friend's not gonna use it anymore," Pete said.

Pete showed Judd another route home. "You'll want to avoid the place you just came from."

"Actually, I'd like to go back the other way."

"You've gotta be outta your mind!" Pete said.

Judd explained the situation with Marlene. "I have to know if she accepted Christ."

"Don't you think that's too dangerous?" Pete said. "People have to make their own decisions."

"True. But I have to know."

"Then you won't go alone," Pete said.

"What do you mean?"

"We'll get close enough; then you point her out to me. I'll see if I can talk to her."

Judd smiled and nodded. He noticed a bruise on Pete's forehead. "I didn't see this the other day," Judd said.

"Must have smacked my head when they were transporting me," Pete said. "Besides, you've got a smudge of your own."

Judd looked in the mirror but didn't see anything.

Lionel paid attention as Commander Blancka warned the kids. "We don't know about radiation with the meteors," he said. "Best to stay away from them. Avoid looking like an authority. Blend in. Make friends. But always remember you have the power to enforce the Global Community's rules."

"Do we go back to school?" a girl asked.

"School as you knew it, no. The Global Community has an education plan for the future. Central learning stations are being built as we speak. GC-approved instructors will teach via satellite links from New Babylon. You'll uplink for tests and research. Everyone will be required to participate."

When Commander Blancka completed his speech, he told the kids to be ready to leave the following morning. "You Monitors will be airlifted by helicopter."

"Why do they have someone that high up in charge of us?" Conrad asked after the meeting was over.

"You heard him," Lionel said. "What we're doing's important."

"But we're kids," Conrad said.

"We're GCMM now," Lionel said. "Get used to it."

Conrad pulled out his gun and twirled it on his finger. Lionel grabbed it angrily. "You know that's dangerous!"

Conrad took his gun and holstered it. "It's not loaded," he said. "Besides, who died and left you in charge?"

Lionel stared at Conrad. "If you don't think this is serious, why don't you quit?" he said.

"So, your first job is to monitor the Morale Monitors?"

"If I have to," Lionel said.

Conrad walked away.

Vicki helped in the main tent. The suffering was unbelievable. Finally she spotted Darrion and Shelly. She excused herself and caught up with them. Shelly looked exhausted. Darrion sat with elbows on knees. She didn't look up when Vicki ran to them.

"What happened?" Vicki said.

Shelly shook her head. "Long story. Bad ending."

"Mom's gone," Darrion said. "They had her locked in a cell. After all this time they were still questioning her."

"They wouldn't show us the facility," Shelly said. "It was roped off and patrolled. We stayed till dark to get a look."

"There's no way she could have survived," Darrion said. "The place was knocked flat. The whole thing must have come down on her."

"I'm sorry," Vicki said.

"We did get a look at the logbook," Shelly said. "Judd and Taylor Graham were taken away on the morning of the quake."

"So there's a chance they're still alive," Vicki said.

Shelly nodded. Vicki noticed something strange on Shelly's forehead. Shelly rubbed at the smudge, but it didn't come off. "What's it look like?" Shelly said.

"Like what they do in Catholic churches around Ash Wednesday," Vicki said.

"Maybe I tripped or something," Shelly said. "It was a long night. What about Ryan?"

Vicki told them. Darrion hung her head. Shelly lay back on the ground. "I can't even cry anymore," she said.

Vicki took them to the grave. Phoenix hadn't moved. The three girls stood in silence. Vicki wondered about Lionel. And Judd.

Judd described Marlene and told Pete where he might find the group. Pete dropped Judd off at a gas station that was still standing.

"I'll wait for you here," Judd said, taking the laptop with him.

The service station owner sat in a lawn chair near the gas pumps and held a large dog by the collar. The dog lunged at Judd. Judd saw the butt of a gun sticking out of the man's belt.

"You best move on," the man said, spitting in the dirt. "All the food's gone."

"Can I use your rest room? My friend will be back for me soon."

The man nodded to the corner of the building.

Judd noticed a telephone behind the counter when he returned. A light blinked on one of its lines.

"Is that phone working?" Judd asked.

"They're tryin'," the man said. "Comes and goes."

"Would you mind if I tried to hook up my computer?" Judd said.

"It'll cost you."

Judd had no wallet. No identification. The Global Community had taken all he had. He had scrounged for food since the earthquake. He wondered how he would live without money.

The man rolled his eyes when he saw Judd pat his pockets. "Local call?" the man said.

"Yeah," Judd said, "I just need to get the access number."

"I don't understand those things. Go ahead and use it if you have to."

Judd tried several times to dial out but got a busy signal each time. On the fifth try he got a ring and located the number for a dial-up line.

The computer was old and slow, but Judd felt like he was holding a gold mine. It was his first cyber contact with the outside world since he'd been arrested.

Judd first downloaded his messages but saw none from Vicki, Lionel, or Ryan. Next, he located a Web site with a people search. The Global Community was already tracking the number of deaths. He entered Vicki Byrne's name and held his breath. The computer ground slowly, then showed Vicki in the "no known whereabouts" listing.

At least she's not confirmed dead, Judd thought.

Judd entered Lionel Washington's name. "Injured." Judd typed in Ryan's name. "Confirmed dead."

Judd gasped. Could it be true? Could Ryan really be dead?

He typed in his own name. "No known whereabouts."

He checked the adult Tribulation Force. Rayford Steele was "confirmed alive." Chloe and Buck Williams were not accounted for. The same for Loretta and Donny Moore.

When Judd typed in Amanda Steele's name, he again gasped as he read, "Subject confirmed on Boston to New Babylon nonstop, reported crashed and submerged in Tigris River, no survivors."

Judd figured Amanda had been flying to see Rayford in New Babylon. The report said she hadn't made it. Judd hung his head. When would the death toll stop?

Judd called up his E-mail again and looked at the multiple lines of messages. He heard a click of the modem and realized the phone was dead. One message interested him. It was from Pavel, the boy from New Babylon he had met online. He tried to dial up again, but the line was dead. Judd wondered if Pavel had made it through the earthquake. If it was the worldwide quake the Bible talked about, being outside when it hit was probably the boy's only chance.

Judd tried to dial up again but couldn't get through. He heard a loud rumbling and saw at least ten motorcycles pull into the gas station. The dog barked, and the owner reached for his gun.

"No!" Judd shouted.

6

JUDD'S shout startled the owner and the riders. The group turned and stared at Judd as he ran toward them.

"Don't do this," Judd said.

"Stay out of it, kid," the biker nearest the owner said. He was huge and had long red hair.

"They think they're comin' in here and stealin' my gas," the owner said. "Over my dead body."

"Whatever it takes," the biker snorted.

The dog barked wildly as the hairy man got off his bike and approached the owner.

"I'm warnin' you," the owner said.

Judd heard another cycle. A trail of dust lifted in the distance. A moment later, Judd saw Pete flying along the path he had taken toward town.

"Is that who I think it is?" a girl on the back of one bike said.

"Sure looks like him," the hairy man said.

Pete took his time climbing off the cycle. Even the dog stopped barking. Pete pulled off his helmet and ambled toward the others.

"Pete?" the hairy man said.

"What's up, Red?"

"Just looking for a little gas, that's all."

Pete stopped in front of the owner and pawed at the ground with his boot. "This looks like an honest businessman," Pete said.

"Cash only," the owner said.

"Don't do this," Red said to Pete. "You get in our way, and there'll be trouble."

Pete stepped nose to nose with Red. Their combined weight was surely more than 600 pounds.

"I'm trying to keep you from doing something you'll regret," Pete said. "Now pay the man or leave."

Red clenched his teeth and his fists. Finally he turned and waved a hand. "Come on. We'll fuel up later."

As the dust settled from Red's gang's departure, the owner turned to Pete. "Sure am glad you two came along," he said, giving a toothless smile. "Fill your tank. It's on me."

"It was nothing," Pete said. "But get ready. I don't think you've seen the last of them."

"Did you find her?" Judd said.

Pete nodded, then asked the owner, "Mind if we use your office to talk?"

"Go right ahead," the owner said.

"I found the people," Pete said when they were a safe distance away. "Told them I was looking for a skinny kid who stole my motorcycle."

"Thanks a lot!" Judd said.

"They're still looking for you. Said you took some stuff and ran from the GC."

"I was hungry," Judd said. "I took a few pieces of bread. Give me a break."

"I saw the little lady you talked about."

"Talk with her?"

"Couldn't," Pete said, moving closer. Pete was only a few inches away. "But I saw the weirdest thing."

Judd stepped back. "What's the matter with you?"

"She's got the same kind of smudge on her forehead that you do."

Judd found a broken mirror in the bathroom but couldn't see the smudge. "Let me see your head again."

Pete leaned forward in the light and pulled back his long hair. Judd studied the mark closely. "This isn't a bruise like I thought," he said. "It's some kind of stamp or a mark. Maybe they put it on you at the shelter to keep track of patients."

"I don't remember it if they did," Pete said.

"It's almost like one of those 3-D images."

"You're right," Pete said, looking at Judd. "Holy cow, it looks like a cross."

"You see that on my forehead?" Judd said, looking in the mirror again.

"Yeah. I can see yours and you can see mine, but not in a mirror. What do you think it is?"

Judd's mind raced. "The pastor I told you about, Bruce Barnes, taught about a mark people would have, but that was supposed to be given by the Antichrist.

People will have to take it in order to buy and sell stuff."

Pete threw up his hands. "Hey, don't look at me. I'm new to this."

Judd ran to the computer and tried the dial-up. This time he got through and went straight to Tsion Ben-Judah's Web site.

"And Marlene had this same thing on her head?" Judd asked.

"Plain as day," Pete said.

Judd did a search of Tsion's Web site. "Bingo," Judd said. Pete looked over his shoulder as Judd read, " 'Many of you have noticed a mysterious mark the size of a thumbprint on the forehead of other believers. Do not be alarmed. This is the seal, visible only to other believers.' "

"A seal?"

"Yeah, like a stamp of approval," Judd said.

"And other people don't see it?"

"Go try it out," Judd said.

Pete walked outside to the owner. Pete pulled back his hair and said, "You see anything on my forehead?"

"Some lines and hair is all I see," the owner said. "Is there supposed to be something up there?"

"I guess not," Pete said. He came back to Judd, shaking his head. "This Bible stuff is gettin' weird."

"Listen to this," Judd said. " 'The seventh chapter of Revelation tells of "the servants of our God" being sealed on their foreheads.' "

"Why would God do that?"

"I don't know. I'm just glad he did. Now we know

Marlene is a true believer. She has the mark. She must have prayed after I left."

"I wonder if it'll help us in the future," Pete said.

"How?"

"I assume it'll be good to know who's on our side and who's not," Pete said.

Vicki collapsed in her tent. She had been working nonstop for hours. The number of injured and dead was staggering. Men and women walked in a daze looking for friends and family. Grown men thrashed about, saying they wanted to die.

Vicki was almost asleep when Shelly opened the tent. "There's a man out here to see you."

"Who is it?" Vicki said.

"I don't know, but I told him you were taking a rest. He said I should come wake you."

Vicki gasped when she saw the man. Chaya's father, Mr. Stein, stood a few yards from the tent.

"Vicki," Mr. Stein said.

Vicki rushed to him. "I haven't seen Chaya. She went to your house to—"

Mr. Stein held up a hand. "I was with her at the house. I made a solemn vow to find her friends. I'm here to keep that promise."

"What happened?"

"Chaya is dead," Mr. Stein said.

Vicki fell to her knees. "No," she choked.

Mr. Stein knelt beside Vicki. "We were in the house

59

together when the earthquake hit," he said. "We were trapped many hours. If they had found us earlier, she might still be alive."

Vicki closed her eyes. "I'm so sorry."

"I have lost everything. My wife. My daughter. My home and all my possessions." Mr. Stein looked away. "But what good are possessions when the people you love are gone?"

"Were you able to talk with her before. . . ."

"You know I did not want to speak with her again," Mr. Stein said. "We had great differences. But in those hours, I understood how wrong I was."

"Wrong about what?"

"For shutting her out. She was my flesh and blood."

"Did you talk?"

Mr. Stein nodded. "She tried to convince me that her belief in God was right and mine was wrong. Until the very end she was talking about her belief in Jesus as Messiah."

"She prayed for you constantly," Vicki said.

"She was misguided."

"A funeral. Would it be all right with you if—"

"There is no need," Mr. Stein said. "I buried her yesterday."

Vicki felt crushed. Ryan. Mrs. Stahley. Donny Moore. All dead. And now Chaya, the person who had the best grasp of the Bible of any in the Young Tribulation Force.

"Why, God?" Vicki whispered.

"I thought you had it figured out. Your God was supposed to have a plan. He wants good things to happen, right?"

Vicki shook her head. "Mr. Stein, whether you believe it or not, your daughter loved you. And God loves you. He wants you to know him not just by rules and laws, but—"

Mr. Stein put up a hand. "I did not come for another sermon. I made a promise to find you, and I kept my word."

Mr. Stein turned to leave.

"The Bible doesn't say God will only cause good things to happen," Vicki said. "It says he takes everything that happens and works it for good to those who love him."

Mr. Stein frowned. "I am through arguing."

Vicki put her face in her hands.

"Do you have need of anything?" Mr. Stein said.

"We're like everyone else now. No house. No food. We'll make it somehow."

Mr. Stein handed her a card. "I don't know when the phone lines will return, but if you have need, call me or come see me. My office escaped serious damage. I may be able to help you in some way."

———————————

Lionel and Conrad packed for their trip north. The group waited near two choppers where Commander Blancka and his staff would transport them. Lionel knew he and Conrad would be in the Chicago area, along with Felicia and another girl, Melinda.

"How do they expect us to cover an area that big with four people?" Conrad said.

"Remember," Lionel said, "they're testing the program. If it works, they'll expand it."

"I've heard there's a lot of looting in Chicago," Conrad said. "Think we'll get mixed up in that?"

"I talked with the instructor after the commander left. He said we aren't peace officers, but in an emergency, you never know."

Conrad pulled a sheet of paper from his pocket. "I found that rabbi guy's Web site on the Internet."

"So?"

Conrad pointed to a paragraph at the bottom of the page. "This caught my eye. It says the good people are supposed to have some kind of a mark on their forehead."

Lionel smirked. "Why are you wasting your time on this? I don't see any mark on your forehead; do you see one on mine?"

"Guess not," Conrad said.

Lionel crumpled the paper and threw it away. "Get some sleep tonight. We've got a long flight tomorrow."

Conrad left. Lionel tried to sleep but couldn't. He went into the bathroom and looked in the mirror. There was no mark.

Judd finally opened his E-mail and checked the message from Pavel. The boy had miraculously survived the wrath of the Lamb earthquake along with a nurse who was attending him.

"The nurse insisted we go outside," Pavel wrote.

"Animals were going crazy. Then the earth started shaking. We were near the main building where Nicolae has his office. After a few moments, it crashed to the ground."

Pavel asked Judd to write if he had survived. Judd logged on and sent a message to see if Pavel might be online. In a moment, Judd heard a ding and saw Pavel's response.

"I'm so glad to know you're OK," Pavel wrote. "Shall we put on the video link?"

"Stay with text, I'm on an old machine," Judd wrote. Judd briefly explained what had happened to him and how he was trying to get back to Chicago. "What about Carpathia?" Judd wrote.

"Alive and well," Pavel wrote.

"Any news on his pilot? His name is Rayford Steele."

"Haven't heard, but if the rabbi is right, your friend should be safe. Tsion Ben-Judah believes the Scriptures say the Antichrist will stay alive until a little over a year from now. If the pilot is close to Carpathia, it may be the safest place."

"What about your father?"

"He's OK. And he tells the strangest story about Nicolae. Carpathia escaped certain death when he took a helicopter from the roof of his office. But his right-hand man didn't make it."

"Leon Fortunato?"

"Exactly. How did you know?"

"I met him once," Judd typed, smiling.

"My father said Fortunato is telling the story everywhere that Nicolae raised him from the dead!"

"That can't be!"

"My father was in Nicolae's shelter. It's a huge underground facility big enough for Nicolae's airplanes. Suddenly, the potentate walks in with Fortunato. Leon was covered with dirt."

"That doesn't prove anything."

"Fortunato tells it like it is fact," Pavel wrote. "He told the staff he fell to the bottom of the building, struck his head, and died. The next thing he remembers, he hears Nicolae's voice saying, 'Leonardo, come forth.' "

A chill went down Judd's spine. "Those are the same words Jesus used to call Lazarus from the grave. Sounds like a counterfeit to me."

"I know from reading different passages that a person dies once," Pavel wrote. "There are no second chances. But still, Fortunato lives."

"There has to be an explanation."

"I'm afraid people will be fooled," Pavel said. "The potentate will soon broadcast live to the world."

"I'm not in a place where I can see or hear anything from the media."

"I'll send you the text of his message once it is complete. My greatest fear is that people will proclaim Nicolae divine."

"Let's pray it doesn't happen," Judd said.

Judd heard the rumble of motorcycles and signed off. "Hopefully, I'll write you from Chicago."

Pete moved to the front window. "They're back."

"Maybe we should get out of here," Judd said.

"And let that old man fend for himself? I know how these people operate. They're like wolves. The old guy'll be so scared he won't be able to shoot anything. I'm not leaving him alone."

"How do you know so much about these people?"

"I used to be one of them."

7

THE OWNER of the gas station darted inside and shut off the gas pumps. Pete brought his bike inside and closed the garage doors. "Put your laptop away," Pete said as he went out the door. "We might have to get out fast."

"What's he gonna do?" the owner asked Judd.

"You got me," Judd said.

The gang pulled in and circled around Pete. The group had grown to twenty bikes. Judd couldn't hear what they were saying, but Red shouted, and Pete stood his ground.

The owner pulled his gun, and Judd put out his hand. "A little fuel isn't worth getting killed."

"This is all I got left," the owner said. "I'm not lettin' a bunch of cycle goons take it away."

Judd watched Red get off his bike and grab Pete by the hair. He jerked it back from his face and pointed. The others laughed.

"I'm not lettin' him die out there," the owner said, heading for the door.

"Wait!" Judd shouted. "Let it play out."

Red let go and stepped back. Pete seemed animated, gesturing and talking loudly. A few bikers stared at him. Others shook their heads and laughed.

Judd froze. He knew the danger outside, but he couldn't let Pete get killed.

"I'm going out there," Judd finally said. "If we need you, I'll signal you like this." Judd scratched the back of his neck.

"Got it," the owner said. "Now be careful."

Judd opened the door slowly. Pete still talked. The bikers sat with arms folded. When Judd got close to the pumps, he heard Red say, "Since when did you become perfect? Have you forgotten what you used to do?"

"I'm not perfect," Pete said.

A woman in the group spoke up. "How 'bout you and Rosie? You two were livin' together."

"I know what Rosie and I did was wrong," Pete said. "Believe me, I'd give anything to be able to talk with her like this."

Judd couldn't figure out what Pete was doing.

Pete turned and saw Judd. He smiled and said softly, "Bet you didn't know if this Christian thing would stick with me, huh?"

"I liked the old Pete better," someone said.

"Yeah, the boozin', cussin', fightin' Pete," another said.

"Look, I don't know all the verses and everything,"

Pete said. "This guy does. His name's Judd. He's the one who helped me."

Red got back on his motorcycle and kicked it to a start. "Don't want your religion," he said. "And next time you get in our way, you'll pay."

The other cycles rumbled to a start and followed Red. Pete watched the trail of dust and shook his head.

"You told them about God?" Judd said.

"They need to hear it as much as I did. They don't want to hear it, though."

"You didn't want it for a lot of years," Judd said.

"Maybe someday they'll listen."

Vicki awoke to bright sunshine. A man was speaking through a bullhorn. Darrion and Shelly followed her out of the tent. Vicki felt grungy and wished she could take a shower.

"All able-bodied people should move to the media tent for a special announcement," the GC guard was saying. "Potentate Nicolae Carpathia will make a statement via satellite shortly."

"You think he can use an earthquake for his own good?" Shelly said sarcastically.

"He'll use anything and everything," Vicki said.

The three girls reached the tent and watched a Global Community newscaster give the latest. "The number of dead and injured worldwide is staggering," the man said. "These pictures show the extent of the damage."

Video clips of major cities flashed on the screen. A

shot of Paris showed the Eiffel Tower in ruins. The Leaning Tower of Pisa was no longer leaning but flat on the ground. Shots of New York, Los Angeles, and Chicago made Vicki shudder.

"Other natural phenomena occurred during the earthquake," the newscaster said. "This amateur video was shot in New Babylon during the earthquake."

Vicki gasped. The camera was shaky, but there was no mistaking the fire in the sky. The moon had turned blood red.

"No matter how much they try to explain that away," Darrion said, "we all know that the moon turning that color is not a natural phenomenon."

Nicolae Carpathia's face flashed on the screen. He looked grim but composed. "Brothers and sisters in the Global Community, I address you from New Babylon. Like you, I lost many loved ones, dear friends, and loyal associates in the tragedy. Please accept my deepest and most sincere sympathy for your losses on behalf of the administration of the Global Community.

"No one could have predicted this random act of nature, the worst in history to strike the globe. We were in the final stages of our rebuilding effort following the war against a resistant minority. Now, as I trust you are able to witness wherever you are, rebuilding has already begun again."

Nicolae told viewers that New Babylon would become the center of the world for banking, government, and even Enigma Babylon One World Faith.

"Told you he'd use the earthquake to his own advantage," Vicki smirked.

"It will be my joy to welcome you to this beautiful place," Nicolae continued. "Give us a few months to finish, and then plan your pilgrimage. Every citizen should make it his or her life's goal to experience this new utopia and see the prototype for every city."

The screen switched from Nicolae to a virtual reality tour of the new city. It gleamed, as if already completed. The tour was dizzying and impressive. Carpathia pointed out every high-tech, state-of-the-art convenience.

"Looks pretty impressive," Shelly said.

"It's a fake," Vicki said. "The guy can only attempt to copy what God does."

The potentate continued with a stirring pep talk. "Because you are survivors, I have unwavering confidence in your drive and determination and commitment to work together, to never give up, to stand shoulder to shoulder and rebuild our world.

"I am humbled to serve you and pledge that I will give my all for as long as you allow me the privilege. Now let me just add that I am aware that, due to speculative reporting in one of our own Global Community publications, many have been confused by recent events."

"What's he talking about?" Shelly said.

"Must be Buck Williams's magazine article," Vicki said.

"While it may appear that the global earthquake coincided with the so-called wrath of the Lamb, let me clarify," Nicolae said. "Those who believe this disaster was God's doing are also those who believe that the disappearances nearly two years ago were people being swept away to heaven.

"Of course, every citizen of the Global Community is free to believe as he or she wants and to exercise that faith in any way that does not infringe upon the same freedom for others. The point of Enigma Babylon One World Faith is religious freedom and tolerance.

"For that reason, I am loath to criticize the beliefs of others. However, I plead for common sense. I do not begrudge anyone the right to believe in a personal god."

"Gee, thanks," Darrion muttered.

"However, I do not understand how a god they describe as just and loving would capriciously decide who is or is not worthy of heaven and effect that decision in what they refer to as 'the twinkling of an eye.'

"Has this same loving god come back two years later to rub it in? He expresses his anger to those unfortunates left behind by laying waste their world and killing off a huge percentage of them?"

"Look at that smile," Vicki said. "Makes me sick."

"I humbly ask devout believers in such a Supreme Being to forgive me if I have mischaracterized your god," Carpathia continued. "But any thinking citizen realizes that this picture simply does not add up.

"So, my brothers and sisters, do not blame God for what we are enduring. See it simply as one of life's crucibles, a test of our spirit and will, an opportunity to look within ourselves and draw on that deep wellspring of goodness we were born with. Let us work together to make our world a global phoenix, rising from the ashes of tragedy to become the greatest society ever known. I bid you good-bye and goodwill until next I speak with you."

People around the tent stood and clapped. Vicki shook her head and remained seated. When the others sat, Vicki recognized a familiar face.

"Isn't that the guy who was at Judd's graduation?" Shelly said.

"Leon Fortunato," Vicki said.

Fortunato seemed friendly and looked straight into the camera. "I want to tell you an incredible story," he said. "So incredible that I would not believe it if it had not happened to me.

"I was in the top floor offices of the Global Community when the earthquake hit. Unlike the potentate, I was unable to escape. But I am glad he did, because if it were not for him, I would be dead.

"The building collapsed around us," Leon continued. "I wish I could say I was brave during this time, but like the rest, I went screaming into the rubble. I fell headfirst, and when I hit the bottom, it felt and sounded like I'd cracked my skull. The weight of the whole building came down on me, breaking my bones. My lungs burst. Everything went black."

Fortunato stopped. Vicki watched the crowd in the tent. They were leaning forward, listening to every word.

"I believe I died," Fortunato said. "It was as if someone pulled the plug on my life."

Another pause. "And yet, here I am. Alive. You ask me how? I say it was my friend Nicolae. I was not conscious of anything, like the deepest sleep a person could ever have. And then I heard a voice calling my name. I thought it was a dream. I thought I was a boy again and my mother was softly calling my name, trying to wake me from sleep.

"Then I heard the loud, strong voice of your potentate. He cried out, 'Leonardo, come forth!' "

"I don't believe it," Vicki said.

"What?" Darrion said.

"Those are the same words Jesus used with Lazarus to bring him back from the dead," Vicki said.

A woman turned in front of the girls and shushed them.

Leon Fortunato wiped his brow and composed himself. "I'm sorry for being emotional," he said. "My only regret was that there were no witnesses. But I know what I experienced and believe with all my heart that this gift our Supreme Potentate possesses will be used in public in the future. A man bestowed with this power is worthy of a new title. I am suggesting that he hereafter be referred to as His Excellency Nicolae Carpathia. I have already instituted this policy within the Global Community government and urge all citizens who respect and love our leader to follow suit.

"As you may know, His Excellency would never require or even request such a title. Though reluctantly thrust into leadership, he has expressed a willingness to give his life for his fellow citizens. Though he will never insist upon appropriate deference, I urge it on your part."

"That's all I can take," Vicki said. "Come on."

Outside the tent, Shelly asked Vicki what she thought of Leon Fortunato's statement.

"Look," Vicki said, "God does miracles; there's no

question. All the enemy of God can do is copy the miracles. He fakes it. With the mind control Carpathia has, I wouldn't be surprised if he planted those thoughts about Fortunato being raised from the dead."

"But you heard him yourself," Shelly said. "He climbed out from the bottom of that building."

"Right," Vicki said, "and he claimed to have broken all kinds of bones and burst his lungs. Did those just heal over?"

Darrion spoke up. "The point isn't whether it's true or not," she said. "People are going to believe it. They're going to think Carpathia is some kind of Messiah himself."

Lionel and the others watched the speeches by Carpathia and Fortunato. Several outbursts of clapping and cheering were stopped by Commander Blancka. When it was over, the group rose to its feet. Everyone but Conrad.

"What's the matter with you?" Lionel said.

Conrad shook his head. "I'm just not in the rah-rah mood," he said.

"Didn't you hear?" Lionel said. "Carpathia actually raised somebody from the dead. Don't you know what that means?"

"Yeah, a new GC health care plan. Somebody dies, and Nicolae brings them to life again."

"You don't get it," Lionel said.

"I do get it," Conrad said. "I just have a hard time believing it. Let me ask you this. There were other dead people in that building who worked with Carpathia. If he's the wonderful leader everybody thinks he is, why did he only raise one person from the dead? Why not the whole bunch?"

Lionel stammered. He hadn't thought of that angle. Finally, he said, "You have to decide whether you're in or out."

Conrad shook his head. "I'm in. But only until I can find my brother."

It was evening when Judd and Pete neared New Hope Village Church. As Pete drove his motorcycle over chunks of asphalt and concrete, Judd looked at what once was a beautiful place of worship. Now, half the building was underground. The entire sanctuary appeared to have turned and was sitting at a weird angle.

The last time Judd had been in the church was at Bruce's funeral. How his life had changed since then. Now he was on the run from the Global Community.

"This is where my new life really started," Judd said. "After the disappearances, I met Bruce here."

"It's a shame. Looks like it was quite a church."

Judd got off the cycle and looked around the parking lot. Loretta's place was not far. He wondered if she was alive. And Vicki. Where could she be?

Pete broke Judd's silence. "I'm glad you made it back, and I hope you find what you're looking for."

"You're leaving?" Judd said.

"I want to check on that old guy at the gas station. We never got to tell him what you told me."

"You need to study and get grounded," Judd said. "Stay here."

"Can't. I have a few loose ends to tie and lots of people who need to hear what I know."

Judd put out his hand. "I hope this won't be the last time we see each other."

"It won't be," Pete said. "You can count on it."

AFTER an overnight stay in Indianapolis, Lionel and
Conrad continued their flight to Chicago with Felicia and
Melinda. Commander Blancka talked with his staff as
they neared Glenview Naval Air Station.

Conrad tapped Lionel on the shoulder and motioned
toward the commander. "Looks like something's up."

When they landed, the four kids hopped out, grabbed
their belongings, and moved away from the chopper. A
few minutes later Commander Blancka rushed up to them.

"We have a situation. I know you're prepared to work
behind the scenes, but we need your help."

"What's up?" Lionel said.

"Looters. They're goin' wild. The GC needs all the
help they can get. Are you up for it?"

"You bet, sir," Lionel said.

The others agreed. Commander Blancka told them to
stay in radio contact and passed them to another GC offi-

cer. The man scoffed when he saw the kids. Commander Blancka bristled, and the guard escorted the four to a helipad. The chopper flew over a crumpled tollway and a river.

Conrad pointed to their left. "O'Hare's over there," he said. "Not much of it left."

They passed a forest preserve, then landed in a crumpled parking lot. A crooked sign said Woodfield Mall. The upper level of the huge building had collapsed. Several stores on the lower levels were intact. Lionel and the others walked over broken glass to get inside. Empty shelves and overturned tables littered store floors. The looters had done a job.

The guard stepped through water from a broken fountain and met another GC patrol. "I didn't know we were getting a bunch of kids," he muttered.

"You heard the commander," Lionel said. "We know what we're doing."

"If you four can contain this area," the patrol said, "it'll give the rest of us a chance to work some other problem spots."

"What happens if we see somebody stealing something?" Melinda said.

The guard rolled his eyes. "You could try to talk them out of it," the guard said, "but our orders are to shoot. I suggest you do the same."

Judd slept near New Hope Village Church. He awoke stiff and cold. The nearest house was Loretta's. He could tell someone had dug through the roof to get inside. A few garden tools lay at the back of the house. He shouted but no one answered.

He was amazed to find an empty crater where his own house had been. A meteor had struck it, and nothing was left but debris and the huge hole. In an open field he found the swing set he and his father had put together for his little brother and sister. Concrete was still attached to the foot of each post.

Judd bent to inspect the swings and found what he was looking for. He had written his initials in the concrete. On another leg of the swings he saw his little brother's handprint. Over it he had written "Marc." He saw the same on the next leg where Marcie had written her name and pushed her hand deep into the cement.

Judd knelt and inspected the last post. It was chipped, but he could still make out the letters "Da—." Judd put his hand in the imprint of his father's hand and closed his eyes. Judd's hand almost fit perfectly.

"I wish you were here now, Dad," Judd said. He thought of his father, brother, and sister. It seemed so long ago, like another world. It *was* another world.

Judd thought of his other family. Lionel, Ryan, Vicki, and Bruce. Judd guessed Ryan and Lionel would have stayed at his house. That would explain why Ryan was listed as dead. But how would Lionel have gotten away? Judd still held out hope for Ryan as he traced his way back to the church. After several wrong turns, he found the rubble of Vicki's place.

"Halt!" someone behind him shouted.

Judd turned to see a Global Community squad in a covered vehicle. "What are you doing?"

Judd knew the GC would shoot if he ran. He played it cool. "Looking for some friends of mine," Judd shouted.

"This area's been evacuated," a man said. "Check the shelters."

Judd gave a sigh of relief when the GC squad drove past him.

After the men flew away in the chopper, Lionel and the others paced in front of the darkened windows. One jewelry shop was completely gutted. Another that sold fine luggage had nothing left but some boxes high on the wall. Escalators tilted, and the silence was eerie.

"I hear they wasted Chicago at the start of the war," Conrad said. "Now this."

"What war?" Lionel said.

Conrad told Lionel the details of the war between the Global Community and the militia. "My brother said the GC was just waiting for a militia uprising. They wanted to blow them away and make it look like the Global Community was just defending themselves."

"Who's your brother?" Felicia said.

"His name is Taylor Graham," Conrad said. "Works for Maxwell Stahley in GC security."

"Stahley's dead," Felicia said. "You haven't heard?"

Conrad looked upset. "He was alive when they took me down South," Conrad said. "Was it a plane crash?"

"They found him in a building in some suburb," Felicia said.

Lionel held up a hand. The four stood in front of an upscale dress shop. "Somebody's in there," Lionel said.

"I see some things I wouldn't mind wearing," Melinda said. "But I don't see any looters."

Lionel climbed through the broken window. Glass crunched under his feet. He heard shuffling inside.

"Come on!" Lionel shouted to his friends. Lionel cupped his hands and yelled, "Halt! In the name of the Global Community, or we'll shoot."

"I'll cut through the next store and meet you in the back," Conrad whispered.

Melinda and Felicia were right behind Lionel, hurtling past the racks of expensive clothes. Lionel hit the ground and saw two people running for the rear exit.

"Stop right there or we'll shoot!" Lionel repeated.

The two kept running. Lionel pointed the gun to the ceiling and shot. Melinda screamed and lost her balance, sending Lionel headlong into a display.

"Are you OK?" Felicia said, helping Lionel up.

"Yeah," Lionel said, but he wasn't. He had a welt under his ear, and something was going on in his head. Things were coming back. About Chicago. About his life before the Global Community.

Vicki, Shelly, and Darrion were busy at the shelter. Vicki could tell the nurses appreciated the help. Hundreds of people poured in each day. Some were looking for a meal. Others were injured and needed medical help.

Vicki didn't want to think about the future. Each question made her stomach tie in knots. Where would they live? What would they do for money? She tried to concentrate and push the questions out of her mind, but they kept coming back.

Vicki heard Shelly shout first. Then Darrion called her name. Vicki asked the woman she was helping to stay where she was. She stepped out of the medical tent and spotted Darrion and Shelly. Both were smiling. Behind them was a man in dirty jeans with a few days' growth of beard.

"Vick," the man said.

"Judd?"

Judd ran to her. Vicki hugged him tightly.

"I've been looking all over," Judd said. "I'm so glad I found you."

"The GC wouldn't tell us anything. How'd you get away?"

"Long story," Judd said. "Is there someplace we can talk?"

Shelly winked at Vicki and said she would take over in the medical tent. Vicki and Judd walked toward the church.

Lionel ran out the back door, his head pounding. Felicia and Melinda were behind him. Lionel went from the darkened back room to bright sunlight. When his eyes adjusted, he saw two men struggling with Conrad. Lionel pointed the gun but couldn't get a clear shot. Before he could reach his friend, one of the men had wrestled the gun from Conrad.

"Stay right there if you want to live," the man said.

"Put the gun down," Lionel said.

"Yeah, right," the man said. "Who do you kids think you are anyway, the cops?"

"We're with the Global Community," Lionel said, keying the microphone on his shoulder. He gave their position and requested help.

"That was a mistake," the man with the gun said. He leveled the gun at Lionel.

Lionel fired at the knee of the gunman. The man stared at him, then shook his head. To Lionel's surprise, the man dropped the gun and walked toward the parking lot. Lionel knew he couldn't have missed, but the man kept walking.

Conrad scampered to retrieve the gun.

"Stay where you are!" Lionel yelled.

The men kept walking. Lionel heard a chopper. Above the building he saw Commander Blancka give him a thumbs-up. Lionel motioned toward the men, but the commander ignored him. The chopper landed nearby, and the commander jumped out.

"They're getting away, sir," Lionel said.

"No, they're not," Commander Blancka said. "They're being debriefed."

"What's going on?" Conrad said.

"It's one thing to know how to fire a gun and hit a

target," the commander said. "It's another to use it against a person."

"You mean that whole thing was staged?" Melinda said.

"Our guns were loaded with blanks," Lionel said.

"It was your last test, and you passed," the commander said.

Conrad looked depressed. "I don't think I did very well."

"We put you in a situation you weren't prepared for," Commander Blancka said. "Hopefully you learned something."

The commander ushered them to the chopper. "Here's where we have you set up," he said, pointing to a map. "Mount Prospect is just east of us. We're putting all four of you there. We've heard reports of some resistance in the high school.

"As I told you, school as you've known it won't exist in the coming months. What we hope you'll do is get situated and blend in with the community."

"Where will we stay?" Lionel said.

"Just like everybody else who lives there," the commander said. "You'll stay in a shelter until homes and apartments can be rebuilt."

Judd told Vicki about the earthquake and watching Taylor Graham fall to his death. It felt like Judd could tell her anything. He explained about the mark of true believers, and Vicki gasped when she saw the mark on Judd's forehead.

"You're right," Vicki said. "We all have the mark."

Vicki listened and asked questions about Pete and how Judd made it home. "You're lucky to be alive," she said.

"I feel like God's been watching out for me the whole time. What happened with you?"

Vicki explained about the *Underground* and how Mrs. Jenness had caught her. Judd couldn't believe Vicki's ordeal on the bridge.

"And I thought I had it tough," Judd said. "What about Lionel and Ryan?"

Vicki looked away.

Judd took her by the shoulders and looked into her eyes. "I read something on a Web site, but I want to hear it from you. Is Ryan dead?"

Vicki pursed her lips. "I feel like it's my fault. I told him to stay in the house. If he'd have been outside maybe he'd still be alive."

"Then he is dead?"

"They found him in the basement of my house. His back was hurt, and he had some kind of infection."

Vicki's voice broke. She put her head on Judd's shoulder. "I found him at a makeshift hospital. He'd written me a note the night before."

"Do you still have it?" Judd said.

Vicki pulled the crumpled piece of paper from her back pocket. "I got to talk with him before he died."

Judd opened the paper. He wiped away a tear as he read it, then sat on a fallen tree. "It doesn't seem real," he said.

"I had to get help bringing his body here." She pointed to the church. Judd saw a fresh mound of earth. Phoenix was perched on top.

Judd walked slowly toward the grave, then knelt beside it and stroked the dog's back. Phoenix whimpered and put his head on Judd's knee.

"It's not your fault," Judd said to Vicki. "You were just trying to protect him from the GC."

"But he died! And he's never coming back!"

Judd sat with the feeling. First his family. Then Bruce. Now it was Ryan. Judd kept seeing Ryan's face. He had called him a little guy for so long. He thought of Ryan's fights with Lionel, his love for Phoenix, and their trip to Israel together. That trip had shown Judd what Ryan was made of.

"You haven't told me about Lionel."

"Somebody from his family came and took him down South," Vicki said.

"I thought his family was gone," Judd said.

"Apparently a few of them were living and wanted him home. We haven't heard anything since he left."

"Weird," Judd said.

"At least you're back," Vicki said.

"But I don't know how long I can stay," Judd said. "The GC network will be up and running soon. The first place they'll look will be here. I think we need a permanent place to hide."

"You must be starving," Vicki said. "Let's go back to the shelter."

"Gimme a minute with him, OK?" Judd said.

Vicki walked to the edge of the parking lot while Judd put a hand on Ryan's grave.

"I feel real stupid," Judd said. "I mean, I know you can't hear me. So this is probably more for me than it is you.

"I'm sorry. Sorry I treated you like a kid. You were the best of us. You loved God with everything you had. You went out and found those Bibles. You saved me and Vicki that time under the L tracks.

"I'm gonna miss you. And it hurts like everything to let you go. But I know I have to say good-bye. I just wish I could see you one more time and tell you. . . .

"You were like . . . no, you *were* my brother. You are my brother. And I'm gonna see you again."

Vicki patted Judd on the back when he walked back to her. "I've done that a couple of times myself."

They moved toward the shelter. Judd said he would sleep outside near a fire. When they reached camp, Vicki relieved Shelly in the medical tent. As Vicki helped an elderly patient roll over, someone in the corner shouted, "That's her!"

Vicki finished with the patient and hurried to see what the problem was. Vicki finally realized the girl was talking about her.

"Nurse, get a guard," the girl said. "She's the one. That's the girl who killed Mrs. Jenness!"

9

VICKI was stunned. It wasn't true, but there was no way to prove her innocence. Anyone who might have seen her trying to rescue Mrs. Jenness could easily have thought she was trying to get rid of the woman.

A nurse came and quieted the shouting girl.

"I'm telling you, she's the one who offed Mrs. Jenness."

The nurse looked at Vicki. "Do you mind telling me what this is about?"

Shelly whispered to Vicki, "That's Joyce from Nicolae High. Let me see what I can do."

Vicki finally recognized her. Shelly tried to calm her, but Joyce kept shouting and calling Vicki a murderer.

"Were you in a car with Mrs. Jenness?" the nurse said.

"Yes. The earthquake hit as we were crossing a bridge. But I tried to save her, not kill her."

Joyce spoke up. "I was there when Mrs. Jenness drove away with you. I know you were in that car. This morning

I met a lady who was near the bridge when it collapsed. She described Mrs. Jenness's car perfectly and said when it went in the water there was a girl on top trying to push Mrs. Jenness back inside."

"That's not true!" Vicki said.

"She killed her!"

"I was trying to save her life."

"Calm down," the nurse said.

"I want a GC guard notified right now," Joyce said. "She's a murderer!"

Vicki saw Judd talking to a woman in the corner. A moment later the woman walked up and demanded silence. Vicki saw a smudge on her forehead. "There will be no more fighting about this." The woman looked at Vicki. "You go back to your tent."

"If you won't do anything about it," Joyce shouted, "I'm going to the authorities!"

"Give her something to calm her," the woman said.

"No!" Joyce shouted as the nurse grabbed a needle. "I'll get you for this, Byrne!"

Lionel and the others were flown to Mount Prospect by helicopter. They checked in at a shelter but were turned away.

"Head over to Nicolae High," a worker said. "They have more room there."

"That's where we're supposed to wind up anyway," Conrad said.

While walking, Lionel looked for anything familiar.

The streets and buildings were a mess. But the incident at the mall had stirred him. He now recalled the GC attack on Chicago. He remembered the day it happened and the sound of the bombers overhead. The explosions. The fear he had as he listened. But he couldn't remember the people, and he knew the people were the most important part of the puzzle.

"Do you still have those diaries?" Lionel asked Conrad.

"Didn't have room to pack them," Conrad said. "I brought your Bible, though. Been reading it."

Lionel looked at the inscription in the Bible as he walked. *Who is Ryan?* Lionel thought. *And what does he have to do with all this?*

"You think you're gonna find your friends?" Conrad said.

"The thought's crossed my mind," Lionel said.

When they neared Nicolae High, Lionel stopped the others. "We have to be careful not to come on too strong. We don't want to try and impress people with how important we are."

"Is that what you think we want to do?" Felicia said.

"I'm not saying—"

"You're not the boss of everybody," Melinda interrupted. She rolled her eyes.

"Like it or not, the commander put me in charge," Lionel said. "And I want it understood. We might not have anything to report for months. It's like going undercover."

"Give us some credit," Felicia said. "We went through the training too."

They walked in silence to Nicolae High. Lionel talked with a staff worker. "This place has been turned into a morgue," the man said. "We've had a hard time keeping track of all the bodies."

"Where are people staying?" Conrad said.

"We have four shelters in the area," the man said, pointing them out on a crudely drawn map. "Get to any of these and you'll find food and a place to stay warm."

"Are any teachers or administrators of the school still around?" Lionel asked.

"Plenty of them. They're under all those sheets."

Judd called a meeting of the Young Trib Force that evening. He commended Vicki, Shelly, and Darrion for the way they had handled themselves during the past few days.

"It's clear we need a place to hide," Judd said. "The GC will be looking for me, and this thing with Joyce could blow up in Vicki's face."

"What's the deal with her anyway?" Darrion said.

"I knew her from school," Shelly said. "After the disappearances, we hung out together. When I became a Christian, she turned on me."

"I remember talking with her," Vicki said. "Joyce said she believed Jesus came back. She thought it was the only explanation."

"So she's a believer?" Darrion said.

"No," Vicki said. "She said if the disappearances were God's idea of how to do things, she wanted no part of it.

Then she told me not to waste my breath trying to convince her."

"So she's chosen not to believe," Darrion said.

"Exactly," Vicki said.

"That may be why she's trying to pin murder on you," Judd said. "She must hate anything that reminds her of the truth."

Judd put together a list of people they knew who were missing or dead. They were all concerned about John and Mark. Vicki asked Judd to explain what he knew about the mark on their foreheads.

Judd noticed a strange young man walking toward them.

"Vicki!" Charlie shouted. "They kicked me out. Boom, just like that, out the door, on the street, no more Charlie in the store, or hospital, or whatever it is. Said I had to find my own place to stay."

"What about the nurse?" Vicki said.

"She got in trouble," Charlie said. "Lost a patient. I think it was that kid I carried for you."

"Oh, no," Vicki said.

"Oh yeah," Charlie said. "They kicked me out and told me not to come back."

Vicki introduced Charlie to the rest of the group. Charlie shook hands with Judd, but his hand was limp.

"What're you guys looking at each other's heads for?" Charlie said.

Judd looked at Vicki. Vicki shrugged.

"We're talking about . . . something that we all have in common," Judd said.

"You're in a club?" Charlie said. "Can I be in too?"

"Well," Judd said, "it's not really a club. It's more like—"

"You guys look like friends," Charlie said. "Happy. I want to join. Now what's with your head?"

"We all have a mark," Vicki said. "It means we're for real."

Charlie squinted at Vicki and looked her over. "You guys are crazy. There's nothin' on your head."

"You can't see it," Vicki said. "Only those who believe can see it."

"This is really weird," Charlie said.

Judd wondered if they were telling Charlie too much. He took Vicki aside.

"He's the one who helped me carry Ryan," Vicki said.

"I just don't want to take a chance and tell him stuff that might get us in trouble."

"How can we keep it from him? Isn't that why we're here?"

"Of course it is, but we have to make sure we can trust the people we tell."

"Oh yeah," Vicki said. "I haven't seen that in the Bible lately. Besides, you were talking about this stuff to a woman who's with Enigma Babylon One World Faith."

"She was asking questions," Judd said. "I had no choice."

"Charlie's asking questions too."

Charlie interrupted and pointed to Shelly. "That girl says if I believe like you guys, I get something on my head too. Can I get it now, or do I have to pay something?"

Lionel and Conrad unpacked two tents the Global Community had given them while Melinda and Felicia checked out the shelter for food.

"Recognize anything around here?" Conrad said.

Lionel was cautious. "Some stuff came back about the war when we were at the mall, but none of this looks familiar."

"How about the high school?" Conrad said.

Lionel shook his head.

"It was pretty messed up. Maybe we'll find somebody who knew you."

Felicia and Melinda were out of breath when they returned.

"Where's the food?" Lionel said.

"Just got a lead on something," Felicia said. "I met a girl in the medical tent who says somebody committed a murder during the earthquake."

"That's out of our league," Conrad said.

"The girl says the person who killed this lady is one of those religious nuts we're supposed to be looking for," Felicia said. "And get this. The girl was accused of trying to push her beliefs on people at Nicolae High."

"Sounds like it'd be worth checking out," Conrad said.

"How'd you find this girl?" Lionel said. "She just walked up to you and spilled her guts?"

"She said nobody's listening to her," Melinda said. "I told her we were with the Global Community."

"You what?!" Lionel said.

"I didn't say we were officially with them or

anything," Melinda said. "I just said we could look into it if she wanted."

Lionel shook his head. "Let's go back over there and get the story."

Judd thought Charlie seemed a little odd. Slow. He looked away when he talked to Judd, and he had a funny walk. But Vicki was right. Those things didn't disqualify him from knowing about God.

"First thing I need you to know," Judd said, "is that this isn't a club you join. Do you get that?"

"Not a club, got it. What do I have to do to get one of those things on my head?"

Judd rubbed his neck. "You can't do this just because you want a thing on your head, Charlie."

"Come on, tell me. I want to see everybody else's."

"Then we have to talk seriously about what we believe."

"Believe about what?"

"About God. About what happened to the people who disappeared."

"My sister got killed in the big shake," Charlie said.

"That's what Vicki said. I'm sorry."

"They kicked me out of the store where she worked. Told me not to come back."

"You can stay with us for a while."

"Right. So what am I supposed to believe?"

Judd sighed. "Did your sister ever take you to church?"

Lionel told the others to wait outside while he talked
with Joyce. "I don't want it looking like we're here on
some kind of official business."

Joyce was still groggy from the medication, but she
was able to talk. She repeated her story, then added, "The
girl's name is Vicki Byrne."

Lionel thought about the name. It sounded familiar.

"I was near the office when Mrs. Jenness took Vicki
out to the car," Joyce said. "I know she killed her. She's
probably bolted by now."

"Why would she kill your principal?" Lionel said. He
wrote the name *Mrs. Jenness* on a piece of paper.

Joyce cocked her head. "Do I know you? You don't go
to Nicolae High, do you?"

"Not anymore," Lionel said. "Finish your story."

"Mrs. Jenness had the goods on her. She found something and was taking Vicki away."

Lionel noticed someone on the other side of the tent.
A girl with red hair was looking at him. She smiled when
Lionel spotted her and waved. Then she rushed toward
him.

Joyce sat up in bed and screamed, "That's her!"

The girl with red hair stopped, then turned and ran
out of the tent.

Vicki was out of breath when she found Judd. She interrupted his conversation with Charlie. "I saw him. He's
here!"

"Who?" Judd said.

"Lionel! He was in the tent talking with Joyce."

Judd stood. "I'll be back," he said to Charlie.

"That's good," Charlie said. "I can wait. Go find your friend. I'm cool with that."

Judd wondered if it really was Lionel. His heart raced as he neared the medical tent.

"Go get her!" Joyce shouted.

"She won't get far," Lionel said.

"Your friend said you're with the Global Community. You can do something about her, can't you?"

Lionel frowned. "Sometimes my friends get carried away."

"But she told me if this really was a murder, the GC would look into it. She promised."

Lionel studied Joyce. It was possible they had been in the same hallway together only a few weeks ago at Nicolae High. Her locker could have been a few feet from his own.

"Don't you believe me?" Joyce said. "She's a murderer!"

JUDD recognized Lionel right away. Lionel wore different clothes and seemed surprised when Judd approached.

"Good to see you again," Judd said, smiling.

Lionel backed away. "Do I know you?"

"Of course you do."

Lionel paused. "Are you Ryan?"

Judd laughed. "This is a joke, right? It's Judd, remember?"

"That guy was in on it too," Joyce said. "Judd Thompson. Last year at graduation he gave this speech, and the GC—"

"I'll handle this," Lionel said. He turned to Judd. "How do I know you?"

Judd shook his head. "You stayed in my house. I drove you to school. We ate meals together. Went to church. Don't you remember any of that?"

Lionel looked down. "I remember reading something about you in my diary."

Vicki couldn't stand it any longer. She didn't care about Joyce, she was going to see her friend. She rushed up and gave Lionel a hug.

"That's her," Joyce shouted. "Somebody arrest her!"

"Enough," Lionel said.

Lionel bristled and Vicki pulled away.

"What's wrong?" Vicki said.

"He doesn't remember us," Judd said.

"That's crazy," Vicki said.

"I had an accident during the earthquake. I could remember stuff about the camp, but not anything before that."

"What camp?" Vicki said. "You went down South to be with your family, didn't you?"

Lionel frowned.

"A man from your family came to our school," Vicki said. "You had a hard time deciding, but you finally went. We didn't hear any more from you."

"I demand you do something," Joyce said.

Lionel held up a hand. "Give me a minute to think, OK?"

Lionel walked away. Images and thoughts swirled in his head. The school. A man taking him to a seedy hotel in Chicago. A van ride. Getting chased through a swamp. It was all coming back slowly and in pieces.

102

But Lionel also saw Commander Blancka's stern face. Lionel had pledged to serve the Global Community. If Joyce was telling the truth, he should report Judd and Vicki. If they were really his friends, he should help them. He felt trapped.

Judd and Vicki moved away from Joyce.

"What's going on with Lionel?" Vicki said.

"We can't worry about him. We have to figure out what's best for us. Maybe we should get out of here before something bad happens."

"And leave Lionel?" Vicki said. "No way."

Another boy joined Lionel, and the two returned. "This is Conrad," Lionel said.

Judd stared at the boy. He recalled Taylor Graham talking about a brother named Conrad.

"What's your last name?" Judd said.

"Why do you want to know?"

"Is it Graham?"

Conrad looked startled, then composed himself. "How'd you know that?"

"I knew your brother," Judd said.

Conrad's eyes widened. "You knew Taylor? How is he?"

Lionel held up a hand. "You can talk later. Right now I want to get to the bottom of the murder question."

"You don't actually believe her, do you?" Vicki said.

"I don't know what to believe," Lionel said. "Step outside the tent. I want to get more information."

Vicki walked away with Lionel. Joyce shouted behind
them. "Why are you taking information? Are you some
kind of police officer?"

"I'm a citizen of the Global Community like you,"
Lionel said.

Vicki took Lionel by the shoulders. "Look at me.
You're talking crazy. Don't you remember? Your mother
worked for *Global Weekly*. Then your whole family disappeared. I knew your sister, Clarice. We rode the bus
together."

Lionel put away his notebook and pen.

"You and I met Bruce on the same day," Vicki said.

"Go back," Lionel said. "Tell me more about my
family."

Judd walked outside with Conrad.

"You really knew my brother?" Conrad said.

"I'll tell you about your brother if you'll tell me about
Lionel," Judd said.

Conrad nodded. "We've spent the last few weeks in a
Global Community camp down South. They trained us to
become GC Morale Monitors."

"Morale Monitors?" Judd said.

"We're supposed to blend in and report anyone suspicious to the GC command."

"Suspicious?"

"Yeah, like religious fanatics who talk about Jesus
coming back," Conrad said.

Judd scowled. "Why doesn't he remember us?"

"Probably a combination of the mind control the GC used and the fact that he got conked on the head. Pretty much wiped out his hard drive, if you know what I mean. Before the accident, he was talking about going along with the GC program until he could get back up here to his friends. Now he's pretty much following them lockstep."

"Why are you telling me this? You're one of them, right?"

Conrad glanced about. "I've been reading Lionel's Bible and some of the materials he brought with him. I even got on the Internet and found that rabbi's Web site. I want to know more."

The more Lionel listened, the more sense Vicki made. His family had disappeared and left him behind.

"Didn't I have a relative?" Lionel said. "A guy?"

"Uncle André."

"Yeah," Lionel said. He closed his eyes as Vicki continued.

"He's dead. He had a run-in with some bad guys. That's when Judd took us all into his house. We had meetings just about every day with our pastor, Bruce Barnes."

Lionel shook his head, his eyes still shut. "I'm not remembering any of that."

"You and Ryan used to fight like cats and do—"

"Who did you say?"

"Ryan. You and Ryan used to fight over the stupidest things."

"Where is he?" Lionel said.

"Come with me," Vicki said.

Judd told Conrad the story of meeting Taylor Graham and flying to Israel. "We didn't know it at the time, but your brother was trying to protect you."

"He knew I was being held."

"Yes, but he protected us too. He was a good man."

"Was?"

"I can't be sure, but I think your brother didn't make it through the earthquake."

Conrad frowned. Judd described Taylor's fall into the gorge. It was the last Judd saw of him.

"If anybody could survive that, it's my brother," Conrad said. "Where'd Lionel and the girl go?"

Lionel sensed Vicki and Judd were telling the truth. In the back of his mind he saw Commander Blancka. The man would want to know everything. If Lionel contacted them, it would only be minutes before the GC converged on them.

"Do you know those two following us?" Vicki said.

Lionel turned and saw Melinda and Felicia. "They're in our group."

When they reached the church, Vicki led Lionel to Ryan's grave. Phoenix still stood watch, jumping up and growling when the group drew closer.

"Ryan's name was in my Bible," Lionel said.

"He found a bunch of them and gave you one. This is his dog, Phoenix. He named him that because—"

"—because he found him in the ashes," Lionel said. "You remember?"

"No, just the story about the bird rising." Lionel kicked at the dirt around the grave. "Maybe if I saw his face. Do you have a picture?"

Vicki took Lionel by the shoulders again. "Look at my forehead. Do you see that mark?"

Lionel shook his head. "I've already looked. I don't have that on my head."

"You do," Vicki said. "I can see it. Look at my forehead."

Lionel squinted, leaned closer, and said, "Yeah, it looks like a bruise or a smudge."

"When you asked God to come into your life, he sealed you. This is the sign of that seal. He's not gonna let you go because you bumped your head."

Lionel put his head in his hands and sat on the grave. "This is too much."

"Do you believe me?" Vicki said.

"It doesn't matter whether I do or don't. I have to file a report."

"You don't have to. Think about it. If we're really enemies of the GC and you're our friend, you're an enemy of the GC."

"What if you're lying?"

"Why would I?"

"To get out of the murder rap."

"It's Joyce's word against mine," Vicki said. "You can't believe her."

"Not true," Felicia said, coming up behind them. "We found the other witness."

"Where?" Lionel said.

"At the next shelter," Felicia said. "She told us she saw Vicki on top of Mrs. Jenness's car, trying to push her under the water. And it worked. The woman's dead. They just found her car this morning. Her body's still in it."

"What are you going to do, Lionel?" Melinda said.

"Just leave us alone a minute, OK?"

Melinda and Felicia walked away. Lionel rammed his fist into the grave. Phoenix barked and jumped up. His ears stood straight.

Lionel pulled Vicki close. "If I turn you in and you really are my friends, I'll have betrayed you. And I'll have betrayed the memory of my friend."

Lionel grabbed a fistful of dirt and held it in his hand. Judd and Conrad came close.

"You have to believe them," Conrad whispered to Lionel.

Lionel rubbed his eyes. Images flashed through his brain. A boy on a bike riding next to him. Running through a school hallway at night.

Lionel looked up. "We fought about something, didn't we?"

"You and Ryan fought about everything," Judd said.

"We were putting something in the back of a car," Lionel said, his eyes darting back and forth. "The other kid grabbed me around the neck and wrestled me to the ground."

"You were loading Bibles," Judd said. "I had to separate you."

"He had a stash somewhere. . . ." Lionel said, his voice quickening. "He'd go off and wouldn't come back for hours."

"We found it in the church," Vicki said. "Hundreds of them were stacked up in there."

". . . and the man showed us a tape . . . Bruce . . . it was right in there that I finally understood about God. . . ."

Lionel felt the emotion rising. Things were getting clearer, like a blindfold suddenly lifting. The closeness of his friends had brought everything back.

Lionel looked at Judd. "The rabbi?"

"We don't know where he is," Judd said, "but we assume he survived the quake."

Vicki handed Lionel the note Ryan had written. Lionel scanned it, then fell beside the grave of his friend. "I wasn't here for him."

Melinda and Felicia returned. "Excuse us, but we've got a situation here," Melinda said, pointing to Vicki and Judd. "She's accused of murder, and there's evidence he's against the Global Community."

"There's no way Vicki would have killed Mrs. Jenness," Lionel said.

"Are you taking their side?" Felicia said.

"I just want to sort this thing out," Lionel said.

"Let them explain their case to Commander Blancka," Melinda said.

"I'm not reporting anything until—"

Lionel was interrupted by the *thwock-thwock-thwock* of rotor blades. He could hear the chopper but couldn't see it yet.

"We filed a report a few minutes ago," Melinda said.

Lionel looked at Vicki and Judd. The memories were flooding back now. He was finally home, finally back with the people he loved. And they were in more danger than they had ever been in before.

LIONEL saw the chopper and had to do something. Judd and Vicki looked scared. *They should be*, Lionel thought. *I have to get rid of Melinda and Felicia.*

The two Morale Monitors started toward the chopper, then turned.

"You two go and get Blancka," Lionel said. "We'll let him sort out this mess."

"They could run," Melinda said, nodding toward Judd and Vicki.

"I'm staying," Felicia said.

Lionel grabbed his gun. "If they run, I'll shoot 'em."

The girls hesitated.

"Conrad and I can handle these two," Lionel said. "Go! The commander will be waiting."

Melinda and Felicia ran toward the chopper, and Lionel put away his gun. "We have to hurry. Conrad, I'm assuming you're with us."

"I don't know about this God stuff," Conrad said, "but I'm with you."

"Vick and I need to get out of here," Judd said. "Question is whether you guys go with us."

"We should work behind the scenes for now," Lionel said.

"You're crazy," Conrad said. "I don't want to stay here." Lionel shook his head.

"It's almost dark," Judd said. "They won't be able to see us soon."

"We could hide or find what's left of my house," Vicki said.

"No way," Conrad said. "The chopper's high-tech. Lights, night vision, even heat sensors. They'll spot you in two minutes."

"Time's running out," Vicki said. "If we stay here, that commander guy—"

Judd cut her off. "Ryan's place. Under the church."

"You think we can get in there?" Vicki said.

"It's worth a shot," Judd said. "Could the chopper find us under all that concrete?"

"Yeah," Conrad said. "It wouldn't be easy, but they'd still spot you."

"Not if they think we ran," Judd said. "You two cover for us and send them the wrong way."

"If they'll believe us," Conrad said.

Judd took Lionel's flashlight. It was pitch black inside the church basement.

"You sure this is where Ryan's hideout was?" Vicki said.

"We're close," Judd said.

"Look stable?" Lionel said.

"Can't tell," Judd said, pulling at loose stones and dirt.

"Another tremor and you guys will be smashed," Conrad said.

Judd held the light while Vicki climbed through the opening. A block fell near Vicki with a sickening thud and she froze. Gathering herself, she continued.

When she reached the bottom she called out, "There's an old steel desk down here that should protect us."

Judd followed her inside. When he heard chopper blades, he turned. "What about you guys?"

Lionel pushed him. "We're OK."

"No," Judd said. "If those girls find us gone, they'll know you helped." Judd climbed out of the hole.

Lionel looked over his shoulder. "Get back inside!"

Conrad held out his gun to Judd.

"What?"

"Take it and smack me underneath the eye," Conrad said. "I'll tell them you overpowered me."

"I can't hit you."

"You're saving us both," Conrad said.

Judd took the gun and carefully hit Conrad just under his eye.

Conrad frowned. "My grandmother can hit harder than that." But his eyes watered and a red mark rose on his cheek.

"Get in there!" Lionel said, ripping the radio from

Conrad's shoulder and tossing it into the hole. "Sit tight and keep an ear on that. We'll be in touch."

Judd climbed into the darkness and followed Vicki's voice to the steel desk.

A shot rang out. Then two more.

"What was that?" Vicki said.

"Lionel," Judd guessed. "Hope he knows what he's doing."

Lionel had keyed his microphone when he fired. He wanted the commander to believe he and Conrad were hot after Judd and Vicki. But he also wanted to scare Phoenix away. It worked. Phoenix darted into the rubble of the neighborhood and disappeared.

Lionel keyed his mike. "This is Washington! The suspects are getting away! Graham got knocked down!"

Commander Blancka sounded enraged. "What's going on down there?"

"The guy hit him, sir," Lionel said, waving for Conrad to run with him. Lionel was out of breath. "He grabbed Conrad's gun! I got a couple of shots off!"

Lionel heard Melinda protest in the background. Commander Blancka said, "Where are they now?"

"We're in pursuit," Lionel said. "East of the ruined church. Send the chopper!"

Silence.

Come on, Lionel thought, *believe me!*

A few moments later the commander barked, "Washington and Graham, bring it in."

"They're getting away!"

"That's an order!"

Judd squeezed under the desk with Vicki. He turned the radio down. The dust made him cough. It felt good to be close to Vicki again.

There was a long silence. Vicki finally spoke. "I can't believe Ryan's not coming back. Why would God let that happen?"

Judd shook his head. "I remember how hard it was for Ryan when Bruce died. It was hard on all of us, but him especially. Now I know how the little guy felt."

"He hated you calling him that," Vicki said.

Judd nodded. "He had a lot of heart. He never gave up."

Vicki sniffed, and Judd could tell she was wiping her eyes. "Sometimes it feels like God doesn't care," she said. "Like he's a million miles away."

Judd's leg cramped and he scooted lower under the desk. He braced himself on the bottom of the desk drawer and felt paper taped to the underside. Carefully, he loosened a thick packet.

"What is it?" Vicki said.

Judd put the envelope on the floor and cupped his hands around the end of the flashlight. In the dim light Judd saw Ryan's name on the front of the envelope. Judd tore it open and looked inside.

"Verses," Judd said as Vicki held the light. "Bruce's handwriting."

Judd read aloud, "Ryan, if you ever lose hope, this will help you. Isaiah 40:30-31."

Even youths will become exhausted, and young men will give up. But those who wait on the Lord will find new strength. They will fly high on wings like eagles. They will run and not grow weary. They will walk and not faint.

Judd stuffed the envelope in his pocket. "There's a whole stack of those. And stuff Ryan wrote about talking to people about Christ."

"We'll read it later, right?" Vicki said.

"For sure."

———————————

It was dark when Lionel and Conrad reached the commander. Melinda and Felicia stood near him with arms folded.

Before the commander spoke Lionel said, "Start east of the church."

"We'll handle it," the commander said, inspecting Conrad's eye. "How'd you get this?"

"Guy hit me with my own gun," Conrad said. "Made Lionel put his down too."

"Lucky he didn't kill you," the commander said. "Where's your radio, Conrad?"

"Must have lost it in the struggle."

Felicia smirked. "Or maybe you two gave it to them."

Lionel turned on her. "We almost get killed, and you—"

"Enough!" Commander Blancka said. He radioed the

chopper pilot. "Search the area. Let us know when you have something."

"I'm telling you, sir," Felicia said, "these two were like big pals with Lionel. Why wouldn't they take his gun?"

"How should I know?" Lionel shot back.

"He's helping them," Felicia said.

"Enough," the commander said.

"Sir, request permission to help in the search," Lionel said.

The commander said, "You're here at base until this gets straightened out."

"But, sir—"

"You're staying. Is that clear?"

The radio squawked. "Got something, sir."

Vicki held her breath as the chopper flew overhead. Judd whispered, "Sorry to get this close, but the smaller we are the better."

"It's OK."

Vicki was glad Judd was back and safe, but their troubles were starting again. She had told God she would do anything to help others come to know him, but she wanted just one day where everyone she loved was safe. Every time she thought of Ryan she felt a pain in her chest.

The chopper hovered, then turned south and away from them.

"What happens if they catch us?" Vicki said.

Judd put his head against the desk and sighed. "Lionel's smart. He'll lead them the other way."

"Then where do we go?" Vicki said. "Every place we know is flattened. The GC are crawling all over the shelters. They're sure to spot us there."

"How about Darrion's house?" Judd said. "That bunker Mr. Stahley built under the hill was like a steel fortress. If the hill hasn't collapsed around it, we might be able to get inside."

"That's pretty far away," Vicki said. "I don't see how we can get there on foot."

"We'll have to find a vehicle," Judd said. "What do you think?"

"I'm willing to give it a shot. We just need to—"

Judd put a finger to Vicki's lips. "Someone's outside."

JUDD'S heart beat furiously. Someone was trying to get in. Dirt and rocks fell.

Judd picked up a stone. He wouldn't be taken prisoner by the GC again. Judd thought about running. If the chopper pinpointed their position, they were easy targets.

Vicki grabbed Judd's arm and whispered, "What if it's Lionel?"

Judd shook his head. "He would have said something."

Judd eased out for a better look. The ghostly moon glowed through the hole. Suddenly, a figure appeared in the entrance. Judd braced himself and tried not to breathe. The figure stepped toward the hideout, then backed away.

A high-pitched whine, then breathing. Judd stood. "Be right back," he said.

"Don't," Vicki said.

But Judd crawled away. He returned and plopped Phoenix down between them.

"Hello, boy!" she said. Phoenix licked Vicki's face.

Judd placed Phoenix on top of the desk and said, "Stay!" Phoenix put his head down and whimpered.

"Maybe they'll see him and not us," Judd said.

"I wish he'd brought us something to eat," Vicki said.

Lionel stayed with Commander Blancka's aide while the others followed the chopper. He and the aide set up a tent for the commander.

A few minutes later the group trudged in. Conrad winked at Lionel. The commander held Vicki's friend Charlie by the shirt and dragged him inside.

When he first met the boy, Lionel thought Charlie was strange. Charlie wouldn't look him in the eye. His hands and feet were always moving.

"I told you I don't know where they are," Charlie said nervously.

"Let's start over," the commander said. "How do you know them?"

"I met the girl at the store, or the hospital, whatever you want to call it," Charlie said. "My sister was killed in the big earthshake. So I went over—"

"Focus!" the commander shouted. "How did you know this guy and girl?"

"I helped the girl," Charlie said, shaking. "We carried the kid over here and buried him one night. Real spooky."

"You buried a body?" the commander said.

"She asked me to help, so I did."

The commander looked to Melinda and Felicia. "Is that the girl accused of murder?"

"Yes, sir," Melinda said. "Sounds like more than one."

Lionel knew Vicki hadn't killed Mrs. Jenness, and to think she had harmed Ryan was crazy. But he couldn't say anything.

Conrad tugged Lionel's sleeve and nodded toward the door. "Back in a few," he whispered. "Cover for me."

Lionel nodded. Conrad slipped into the night as the commander continued with Charlie. "What did you do after you helped them bury the body?"

"I talked with that guy about his head," Charlie said.

"His head?"

"They had a club and I wanted to join. If you made it, they put something on your head that people outside the club couldn't see. If I believed like they do I'd get a thing on my head. Something about God and how all the people disappeared."

Lionel was sweating. Charlie knew Vicki and Judd were his friends. Would he tell the commander? Lionel tried to stay out of Charlie's sight.

"I got kicked out of the store where my sister worked," Charlie continued, "so I came here. They told me to wait, and I did till that big helichopper came. Didn't like all the noise. I ran away."

"And you have no idea where they are now?" the commander said.

"Last I saw they were down by that kid's grave. The

121

girl cried. She gave me this." Charlie held up a Bible. "I think she was real sorry about him dying."

"Sorry for killing him," Melinda said, "or sorry she might get caught."

Lionel fumed.

The commander threw the Bible in the corner. "We'll go to the church." He looked for Conrad.

"He went to get his eye checked, sir," Lionel said.

"Keep an eye on that guy," the commander told Lionel. "Send Graham our way when he gets back."

Judd told Vicki more about his escape from the GC. "I told the people in the cave my name. I figure they passed it on to the GC."

"But the quake knocked out most of the communication lines," Vicki said.

"They're going up all over," Judd said. "It's like Carpathia was ready for this. The information will get back that I'm not dead. If they catch me now, who knows where they'll send me?"

Phoenix growled and the hair on his back stood straight. "Easy, boy," Judd said. "We need you right where you are."

Someone fell into the room with a thud. Phoenix barked, and Judd and Vicki stared into the beam of a flashlight.

"Good," Conrad said. "I thought you might have run." He brought them up-to-date.

"That Charlie is bad news," Judd said.

"He's sweet," Vicki said. "He deserved to hear the truth."

Judd said, "Conrad, you'd better get back before they miss you."

"Not yet," Conrad said. He sat cross-legged in front of the desk. "By daylight we might be able to move you."

"You think it'll be safe then?" Judd said.

"Lionel will have a plan." Conrad scooted closer. "I also came down here because I want to know more."

"About what?" Vicki said.

"About God. You know, the forehead stuff."

Phoenix sat up again and bristled.

"Guess we can't talk now," Conrad said. "Later?"

"I don't think we'll be getting much sleep," Judd said.

"If we have to run," Vicki said, "tell Lionel we'll try to make it to the Stahley house. He should tell Darrion and Shelly to meet us there."

"I don't know where that is, but Lionel will, right?" Conrad said.

"Right. Darrion can lead you there if she needs to."

"Sit tight as long as you can," Conrad said as he crawled through the entrance. He looked back at Phoenix. "And keep him quiet."

Lionel sat Charlie down and looked at him sternly. "You know Vicki didn't kill Ryan."

"I know, but the big man talks mean, and I'm scared he's going to yell at me."

"You have to tell the truth."

"You're one of them, aren't you?" Charlie said.

Lionel nodded. "But don't tell the commander, OK?"

"I won't if you tell me how I can get a thing on my head."

Lionel pulled up a chair. "Charlie, this isn't a club. And you can't be part of the group if all you want is something on your head."

"Then how can I join?"

Lionel struggled to remember his own story. His past with the other kids had flooded back quickly. Now, as he talked with Charlie, he relived the moment when he finally understood the truth.

"I treated church like a club when I was a kid," Lionel said. "It was just a place to hang while my parents sang and did their Bible study."

"So you didn't have the thing on your forehead back then?"

"Charlie, stop talking about the mark and start listening."

"Right, got it. Start listening."

"The thing I missed was that God is real. He made you and me for a purpose. And he wants us to know him."

"I believe that," Charlie said. "I don't think we got evolved or came from monkeys or whatever they say we came from."

"Good," Lionel said. "But it's not enough just to believe God exists. He offers each of us a gift."

"You mean the thing on—"

"Stop with that!" Lionel shouted. Charlie shrank in his chair. "God offers everybody forgiveness. When I first met Judd and Vicki, I didn't even know I needed it. I was so scared because all my family had disappeared. Deep down I knew I'd missed the most important thing. I had never asked Jesus to forgive me. That's the gift. If you ask God to come into your heart and forgive you—"

Commander Blancka's aide returned.

Vicki held Phoenix and tried to keep him quiet. She strained to hear voices outside.

"This is where they were standing," a girl said.

"And this is the grave?" a deep-voiced man said. "Dig it up."

Vicki looked at Judd in horror. Judd put a finger to his lips.

Vicki heard Conrad, out of breath. "Sir, I saw movement near a house about a hundred yards back."

Commander Blancka radioed the pilot the information, and Vicki heard chopper blades.

"Located your radio?" Commander Blancka said.

"Not yet, sir," Conrad said.

"That's easy enough," the commander said. He keyed his microphone. "Commander Blancka requesting a radio locate."

"What's that, sir?" Conrad said.

"The radio has a homing device. Lets us find you."

The radio squawked. "Commander Blancka, we need the ID number for the radio."

Vicki quickly turned off the radio. They had to get rid of it.

LIONEL heard the commander's call and knew Judd and Vicki still had Conrad's radio.

"Where you going?" the aide said as Lionel stood to leave.

"I'm done baby-sitting. I'm going to catch these two."

"But the commander—"

"When I turn them in, he'll be glad," Lionel said as he rushed through the door of the tent. "Keep an eye on Charlie."

As he ran toward the church, Lionel formed a plan. He would tell the commander he had helped Judd and Vicki escape. They were long gone. The GC would court-martial him or worse, but Lionel didn't care.

Lionel felt guilty. If he had only said no to the man who had taken him south. If he had resisted the GC training after his accident. He shook his head. He couldn't think about that now. He had to get to the commander before anyone found Judd and Vicki.

Lionel's radio squawked. "We've got that locate you wanted on the radio, sir."

"Give me the coordinates," Commander Blancka said.

"Sir, the unit is moving."

"That means they're on the run!" the commander said. "Where are they?"

"From the description of your own location, I'd say they're only a few yards away."

Lionel's heart sank. The underground shelter had become Judd and Vicki's prison. Lionel had given them Conrad's radio. *How could I be so dumb!* he thought.

Lionel swore.

So, he thought, *there's some of that still in me.* He picked up his pace and neared the group. The helicopter was in position over the church with its lights trained on the commander and the others.

"Somebody's running!" Melinda shouted, drawing her gun.

Lionel shouted and held up his hands.

"What are you doing here?" the commander shouted. "I told you—"

"Sir, I have something I need to tell you," Lionel said.

The pilot said, "They're a few yards to your right."

"Sir," Lionel said.

"Hang on to it!" the commander shouted.

"This is important, sir," Lionel said.

"Commander, look!" Conrad shouted, pointing to a figure in the shadows.

Melinda and Felicia pointed their guns toward the figure. Lionel fumbled with his own gun, then turned,

hoping he wouldn't see Judd and Vicki with their hands up. He gasped when he saw Phoenix bounce out of the shadows and into the beam of the searchlight. Conrad's radio was neatly tied around the dog's neck. Phoenix sat and put his paw in the air.

"It's a dog!" the commander shouted into his radio. "They're not here! Keep looking!"

The chopper flew away. Melinda and Felicia moved toward Phoenix, their guns still up. Phoenix growled. "He might be booby-trapped," Felicia said.

"Booby-trapped, my eye," the commander said. He strode past them and unhooked the radio from the dog's back. "They're taunting us with this dog, trying to make us look like fools. They're probably miles from here at one of the shelters by now. Probably gettin' a good night's sleep while we're out here hunting them down."

"What should we do, sir?" Conrad said.

"We're gonna find 'em," the commander said. "Not one of us is going to stop until we find those two."

Felicia objected when the commander told each of them to go in a different direction. "I don't trust Lionel," she said.

"Fine," the commander said. "He goes with you."

"But—"

"No buts!" the commander barked. "Graham, strap your radio on and follow this dog. See if he leads you anywhere. And Washington, what was it you were going to say a minute ago?"

"It's not important now, sir," Lionel said.

Vicki trembled. "Do you think it worked?"

"The chopper moved away," Judd said. "That's a good sign."

They sat still a few minutes, waiting for someone to burst into their hiding place, but no one came.

They had outfitted Phoenix with the radio and pushed him out the entrance. In the noise and confusion they had gone unnoticed, and Phoenix had done exactly what they wanted. He had gone away from the church.

"What now?" Vicki said.

"We wait," Judd said.

"But they'll see us through the chopper's heat sensor," Vicki said. "I think we ought to bolt while we have the chance."

"That's what they want us to do," Judd said, "lose our cool and run."

Vicki frowned. "I'm not losing my cool; I'm looking for our best options."

"I didn't mean it like that," Judd said. "They think we're on the run. We'll hide here until Lionel tells us to move."

"What if we split up?" Vicki said. "Wouldn't that give us a better chance?"

"Not with that chopper," Judd said. "I think we should stick together and wait to hear from Lionel."

Vicki felt cramped under the desk. "Let me outta here," she said. "My legs are going to sleep."

Vicki shoved her way out and knocked over a pile of rocks.

130

"Watch it!" Judd said.

"Just because you're a year older doesn't mean you can boss me around," she said. "You're doing the same thing you did with Ryan! You bossed him and made him feel like a jerk!"

Judd hung his head. "I want to talk, but if you don't whisper, you'll lead them right to us."

"You're doing it again," Vicki whispered. "You don't think I know we need to be quiet?"

"We have a different opinion about our next move," Judd said, "but we're on the same team. We both want to get out of here alive and stay away from the GC."

"We do have that in common," Vicki said.

Judd sighed and turned his head.

"What is it?" Vicki said.

"The truth is, I feel a sense of responsibility for you."

Vicki bristled.

"Not like you're my child," he continued, "but my friend who I wouldn't want anything bad to happen to." Judd's voice cracked. "Vicki, I really care about you. And believe me, I've kicked myself a thousand times for the way I treated Ryan."

"I know you care," Vicki said.

"It's your call," Judd said. "If you want to run, I'll go with you."

"We'll stay," Vicki said as she crawled under the desk. "I'm sorry for saying that about Ryan."

Judd nodded and sat beside her. She put a hand on his shoulder. He seemed so tired.

Judd awoke twenty minutes later as Conrad slipped into their hiding place.

"I could only talk to Lionel for a minute, but he agreed with me," Conrad said. "We'll create a diversion after I leave and get you two out of here. This place is going to be crawling with GC by morning."

"Are we that important?" Vicki said.

"The commander's taking it personally. He wants you two bad."

Conrad went over the plan and made sure their watches were in sync. He also said they would find Shelly and Darrion and get them to the Stahley mansion as soon as possible.

"Something else," Conrad said. "If the GC get close, remember, they have guns. We have orders to shoot to kill."

Judd looked at Vicki.

"And if they catch you, don't do anything stupid. Lionel and I will figure out something."

"What if the Stahley place is destroyed?" Vicki said.

"There's a picnic area in the forest preserve behind it," Judd said. "We can meet there."

The commander's voice blasted over the radio. "Graham, where are you?"

"Still following the dog, sir. No sign of them yet."

"Roger. Keep an eye on him. Out."

Conrad rolled his eyes. "I have a few minutes before

we put the plan in motion. Would you mind telling me more about the God thing?"

"How much do you know?" Judd said.

"I've checked out the rabbi a couple of times on the Web. I know all the stuff that's happening was predicted in the Bible."

"It took us a while to figure it out," Judd said. "A pastor who got left behind helped us. He's gone now, but the message is the same."

"Which is what?" Conrad said.

"God came back for his true followers, and a lot of people who thought they were religious didn't make it."

"Why not?"

"Because it's not about being religious," Judd said. "It's about a relationship with God through Jesus Christ."

"What does that mean?" Conrad said.

Vicki jumped in. "I had the same question. My parents changed big-time and wanted me to. They kept saying I should accept Jesus. It wasn't until they disappeared that I figured it out. Accepting him means you admit you can't get to God on your own. You ask him to forgive you for the bad stuff you've done. And with me there was plenty of bad stuff."

"Me too," Conrad said.

While Vicki told more of her story, Judd turned on a flashlight and grabbed a small Bible from Ryan's stash. He showed Conrad verses in Romans that said everyone had sinned.

"I read that on the Web site," Conrad said, "but it didn't make sense until now."

"You can pray anywhere," Judd said. "Even here."

"Yeah," Conrad said. "How do I do it?"

Judd led Conrad in a short prayer. "God, I know I've sinned. I'm sorry. Please forgive me. I believe Jesus died for me and came back from the dead. I accept your forgiveness right now. Come into my life and change me. Amen."

Judd handed Conrad a Bible. "Did you get to talk to my brother about any of this?" Conrad said.

"Ryan and I got to talk about God with him," Judd said. "He heard the truth."

"But he didn't believe, did he?"

Judd turned his head. "He didn't tell me he believed, but only God knows his heart."

Conrad nodded and pointed to Vicki's forehead. "I can see it," he said. "No matter what happens now, at least I know I'll see you guys again."

Lionel glanced at his watch. The plan would go into effect in two minutes. He hoped Conrad had made it to the hiding place.

Felicia and Melinda continued to eye him as they walked through the rubble. They had searched two shelters and were heading to a third when Conrad's call came in.

"This is Graham," Conrad said. Phoenix was barking wildly in the background. "I think I just spotted them. Their dog's goin' crazy over here."

"Location!" Commander Blancka shouted.

Conrad gave his position. Conrad was leading them away from the area Judd and Vicki would need to travel.

"We got 'em now!" the commander shouted.

The chopper flew overhead, its lights filling the sky. Lionel wondered how Conrad had gotten Phoenix to bark like that.

––––––––––––––––––

Judd counted down the minutes. Vicki nervously paced in front of the opening.

"It's time," Judd said.

"You go first," Vicki said, helping Judd up to the ledge that led to the opening.

As he reached back to help Vicki up, the earth trembled. The concrete wall he was standing on swayed. A large beam fell, and with it came bricks and mortar.

Vicki let go of Judd's hand and fell back. Judd was thrown forward, outside the church. As quickly as the aftershock had started, it was over, but the hole Judd had crawled through was blocked by debris.

Judd whispered Vicki's name, but she didn't respond. He grabbed handfuls of dirt and rocks and pulled bricks from the opening. He felt like he was clawing for his life.

When the hole was big enough, he stuck his head through. He whispered again, and this time he heard a faint coughing coming from the floor.

"Vick, can you hear me?"

"There's something on my leg," Vicki choked.

"Hang on. I'll get you out!"

"No," Vicki said. "This is your chance. Go!"

"If you think I'm leaving you now, you're crazy," Judd said, frantically moving debris from the entrance.

"Even if you could get me out—"

"Save your breath," Judd said. "I'm almost through." He carefully squeezed through the hole. "I can't see you, Vick. Talk to me."

"I can't move my right leg at all," Vicki said.

Judd felt along the mound of dirt until he touched Vicki's hand.

"I got you now," Judd said, pulling at the dirt and rocks. A few minutes later only the beam trapped her.

"I have to get some leverage to get you out," Judd said. He found a stick outside and brought it in, but it broke in half when he tried to move the beam.

"Time's running out," Vicki said.

"Hang in there. I've almost got it."

The tree branch lifted the beam, and Vicki managed to slide backward before it fell. Vicki got up and hobbled toward the entrance. "I can't put any weight on my leg," she said.

Judd climbed outside and pulled Vicki through. Judd felt her ankle.

Vicki winced. "That's it."

"It doesn't feel broken," Judd said. "But it's bad."

"Let me see if I can walk on it again."

Vicki stood but crumpled to the ground in pain. "It's no use. I can't go."

"I'll carry you," Judd said.

"I'll slow you down."

"I'm telling you, I'm not leaving you."

As Judd lifted Vicki into his arms, he heard the sound of the chopper, then footsteps nearby. He reached for his rear pocket and felt for Conrad's gun. It was still there.

14

LIONEL ran with Melinda and Felicia toward the chopper. The earth tremor answered his question about Phoenix. The dog was going wild because of the shudder of the earth. Lionel hoped Judd and Vicki had gotten out of the church.

The radio was busy with reports about the quake. Commander Blancka said, "Keep going and find them. I'll join the chopper." He gave his location and asked the pilot to pick him up.

Melinda led the group with a flashlight and a global positioning device the commander had given her.

"Where are you going?" Lionel said.

"Conrad should be due north if my GPS is right," Melinda said.

Lionel looked in horror. Melinda was taking a short-cut toward Conrad's position. She was leading them straight through the demolished parking lot of New Hope Village Church.

Judd had carried Vicki only a few yards when he saw the beam of the flashlight and heard voices. It sounded like Lionel, but someone was with him. Judd ran to a fallen tree and placed Vicki on the other side. He tried not to breathe.

"How much farther?" a girl said.

"About half a mile," another girl said.

The three Morale Monitors passed a few feet on the other side of the downed tree. Judd heard Lionel say, "I hope that aftershock didn't damage the shelters."

When the three passed, Vicki tried to walk but stumbled in pain. "I don't want you to have to carry me all the way to the Stahley place."

"You're light," Judd said. "It's not a problem."

But Judd knew Vicki was right. No matter how light she was, he couldn't carry her that distance. As he ducked in and out of crumpled subdivisions, he frantically looked for a bike, a motorcycle, or anything that would help them get away. After ten minutes, Judd put Vicki down and fell to his knees, exhausted.

"You can't do this," Vicki said. "Leave me here and come back later."

"No way," Judd said. "Just let me catch my breath."

Lionel knew they needed to give Judd and Vicki as much time as possible. As they topped a hill, the helicopter's searchlight scanned a row of houses.

"There he is!" Melinda shouted, pointing at Conrad.

Conrad held Phoenix by the collar. Commander

Blancka had just arrived. Phoenix growled and barked at the man when he came close.

"All right, where'd you see them?" the commander said.

"I saw two people in there," Conrad said, pointing to a small, white house a few yards away. "The dog was going crazy."

"Did you see them run in or come out?" the commander said.

"No, sir, they were moving around inside."

"Then we've got 'em!" The commander barked orders to the chopper. It trained its searchlight on the house as the others took position.

Suddenly, the door opened and a man in his night-clothes walked out. A woman in a robe held a baby. The man put his hands up and squinted.

"On the ground!" the commander shouted through a bullhorn.

The man fell to the ground and put his hands behind his head. The woman came outside and sat beside him with the crying baby. The commander waved the chopper away.

"We didn't do anything," the man said.

"Is that them?" the commander shouted.

"No!" Melinda shouted.

"Maybe they're inside," Lionel said.

The woman cried and shook her head. "Someone flashed a light in our bedroom window, then we felt the earthquake."

"Search it," Commander Blancka yelled.

Lionel followed the others inside. He knew Judd and Vicki hadn't been there.

"I thought I saw them, sir," Conrad said. "The dog went wild, and—"

"Don't think anymore!" the commander said. "Let the dog loose."

Conrad let go of Phoenix's collar. Phoenix sat. The commander kicked at him and yelled, "Go find your friends!"

Phoenix dodged the commander's boot, and the man lost his balance and fell. Phoenix ran into the night. The chopper followed with its searchlight. Phoenix sniffed at the ground and headed back toward the church.

Judd found that carrying Vicki over his shoulder made running easier. She said she didn't mind, but Judd knew the jostling couldn't be comfortable.

Judd passed a house with a four-wheel-drive vehicle parked in front. A light was on in the living room, and Judd spotted someone sitting in a chair.

"Just act like you've passed out," Judd told Vicki.

"A few more minutes and I won't have to act," Vicki said.

Judd kicked at the door. "Hello? I need help!"

Judd peered through a broken windowpane. A man walked into the front hallway.

"Hi. My friend was hurt in the aftershock, and I was wondering—"

"Go away," the man said.

"I need to get her some help!"

The living room light went out. Judd reached inside the broken window.

"What are you doing?" Vicki whispered.

"Looking for a key to that car," Judd said.

When he couldn't find the key, he carried Vicki down the street. Two blocks later he spotted a crumpled bicycle with something attached behind it.

"It's one of those kid carriers," Vicki said.

"It might work," Judd said.

Judd quickly unhooked the carrier. Vicki fit in the stroller, but she had to keep her feet in the air. Judd pushed her a few yards but noticed the front wheel was bent. The ground was so uneven that Judd abandoned the idea and picked Vicki up again.

"Do you know where we are?" Vicki said.

A dog came at them. Judd kicked at it and kept moving. "About a third of the way there. If we can make it by daylight, we've got a chance."

Lionel had to make a tough decision. If he let Phoenix continue, the dog would lead them straight to Judd and Vicki. He thought of shooting Phoenix. It would keep his friends safe a little while longer.

What am I thinking? Lionel thought. I can't shoot Phoenix, no matter what.

Lionel caught up with Conrad. "Nice try."

"I thought that might hold them off longer," Conrad said. "It was murder trying to find a house with somebody in it and hold that dog back at the same time. What do we do now?"

"Hang back and see how this plays out. Judd and Vicki might get away. If the worst happens and they get caught, we can pull our guns on the GC."

"You forgot," Conrad said. "I don't have a gun. Judd got mine."

"If you have to, disarm Melinda or Felicia. Take them by surprise."

"Do you really want to take on Blancka like that?" Conrad said. "I'm through with the GC myself, but there's no way you can work from the inside if you pull a gun."

The chopper followed Phoenix through the twisted wreckage. Phoenix kept his nose to the ground and darted through the rubble. Without the chopper it would have been impossible to keep up with him.

A call from headquarters came over the radio. Someone had just reported two prowlers running through the neighborhood west of New Hope Village Church. Commander Blancka asked for the exact location and got it. He instructed the chopper pilot to abandon the dog and go for the prowlers.

Judd kept moving. He jogged through backyards and parking lots. He looked for grass. The roads were terrible. Huge chunks of asphalt heaved up.

Dogs were not an enemy, but they seemed so spooked at the aftershock that every one of them barked. More than once Judd stumbled and nearly fell. He hit his head on a low-hanging tree limb, and Vicki's clothes got caught in the branches.

Then the sound Judd feared most. The chopper.

Judd saw light a short distance away and ran toward it. He knelt in the grass a few yards from a series of tents.

"It's another shelter," Vicki said, as Judd gasped for breath.

"The chopper's right behind us. If we don't figure out a better way to get around than this, we're sunk."

"Maybe we can buy some time if we hide in there," Vicki said.

Judd felt the beating of chopper blades, and the wind picked up.

Lionel met with Conrad while they waited for orders from Commander Blancka. Conrad took Lionel's flashlight and turned it on his own face.

"See anything new?" Conrad said.

Lionel shook his head. "What?"

"Don't you see anything right here?" Conrad said, pointing to his forehead.

Lionel smiled. "All right, brother! Good to have you on board."

Vicki hopped to the rear of the tent and fell to the ground. She scooted under the edge and held the flap for Judd. There was little light inside.

145

"Feels creepy in here," Vicki whispered.

Judd put a finger to his lips.

When her eyes got accustomed to the darkness of the room, Vicki gasped. "Nobody's going to hear us in here. They're all dead."

Sheets draped the bodies around the room. By the size of the bodies Vicki could tell some were young, others older.

"I bet we're near the high school," Vicki said. "This has to be the morgue."

Judd shuddered. "Sorry."

"It's perfect," Vicki said. "Nobody to rat on us."

The chopper hovered over the shelter. People ran from tents and scrambled out of sleeping bags. A car drove up a few yards away.

"I want all of these tents searched," a man yelled. "Washington, you two check here. You two, that tent."

An older woman shouted, "What's going on here?"

"Commander Blancka, Global Community. We're looking for two suspects."

"Everyone in camp is registered," the woman said. "Would you like to see the records?"

"No, ma'am," Commander Blancka said. "We're gonna eyeball every person here to make sure."

Vicki looked at Judd. The tent flap opened.

"That's the morgue," the woman said.

"Ick," a girl said. "I'm not goin' in there."

"Washington," Commander Blancka said, "you check the morgue."

146

Lionel lifted a few sheets and looked at the faces of the dead. He shook his head and was about to leave when he heard hissing.

"Psst, over here!"

"You guys are in deep," Lionel whispered as he grabbed two sheets at the front of the tent and handed them to Judd and Vicki. Judd explained the situation.

"You can't stay here," Lionel said. "They'll be taking the bodies out of here in the morning."

"Think we can get the commander's jeep?" Judd said.

Lionel smirked. "Oh, that would be too cool. But there's no way."

"If you could create one more diversion, I might be able to get it."

"But the chopper'd be on you in a second," Lionel said.

"It's worth a shot, don't you think?" Judd said.

The tent flap opened and two men came in carrying a body. Lionel covered Judd and Vicki and stood.

"Another stiff to check out?" Lionel said.

The men didn't answer. They put the body down, covered it, and left.

"OK," Lionel said. "Here's what I'll do."

The helicopter circled the camp with its light still on. Lionel approached the commander slowly. Melinda and Felicia were searching tents nearby.

"Sir, I found something kind of strange in the

morgue," Lionel said loudly enough for everyone to hear. "I wonder if you'd take a look."

Lionel led the group into the tent and took them to the side where Judd and Vicki had entered.

"I found one of the tent pegs out and these two sheets."

"I'll bet they crawled in here and pretended to be dead," Melinda said.

"Good call," the commander said.

"Sir, I wasn't able to search all these bodies. I think we ought to do that now."

Commander Blancka lifted the two sheets. He pulled the edge of the tent up and cursed.

"My jeep! They're in my jeep!"

15

WHEN Judd got the jeep rolling, he handed the microphone to Vicki and said, "Push this and hold it. It'll jam the frequency of the pilot. Then keep quiet."

Vicki keyed the microphone just in time. The jeep was barely past the morgue when Vicki saw Commander Blancka and the others rush out.

Vicki tapped Judd on the shoulder and pointed behind them. Judd nodded, pointed to the microphone, and gave Vicki a thumbs-up.

Judd drove onto roads he would never have thought were passable. The jeep rolled up embankments and over downed power lines. He kept the car going toward the Stahley mansion, zigging and zagging past collapsed buildings and burned-out cars. The helicopter remained over the shelter. Judd looked at the gas gauge. The tank was almost empty.

Lionel watched a frantic Commander Blancka try to con-tact the pilot. Blancka called several times but got no response. The man ripped the radio from his shoulder in disgust. "They're jamming us! Somebody get his attention!"

The man waved his arms. Melinda and Felicia joined in, shouting and yelling.

Conrad rolled his eyes and pulled Lionel aside. "You know where I stand with you guys. Now that I'm one of you, there's no way I can stay inside the GC."

"Why not?"

"It's clear what's ahead. We're coming down to the end. Just a little more than five years and the game's up, right?"

"Sure, but what's that got to do—"

"We're looking at one huge countdown clock," Conrad said. "I'm choosing sides now, and it's not with the GC."

"But choosing sides doesn't mean you leave your friends when they're in trouble," Lionel said.

"I don't want to leave them, but—"

"If it were just you and me," Lionel said, "I'd be out of here in a second. But I'm thinking about Judd and Vicki."

"All right. But when we know they're safe, I'm gone."

The girls waved wildly at the chopper. Melinda finally made it to the searchlight and pointed toward the camp. The chopper turned.

"It won't be long now," Lionel said. "I hope Judd's far enough away to ditch the jeep and make it on foot."

Judd drove fast, twisting and winding through the churned-up roads. A few spots had already been repaired by GC crews, and on those Judd was able to make good time. But most roads were like a giant jigsaw puzzle that had been shaken apart.

Vicki tightly wrapped a rag around the microphone and put it under the seat.

"How much gas do we have left?" she said.

"Not much," Judd said. "They've probably made contact with the chopper by now."

"Do you know where you're going?" Vicki said.

"I know the right direction," Judd said. "Don't recognize these roads, though."

They came to an intersection littered with debris. Judd drove around it until he came to a house in the middle of the street. "Cover your head," he said.

"You're not actually going through there, are you?" Vicki said.

Judd floored it and broke through the brittle wall and out the other side.

Vicki threw pieces of wood from the jeep. "I know where we are now," she said. "This is how I came back after leaving Mrs. Jenness."

Judd rolled over two yellow bumps, and Vicki told him it was all that was left of a fast-food restaurant.

"The river's that way," Vicki said.

When Judd crested the hill he couldn't believe his eyes. Twisted pieces of metal were all that was left of the bridge. The road ended at the edge of the river.

"How did you ever survive that?" Judd said.

Vicki shook her head. The memory of her ordeal with Mrs. Jenness was fresh.

"If I'm right, the river runs through the forest preserve," Judd said. "That means we're not far. That's the good news."

"And the bad news?"

"The Stahley place is on the other side of the river. We're going to have to find a way across."

"There's probably not a bridge within miles that survived the quake," Vicki said.

"Then we'll have to swim. Or get a boat."

Vicki turned in horror. "Look!"

The chopper hovered in the distance, its searchlight darting across the road. Judd stopped the jeep. "Quick," he said, "get under what's left of the bridge!"

"I'll try," Vicki said. She hobbled out and headed for the riverbank.

Judd turned the jeep around, unwrapped the rag from the microphone, and pushed in the cigarette lighter. He unscrewed the gas cap and stuffed the rag into the hole. He looked for a stick or a piece of wood long enough and finally found a tire iron behind the backseat.

Judd checked the sky. The chopper was closing ground. He looked back and saw that Vicki was almost hidden.

I hope there's enough gas in there! he thought.

When the lighter was red-hot, Judd lit the rag. He wedged the tire iron against the accelerator and put the jeep in gear. He hoped the car would travel a good distance from the river before it overturned, but it only went a few hundred feet before the front wheels turned and the jeep ran straight into a demolished house. Seconds later an explosion rocked the street. The jeep burst into flames.

Judd ran from the wreck as the chopper flew near.

———————

Lionel stayed close to the commander and listened for news from the pilot. The commander had gone to a different radio frequency, and the chopper immediately pursued the jeep.

"We've got something here, Commander," the pilot said a few minutes later.

"Go ahead."

"An explosion. I'm just getting to the site now. Yeah, it looks like it's your vehicle. It crashed into a house. It's on fire, sir."

"Put down as close as you can and see if those two are in there," the commander said.

"If they are, they're toast," the pilot said. "I don't see any bodies outside the building."

Lionel glanced at Conrad. Conrad shook his head. Melinda and Felicia looked excited.

———————

Vicki couldn't see the chopper, but she heard it and tasted dust. The pain in her leg was so great she had to concentrate on putting one foot in front of the other as Judd helped her move along the side of the river.

"Why'd you blow it up?"

"Thought about sending it into the river," Judd said, "but I figured it was better they find it burning. Might give us a few more minutes to run."

"This is not running," Vicki said.

"You're doing fine," Judd said.

"Any chance they might think we're dead?"

"I hope so," Judd said. "It'll take a while to sift through the wreckage. How's the ankle?"

"Hurts," Vicki said, "but you were right about the sprain. If it was broken, I wouldn't be able to walk at all."

The river had changed since Vicki had last seen it. The bank was much steeper. The river was wider and swollen. In places, the earth had shifted, creating small waterfalls. The water looked much too swift to swim.

"How much farther?" Vicki said.

"Maybe a mile or two."

Judd moved to the edge of the water, then returned. "Too deep to cross. Keep moving."

Vicki saw whitecaps in the moonlight as the river rushed past. Pieces of the bank were still crumbling into the water.

"Look at that," Judd said, pointing to the middle of the river.

Vicki saw a front porch sticking out of the water, being swept downstream. The white picket fence on the porch was still attached, but the rest of the house was underwater and rolling. When it reached the first water-fall, the house hung on the edge, then with a sickening crunch, crashed over the side and broke apart.

It was difficult to walk along the churned-up ground.

Vicki slipped several times and had to be helped to her feet. "Let's move to the top of the bank," she said.

"We'll be too easy to spot up there," Judd said.

"If he's got night vision, it won't matter," Vicki said. She took another step and her ankle gave way. She plunged down the hill, grabbing at dirt and grass as she tumbled. But she couldn't hang on. With fistfuls of dirt, she splashed into the chilly water.

Lionel heard the call from the pilot and rushed to the commander's side.

"Go ahead," the commander said.

"Heat's pretty intense here, sir. I don't see any bodies inside or out. Looks staged."

"Those vehicles don't just burst into flames," the commander said. "Continue the search. We've got a second chopper on the way to help you."

Judd heard Vicki cry out. He turned as she flipped and rolled down the embankment. A splash. Vicki was in the churning water.

Judd scampered down the hill. His foot caught on a tree root and he, too, tumbled headfirst into the water. The current was swift and took him under. He surfaced and yelled for Vicki, but she didn't answer. Then a strange sound mixed with the gurgling water in Judd's ears. It was the *thwock, thwock, thwock* of the helicopter.

For a moment, Judd felt a sense of relief. The GC chopper could rescue them. But Judd knew once he was in the hands of the GC, he and Vicki would be separated and probably punished.

The chopper darted over the water, the blades whipping up waves and making the swimming harder. It flew from bank to bank. Judd went under and stayed as long as his lungs could stand it.

Vicki was underwater for what seemed an eternity. She didn't have time to take a breath when she fell in. The current pushed her downstream into the roots of a tree. The water was black and icy. She struggled to get free, breaking a branch that snagged her clothes, but soon she was caught on another. Finally, the current took her away from the tree, and she rose to the surface.

Vicki gasped for air. She grabbed for the bank, but it was too far away. The swirling water took her under again. When she surfaced, she called out for Judd.

Vicki's cry was close. Judd turned and saw her shadow against the searchlight. This was their chance.

Judd swam with all his might, and the current pushed Vicki toward him. He screamed and reached out for her.

Judd touched her hand once, then took two more strokes to get closer. *Just a little more*, he thought.

As he strained toward Vicki, a piece of the splintered

house hit him and forced him underwater. When
he surfaced, he barely heard Vicki's cry above the noise.

Vicki screamed for Judd, then lost sight of him. A bright
light blinded her as the water kicked up around her.

"Stay where you are," a voice boomed overhead.

Like I can control where I'm going, Vicki thought.

Out of control, Judd twisted and turned in the river. He
tried to swim to shore, but just as he felt he was making
progress, the current pulled him under.

When he surfaced, a section of roof hurtled toward
him. He couldn't dodge it, and it was too big to swim
under, so Judd grabbed the edge and tried to crawl on. As
he did, he sent shingles plopping into the water. Finally,
Judd made it to the center of the spinning roof.

Where's Vicki? he thought. He didn't know which was
worse—being found by the GC or being at the mercy of
the river.

He spotted the chopper hovering near the spot where
they had fallen in. Judd kicked himself for not being
more careful. If only they had walked farther up the bank.
If only he had held on to Vicki.

The roof spun completely around, and water washed
over him. When Judd could see again, he noticed a rescue
line dangling from the chopper. The pilot was shouting
something through his loudspeaker. "Don't get on, Vick!"
Judd screamed.

Vicki went under and swam toward the shore, but the current was too swift. The chopper hovered closer and dropped a lifeline.

"This is the Global Community!" the pilot shouted. "You are under arrest. Grab the harness and put it around you."

Vicki went under again and kicked as hard as she could. Swimming was easier than walking, but her ankle felt like it was on fire. When she surfaced, the pilot moved into position.

"Grab the harness," the pilot said. "This is your only chance. There's a huge waterfall around the next corner. You don't want to go over that. Grab on and I'll pull you up."

What about Judd? Vicki thought.

"No!" Judd shouted as he watched the chopper pull Vicki from the water. He slammed his fist on the roof of the house and rolled off. When Vicki was in, the chopper flew slowly toward Judd. Before he was spotted, Judd dove underneath the floating roof. He found a pocket of air and stayed there until the chopper passed.

The roof picked up speed. When Judd surfaced, he thought the chopper was back. But this wasn't the sound of rotor blades. This was a roar. He swam against the current and watched in horror as the roof of the house disappeared over the edge of a chasm.

16

LIONEL stiffened when he heard the pilot's voice.

"We've apprehended one of them," the pilot said. "We have a female in custody. Search for the male is negative. I think he might have drowned."

"Bring the girl back and keep going," Commander Blancka said from the other chopper. "Morale Monitors on the ground, the GC has taken over police headquarters on Maple Street. I want the two girls to head this up. Get everything you can out of her."

Lionel clicked his microphone. "What do you want Graham and me to do, sir?"

"Stay where you are. We'll pick you up."

"This changes everything," Lionel said to Conrad. "Vicki will have no hope unless we help her."

"I'm no chicken, but I'm not a hero either," Conrad said. "And if Vicki's at this police station halfway across town, what are we supposed to do?"

"I don't know yet," Lionel said. "But there's no way I'm letting Blancka decide her fate."

"What about Judd?" Conrad said. "You think he's still alive?"

Lionel hesitated. "Judd'll be all right. He can take care of himself."

Judd tried to swim against the current but couldn't. With nothing to hold on to he took a deep breath, held out his arms, and plunged over the fall into the darkness.

He hit the surface with his feet, and water surrounded him. He sank deeper and deeper. He was afraid he would black out and drown from the fall. With his lungs nearly bursting, he reached the soft bottom and tried to push up. His feet stuck in the muck. Judd struggled and finally kicked free. He rose to the surface and gasped for air.

The water was calm now. The current carried him slowly downriver. Judd found a piece of wood and clung to it with his remaining strength.

Judd watched the riverbank for anything familiar. After a half hour of drifting, he let go of the wood and swam to shore. He climbed through the mud to the top of the bank. Something slick passed him.

Snake.

A chill went through him, and he clawed his way to the top. Judd tried to get his bearings. He knew he had to go west to get to the Stahley place, but which way was west? The stars were brilliant in the sky. Since the earthquake, they seemed brighter. Without the haze from the city, Judd found the North Star easily.

Once again Judd heard the helicopter. He ran. This time it would be looking for his body.

They're not going to find it, Judd thought as he took off into the forest.

Vicki shook from the cold as she hobbled into the police station. Commander Blancka led the way into the interrogation room. Melinda and Felicia followed.

"Young lady, I'm going to give you a chance," the commander began. "If you cooperate, that'll be taken into consideration when it comes time to sentence you."

Vicki said nothing.

"If you refuse to cooperate, refuse to give us information, I'll have no choice but to be severe with my punishment." The commander looked at Vicki without emotion. "And I can be severe."

After the commander left, Melinda said, "We know your name is Vicki Byrne. Why did you kill Mrs. Jenness?"

"I didn't kill her," Vicki said. "I told you that."

"We have witnesses."

"You have one person who says she thinks she saw something. It won't stand up."

Melinda smiled. "You don't understand. This isn't a court. There won't be a trial. Whatever Commander Blancka decides is final."

"I have a right to a fair—"

"You lost your rights when you disobeyed the Global Community," Felicia said. "They could have left you in the water to die. Or shot you for stealing GC property. If the commander decides you murdered that lady, he's told us what will happen."

"And what's that?" Vicki said.

Melinda leaned close. "Death."

Judd huddled in a thicket of bushes. The chopper stayed near the river.

The forest had felt the effects of the earthquake just as the city had. Trees were uprooted. Whole sections of the forest had been swallowed. Judd recognized what was left of the access road and ran toward a meadow. He found the small grove of trees where he had knelt with Ryan and Taylor Graham. Judd found the remote entry box and pushed the button. He glanced at the hill. Nothing happened. He pushed the button again. Still, nothing happened.

Judd looked around for any sign of the GC. He couldn't see the house, but he assumed it was deserted. Both Mr. and Mrs. Stahley were dead. There was no reason to guard it unless they were still looking for Darrion.

Judd ran to the door built into the hill. He tried to find an opening, but the shifting ground had sealed the entrance. Digging would take hours.

He walked around the meadow and onto the Stahley property. The huge fence that surrounded the property was on the ground. The security gate at the front of the

property was also in shambles. Judd hoped the earthquake had scared off the dogs.

Judd climbed through broken glass on the patio area.
The swimming pool was empty. Judd leaned over and
saw a huge crack in the bottom of the pool. The roof had
collapsed over the kitchen, but the house hadn't been
damaged like many Judd had seen.

Looters had been there. The refrigerator was open,
food strewn around the kitchen. The high-tech television
and stereo equipment were gone from the living room.

With the sun coming up, Judd felt exhausted. He
wanted to see the hideout downstairs. If the equipment
was still there, and if the phone lines were up, he might
be able to contact others in the Trib Force. Someone had
to help Vicki.

Judd put his head down on the couch. *I'll just lie down
for a moment,* he thought.

As soon as he put his head down, he was asleep.

Though the commander ordered him to stay, Lionel left
to find Darrion and Shelly. He found them sleeping at a
nearby shelter. He woke them and explained what had
happened to Vicki.

"What about Judd?" Shelly said.

"We don't know," Lionel said. "We hope he got away.
There's a chance he could have drowned."

Shelly shook her head.

"We have to help Vicki," Darrion said. "Is there any
way to hire a lawyer or have someone negotiate for her?"

"It's worth a shot," Lionel said. "Commander Blancka has full power from the Global Community. He's the judge and jury."

"Who could we get?" Shelly said. "I don't know any lawyers."

"What about Mr. Stein?" Darrion said. "Vicki said he offered to help any way he could."

Lionel told Shelly and Darrion to get Mr. Stein. If they couldn't find him, they were to go to Darrion's house. As soon as Vicki's case was settled, the remaining members of the Young Tribulation Force would meet there.

Judd awoke at noon, hungry and aching. He stumbled to the kitchen and found an unopened box of crackers. That eased his hunger for a while. He hoped the earthquake hadn't damaged the secret entrance to the underground hangar.

He found a picture of the Stahleys hanging at a weird angle. He pried the secret entrance open and crawled onto the landing behind the wall. The ladder that led to the secret room had fallen, so Judd scampered back to the kitchen and found a piece of rope. He climbed into darkness and activated the entrance.

Inside the chamber Judd found the safe still open. He had taken the secret documents but left gold coins and a stack of bills. The door to the safe was still open, and the money and gold were gone. He pulled Ryan's packet from his pocket, still damp, and placed it inside the safe.

Judd checked the hangar for the stash of food Taylor

Graham had shown him. It was still there. He went back
to the computer room and picked up the phone. Dial
tone. That meant he could access the Internet.

A few minutes later he was viewing Rabbi Tsion Ben-
Judah's Web site. Judd sent an urgent message to the
man, hoping he would be able to help with Vicki. While
he waited, Judd read the rabbi's latest posting. Thousands
of messages had poured in since the earthquake. Many
identified themselves as members of the 144,000 Jewish
witnesses. An on-screen meter showed the number of
responses as they were added to the central bulletin
board. The numbers whizzed past.

Judd only wanted to spend a few minutes on the
Net, but he couldn't stop reading Dr. Ben-Judah's
message. The main posting was based on Revelation 8
and 9. Tsion believed the wrath of the Lamb earthquake
began the second period of the Tribulation. Tsion
wrote:

There are seven years, or eighty-four months, in all.
You can see we are now one quarter of the way
through. As bad as things have been, they get worse.

What is next? In Revelation 8:5 an angel takes a
censer, fills it with fire from the altar of God, and
throws it to the earth. That results in noise, thunder,
lightning, and an earthquake.

That same chapter goes on to say that seven
angels with seven trumpets prepared themselves to
sound. That is where we are now. Sometime over the
next twenty-one months, the first angel will sound,

165

and hail and fire will follow, mingled with blood, thrown down to the earth. This will burn a third of the trees and all the green grass.

Judd knew he needed to make contact with someone about helping Vicki, but he couldn't stop reading. He was looking at what he would have to experience if he survived.

Later a second angel will sound the second trumpet, and the Bible says a great mountain burning with fire will be thrown into the sea. This will turn a third of the water to blood, kill a third of the living creatures in the sea, and sink a third of the ships.

Judd was stunned. He shook his head and tried to imagine all those things taking place. The world would be in even greater turmoil than it was now, after the worldwide earthquake. He read on.

The third angel's trumpet sound will result in a great star falling from heaven, burning like a torch. It will somehow fall over a wide area and land in a third of the rivers and springs. This star is even named in Scripture. The book of Revelation calls it Wormwood. Where it falls, the water becomes bitter and people die from drinking it.

Judd heard a ding and a window popped up saying he had an E-mail. It was Dr. Ben-Judah.

"Judd, I have been praying for you and your friends. Is everyone all right?"

Judd brought Tsion up-to-date and gave him the bad news about Ryan. There was a long pause.

"I am sorry you have to go through such a painful experience. Losing a friend like Ryan is very difficult. His love for God's Word was an encouragement to me. I will miss him greatly."

"What about the adult Trib Force?" Judd wrote.

"Buck is searching for Chloe even now," Tsion wrote. "Please pray. Rayford is alive in New Babylon. Unfortunately, his wife, Amanda, was on a flight that is reported missing. Rayford still holds out hope that she is alive, but the reports are not encouraging."

"What about Loretta and Donny at the church?"

"They are both in the presence of Jesus," Tsion wrote. "Donny's wife as well."

Judd shook his head. Loretta had been like a second mom to him. He told Tsion about Vicki, and the rabbi said he would stop everything and pray for her.

"O God," Tsion wrote, "you have delivered your servants from the lions, from the furnace, and from the hands of evil authorities. I pray you would deliver our dear sister from any harm now. May your peace wash over her and may she remain faithful to you in every word and action."

Vicki wondered when Melinda and Felicia would tire. She was barely able to keep her eyes open as they asked question after question. Finally, they escorted her to a cell.

Vicki put her head down on a cot. Her ankle was

swollen and turning blue, but it didn't hurt as much. Her clothes had dried so she wasn't cold anymore.

She knew she should feel afraid, but she didn't. When she had asked God to forgive her, she didn't know how dangerous that decision would be. Now, if she had to give her life for the cause, she felt OK. Ryan had done it. Bruce had given his life as well.

If God wants me to go through the same thing as them, then so be it, she thought. She closed her eyes and for the first time in days slept soundly.

17

JUDD was thrilled to talk with Dr. Ben-Judah. When Judd asked where Tsion was staying, the rabbi replied, "I think it is safer if neither of us knows where the other is."

Tsion signed off. Judd e-mailed Pavel, his friend in New Babylon. Pavel had read Tsion's Web site and talked with Judd about receiving Christ. Judd was grateful this new believer had survived the earthquake. While he waited to make contact, Judd revisited Tsion's Web site. The rabbi wrote:

> How can a thinking person see all that has happened and not fear what is to come? If there are still unbelievers after the third Trumpet Judgment, the fourth should convince everyone. Anyone who resists the warnings of God at that time will likely have already decided to serve the enemy. The fourth Trumpet Judgment is a striking of the sun, the moon, and the

stars so that a third of the sun, a third of the moon, and a third of the stars are darkened. We will never again see sunshine as bright as we have before. The brightest summer day with the sun high in the sky will be only two-thirds as bright as it ever was. How will this be explained away?

Judd shook his head. "People explained away the fact that Jesus came back from the dead, too," he muttered. He read on with chills. What Tsion was writing would one day come true.

In the middle of this, the writer of the Revelation says he looked and heard an angel "flying through the midst of heaven." It was saying with a loud voice, "Woe, woe, woe to the inhabitants of the earth, because of the remaining blasts of the trumpet of the three angels who are about to sound!"

Tsion said he would cover more in his next lesson and ended with an encouraging message. The rabbi said he believed there was a time coming when many would believe in Christ. Tsion called it a "great soul harvest." He wrote:

Consider these promises. In the Old Testament book of Joel 2:28-32, God is speaking. He says, "And it shall come to pass afterward that I will pour out My Spirit on all flesh; your sons and your daughters shall prophesy, your old men shall dream dreams, your young men shall see visions. And also on My

menservants and on my maidservants I will pour out
My Spirit in those days."

I wonder if that means me? Judd thought. He continued.

"And I will show wonders in the heavens and in the
earth: blood and fire and pillars of smoke. The sun
shall be turned into darkness, and the moon into
blood, before the coming of the great and awesome
day of the Lord.

"And it shall come to pass that whoever calls on
the name of the Lord shall be saved. For in Mount
Zion and in Jerusalem there shall be deliverance, as
the Lord has said, among the remnant whom the
Lord calls."

Judd read on. Tsion wrote that Revelation makes it
clear that the judgments he mentioned would not come
until the servants of God had been sealed on their foreheads.

"That's just happened," Judd said, putting a hand to
his forehead.

We are called by God to be servants. The function of
a servant of Christ is to communicate the gospel of
the grace of God. Although we will go through great
persecution, we can comfort ourselves that during
the Tribulation we look forward to astounding
events outlined in Revelation.

Revelation 7:9 quotes John saying, "After these

things I looked, and behold, a great multitude which no one could number, of all nations, tribes, peoples, and tongues, standing before the throne and before the Lamb, clothed with white robes, with palm branches in their hands. . . ."

These are the tribulation saints. Now follow me carefully. In a later verse, Revelation 9:16, the writer numbers the army of horsemen in a battle at two hundred million. If such a vast army can be numbered, what might the Scriptures mean when they refer to the tribulation saints, those who come to Christ during this period, as "a great multitude which no one could number"?

Judd sat back. He saw the logic. God was about to do something incredible on the earth and if he lived, Judd would get to see it.

Do you see why I believe we are justified in trusting God for more than a billion souls during this period? Let us pray for that great harvest. All who name Christ as their Redeemer can have a part in this, the greatest task ever assigned to mankind.

———————————————

Vicki awoke. She couldn't tell whether it was morning or evening. The only window was toward the back of the jail area, out of her sight. She had slept soundly and awoke refreshed and hungry. Her ankle was tender, but she could at least stand on it without falling over.

An hour later a GC guard brought her some bread and soup. "Can you tell me what time it is?" Vicki said.

"Almost six," the man said.

"A.M. or P.M.?" Vicki said.

"P.M., miss," the guard said. "And you have a visitor waiting. They're getting him cleared right now."

Vicki couldn't imagine who it was. It couldn't be Judd, unless he was wearing some kind of disguise. A few minutes later Vicki heard the clicking heels of a well-dressed man. The guard opened the door, and the man stood in the shadows. He took off his hat and stepped forward.

Vicki gasped. "Mr. Stein!"

Pavel contacted Judd a few minutes later. Judd brought him up-to-date with all he had been through.

"I'm glad you're safe for now," Pavel wrote. "Many things are happening here as well."

"Like what?" Judd wrote.

"The rebuilding effort is going strong. Thousands are working with Cellular-Solar to get the communications network up. Some are being forced to help rebuild airports."

"Carpathia cares more about people traveling and talking with each other than he does about the sick and dying," Judd wrote. "The people at the shelters are doing the best they can. That's where the relief effort should be going."

"You are right," Pavel wrote, "though everyone here has been glowing about how Nicolae is handling the disaster. They talk of him as if he were a god. In fact, that may be what he thinks he is."

Judd sat forward. "What do you mean?"

"My father survived the quake. He said strange things about Nicolae. There are people who believe he is more than human."

Mr. Stein smiled. The guard would not allow him inside the cell. Instead, he sat on a stool outside.

"How are you?"

"Considering I almost drowned, I'm OK," Vicki said. "How did you know I was here?"

"A little bird," Mr. Stein said. "No, make that two. They told me what happened and that you were in trouble."

"That's an understatement," Vicki said. "Are you a lawyer?"

"No, but I know enough about the legal process to help. I would contact one of my lawyer friends, but I'm not sure there is time."

"Why?"

"This commander who will make the decision about you seems to have made up his mind. I told him I wanted to represent you, and he asked why I would bother. He seems very anxious to move ahead."

"Which means what?" Vicki said.

"If there is any arguing or convincing that will be done, it has to be done now."

"And you're going to try?"

174

"Unless you have another idea."

Vicki shook her head.

"First, you must tell me if you are guilty of the charge of murder."

Vicki explained what had happened with Mrs. Jenness. Mr. Stein listened intently and took a few notes. He scratched his chin when Vicki told about trying to pull Mrs. Jenness from the sinking car.

"This woman was your enemy," Mr. Stein said. "She was against you and those you were working with."

"I didn't really see her as an enemy," Vicki said. "She didn't know the truth. I always hoped we would some-day be able to break through to her. That's what I was trying to do when the earthquake hit. I was telling her that Jesus is—"

"Enough," Mr. Stein said. "I know your position by heart. Now tell me this: Why would you go back to help her? If you had saved her, she would have handed you over to the Global Community."

"A person's life is worth a lot more than my comfort or safety," Vicki said. "I tried to help her because she needed it. Sure, she could have turned me in, but if I hadn't tried, I couldn't live with myself."

Mr. Stein frowned. "I'm asking these questions because this is what the commander will ask. You're saying you helped Mrs. Jenness because . . . "

"There's a verse in the Bible that says there's no greater love than for a person to lay down his life for a friend," Vicki said.

"But she wasn't your friend," Mr. Stein said.

"Exactly," Vicki said. "And I wasn't a friend of Jesus when he gave his life for me. I was sinful and against him, and he still died for me."

"So you used that example to give you the strength to help Mrs. Jenness."

Vicki hung her head. "I only wish it would have worked."

Mr. Stein leaned forward. "I can't lie to you. When I talked to the commander and the young ladies he employs, they were rounding up the witnesses who say you actually murdered this woman."

"They have a girl who hates me and would say anything to get me in trouble, and they have another lady who saw me on the bridge in Mrs. Jenness's car."

"I admit the evidence is slim, but it is your word against the two of them. And Mrs. Jenness is dead. Is there anyone you can think of who could testify on your behalf?"

"Anyone I'd ask would be in bigger trouble because of it," Vicki said, leaning forward. "I want you to know, if I had it to do over again, I'd take the same chance. I don't care what happens. They can lock me up if they want."

"It will be much worse than that," Mr. Stein said.

Someone knocked on the door and motioned for the guard.

"Let me do the talking," Mr. Stein said.

Judd shuddered. "Are you sure no one can trace this?"

"I'm sure," Pavel said. "I'm using a line my father had

installed that cannot be accessed. When I am done, I take my computer back to my room."

"All right," Judd said. "What are the people in the inner circle saying about Nicolae?"

"Leon Fortunato, Carpathia's right-hand man, says he thinks the potentate could be the Messiah."

Judd blinked at the screen. "What does he base that on?"

"Fortunato thinks that because he was raised from the dead, Carpathia has to be some sort of deity."

"And what does Nicolae say about it?"

"He doesn't confirm it or deny it," Pavel said. "My father overheard one of Nicolae's conversations. The potentate said it was not time to make the claim that he is the Messiah, but he wasn't sure it was untrue."

"He thinks he's the Messiah, the savior of the world?"

"He said he knows there are people who say he is *the* Antichrist. He would love to prove them wrong."

"What does your father think?" Judd said.

"He looks at what Nicolae Carpathia has accomplished and says he wouldn't be surprised if Nicolae was sent by God."

Judd shook his head. "And what do you think?"

"I believe there is the one true Messiah and Savior," Pavel wrote, "and that man is Jesus Christ. Nicolae Carpathia is our enemy."

The guard opened the cell door. Melinda led Vicki and Mr. Stein into a conference room.

"When will we be able—," Mr. Stein said, but Melinda waved a hand.

"You can talk with the commander when he gets here," she said.

Vicki waited nervously, then closed her eyes.

"Are you tired?" Mr. Stein asked.

"I'm praying."

Mr. Stein sighed. "I think you had better do more than that."

"There's nothing more powerful I can do," Vicki said. "For some reason God wants me to go through this. I don't know why."

"Why would God want you to be jailed or killed for something you did not do?"

Vicki thought for a moment. *Maybe that's it.*

"In the New Testament there were many people who were killed or sent before authorities," Vicki said. "God said he would give them the right words to say. Maybe the commander or those two girls need to hear the message. Maybe one of them will be used by God to do something great for him."

"You need to be thinking of yourself," Mr. Stein said.

"I thought of myself my whole life," Vicki said. "That got me left behind."

Commander Blancka came in and glared at Vicki.

18

VICKI watched the commander carefully. He didn't look capable of kindness. His voice was low and gravelly.

"I'll review the charges, then you'll have a chance to respond," the commander muttered. "But this is not a trial. Under the Global Community statute during states of emergency, I'm the judge, the jury, and the one who will pass sentence."

Vicki nodded. Mr. Stein put a hand on her shoulder.

"Vicki Byrne, you're charged with the murder of Mrs. Laverne Jenness. You're also charged with stealing and then destroying Global Community property. You won't give us information on an escapee of a GC reeducation camp, a person whose name is Judd Thompson. That means you're harboring a criminal and subject to the same penalty as the accused.

"You're also charged with crimes against the Global Community and a number of smaller charges—"

"What crimes?" Mr. Stein interrupted.

Commander Blancka looked up. "You will not interrupt me!" he said. "Who are you anyway?"

"My name is Mitchell Stein. Vicki is a friend of the family. I am here to help in her defense."

"As I said, this is not a trial."

"Call it what you will, sir, but your decision will greatly affect my friend's life. She deserves representation."

"We'll find out what she deserves," the commander said. "I have statements from three people. One says Vicki was the last person seen with Mrs. Jenness before her body was found. Another woman says Vicki was seen on the roof pushing Mrs. Jenness inside the car."

Vicki shook her head.

"And the third witness says he helped Vicki dispose of a dead body."

"Commander," Mr. Stein said, "I think it would be helpful to hear Vicki's side of the story."

"I've read her statement," the commander said. "It's her word against the others. The fact that she ran from us, stole our vehicle, then destroyed it, and that she's been charged with speech against the Global Community in the past is pretty strong evidence, don't you think?"

Mr. Stein cleared his throat. "I am concerned that you do not have the entire story. Surely, if you are going to decide whether such serious charges are true, you should hear from the accused rather than what someone else said."

Vicki looked at Melinda and Felicia. Both girls scowled.

"Vicki is a young woman of faith," Mr. Stein continued. "This is something the Global Community has encouraged."

"The GC hasn't encouraged anyone to commit murder," the commander fumed.

"And if you will hear Vicki out, I think you'll conclude that murder was the last thing on her mind that day. She has a heart of compassion, not murder."

"All right," the commander said. "She can speak."

———

Judd heard a noise upstairs and muted his computer speakers. Someone was inside the house. *Could be GC, could be burglars*, Judd thought.

Moments later someone climbed down the rope to the secret entrance. Judd looked for a weapon to defend himself, then hit the light switch. The ceiling moved. Judd flipped on the light. It was Darrion and Shelly.

Judd welcomed them.

"We've got a surprise," Darrion said, pointing to the opening. "Look who we found."

Mark stuck his head into the room and grinned. "You were going to attack us with a computer keyboard?" He smirked.

"It was the only thing I could find," Judd said, putting the keyboard down. "Thought you might be the GC."

Mark crawled through and gave Judd a hug.

"Have you heard from John?"

"Who's John?" Darrion said.

Judd told Darrion about meeting John and Mark at Nicolae High.

"He was away at school when the quake hit," Mark said. "I've looked on every list of dead and injured I can find but I don't know anything for sure yet." Mark paused. "I heard about Ryan. I'm sorry."

Judd nodded and bit his lip. "What happened to you?"

"Long story," Mark said, pulling up a chair. "I was at my aunt's house when it hit. She has a dog that doesn't bark at anything. Too lazy. Well, this thing had him running back and forth in the front room, whining and barking. I figured it out before it hit, but I had a hard time convincing my aunt to follow me outside.

"When the roof in the kitchen started cracking, she believed me. I pulled her out just as the wall buckled. We got down the stairs before they collapsed. Then the whole neighborhood went. It was like trying to walk on concrete water."

"Was your aunt hurt?" Judd said.

"She ran back for the dog in the backyard," Mark said. "Glass from next door hit her in the face and neck. Lots of blood. I grabbed the dog in one arm and held her up with the other."

"Between the attack on the militia base and the earthquake, you've had some pretty close calls," Judd said.

Judd brought them up-to-date on what he knew about the Trib Force. They still hadn't heard if Chloe was alive, or whether Rayford's wife, Amanda, had been on the plane that had crashed during the earthquake.

"I just hope the next people we see coming through that opening are Lionel and Vicki," Judd said.

Lionel listened outside the conference room. He didn't want to go in unless Commander Blancka called him.

"We need to plan for the worst," Lionel said. "If she's convicted, we have to be ready."

"For what?" said Conrad.

"To spring her."

Vicki felt nervous, but Mr. Stein's smile calmed her.

"Vicki, why don't you tell the commander about the morning of the earthquake?"

Vicki nodded. "Mrs. Jenness caught me before school with some papers," she said. "I was trying to warn people about the earthquake."

"Wait," the commander said. "You knew there was going to be an earthquake?"

"It's predicted in the Bible," Vicki said. "I didn't know it was going to hit that morning, but it was the next event that was supposed to happen. I can show you if—"

The commander waved a hand. "No, just go ahead."

"Mrs. Jenness was angry. She destroyed the papers, and we headed toward a GC facility."

"Is it true you spent some time away from school because of a behavior problem?" the commander said, glancing toward Melinda.

"Yes," Vicki admitted. "The school thought I was behind the *Underground* newspaper so I was sent away."

"So you were guilty and trying to hide it?"

"Yes," Vicki said.

"Tell us about what happened on the bridge," Mr. Stein said.

Vicki told them the truth about trying to save Mrs. Jenness's life. When she was through, the commander leaned forward. "You must think I'm crazy," he said. "You actually think I'll believe you tried to save a woman who was trying to put you away?"

Mr. Stein stood. "Commander, I had a hard time believing it myself. Then I took a look at this girl's background. She stayed in our home for a brief time.

"Vicki lost her father, her mother, and her younger sister in the vanishings. The family had gone through some sort of religious awakening. Everyone but Vicki. The disappearances upset her. She couldn't think straight. So she came up with this idea of God taking her family away."

"Wait a minute," Vicki said.

"Quiet, I want to hear this," the commander said.

"To strengthen her belief she began to tell others about it. The more people she told, the more convinced she became it was true. This student newspaper is a good example. She knew it would be a disaster if she were ever caught. But she wanted to spread her message."

"How does this fit with Mrs. Jenness?" the commander said.

"You have to understand her belief," Mr. Stein said.

"She thinks Jesus was the Messiah. She bases everything in her life on the notion that Jesus came to take away true believers—and will come again. She lives by his teachings, prays to him, even memorizes the words of the Bible."

Mr. Stein smiled and rummaged through his briefcase. "When I asked her the same question about saving Mrs. Jenness's life, she quoted a verse to me." He flipped open a Bible. Vicki saw it was Chaya's.

"Here it is," he said. " 'The greatest love is shown when people lay down their lives for their friends.' "

"And that convinced you she tried to save Mrs. Jenness?" the commander said.

Mr. Stein took off his glasses and walked toward the commander. "Sir, you may call this young lady misguided. You can say she is confused, that her beliefs are wacky, or that she's sick. But her life is controlled by the notion that Mrs. Jenness needed to believe the same way Vicki does to have any hope of heaven."

"And that kind of belief is dangerous to the unity of the Global Community," the commander said.

"You must be the judge of that, sir," Mr. Stein said.

"And I will be."

Vicki stood. "I want to say something."

The commander put his hand to his forehead and squeezed. "Sit!"

"I know what Mr. Stein's trying to do," Vicki said. "He's trying to make it look like I'm mental. I'm not. Take a look around you. People have disappeared. Treaties have been signed. There's been a worldwide earthquake, something the experts said would never happen. All of it was predicted in the Bible. If you ignore this and go on like it hasn't happened, then I say *that's* crazy."

"Do you see what I mean?" Mr. Stein said.

"Stop trying to make me out to be insane!" Vicki shouted.

"Can I have a moment with her, sir?" Mr. Stein said.

Judd grilled Mark about what he had seen.

"Buck Williams is the only person I've seen from the Trib Force," Mark said. "And I only saw him as he passed in his Range Rover."

"So you stayed at shelters?" Judd said.

"I helped my aunt get to one, then a bunch of GC guys came through and loaded anybody healthy onto the back of a truck."

"You must have been scared out of your mind," Shelly said.

"They had no idea who I was," Mark said. "They were just looking for anybody who had the strength to work."

"Let me guess," Judd said. "Cellular-Solar."

"You got it," Mark said. "They worked us all that day and into the night clearing the way for the new communication towers. We cut down old ones and dug holes for new ones. They've got cell towers and satellite receivers just about everywhere."

"How did you get here?" Judd said.

"Saw my chance to run and took off," Mark said.

"I came back to check on my aunt and found Shelly and Darrion."

"How's your aunt?" Judd said.

"She'll live, but it'll be a while before I can move her," Mark said.

Lionel stood as Vicki and Mr. Stein walked into the hallway. He had heard most of the conversation and thought the commander might be changing his mind about Vicki.

"You're trying to make me look like a fool," Vicki whispered to Mr. Stein.

"I'm trying to save your life," Mr. Stein said. "Which do you care more about, your reputation or your survival?"

"I don't care what people think about me," Vicki said, "but you're trying to make what I believe look sick."

"If he lets you go, what does it matter?"

"It's not the truth!" Vicki shouted.

Lionel approached. "Vick, it may be a way out for you," he whispered.

"I can't believe you'd go along with this," Vicki said.

"I just want you to get out of here alive."

"And so do I," Mr. Stein said.

The door opened. Melinda and Felicia scowled.

"All right, time for you to get back inside," Lionel barked. He followed them inside.

Melinda whispered something to the commander, then turned and glared at Lionel.

"You have something to say?" the commander said to Mr. Stein.

"Yes," Mr. Stein said with a sheepish look. "Vicki wants to make sure I do not represent her in any way as being sick or crazy."

"Right," the commander said. "Washington!"

Lionel jumped to his feet. "Yes, sir!"

"I'm told you know this girl and her friend who took the jeep."

Sweat rolled down Lionel's forehead. He wiped it away. "Before I went south to the camp I did."

"Have any idea where this Judd Thompson might be?"

"Believe me, sir," Lionel said, "if I knew where Judd was, I'd be there right now."

"Have any comment about this Byrne girl before I decide what to do with her?"

Lionel hesitated. He looked at Vicki. "I don't have any comment, sir, except to say that I know she'll get what she deserves in the end."

Lionel turned and saw a look of surprise on Melinda's face.

The commander shuffled papers and cleared his throat. Before he spoke, a guard entered the room and approached him. The two talked quietly, then the commander hurried to the back door.

"Take her back to her cell," the commander said. "I'll give my decision tomorrow morning. Meet here at 0800 hours."

19

VICKI was taken to her cell. Mr. Stein followed and was allowed inside.

"What happens now?" Vicki said.

"Your guess is as good as mine," Mr. Stein said. "Sounds like the commander will decide between now and tomorrow morning."

"Do you think there's a chance—?"

"If he believes you are a little off in the head," Mr. Stein said, "he might just send you to a reeducation camp."

"And if not?"

"I don't want to think about it."

"I'm not afraid to die for the gospel," Vicki said.

Mr. Stein shook his head. "I'll never understand why fanatics say things like that. You think it impresses me. It doesn't. There are many people who would give their lives for something foolish."

"The point isn't whether I would die for my faith," Vicki said. "The main thing is whether what I put my faith in is true."

"You sound like my daughter."

"If they said it was illegal to talk about God," Vicki said, "I would die giving you that message. But I'd rather live to see you accept your Messiah. That's what Chaya was praying for all along."

"They're coming for you tomorrow morning," Mr. Stein said, "and the best you can hope for is to go to a reeducation camp. Why would you be concerned about me when you're facing that?"

"Lionel said it best."

"He was against you."

"No, I understood. He said he knew I'd get what I deserved. Because of Jesus, I have the hope of heaven. The Global Community can't take that away."

"I wish I were as confident as you about the future," Mr. Stein said.

Vicki scribbled the address for Tsion Ben-Judah's Web site on a scrap of paper. "Please, when you get home tonight, look this up. I don't know if the rabbi survived the earthquake, but I'm sure his postings from the past few months are there."

"This is the man who was on television," Mr. Stein said. He rose and called for the guard. "I'll be back in the morning."

"You saved Chaya's Bible," Vicki said. "Why?"

Mr. Stein bowed his head. "Losing Chaya so soon after her mother's death was difficult. So I kept it. I can't tell you why."

"Have you read it?" Vicki said.

"I looked up the verse you talked about, but only for the purpose of helping you."

"You're a man of your word," Vicki said. "You promised Chaya you would find me, and you did. Now promise me something. No matter what happens to me, promise you'll look at that Web site and then read the Gospel of Matthew. It was written to Jewish people."

"I can't promise—"

"It would mean a lot to me," Vicki said.

The guard opened the cell door. Mr. Stein flipped to the first book of the New Testament and smiled. "I am a klutz when it comes to computers. But I will try to read this Matthew passage."

"I have your word?"

"You have my word."

Vicki smiled.

Judd tried to find out about Vicki through the Internet, but there was nothing. He e-mailed Tsion and asked the rabbi to pray. Judd suggested contacting Buck Williams, but Tsion said Buck wasn't available. He was still frantically looking for Chloe.

The kids talked about Ryan and traded stories. There were laughter and tears. Finally, Darrion said, "I think Shelly and I should go back to get Vicki."

"No way," Judd said.

Shelly said, "Darrion's right. It's dark. No one would see us. If they do, we'll say we're just looking for shelter."

"The GC have orders to shoot anyone moving around at night," Mark said. "We'd have to wait till morning."

"Vicki may not have that long," Darrion said.

"They'll probably send her to a reeducation camp like they did me," Judd said. "We can work on getting her out after she's sent there."

"Probably doesn't cut it," Darrion said. "That girl Joyce and the other two Morale Monitors have it in for her. If they believe she murdered her principal, they might give her the death penalty."

The four kids were silent. Judd thought of Vicki waiting in a cell. Or maybe they had already passed the sentence.

"We only have two options," Judd said. "We can try to find her and get her out, or we can wait and let Lionel and Conrad try. They're inside the GC machine."

"He's right," Mark said. "We have to trust Lionel and Conrad."

Lionel and Conrad secretly met outside the Global Community station.

"What happens if we get her out and then get caught?" Conrad said.

"We'd probably be shot for deserting," Lionel said.

Conrad sighed. "I don't see how we can let her go in there tomorrow morning. But I don't want the commander to pull the trigger on me either."

"He won't have the chance," Lionel said. "If my plan works, we'll be out of here by midnight. We can make it to the hideout before sunup."

"What if somebody sees us?"

"We're Morale Monitors," Lionel said. "We're searching for the other kid."

Conrad nodded. "All right, what's the plan?"

Judd and the others searched for blankets and pillows. Darrion said she was going upstairs to find a change of clothes. Mark surfed the Web for any information about Vicki. A few minutes later he called for Judd.

"Take a look at this on the Enigma Babylon page," Mark said.

Judd watched as an image of a smiling Pontifex Maximus Peter Mathews appeared on the screen. The man wore a huge hat and a funny outfit. Underneath was a message to "every soul on earth."

"Wherever you are in the world, whatever you're going through, know that Enigma Babylon One World Faith will be there. When disaster strikes, when governments fail, when your life crumbles before you, trust in Enigma Babylon."

"Looks like a commercial, doesn't it?" Mark said.

"The sad thing is, people will buy into it," Judd said.

Judd read on. "Don't be fooled by those who would cause you to fear for your future. Do not be led away from the hope of a new world order. Be part of a new breed of global citizenship."

"From reading that you'd think this Pontifex guy was competing with Carpathia," Mark said.

Judd sighed. "We've got bigger problems than Enigma Babylon right now."

Mark turned his chair toward Judd and spoke softly. "You're worried about her, aren't you?"

"I'm going out of my skin because there's nothing I can do. I want to march down there, grab Vicki, and run. But I know I can't."

Shelly burst into the room. "Have you guys seen Darrion?"

"I thought she went upstairs," Judd said.

"I've looked," Shelly said. "She's not upstairs or in the hangar."

Lionel found Melinda alone in a snack room at the station. He bought a drink and sat at a nearby table.

"Where's Felicia?" Lionel said.

Melinda didn't look up. "Went back to the shelter to get our stuff. We're staying here tonight."

"It'll be more comfortable than sleeping on the ground," Lionel said.

Melinda looked up. "What's with you? Why the small talk?"

"I'm really sorry about everything," Lionel said. "You guys were right. If I'd have listened to you, we'd have both of them in custody and the commander wouldn't be out a jeep."

"He told us he was going to have a talk with you tomorrow after the sentencing."

"I deserve it," Lionel said. "I just don't want this to break up the team."

Melinda eyed him warily. "You mean it?"

Lionel nodded. "Let me buy you some hot chocolate or something."

"Sure," Melinda said.

Lionel put money in the machine and turned his back to Melinda. "So why'd the commander rush out of here?"

"Didn't tell us," Melinda said, "but you know it has to be important. I think he wanted to finish with this girl tonight."

Lionel stirred the drink and handed it to her. "Know what I think? I say Vicki's in that cell thinking this is the last night of her life."

"It probably is."

"But what if it isn't?" Lionel said, dragging his chair close. "What if the commander buys into what that Stein guy says, that she's crazy or something."

"The commander's too smart for that—"

"Even in situations like this, you can't execute crazy people," Lionel said. "There's a chance he could send her to a reeducation site."

Melinda sipped her hot chocolate and shook her head. "He wouldn't do that. He can't. The girl murdered that principal."

"Melinda, there's a chance the commander might let her go. If he was going to give her a harsh sentence, why wouldn't he have done it before he ran out of here?"

Melinda took another sip.

"Now if I'm that girl," Lionel said, "and I'm thinking this is the last night of my life, I'd do or say anything to get out of it."

"What are you suggesting?"

"The commander wants the guy, Judd, right?"

"He'll find him."

"Eventually. But what if we get the information ourselves?"

"We don't have the commander's OK," Melinda said. "They won't even let us in to talk with her."

Conrad walked into the snack room. "What's up?" Lionel filled him in.

"No way," Conrad said. "I'm in enough trouble with the commander as it is."

"This could get us all some points," Melinda said. "If we get the information, we can deliver this Judd guy by the time the commander passes sentence."

"Exactly," Lionel said.

Conrad crumpled his can of soda. "Call me chicken or whatever you want, I'm not going down there."

Melinda drank the last of her hot chocolate. "I'm in. Let's go."

Judd led Shelly and Mark through the darkened house. Judd found the staircase that led upstairs. It was pitched at an angle and didn't look safe.

The three called for Darrion, but there was no answer.

"She told me her room was upstairs," Shelly said.

"Let me go first and see if it's safe," Judd said.

When he got to the middle, the staircase cracked and collapsed. Judd grabbed the railing overhead and pulled himself up. "You guys OK?" he said.

"Didn't hit us," Mark said. "See if you can find her room."

Judd knew where Mr. Stahley's office was. He went in and looked through the drawers. On the other side of the house he found Darrion's room. He tried a light, but the bulb was broken. The moonlight shone through the window. Judd saw clothes on the floor. He rushed to the stairs and used the railing to let himself down.

"She changed clothes upstairs," Judd said.

"The front door was open a bit," Mark said. "You think she's gone?"

"I think it's worse than that," Judd said. "Mr. Stahley's revolver is gone."

"You think Darrion has a gun?" Shelly said.

"Unless the looters got it."

An engine revved outside. Judd flew out the door in time to see a motorcycle bouncing through the grass near the entrance to the estate.

"Is that Darrion?" Shelly said.

"Has to be," Mark said, "but where'd she get the bike? Everything in the garage was gone."

"Stahley had all kinds of hiding places," Judd said. "Probably had the bike stashed for an emergency."

"Where do you think she's going?" Shelly said.

"She's trying to rescue Vick," Judd said.

Lionel knew he had to get Melinda into the cell quickly. Getting past the guard would be their major problem. But which tactic? Make the guard sympathize with them or play hardball?

"I don't have authorization to let you in," the guard said.

"The reason you don't have authorization is Commander Blancka had to leave on important business," Lionel said. "He expects us to get the information from the girl tonight."

"Why do you think he delayed the sentencing?" Melinda said, scowling at the guard.

"I'd let you in if I had—"

"That's fine," Lionel said. "When the commander comes back here in the morning and finds out you wouldn't let us in, it's your problem, not ours."

Lionel pulled at Melinda's arm. "Let's get out of here."

"Wait," the guard said. "So, you just want to go talk with her, right?"

Melinda turned. "This guy who blew up the commander's jeep—she knows where he is. Now's our chance to get it from her."

"OK," the guard said. "I'll let you in. But you have to leave your weapons here and sign in."

Mitchell Stein opened his laptop. He took the scrap of paper and typed in the address. Reading the words of a traitor to his faith turned his stomach, but a promise was a promise.

Mr. Stein read through some of the E-mails that had poured in since the earthquake. "These people are like sheep," he muttered.

He clicked on an icon that took him to a separate section written by Rabbi Ben-Judah.

> For those of you who still doubt our message, or who need the information to make an informed decision, I have written the following. The texts are found in the book of Romans, a logical layout of what we believe, written by the apostle Paul. Scholars have long been amazed at the sound reasoning and unity of thought contained in this book.

Mr. Stein wanted to stop, but something drew him to the words on the screen.

> Early in the book, Paul writes, "From the time the world was created, people have seen the earth and sky and all that God made. They can clearly see his invisible qualities—his eternal power and divine nature. So they have no excuse whatsoever for not knowing God."
> If it is true that God has put the knowledge of himself on our hearts, what would keep a person from understanding the true and living God? The answer is found two chapters away. "For all have sinned; all fall short of God's glorious standard." A little further in the book Paul writes, "For the wages of sin is death, but the free gift of God is eternal life through Christ Jesus our Lord."

Mr. Stein read on about God's Law and how people had tried to make a way to God themselves. The rabbi wrote:

It will not work. God's Law is holy and perfect and can accept nothing but perfection. You and I are imperfect. The more you read about God's Law, the more you understand how imperfect we are.

That is true, Mr. Stein thought.

The only way to God is through accepting the gift he has given in Jesus. He lived a perfect life. He died in our place. He took the penalty for our sin. "Salvation that comes from trusting Christ . . . is already within easy reach," Paul wrote. "For if you confess with your mouth that Jesus is Lord and believe in your heart that God raised him from the dead, you will be saved. For it is by believing in your heart that you are made right with God, and it is by confessing with your mouth that you are saved."

There were more verses and a prayer the rabbi included at the end, but Mr. Stein couldn't read any further. He sat back in his chair and stared at the ceiling. He had believed his wife and daughter were mistaken. He had thought they were confused about their faith. Now he was confused.

VICKI was glad to see Lionel, then she noticed Melinda behind him. Lionel unlocked the cell door, and the two walked in. Vicki sat up on her cot and looked them over. Lionel and Melinda stared at her.

"What's up?" Vicki said. "Has the commander decided?"

"What do *you* think?" Melinda said. "You counting on him letting you out of here?"

"I don't know what he'll do," Vicki said. "All I know is that I'm innocent."

Lionel laughed. "That's a good one. You're as innocent as those militia people."

Vicki couldn't believe Lionel would turn on her like this. Had he lost his memory again?

"You've only got one hope now, Byrne," Melinda said. "You tell us what you know about this Judd Thomp-

201

son, and we'll have a talk with the commander before he sentences you."

"I don't know where—"

"Think hard before you answer," Lionel said, getting down in Vicki's face. Lionel winked. "Tell us where you and Judd were going before we caught you."

Vicki felt relieved. Lionel was up to something. She wanted to play along but didn't know what to say. Finally, she said, "If I tell you, what happens to Judd?"

"What is he, your boyfriend?" Melinda said. "Do yourself a favor and give him up."

"All right," Vicki said. "If you promise to talk to the commander."

Judd and the others looked in the garage, but there were no vehicles left. The Stahleys' cars had either been stolen or taken by the GC.

"What do you think she'll do?" Mark said.

"Who knows," Judd said. "She's lost her mother and father, and now Ryan's dead. She'll probably risk it and go into the GC camp and wave that gun around."

"She doesn't even know where they're holding Vicki, if she's still alive," Shelly said.

"Vick's alive," Judd said. "She has to be."

Lionel shouted at Vicki. He glanced away and saw Melinda put her hand to her head and wince. Just a few more minutes and his plan would work.

"Judd and I were headed back to the church," Vicki said. "There's an underground hideout there. And we would have made it if that stupid chopper hadn't shown up."

"You were miles from the church when they found you," Melinda said.

"We tried to throw the GC off by driving away," Vicki said.

Melinda sat on the floor. "I don't feel so good." She rubbed her head and moaned.

Lionel knelt beside her. "What's the matter?"

"It's my head," she said, running a hand through her hair. "Everything's spinning. I want to go back to the other room."

"Should I call for the guard?" Vicki said.

"No," Lionel snapped. "Just lie down. You'll be OK in a minute."

Melinda's eyes widened. "You! You put something in my drink!" She reached for a cell bar to pull herself up, but Lionel grabbed her and put a hand over her mouth. Melinda tried to shout, but she was helpless.

"Help me get her to the bed," Lionel said to Vicki.

Vicki grabbed Melinda's arm, and the two dragged the girl to Vicki's cot. By the time her head hit the pillow, Melinda had passed out.

"Listen close," Lionel said. "We're not out of this yet. I'm going down the hall to signal Conrad. You change clothes with Melinda. When Conrad comes, you have to be ready."

"What about the guard?" Vicki said. "He'll know!"

"That's where Conrad comes in," Lionel said. "You have three minutes to make the change."

With tears streaming down her face, Darrion flew into the night. She hated going against Judd and the others, but she couldn't sit still and watch another person she loved die without a fight. Vicki had taken her in and helped her when it seemed the whole world was against her. Darrion couldn't bear the thought of Vicki's execution or even imprisonment.

She felt the gun on her hip and wondered if she would have to use it. She wished she had tried to rescue her mother before the earthquake. She wouldn't make the same mistake again. Still, Darrion had no idea how she would find Vicki or get her out. But she knew she had to try.

Darrion had believed in Christ long enough to know she needed God's help to do anything. But she couldn't think of that now. She didn't even want to pray. God didn't seem to be doing anything to help her friends, so she would take over.

Darrion's father had taught her a lot about motorcycles. But nothing had prepared her for this ride. The road was jagged, and she nearly lost control several times. She slowed when the beam of her headlight shone on water.

I have to cross the river.

She backtracked along the bank until she saw work crews with huge lights working on a bridge. The top of the bridge was intact, but the pavement had crumbled. The GC workers pounded nails in boards.

The workers looked up as Darrion gunned the engine and shot past them across the rickety boards.

"She'll never make it to the end," someone shouted.

But Darrion had been trained well. She picked her way through the shaky maze of boards and steel girders. The lights showed a huge gap between the end of the bridge and the riverbank. She gunned the engine again, shot past the last row of men, and soared into the air.

Lionel ran to the back of the jail and signaled Conrad with his flashlight. A moment later Conrad sent an identical message back.

"Good," Lionel said. "Everything's working."

Lionel quickly moved to the front door and listened for the guard. A cell phone rang. The guard said, "Hello? Hello?"

Lionel ran back to Vicki. Melinda lay limp on the cot in Vicki's dirty clothes.

"What did you give her?" Vicki said. "She's totally out."

"I saved a couple of sleeping pills they gave me after the earthquake," Lionel said. "One pill helped me sleep. I figured two would knock her out."

"What happens—?" Vicki said.

"I don't have time to explain. When I give the word, you hustle past Conrad and me and head for the front door. Don't stop for anybody, got it?"

"Got it," Vicki said. "But—"

Lionel held up a hand. A door opened outside. Conrad shouted something.

"She's in there," the guard said.

On cue, Conrad burst into the cell area and shouted,

"Where's Melinda? Commander Blancka wants her right away!"

"Commander Blancka!" Lionel shouted. "Come on, let's get you out of here."

Vicki ran past Lionel. Conrad blocked the view of the guard.

"Hey, you have to sign out," the guard shouted as Vicki ran out the door.

"I'll sign for her," Lionel said.

"I wonder what the commander wants," Conrad said.

"Must be pretty important," Lionel said as he signed his name and Melinda's.

"Did you get that girl to talk?" the guard said.

"She clammed up," Lionel said. "Went to sleep. We gotta get outta here and see what the commander wants. Thanks for your help."

Lionel and Conrad followed Vicki a few blocks away. They ducked into a darkened alley. All three were out of breath.

"I'm staying," Conrad said.

"No way," Lionel said. "We agreed as soon as Vicki was free, you'd get out of here."

"We need somebody inside," Conrad said.

"They'll pin this on you," Lionel said.

"I'll tell them I got a call from someone who said they were an aide to Commander Blancka. What was I supposed to do—ignore it?"

Lionel bit his lip. The plan made sense, but he knew Conrad was scared of staying with the GC. "Are you sure?"

Conrad nodded. The three put their hands together.

"God go with you," Conrad said.

"You too," Vicki said. She hugged him.

"Let's go," Lionel said.

Vicki's ankle felt much better. She and Lionel ran side by side. Vicki got her bearings and noticed some of the same neighborhoods she and Judd had gone through.

"Someday you're going to have to tell me how you got mixed up with these morale people," Vicki whispered.

"Just get me to the Stahley place and I'll tell you anything you want to know," Lionel said.

As they came over a hill, a light hit them from below. Vicki ducked, then started back. Lionel grabbed her arm.

"Stop or we'll shoot!" a man shouted from below.

Lionel whispered to Vicki, "You're a Morale Monitor, remember that." He put his hands over his head and led Vicki down the hill. When they came close to the GC guards, Lionel said, "We're working with Commander Blancka on finding a missing kid."

"Where's your side arm?" the guard said suspiciously.

Lionel winced. "It's a long story. Commander Blancka said we had to find this guy or we'd get the same punishment. We let him get away."

"Him?" the guard said. "Too bad. I thought I might be able to help you."

"What do you mean?" Lionel said.

"We picked up a girl on a motorcycle about ten

minutes ago," the guard said. "She had a GC-registered side arm. Wouldn't give us her name."

"Doesn't sound like who we're looking for," Lionel said. "We're looking for a Judd Thompson."

"I'll send a report to the other patrols," the guard said. "Give me your names."

Lionel gave him his name and Melinda's. When the guard was gone he said, "That was close."

"What happened to your gun?" Vicki said.

"Left it when we got you out," Lionel said.

"It's a good thing we didn't run away from them," Vicki said. "I just don't want to be out here when they find Sleeping Beauty in that cell."

Judd didn't sleep all night. He paced the floor of the computer room, then moved upstairs when he saw he was keeping the others awake. His body wasn't on the same schedule as everyone else's.

It was nearly sunup when he finally sat on the couch and grew tired. A noise startled him. He heard footsteps in the kitchen, and voices.

GC, Judd thought. *They've caught Darrion, and she led them back here*. Judd scooted down on the couch and reached for his gun. These guys wouldn't take him without a fight.

The voices came nearer. "It's gotta be around here somewhere," one said.

"I thought they said it was near a hallway that led to the kitchen," another said.

Judd peeked over the top of the couch. He clicked the safety off and yelled, "Hold it right there!"

The two scrambled backward and put up their hands. "Don't shoot!" one of them said.

Judd stood and walked closer.

"Judd, is that you?" a girl said.

"Vicki?" Judd said.

Judd finally saw their faces. *Vicki and Lionel.* A wave of relief swept over him. He put the gun away. Vicki ran to him and they embraced. Judd put an arm around Lionel.

"I didn't know if I'd ever see you guys again," Judd said.

"It wasn't easy," Lionel said. He told Judd the story of their escape and meeting the GC patrol. "We had to talk our way across a bridge. I'm glad we're finally safe. All except Conrad."

"And Darrion," Judd said. "She took off last night on her dad's motorcycle."

Vicki gasped. "The patrol said they'd taken a girl on a motorcycle into custody."

Judd sat down hard on the sofa. "Once the GC figure out who she is, she's in big trouble."

"We're all in trouble," Vicki said.

"You think she'd lead them back here?" Lionel said.

"Not on purpose," Vicki said, "but they'd be able to trace that bike."

Conrad and Felicia were waiting at the door the next morning when Commander Blancka walked in. "Why did you want to see Melinda last night, sir?"

"What are you talking about?" the commander said.

"I got a call last night that said you wanted to see Melinda. The man said it was urgent and she should meet you at the helipad."

"I never gave that order," the commander said. He looked at Felicia. "Go check on her."

"I was there all night, sir," Felicia said. "Melinda never returned."

The commander glared at Conrad.

"I went down to the cell to give her the message—"

"What cell?" the commander said.

"Where you were keeping that girl, Vicki. That's where Lionel and Melinda were."

The commander barked into his radio as Conrad continued. "I saw them in the snack room. They were planning on getting information out of that girl. They wanted to find the guy by this morning and impress you."

The guard at the cell block said Melinda and Lionel had signed out late the previous night.

"Bring the Byrne girl here immediately," the commander said.

Mr. Stein came in. Conrad thought he looked upset.

"Have you reached a decision, sir?" Mr. Stein said.

"You'll find out soon enough," the commander said.

"Sir, if you intend to execute this young lady, I must know now."

The commander stiffened. "Sit down and wait."

The guard hustled into the room. Behind him was the groggy prisoner. "She's out of her head. Says she was tricked."

Felicia gasped. "Melinda!"

The commander slammed his fist on the table. He looked at Mr. Stein. "You tricked my guard!"

"I did nothing of the sort," Mr. Stein said.

The commander fumed. "You're all under arrest until I find the person responsible for this!"

21

THE NEWEST member of the Young Tribulation Force shook his head as Morale Monitor Melinda accused him of working against the Global Community.

They don't know where Vicki and Lionel are, Conrad Graham thought as Commander Blancka fumed.

"You helped Vicki escape," Melinda said, still groggy from sleeping pills Lionel had given her the night before.

"You're crazy," Conrad said. "You and Lionel blew that. I told you questioning her was a bad idea!"

"That was part of your plan," Melinda said.

The commander interrupted. "Graham, tell me about the call."

"Some guy said you wanted to see Melinda," Conrad said. "I just delivered the message."

"You didn't verify it?"

"There was no reason," Conrad said. "Besides, everything's been crazy around here."

"He knows something and he's not telling," Felicia said.

Conrad turned on her. "How do we know Melinda didn't set this up with Lionel? Ask her what she was doing in that cell—"

"Lionel drugged her!" Felicia said.

"Enough," Commander Blancka said, glaring at Conrad. "Until I sort this out, you'll stay locked up like Stein."

"But, sir—"

"Take him away!"

Judd and the others inspected the underground hangar and found scattered rocks and dirt. Airplane equipment lay strewn about.

Mark pointed out the steel girders. "That's why we're safe here," he said.

Judd found the wall the GC had cut through to get to him and Ryan. Plaster and flooring from above covered the hole.

"We have only one way in or out," Judd said, showing Mark the collapsed secret door in the hillside.

"We can dig a new opening," Mark said. "Won't be fancy, but we'll have another exit."

The kids grabbed tools. After a few minutes, Vicki threw down her shovel. "Have you guys forgotten Darrion and Conrad?" she said. "They're facing Blancka!"

"Darrion said the same thing about you," Judd said, "and look where she is now."

"At least she cared enough to do something," Vicki said.

"Don't give me that!" Judd shouted. "I risked my life to get back here."

"To do what?" Vicki said. "Save us?"

Mark and Shelly stopped digging.

"Settle down," Lionel said. "We're on the same side, remember?"

"Yeah, but Judd always has to show us who's boss," Vicki said.

Judd shook his head.

"The GC are going to figure out who Darrion is," Vicki said. "We have to get her out."

"They'll probably trace the cycle back here," Judd said. "That's why we're digging."

Vicki rolled her eyes. "My point exactly," she said. "You care more about yourself—"

"If Darrion had listened, she wouldn't be where she is."

"Like you've never made a mistake," Vicki said.

"Judd's right," Lionel said. "Conrad's our best bet to get her out."

"He might not even know they have her," Vicki said.

Judd reached for Vicki's shoulder, but she jerked away.

Lionel stared at them. "Is something going on here?"

Judd scratched his head. "Give us a minute."

Lionel returned to help Mark and Shelly.

"You're upset about Darrion," Judd said.

"That's not all," Vicki said. "We got out of there so fast there wasn't time to bring Phoenix."

"You're worried about a dog?"

"I promised Ryan. Maybe promises don't mean that much to you—"

"Stop it!" Judd said. "I know you promised, but risking your life for Phoenix doesn't make sense."

"You get mixed up with a biker gang and try to jump a motorcycle over a river, and *I* don't make sense?"

Judd took Vicki by the shoulders. "This is partly because of us."

Vicki squinted. "Don't flatter yourself!"

"I care for you, Vicki, but—"

"Get this," she interrupted. "I don't go for arrogant types who think they're always right. If you want to be friends, fine. Other than that, no."

Conrad sat back against the cell door.

"Know anything about Vicki?" Mr. Stein said from the next cell. When Conrad hesitated, Mr. Stein added, "I only want to know that she is safe."

"If the GC don't know where she is, she's OK," Conrad said.

Mr. Stein sighed. "You are one of them, are you not?"

"What do you mean?"

Mr. Stein told his story. His wife and daughter Chaya had believed Jesus was the Messiah before Chaya was killed in the earthquake. Mr. Stein had laughed at them. "Now I'm not so sure they were wrong. I read a part of the New Testament last night, plus some of Tsion Ben-Judah's Web site."

"The Web site got me too," Conrad said. "Then Judd and Vicki explained it, and it all came together."

"I do not know what to believe," Mr. Stein said. "I have so many questions."

Conrad inched closer to the bars. "I don't know that much, but like what?"

"All right," Mr. Stein said, "if Jesus really is the Messiah, how could he forgive someone who has been against him all his life?"

"That's me too," Conrad said.

"But—," Mr. Stein said. "I am a Jew who rejected his Messiah. And the way I treated Chaya! Surely God could not forgive such an offense."

"There are stories in the Bible about people who turned around," Conrad said.

"That is not my only problem," Mr. Stein said. "If this is all true, God has caused millions to die or suffer."

"I don't think he's mean," Conrad said. "I think he's trying to get our attention."

"But there's another problem. If my wife and daughter were right, Nicolae Carpathia is the Antichrist. With all the good he has done, how can I believe that?"

A guard came and took Mr. Stein away. A few minutes later another prisoner was led in. Conrad peered through the dim light to see who it was.

Vicki retreated to a corner. She was crushed but didn't want anyone to know. She had hoped Judd had feelings for her, and several times he had started to say something but never finished. Under the desk in the rubble of New Hope Village Church, she felt close to him. But now he had changed, and Vicki felt foolish.

Shelly came and sat next to Vicki. "Mark punched through the dirt wall about half an hour ago, no thanks to you."

"Sorry."

"What's up?"

Vicki shook her head.

Judd sat by what was left of the Stahley's pool, throwing in clods of dirt and watching them break apart. He wanted to tell Vicki how he felt, but it was clear her feelings weren't as strong as his.

Evening shadows stretched across the Stahley property.

Vicki is too young anyway, Judd thought. But her angry words had hurt him. They had been through so much together. And now this.

Something caught Judd's eye at the edge of the woods. Branches moved and leaves rustled. He sat still. The sounds stopped. Judd relaxed. Then came the squawk of a radio. He dropped and crawled toward the house. Inside, he moved to the window. Nothing.

He quietly called Lionel and told him to watch the other side of the house. Suddenly, Judd spotted two uniformed GC officers heading toward them and more scattered in the woods. A helicopter flew overhead.

Lionel ran to Judd. "How could I have been so stupid!"

218

"What?" Judd said.

"My radio! It has a homing device. I led them right to us!"

Conrad motioned to Darrion. She seemed to recognize him but looked cautious. Conrad pulled back his hair and showed the mark on his forehead. "Do they know who you are?" he said.

Darrion shook her head. "The commander kept saying he couldn't place me. I said I was Laura Grover and that I'd found the motorcycle in a big house. I have to figure a way out of here," Darrion said.

"Hang tight," Conrad said. "They might turn you loose in a few days."

"And if they figure out who I am?"

"Then I'll have to get us both out."

Vicki and Shelly ran to the others when they heard the commotion.

Mark said, "The GC is tracking Lionel's radio. Be ready to run."

Vicki frowned. "Give me the radio."

Lionel handed it to her. "I hope you know what you're doing."

22

JUDD and Lionel helped Mark brace the new exit so it wouldn't cave in. The opening was the size of a window.

Mark stuck his head through the opening. "GC is almost to the house. And they're armed to the teeth."

Judd ran to the computer room. *I gotta get Vicki and Shelly out of there!*

"Are you up for this?" Vicki said.

"This is my acting debut," Shelly said. "Get that picture over the entrance so they don't find you guys."

Judd hurried in. "We have to get out of here now," he said.

"Help me get this picture in place," Vicki said.

Judd pulled out Conrad's gun. "You don't understand—they're almost inside!"

"Help me!" she said.

Judd grabbed the picture, and something cracked. The picture fell.

"Someone's in there," came a voice.

"Hold it in place," Vicki whispered.

"Let's go now," Lionel said.

"What about Judd?" Mark said.

"Do what you want," Lionel said. "I'm heading for the woods."

Mark moved through the opening, but before Lionel could follow, Mark scampered back inside. Lionel heard chopper blades. When the helicopter flew toward the river, Lionel followed Mark outside. They crawled to a small hill. They tucked their arms close to their bodies and rolled to the bottom, then crouched and hurried into a wooded area.

When they stopped to catch their breath, Mark said, "No way Judd can hold them off."

Lionel backtracked and found a drainpipe in a clump of bushes. He pulled out his flashlight and peered inside.

"Judd said there was a landing strip somewhere near here."

The helicopter grew louder.

Vicki heard crunching glass coming from the kitchen. The helicopter hovered, then flew away. Vicki gasped at the click of a rifle.

"Oh, hi there," Shelly said.

"Hands in the air now!" a man shouted.

"What do you want with me?"

"On the floor!"

"You don't have to be so mean," Shelly said. "I just took some crackers."

"Where are the others?"

"Others?"

"The radio!" a man shouted. "It gave you away."

Shelly said, "You can have that thing. I don't want it."

"Where did you get it?"

Shelly filled her mouth with crackers. "This black kid comes up and asks if I'm hungry," she said. "He could tell I was. So he says he'll tell me where to get some food if I do him a favor."

"Washington, sir?" a man said.

"Yeah, let her keep going."

"There's not much more," Shelly said. "He said if I'd take his radio and keep it until somebody found me, he'd tell me where I could get something to eat. Crackers is all I found."

"Was there anyone with him?" a man said.

"A girl," Shelly said. "Redhead. Scrawny."

"Exactly where?" a man said.

"Across the river," Shelly said. "They headed south or west, whatever's away from the river."

Someone radioed the chopper.

"What do we do with the girl?" another said.

"I'll see what Blancka says," the leader said.

Vicki's arms were tired from holding the picture in place.

The chopper blew sticks and leaves into the drainpipe. Lionel and Mark crept deeper into the pipe, a trickle of water rushing past their feet.

"Hope there's no snakes," Mark said.

"Better snakes than the GC," Lionel said.

The boys moved deeper until they could barely hear the chopper. In several places, the earthquake had crinkled the pipe.

"We'd better turn back," Mark said. "We're not gonna find anything."

Lionel heard fluttering wings. "Get down!" he yelled as bats flew past. Lionel shuddered, but he was curious about what might be ahead. They came to a break where dirt blocked their way. The earthquake had opened a hole in the pipe. "Look at this!" Lionel said.

A natural cave stretched several hundred feet.

Judd struggled to hold the picture. He wished Vicki would rest so she could return the favor.

The GC leader sent others searching throughout the house. Judd heard the man talking on his radio in the next room.

Judd told Vicki, "I don't think I can hold this anymore."

Vicki closed her eyes. "We have to."

The painting slipped and banged against the floor. Judd massaged his arms and bent double from exhaustion.

"Did you hear that?" the leader said.

Shelly said, "Stuff's been falling since I got here. The earthquake, you know."

Someone knocked on the wall, and a knife sliced through the picture of the Stahleys. Judd and Vicki squeezed to the side as a flashlight came through.

"Anything?" the leader said.

"Lotsa dust."

The flashlight scanned back and forth as Judd leaned out of its beam.

Shelly screamed. The light went away.

"I saw someone out there!"

The leader took several men and bolted out the front door toward the driveway. Judd propped the picture up as best he could.

"You guys better leave now," Shelly whispered.

"Not without you," Vicki said.

"They'll know something's up. Go!"

Judd and Vicki slipped into the underground computer room. They looked for Lionel and Mark in the hangar.

Lionel and Mark took ten minutes to break through the dirt and rock. When they finally pulled themselves inside the cave, Lionel gave a low whistle. "It's huge."

The cave was twenty feet high. The floor was rocky but fairly level and dry.

"This would make a great hideout," Lionel said.

"Sure," Mark said. "No food, no heat. Just like home."

Lionel noticed a small beam of light coming from the

back of the cave. Mark helped him reach a ledge, and Lionel pulled himself up.

Lionel said, "This could be another entrance."

"No tree roots," Mark said. "We may be right under that landing strip. One good jolt and the whole thing could come down on us."

Judd was alone when Lionel and Mark returned that evening. "The GC bought Shelly's story," he said. "Took the radio and told her to get to a shelter before she gets shot for looting. They headed for the river, but we'd better not risk staying here long."

Lionel told Judd about the cave.

"Let's check it out after dark," Judd said.

Conrad was fascinated by Darrion's story. She had gone from having everything she wanted to having nothing.

"I shouldn't have tried to rescue Vicki," Darrion said. She put her head against the bars. "God didn't seem interested in us, so I tried something on my own."

The door opened and Mr. Stein was led back to his cell.

"They still suspect me," Mr. Stein whispered after the guard left. He rubbed his forehead. "I wish I could talk to Vicki."

"If they suspect you, they might let me go," Conrad said. "Then I could help you both escape."

"They will not let the girl go," Mr. Stein said. "They know who she is."

"Vicki?" Darrion said.

"No, *you*, my dear. They suspect the others are at your house. One group has already been there and gone. They are sending another group tonight."

23

WHILE he ate, Lionel walked through the hangar and gathered supplies. He found a long piece of rope and a metal hook strong enough to hold his weight. He nailed together five other pieces of wood, then screwed the hook in the middle.

"What's that?" Shelly said.

"You'll see tonight," Lionel said.

Lionel looked over Judd's shoulder and read the computer screen. Judd had pulled up Tsion Ben-Judah's Web site. A fast-moving number on the edge of the screen showed how many people were logging on.

"That can't be right," Lionel said. "The numbers are going by too fast."

"I've never seen anything like it either," Judd said.

Judd had logged on to download a Bible, but he found himself distracted by the Web site. He felt guilty for how little he was studying. He knew devotions weren't possible when you were running from the Global Community. Still, he wanted to stay "in the Word" like Bruce had taught them.

From the moment Judd had prayed to receive Christ, he felt hungry for the Bible. He wanted to know all the things he had missed the first time. He wrote verses on scraps of paper and tucked them inside his pockets.

But after Bruce had died, no one checked on him or asked him how things were going. Slowly, with all he had to do, he found it easy to let it slide.

As Judd looked over the message on Tsion's Web site, he wondered who else might be reading it. Perhaps members of the 144,000 witnesses. Perhaps Nicolae Carpathia himself. His friend in New Babylon, Pavel, had told him Nicolae checked Tsion's Web site frequently.

If he's reading this, Judd thought, he has to be seething. Judd read:

> Good day to you, my dear brother or sister in the Lord. I come to you with a heart both heavy with sorrow and yet full of joy. I sorrow personally over the loss of my wife and teenagers. I mourn for so many who have died since the coming of Christ to rapture his church. I mourn for mothers all over the globe who lost their children. And I weep for a world that has lost an entire generation.

How strange to not see the smiling faces or hear the laughter of children. As much as we enjoyed them, we could not have known how much they taught us and how much they added to our lives until they were gone.

I am also sad because the great earthquake appears to have snuffed out 25 percent of the remaining population. For generations people have called natural disasters "acts of God." This is not so. Ages ago, God the Father gave Satan, the prince and power of the air, control of Earth's weather. God allowed destruction and death by natural causes, yes, because of the fall of man. And no doubt God at times intervened against such actions by the evil one because of the prayers of his people.

Tsion went on to say the recent earthquake was an act of God necessary to fulfill prophecy and get the attention of those who don't believe in Jesus. He said he was amazed at the work of the Global Community in setting up communications so quickly. But Tsion said he was shocked at what he saw in the media.

"Do they still have a television around here?" Lionel said.

"Maybe in one of the bedrooms upstairs," Judd said.

Judd continued reading. Tsion grieved the way society had forgotten God at a time when they needed him most.

If you believe in Jesus Christ as the only Son of God the Father, you are against everything taught by Enigma Babylon.

There are those who ask, why not cooperate? Why not be loving and accepting? Loving we are. Accepting we cannot be.

Enigma Babylon does not believe in the one true God. It believes in any god, or no god, or god as a concept. There is no right or wrong. The self is the center of this man-made religion.

My challenge to you today is to choose up sides. Join a team. If one side is right, the other is wrong. We cannot both be right.

But I do not call you to a life of ease. During the next five years before the glorious return of Christ to set up his kingdom on earth, three-fourths of the population that was left after the Rapture will die. In the meantime, we should invest our lives in the cause. A great missionary martyr of the twentieth century named Jim Elliot is credited with saying this: "He is no fool who gives up what he cannot keep [this temporal life] to gain what he cannot lose [eternal life with Christ]."

And now a word to my fellow converted Jews from each of the twelve tribes: Plan on rallying in Jerusalem a month from today as we seek the great soul harvest that is ours to gather.

And now unto him who is able to keep you from falling, to Christ, that great shepherd of the sheep, be power and dominion and glory now and forevermore, world without end, Amen. Your servant, Tsion Ben-Judah.

Lionel returned with a small television. Judd watched him flick through channels. Before the Rapture Judd had seen things he knew his parents wouldn't have liked, but nothing compared to this.

One game show allowed the winner to kill the other contestant. The next channel showed the torture and murder of innocent people. On another, a séance was performed as people tried to communicate with the dead. Enigma Babylon approved of an educational program that taught viewers how to cast spells on enemies. As Lionel flicked the stations, things got worse.

"Turn it off," Judd said.

"Dr. Ben-Judah was right," Lionel said. "This is the bottom."

Conrad explained his plan. Darrion and Mr. Stein agreed to help.

"I just wish I could talk to Vicki again," Mr. Stein said. "I keep thinking about what she and Chaya said to me. I can believe that Jesus was a great man. A good teacher. Even a prophet. But I am still not sure about him actually being God."

Darrion said, "Why would you call him a good teacher if he told a lie?"

"I don't understand," Mr. Stein said.

"Jesus said a lot of good things," Darrion continued.

"Be kind to your neighbor. Do to others what you would have them do to you. But he also said he *was* God. So if you think he was just a good man, you call him a liar."

"I did not say that."

"Saying you're God is crazy, unless it's true," Darrion said. "If he was insane, he's nobody you'd want to follow."

Mr. Stein sighed.

"What she's saying is right," Conrad said. "Jesus taught great things and claimed to be the Son of God. Then he backed that up by doing miracles. Even coming back from the dead. If that doesn't prove he was who he said he was, nothing will convince you."

Mr. Stein put his face in his hands. "The weight I feel is immense. If you are right, I have rejected the Holy One, and I haven't believed my own flesh and blood."

Darrion came close to the bars. "Vicki told me Chaya prayed for you every day. You don't have to feel guilty. She only wanted you to believe."

―――――――――――――

As night approached, Lionel gathered his materials and went to meet with the others. He found Vicki alone. "You want to talk about it?" he said.

Vicki shook her head.

Judd called them together and went over the plan.

"If we have to move, why don't we take all our stuff now?" Shelly said.

"We want to be sure this cave won't collapse," Judd said. "We don't want to lose any of our supplies."

As they left, Mark backtracked and tied a string across the patio doorway to the mansion. He ran it outside to a pane of glass perched above the concrete.

Lionel led the way. Mark helped him carry the equipment that would lower them into the cave. The ground was spongy and filled with crickets.

Judd held the flashlight and searched for the opening as they walked. After several minutes, Mark suggested they go through the drainpipe.

Judd held up a hand. "Hold on," he said.

Looking closely, Lionel spied a hole about the size of a fist surrounded by grass and rocks. Judd and Mark dug out the hole to about three feet in diameter.

Lionel wedged the boards between two rocks and let the rope down. Judd went first and shinnied into the cavern. His voice echoed as he called out, "You guys were right. This is perfect."

Lionel covered the door he had made with mud and grass. He dug out a landing where the kids could climb and then push the door open. When he had finished, he covered the area with extra dirt and a few small rocks.

"How's it look?" Lionel said.

"You'd never know it was there," Vicki said.

A crash behind Lionel sent him to the ground. "What was that?"

"What I was afraid of," Mark said. "Company. Somebody tripped the wire."

Lionel heard a sound that gave him chills.

Dogs.

Conrad watched Mr. Stein. He seemed to be in pain. A guard unlocked Darrion's cell.

"What's going on?" she said.

"We know who you are," the guard said. "Commander wants to see you. They're gonna catch those other two tonight."

"I don't know what you're talking about," Darrion said.

"Sir, tell Commander Blancka it worked," Conrad said.

The guard turned and eyed Conrad.

"Tell him I did what he wanted," Conrad said. "I got the information."

"Of all the dirty tricks!" Mr. Stein screamed.

"You said you were one of us," Darrion said.

"And you were foolish enough to believe me," Conrad said.

The guard looked confused. Mr. Stein grabbed Conrad's shirt and banged him against the cell bars.

"Let him go, now!" the guard shouted.

"Don't trust this little weasel!" Mr. Stein shouted.

"I said, let him go!" The guard pulled his nightstick. Mr. Stein turned Conrad loose.

"I'll report this to the commander," the guard said.

"Just hurry up," Conrad gasped.

Darrion winced when the guard pulled her through the door.

"I did not hurt you badly, did I?" Mr. Stein whispered after they were gone.

Conrad smiled. "Don't worry about it. I'm just a weasel. Where'd you come up with that?"

"Probably the movies I watched when I was younger," Mr. Stein said. "We must pray your plan works."

"Pray?" Conrad said.

"Pray to the God of my fathers, Abraham, Isaac, and Jacob. And pray to the Son of God himself, Jesus Christ."

"Then you believe?" Conrad said.

"My daughter was right. I believe Jesus is the only way and that I cannot come to God except through him."

Conrad smiled.

"I am ashamed to have been so blind," Mr. Stein said. "Chaya's last moments were spent trying to tell me the truth, but I would not listen."

"I can help you with the prayer, if you'd like," Conrad said.

Mr. Stein nodded.

"Just ask God to forgive you for the wrong stuff you've done. Tell him you're sorry for not believing sooner."

Mr. Stein prayed.

"Now tell him you believe that Jesus died for you and rose again. Tell God you don't trust in anything you've done, but only what Jesus has done. Ask him to be your Savior and Lord."

Tearfully, Mr. Stein completed his prayer. "Oh God, please forgive me," he cried. "Come into my life."

Vicki broke into a sweat when she heard the dogs.

"What's going on?" Judd shouted from below.

"Quiet!" Vicki said.

"Everybody in," Lionel said. "We don't have time to figure out who it is."

"What if it's Conrad and Darrion?" Vicki said.

"With dogs?" Lionel said. "No way."

"Get in the cave," Shelly said as she took off for the house.

"What is she doing?" Lionel said.

Lionel helped Vicki onto the rope. She was nervous about climbing that far. When she got to the bottom, she put a hand on Judd's shoulder. "Shelly will be all right. She can do it."

24

THE NEXT morning a different guard returned for Conrad. Darrion had been gone all night.

"Don't believe anything he says," Mr. Stein yelled as the man led Conrad away.

Melinda and Felicia waited outside the interview room and scowled when Conrad sat beside them.

"I wanted to tell you guys what was up, but I didn't want to blow my cover," Conrad said.

"What are you talking about?" Melinda said.

"The commander put me down there so I could listen to those two talk," he said. "I got what he wanted."

"I don't believe you," Felicia said. "You're one of them."

"I was just as surprised as you when Lionel turned up dirty."

The girls turned away.

"I need your help," Conrad said, moving where he

could see them. "I'm going to catch Lionel, the girl, and that other guy."

The door opened. Commander Blancka came outside. "What is this, Graham?"

"Commander, sir, I figured since I was innocent, you put me in with the others to spy. It worked."

The commander cleared his throat. "I didn't. I mean . . . what did you find out?"

"Darrion's definitely one of them, sir," Conrad said.

"We've had someone talking to her all night," the commander said. "She says she doesn't know them."

"If it's all right with you, I'd like to see the look on her face when I tell you the whole story," Conrad said.

The commander motioned the three inside. Darrion looked exhausted. Her eyes were puffy and red. *The commander probably talked about her parents*, Conrad thought.

Conrad knew this would be the tough part. If he could convince the commander he wasn't partners with the others, he had a chance to get Darrion and Mr. Stein out.

Vicki was worried when she awoke and Shelly hadn't returned. She felt stiff and sore from sleeping on the cave floor. In the light of the embers from Judd's fire, she crept to the other side to inspect the drainpipe. Vicki hadn't told anyone, but she was scared she wouldn't be able to climb the rope that led out of the cave. Coming down wasn't so bad, but she had never been very good at climbing in gym class. She couldn't let anyone know. Especially Judd.

Vicki watched the trickling water go through the pipe

and wondered how long they would have to be on the run. Staying in the cave wouldn't be bad if they had food and sleeping bags, but they had none.

Vicki looked at Judd. He was asleep. Part of her just wanted to get out and not have to deal with him anymore. He had yelled at Lionel for letting Shelly go. Vicki couldn't imagine being cooped up with him for a few days, but she couldn't imagine not having him around either.

Lionel stirred and saw Vicki. "She's not back yet?" he said.

Vicki shook her head. "I hope the GC didn't take her away."

"Judd was right. I should've stopped her."

"He was not right," Vicki said. "Shelly can take care of herself as well as anyone."

"What's going on between you and Judd?"

Vicki frowned. "Nothing. That's the problem. I thought he really cared for me but we're too far apart."

"You mean, you're from a trailer park and he's a rich kid?" Lionel said. "I'd say that's not much of an issue at the moment. You're both sleeping in a cave."

Vicki smiled. "It's not the time to let these feelings take over."

"I know one thing," Lionel said. "Judd cares a lot more than you think."

Vicki was startled by a *tick, tick* sound from the pipe behind her. Lionel craned his neck.

"You think we should wake Judd and Mark?" Vicki said.

241

Lionel shook his head. "I'll check it out."

Lionel returned a few minutes later carrying a blanket. Shelly was right behind him. Vicki gave her a hug and watched as Lionel opened the blanket on the floor. Inside were food, a few bottles of water, and the laptop computer from the hideout.

When Shelly caught her breath, she said, "I went to the front of the house. I figured if these were GC, they'd recognize me from before. They were GC all right, but a different group.

"I ran in the front and screamed. The guys about shot me! I told them you guys came back and held a gun on me."

"We're gettin' to be as mean as snakes," Lionel said.

"Don't say that," Shelly said. "I think I saw one as I came up the drainpipe."

Vicki shivered. "What happened next?"

"They asked which way you went, and I pointed toward the woods. They took their dogs down there but came back a few minutes later. Said they were going to stay all night and watch.

"I told them I wasn't going to let you two come back and get me, that I was going to stay with them. They searched the whole house but didn't find the hideout."

"How'd you get out?" Lionel said.

"I thought they'd leave, but they kept looking through their binoculars. I told 'em I was going to sleep and then head for a shelter at sunup."

"They bought it?" Lionel said.

"I guess," Shelly said. "They kept searching in the

garage and near the patio. That's where the dogs kept going."

Judd awakened and welcomed Shelly.

"When they took the dogs upstairs, I slipped behind the picture and into the hideout. I figured Judd could use the computer. I hope it's charged up."

Judd picked up the laptop and inspected it. "Good thinking."

"I came back upstairs and pretended to sleep," Shelly said. "I remembered Mark talking about another entrance to the pipe."

"Are you sure nobody saw you?" Judd said.

"Don't think so," Shelly said.

"You could have led them right to us," Judd said.

"She just saved us!" Vicki screamed, waking Mark. "If she hadn't gone back there, the GC would have tracked us down for sure."

Vicki's voice echoed through the cave. Then came barking.

"Come on," Lionel said. "We have to block the drain!"

"I heard everything," Conrad said, looking straight at Darrion. "She tried to get Stein to be a part of their group."

"What group is that?" the commander said.

"Some religious order," Conrad said. "They go around with stuff on their foreheads."

The commander looked at Darrion. "I don't see anything," he said.

Conrad laughed. "They claim it's invisible."

Melinda and Felicia chuckled.

"Darrion tried to convince the guy, but he wouldn't budge. She told him Judd and Vicki had gone to her house, then went back to the basement of their church."

The commander scribbled notes on a pad.

"You lying double-crosser!" Darrion shouted.

"You're the liar," Conrad said as a guard subdued Darrion.

"What about Washington?" the commander said.

"I'm afraid he's one of them too," Conrad said. "Lionel planned to get Vicki out all along. I should have seen it."

"And Stein?"

"From what I picked up, Vicki was a friend of his family. He's misguided but not guilty of anything."

The commander nodded and whispered to a guard.

"Commander, I don't like this," Felicia said. "From the time Lionel and Conrad met those other two—"

"I appreciate your concern," Commander Blancka said, "but this is valuable information. Go back to the church and search every inch. I want Washington back here to stand—"

The commander's radio squawked. He excused himself, then called Conrad, Felicia, and Melinda into another room.

"Looks like they were at this Stahley girl's house last night," the commander said. "We've got a team waiting in case they come back. I'll assign backup. My guess is you'll find them at this church."

Judd and the others dug furiously. They filled the pipe with dirt and rocks. The dogs barked at the end of the tunnel. When the entrance was blocked, Judd stayed close. The others prepared to leave.

The dogs pawed at the earth on the other side. Two men caught up to them. One cursed. "They must have stayed right here last night."

"Probably took off with the other girl," another said.

The dogs were back at the dirt again, and Judd heard one yelp. The two men left.

"Looks like we're safe for a while," Judd told the others.

Judd asked Lionel to carefully look from the top entrance. Lionel climbed the rope with ease and lifted the opening a few inches. He slid back down and sat by Vicki.

"They're headed back to the house," Lionel said.

Judd opened the laptop while the others ate breakfast. The battery was almost dead.

"We'll only have one shot to see our messages," Judd said.

"You don't have a phone line," Vicki said.

"This works on a regular line and it also has a sat-phone built in," Judd said. He dialed up and logged onto his E-mail. There were hundreds of messages forwarded from Tsion Ben-Judah's Web site. Judd scrolled down the list. A small screen popped up, saying the battery was running out.

Judd scanned the messages and recognized one with a Global Community address. It was from Conrad.

As he opened the message, the laptop went blank.

Judd pounded the floor of the cave.

"What did it say?" Vicki said.

Judd shook his head. "Couldn't read it. Maybe Conrad got Darrion out. Maybe he's in trouble and needs our help."

"We could sneak back up to the house and try to recharge it," Mark said.

"Too risky," Judd said. "But at some point we'll need to communicate with the outside."

"There's gotta be someone who can help us," Mark said.

"There's always your friend with the motorcycle," Vicki smirked.

Judd stared off but didn't say a word.

25

TWO days later, Judd knew the kids were desperate. The GC hadn't discovered them, but they had no food and only the water from the dripping drain. They had tried to keep the fire going, but they were running out of fuel.

"Somebody's going to have to get some wood," Lionel said.

"Won't do any good," Judd said. "No matches."

Shelly put her head on a rock and held her stomach.

"We have to get supplies and recharge this battery," Judd said.

"Maybe they've pulled out," Mark said.

"Wouldn't bet on it," Lionel said. "Probably at least one guard will stay behind for a few days."

"How about digging into the back entrance at night?" Shelly said.

"They'd spot us," Judd said.

"Then we have to create a diversion," Lionel said. He drew a plan in the dirt. One of them would go in for supplies.

"There won't be time to recharge the computer," Judd said.

"Then whoever goes in stays all night. We come back the next night to get him."

"Him?" Vicki said.

"Or her," Lionel said.

"We could just make a run for it," Mark said.

"I know how these guys operate," Lionel said. "They've got a net out for us. They'll be waiting."

The kids agreed to chance the nighttime break-in.

"Who goes?" Lionel said.

"I'm the one who knows the place the best," Judd said.

"We'll draw straws," Vicki said.

Mark held up five splinters of wood. When they had drawn, Lionel held the shortest.

Conrad showed a picture of Lionel and Vicki to a worker at a shelter. The worker shook his head. "Haven't seen them," he said.

Melinda and Felicia joined Conrad. "Any luck?" he said.

The girls shook their heads. "I don't want to go back to the commander and say we've spent two days and have nothing to show for it," Melinda said.

"We could try the high school again," Conrad said.

Felicia frowned. "Like it or not, we'd better head back. Our meeting's in a half hour."

Conrad had tried not to be too friendly with the girls. He wanted them to believe he was on their side, but he didn't want to act like fast pals. Conrad could sense that the girls still distrusted him. At times they whispered to each other. He had read somewhere in the Bible that he was supposed to do good to his enemies, but he didn't know what that meant to people like Felicia and Melinda.

Conrad wanted to talk with Mr. Stein. The commander had released him two days earlier, but a guard was secretly watching the man's house. Conrad feared Mr. Stein might still have questions or doubts. Or he might have changed his mind about Jesus. Conrad had seen the mark on the man's forehead, but he wasn't sure if a person could un-pray a prayer. He couldn't wait to see Judd again. He had a million questions.

Conrad hoped to slip past the guard and visit Mr. Stein late that night, assuming he could get away without Melinda or Felicia seeing him.

Conrad was also concerned about Darrion. He knew the commander had withheld food and water from her. The GC's efforts hadn't worked. But how long could she hold out? Conrad tried to slip her a bottle of water before they met with the commander, but Melinda and Felicia stayed close.

"We've been to fourteen shelters in the area, sir," Conrad told the commander. "Some of them twice. The hospitals haven't treated anyone fitting their description. We found the location of the Washington and Thompson homes and checked there. The Byrne girl was staying with a pastor. The church is empty."

The commander grunted.

"He was killed at the start of the war," Conrad continued, "and it looks like this Byrne took in a bunch of kids. There's nothing left of that house."

"People don't just disappear," Commander Blancka said.

"Heard anything from the Stahley girl's house?" Melinda said.

The commander shook his head. "We've still got guards there, but I don't think they'll come back. My guess is they've found a place they think is safe, and they hope we'll forget about them." The commander looked out the window. "Well, I'm not going to forget. These kids have caused a lot of trouble. The top brass is watching. The whole Morale Monitor program could hinge on what happens here."

"We'll do all we can, sir," Felicia said.

The commander stared at the kids. "We'll break this Stahley girl soon. She has to talk. We'll find the others and make an example of them."

At dinner, Conrad excused himself. He had written a note to Darrion earlier in the day. It read, *You and the others are alive as long as you hold out. Don't give up. I'll try to get you some water tonight.* He put a rubber band around the note and attached it to a candy bar.

He darted behind the former police station. Darrion was in the farthest cell down the hall, and she was the only prisoner. He put his hand through the window and rattled the wrapper. Darrion looked up. Conrad put a finger to his lips. He threw the candy bar as hard as he could and watched it skid to a stop a few feet from Darrion's cell.

Darrion used her blanket to pull the candy closer until she reached it. She ate it hungrily as she read the note. When she was finished, she mouthed, "Thank you," then licked the wrapper.

As Conrad raced back to the tent to finish his dinner, a light rain began to fall.

"What took you so long?" Felicia said suspiciously.

"If you have to know, I got some bad water," Conrad said, taking two bottles from the table. "I've been—"

"That's enough," Melinda said. "Not at dinner."

Conrad shrugged. "You asked."

Melinda leaned close. "You feel up to a little night-time investigating?"

"Sure, where you going?"

"We're gonna hit that Stein guy," Felicia said. "We've got a hunch he has those kids hidden somewhere."

Conrad's eyes widened. "They could have gone there before we put the guard on him. Where's he live, anyway?"

"His house is demolished," Melinda said. "And his daughter died in the earthquake. He's living at his office in Barrington. We leave at midnight."

Lionel asked Judd for his E-mail password, and Judd scribbled it on a scrap of paper. "Look at all you want," Judd said, "but you'll have to go through a lot of forwarded messages from Tsion."

Judd explained how to recharge the laptop, then said, "If you'd rather I go—"

"Oh no, you don't," Vicki said. "Besides, Lionel knows as much about computers as you do."

Judd shook his head as Vicki walked away. "She hates me," he said.

"I don't think so," Lionel said. "You guys can work out whatever's come between you."

Judd changed the subject. "I can't remember, but there might be a battery backup in the desk. If you find one, make sure you—"

"I'll charge it up," Lionel said. "Are you looking for any special E-mails other than Conrad's?"

"His is most important," Judd said. "Write Tsion and tell him to pray."

Lionel climbed the rope and peeked through the entrance. It was raining harder, and water was leaking through the hatch.

"The rain's good for us," Judd said when Lionel returned. "I don't think the dogs can follow as well."

"How much food and water do you want?" Lionel said.

"As much as you can carry," Judd said.

Conrad met Melinda and Felicia near the jail. The girls had signed out a jeep from the commander. The rain was coming down hard as they started toward Barrington.

"Got an idea," Conrad said. "I brought a disk with me to do a data dump from the guy's computer. He might have some information stored."

"Good," Felicia said.

Melinda drove cautiously. Some of the main roads had been bulldozed and were easy to pass. Others were still in rough shape.

The kids were stopped twice at GC checkpoints. When the guards saw they were Morale Monitors, they waved them through.

A light was on upstairs at Mr. Stein's office. Melinda and Felicia walked across the street and found a man watching the building.

"What did he say?" Conrad said when the two returned.

"We're cool," Melinda said. "The guy radioed his buddy around back to watch for anyone trying to sneak out."

Conrad thought it odd that there were two guards and that the one in front hadn't questioned the girls further. Melinda tried the door. To Conrad's surprise, it was unlocked. The girls pulled out their guns.

"Maybe he's expecting us," Conrad whispered.

The office was dark. Conrad shone his flashlight around the room. There were several desks with computers. Some were on the floor. The walls of the building looked stable, though other buildings on the street had collapsed. They found Mr. Stein sleeping upstairs on a couch, an open Bible on the man's stomach.

That's a good sign, Conrad thought.

Melinda nodded toward the computer. Conrad waved them back outside.

"If we wake him up, he might alert the others,"

Conrad said. "I'll get on the computer while you guys check downstairs. Maybe there's some kind of basement where they're hiding."

Conrad pulled a disk from his pocket. When he was sure the girls were gone, he crept to the couch and gently shook Mr. Stein awake.

Conrad put a hand over the man's mouth and whispered, "You have to be quiet. Two Morale Monitors are downstairs."

Mr. Stein nodded. Conrad took his hand away. Conrad was glad to see the mark of the true believer on Mr. Stein's forehead.

"Is anyone hiding here?"

"No," Mr. Stein said. "How is Darrion?"

"Hungry," Conrad said, "but there's no time to talk. I'm loading a message on your computer. It has Judd's E-mail address. Follow the instructions I give and we might be able to get Darrion out alive."

Mr. Stein nodded.

"It's embedded in a file called *Chaya*," Conrad said. "I thought that would be easy for you to remember."

Mr. Stein smiled.

"Now go back to sleep and don't wake up until those two come back," Conrad said.

Conrad put the file onto Mr. Stein's hard drive, then erased the file from his own disk. He began copying files from the computer, but soon realized many of them were from Tsion Ben-Judah's Web site.

I can't let them see this! Conrad thought.

Melinda and Felicia returned.

"Almost finished," Conrad whispered.

"Has he been awake?" Felicia said.

Conrad shook his head.

Felicia kicked the couch, and Mr. Stein jumped like he had just been awakened. "Where are you hiding them?" Felicia screamed.

"What?" Mr. Stein said.

Felicia put her gun to the man's head. "I said, where are you hiding them?"

"Go ahead and pull the trigger," Melinda said.

———————————

Lionel crouched by the bushes near the back patio. The rain was blinding. It was difficult to see even a few feet ahead. Lionel pushed the light on his watch. Three more minutes. He edged closer to the house. He kept the laptop under his shirt and hoped the rain wouldn't damage it. Lionel saw two glowing objects in the house.

As planned, at exactly midnight, Lionel heard the scream and the gunshot. Two dogs barked. Cigarettes fell to the floor. The front door opened. A man shouted orders into his radio.

Lionel ran into the kitchen and nearly lost his balance as his wet shoes hit the floor. He rounded the corner and made it to the slashed picture of the Stahley family.

Lionel moved the picture and climbed through the opening. He prayed Judd and Vicki would be able to get back to the cave in time.

26

JUDD preferred to have Mark join him, but Vicki insisted. The rain matted her hair. It had been Vicki's idea to scream. Judd thought her piercing wail would not only alert the GC but also scare them.

Once Judd made sure the GC guards were after them, they bolted toward the clearing. The rain fell hard. Judd held up a hand to block it. He saw Mark's signal in the distance, a blinking flashlight.

Judd was right about the dogs. They couldn't track as well in the rain. He heard their yelping and turned. Two flashlights scanned the bottom of the hill.

A few yards from the entrance to the cave, Judd picked up the signal again. A flashlight beam crossed their path. Judd's heart sank.

"There they are!" a man yelled.

Judd grabbed Vicki's arm and pulled her away from the hideout.

"To the woods," Judd yelled over the noise of the rain.

Conrad's first instinct was to reach out and grab Felicia's gun, but something made him hold back. The two girls seemed icy cold.

Mr. Stein turned pale. "I don't know what you're talking about," he said.

Felicia gritted her teeth and pushed the gun harder against the man's scalp. "Where are you hiding them?"

"I told you, I haven't seen Vicki or any of the others since—"

"Just get it over with," Melinda said. She glanced at Conrad. "Or maybe he wants to do it."

Conrad understood. In the split second when Melinda caught his eye, he knew the two were trying to trap him. Perhaps they had the commander's approval. That was probably why the guard at the front hadn't put up a fight about them searching the place. The whole evening had been a test.

Conrad shrugged. "You know this isn't gonna look good," he said.

Felicia pulled the gun away slightly, and Mr. Stein took a breath.

"I don't care what you do to the guy," Conrad continued, "but it's clear the commander wants him watched. If you two off him, I don't think the commander will be happy. Like it or not, this guy might be our best shot at finding Lionel and the others." Conrad put the computer disk in his pocket. "It's up to you. I don't mind a little blood."

Felicia looked at Melinda and put the gun away. She pushed Mr. Stein back on the couch.

"The authorities will hear about this!" Mr. Stein yelled.

Conrad jumped on the man, pushing him hard into the wall. "We are the authorities!" he yelled.

Vicki ran after Judd through the pouring rain. They hit the edge of the woods, and both went tumbling into the wet leaves and mud. Lightning flashed, and Vicki saw they were on the edge of a drop-off.

"They'll think we're headed for the drainpipe," Judd yelled. "We have to find a place to hide."

Vicki's heart pounded. She had been upset with Judd for being so bossy. Now she didn't mind. "How about up there?" she said, pointing to a gnarled pile of wood and leaves.

"Good," Judd said. "We can get out as soon as we see them go toward the drain."

Vicki and Judd scampered back up the hillside and covered themselves with wet leaves. The rain pelted them. Vicki was glad to see the dogs enter the woods fifty yards from them. Judd and Vicki lay perfectly still. Lightning flashed again.

When it was clear the men were going toward the drain, Judd whispered, "If they see us, don't stop. Keep running for the cave as fast as you can."

Vicki nodded. Judd ran through the trees ahead of her. She didn't dare look back.

Lionel plugged in the laptop when he reached the computer room. The battery would need an hour or two to recharge. Rummaging through the scattered contents of the desk, he was surprised to find two batteries. He put them next to the laptop and ran to the hangar.

Lionel found the supplies but left them there. Something bothered him. If the GC came back and found his wet tracks leading to the hideout, he was sunk. While the GC were looking for Judd and Vicki there was time.

Lionel looked for some rags and found a stack of blankets near the food stash. He took off his shoes and socks, still dripping from the rain, and climbed through the opening. On his hands and knees, he dried the wet spots. Something in the entryway caught his eye. It had a greenish glow. He inched his way over on top of the blanket.

On the floor next to one of the chairs was a cell phone. The display glowed with the last number the man had dialed.

Suddenly the room lit up with the searchlight of the passing helicopter. Lionel scrambled into the shadows. He stuck the phone in his pocket and crawled toward the hideout.

Back in the computer room he inspected the phone closely. He found the ringer and turned it off. He looked through the list of numbers. One of them said *Comm. B.*

Lionel clipped the phone to his belt and moved to the hangar. He spread three blankets on the floor. In the first he loaded bottles of water. In the second and third he placed the dried and canned food. He tied each blanket and lugged all three to the landing near the picture. He would be ready when the kids returned the following night.

With the physical work complete, Lionel sat at the computer. The battery was 50 percent charged. He pulled out Judd's instructions and opened Conrad's message.

Don't reply to this, Conrad wrote. *Wherever you are, stay there. The GC are still looking, but don't have a clue. I'm trying to get Darrion out, but it might take some time. I'll be in touch as soon as I can. Conrad.*

Lionel smiled and deleted the message.

Conrad got out of the jeep first. "I'm gonna get some sleep."

"Give us the disk," Melinda said.

"No problem," Conrad said. He pulled the disk from his pocket and gave it to Felicia.

"It's broken!" Felicia said.

Conrad grabbed the disk and shook his head. "It must have cracked when I jumped on the guy," he said.

Conrad went toward his room, then ducked behind a building. Melinda and Felicia turned and headed toward the commander's tent.

When they hit the clearing, Judd looked toward the Stahley house. A helicopter hovered with its searchlight trained on the mansion. He hoped Lionel hadn't been caught.

"Keep going," Judd said as he and Vicki stayed close to the ground. The rain came down at an angle, stinging Judd's face.

261

Judd couldn't find the opening or Mark's signal. The dogs bellowed from inside the drainpipe. Vicki tripped over something in the grass.

Mark stuck his head out of the hole. "Thought you guys were goners," he said. "Get in here."

Judd and Vicki crawled onto the ledge with Mark. Shelly made room for them and started down the rope.

"Flashlight's batteries are almost out," Mark said. "I stopped signaling you a while ago."

Before the hatch closed, a flash of lightning lit up the cave. Judd squinted at the floor. He grabbed the light from Mark and turned it on.

"You're gonna run it totally—"

"Shelly, stop!" Judd screamed. "Stay right where you are."

"I can't hang on," Shelly said.

"What is it?" Vicki said.

The dim light barely showed the horror of what lay a few feet beneath Shelly.

"Snakes," Judd said. "The cave floor is full of them!"

Lionel found a message from Mr. Stein. He opened it and read the information about Conrad.

They were just here, Mr. Stein wrote. Conrad left a message. Please write as soon as possible. I have wonderful news.

Lionel pulled out the phone and dialed the number Mr. Stein included at the bottom of his E-mail.

"How did you get a phone?" Mr. Stein said.

"Long story," Lionel said. "Are you sure this line isn't tapped?"

"I don't believe it is."

"Good," Lionel said. "What's the news?"

"My daughter's prayers have been answered," Mr. Stein said. "I have become a believer in Jesus Christ."

Lionel nearly dropped the phone. "That's great," he said.

"I have been reading Dr. Ben-Judah's Web site," Mr. Stein continued. "I tried to contact him."

"Judging from the amount of mail he's getting, that's a long shot," Lionel said.

"I believe God has chosen me to be one of his witnesses," Mr. Stein said. "I want to go to Israel and attend the meeting. It is only a few weeks away."

"Sir, we're in deep trouble here," Lionel said.

"Of course," Mr. Stein said. "How can I help?"

"The message you received from Conrad," Lionel said. "Read it to me." When Mr. Stein finished, Lionel said, "I don't know about letting Darrion go much longer with the commander."

"It sounds as if Conrad has the situation under control," Mr. Stein said. He described the threat on his life by Felicia and Melinda. "If Conrad can get the GC to trust him, he'll have a better chance to get her out. But, as he says here, it may take up to two weeks."

"What about Israel?" Lionel said.

"You are my friends," Mr. Stein said. "I'm sure God will work something out."

"If the GC get your phone records, they'll find out about this call. It won't look good."

"I'm willing to risk anything," Mr. Stein said. "Tell me where you are. I will come get you."

"No," Lionel said. "We've found a safe place."

"Once Conrad sets the plan in motion, do you have anyone to help you surprise the GC while you get away?"

"I'll talk with Judd," Lionel said.

Lionel heard movement above him and whispered, "I'll call you tomorrow night." He turned off the phone and listened as the GC entered the house.

"Don't look down!" Judd shouted to Shelly as she swayed above the cave floor.

"I can't hang on much longer," Shelly said.

"The water must have made them go for higher ground," Mark said.

"Are they poisonous?" Vicki said.

"I don't want to take the chance," Judd said, grabbing the rope and climbing down as quickly as he could. He didn't want to knock Shelly off, but he knew she wouldn't be able to climb up by herself.

Mark held the flashlight. Judd saw Vicki cover her eyes.

"I don't feel well," Shelly said.

"Hang in there, Shel," Judd said. "You've gotta help me climb back to the top."

When Judd got near, he let go with his legs and slid close to Shelly. "Put your arms around me and hold tight," he said.

Shelly grabbed Judd's belt with one hand and tried to

pull herself up. She slipped, but Judd caught her with a hand. Shelly put her arms around Judd's neck.

Judd hung on while Mark and Vicki pulled the rope up an inch at a time. When they made it to the ledge, Judd collapsed. Shelly fell into Vicki's arms, crying.

"Maybe we should have made a run for it," Mark said.

Judd tried to catch his breath. The rain was coming harder, and the chopper wasn't going away.

27

JUDD was drained. The kids couldn't go through another night like this. But Lionel needed them. *What if Lionel was caught?* Judd pushed the thought from his mind.

Shelly, Vicki, and Mark braced themselves at the top of the cave. Judd knew they couldn't stay in that position all night.

"My leg's cramping," Vicki said.

Judd turned on the dim flashlight and scanned the floor. The cave was dry. The snakes weren't leaving. Judd noticed an area under them that the snakes avoided.

"I'm not going down there," Shelly said.

"If you go to sleep, you'll fall," Judd said.

"I'm not going down," Shelly said.

Judd climbed down the rope. He didn't know much about snakes, but he could tell many of them weren't poisonous. He knew that wouldn't make the others feel much better.

Judd noticed a ledge to his left. The rock wasn't wet and there were no snakes. He threw a rock, which hit with a thud. The snakes hissed and moved back. Judd described the ledge, but Vicki and Shelly shook their heads.

"There's room for all of us to stretch out and sleep," Judd said. "We're going to need the rest."

"We need food," Shelly said.

"We'll get it tomorrow when Lionel gets back," Judd said.

"Why don't we sleep in the meadow tonight?" Vicki said.

The helicopter passed again, slivers of light shining through cracks in the opening above them.

"Any more questions?" Judd said.

"So if we go down there, what's to keep our squirmy little friends off us?" Mark said.

"I'll take the first watch," Judd said. "They're just as afraid of us as we are of them."

"Right," Shelly said. "They don't look scared to me."

Judd led the way down and helped Vicki, Shelly, and Mark onto the ledge. The girls were wary of the snakes, but Judd assured them he would keep watch.

Judd turned the flashlight on every minute or so. He threw rocks and sand at the snakes that came near.

A few minutes later, Judd heard the soft breathing of the others as they slept. Judd stretched his legs and yawned. The rainfall overhead and the occasional clap of thunder brought back memories. When a storm would come in the night, he would run into his parents' room and sleep by their bed.

He threw a few more rocks toward the snakes and stretched out by the ledge. The flashlight was almost use-less now. With its dim light he could see only a few feet away.

Judd felt his eyes getting heavier. He shook himself awake. He had to stay awake.

Lionel heard the Global Community guards return. The helicopter widened its search and finally gave up. The GC radios squawked upstairs, but Lionel couldn't make out the conversation from his hideout.

Lionel finished preparing the supplies and checked the computer. He pulled out a blanket and curled up in the computer room. He knew he would need the rest for the night ahead.

He awoke refreshed a few hours later and plugged in another battery. He turned the computer speakers off and logged on to Judd's E-mail. A message from Dr. Ben-Judah caught his eye.

Judd, I know you have been concerned about Chloe, and our prayers have been answered. Buck has returned with her. She has many injuries from the earthquake, but if she hadn't run from her home, she would have died. Thank God she and the baby are all right.

"The baby?" Lionel said out loud. He smiled. So Buck and Chloe were going to have a baby. Cool. Lionel wanted to see Vicki's face when she found out.

Buck is nervous about my plans to travel to Israel, Tsion continued, but I know this is of God. I will go there if it is his will.

*Please pray for this and another matter. Buck and Chloe
have a friend who is in terrible trouble. I won't
go into the details, but this woman needs God in her life.*

Let me know how I can help. I pray for you daily.

Tsion closed with a verse of encouragement. Lionel
put his head on the desk. It had been so long since he
had experienced a normal day. He longed to sit in a
church service with other believers, or in a small group
and talk about the Bible. Lionel couldn't imagine when
that would happen, or if it would ever happen again.

Vicki awoke stiff and cold. She noticed a bit of morning
light coming through the top of the cave. The rain had
stopped. She looked at Judd and gasped. He was asleep,
and several snakes were lying next to him.

Something heavy was on her legs. She lifted her head.
Two huge snakes stretched out beside her. Another had
crawled on top of her legs.

Vicki trembled and tried not to scream. She looked at
Shelly and Mark. The snakes hadn't gotten to them.

"Help," she whispered. She said it three more times
before Mark awoke.

"OK," Mark said, wiping the sleep from his eyes.
"They've just found a warm place. Don't make any
sudden movements."

"Get them off me," Vicki said.

Mark looked behind him and grabbed a long stick.
"Lie back and don't watch," he said.

Vicki closed her eyes. Mark lifted the snake with the

stick. Vicki opened her eyes and saw the snake's head inches from her face. Mark threw the snake to the other side of the cave and it landed with a thud. He pushed the two other snakes away from Vicki, and she scooted closer to Shelly.

Mark climbed off the ledge and put his hand over Judd's mouth. He whispered something to him. Mark picked the snakes off one by one and threw them in the corner. Shelly watched in horror. When the snakes were gone, Judd stood and leaned against the ledge.

Judd shook his head. "I'm sorry," he said. "Couldn't keep my eyes open."

Shelly stood and said, "I'm not staying here another night."

"We have to get Lionel out," Judd said.

"I don't care if I get caught by the GC," Shelly said. "I don't care if they throw me in jail or put me in a reeducation camp. Anything's better than living like this."

"Look!" Mark said, pointing to the other side of the cave.

Vicki squinted and noticed the room full of snakes had disappeared. Only the ones Mark had thrown on the other side remained.

"We have to keep our heads," Judd said.

Shelly jumped down, watching each step closely. "I'm telling you, I'm climbing out of here now."

Judd nodded to Mark. Mark grabbed Shelly and held her by the arm.

"If you don't let go, I'll scream!"

271

"If you climb out of here now, it could endanger the rest of us," Judd said.

Shelly cried. "You don't understand."

Vicki climbed from the ledge and put an arm around Shelly. The girl was falling apart. Vicki didn't want to stay in the cave any more than Shelly did, but Judd was right.

Vicki tried to calm her, but Shelly began to shake and sob. "I have to get out!" she screamed.

Vicki put an arm around Shelly. "What's going on?" she said.

It took Shelly a few minutes to calm down. "I feel so bad," she cried. "I'm trying to hold together, but I can't."

"It's OK that you lost it," Vicki said. "I'm scared of the snakes, too."

"Not like me," Shelly said. "When I was little, my mom left me and went to a bar. I was playing in the backyard. We had a rusty, old slide and a swing. There was this snake sunning itself on the end, but I didn't see it."

"How awful," Vicki said.

"I tried to stop, but I couldn't. I knocked it onto the ground. It probably wasn't poisonous, but it scared me. I cried and cried, but my mom was out drinking. Every time I see snakes, it comes back to me. I'm so sorry."

Shelly put her head on Vicki's shoulder. "It's OK," Vicki said.

After a fitful night's sleep, Conrad reported to the commander's office with Melinda and Felicia. The commander had circles under his eyes, and his jaw was tight.

"The Stahley girl still hasn't talked," the commander said. "Without food or water she should be starving by now."

Conrad knew why Darrion hadn't starved. In addition to the candy bar, he had gotten two bottles of water and some sandwiches to her.

"We're putting a ring around the Stahley place," the commander continued. "There must be something inside that house the kids want."

"Sir, could we have another go at her?" Melinda said.

The commander nodded and looked at his computer. The screen saver was a flying insignia of the Global Community that morphed into the smiling face of Nicolae Carpathia.

"The top brass is asking questions," the commander said. "They've heard there's been trouble. I've been able to cover so far, but they want to know if we can supply Morale Monitors in the new schools."

"When will they need them?" Conrad said.

"Next month," the commander said.

Melinda stood. "Give us another chance," she said. "We'll get something out of her."

While he was on-line, Lionel saw a window pop up. It was Pavel, Judd's friend from New Babylon. Lionel turned on the speakers and looked at the boy.

"You are not Judd," Pavel said.

"I'm his friend Lionel."

"Your face is in shadows," Pavel said. "Lean closer to the camera so I can see your forehead."

When Lionel did, the boy smiled. "It is good to talk with you, my brother," Pavel said. "Where is Judd?"

Lionel explained their situation. Pavel gasped. "I was afraid things would get worse for Judd."

"What's going on over there?" Lionel said.

"Nicolae Carpathia is angered by the response to Tsion Ben-Judah's Web site," Pavel said. "It is being read by millions around the world. The potentate himself has been reading it."

"What for?" Lionel said.

"My father says the Global Community wants to sponsor the rabbi's return to Israel. It's supposed to show how loving the potentate is. I believe he has sinister plans."

"The rabbi's smart," Lionel said. "He won't walk into an ambush. Besides, the GC should look at what Tsion is saying about the one-world faith."

"That is another interesting story," Pavel said. "The potentate is at odds with Enigma Babylon's top man."

"You mean Mathews?"

"Correct. Mathews thinks he and the one-world religion are bigger than the Global Community."

"So Carpathia has competition and he doesn't like it," Lionel said.

"He doesn't like Mathews or Ben-Judah, and he hates the preachers at the Wailing Wall. He's convinced they're speaking to him."

"Wouldn't be surprised if they are," Lionel said.

"My father heard him scream, 'I want them dead! And soon!' "

Lionel shook his head. It had been a long time since

he had seen the prophets Moishe and Eli. They would tell the truth about Nicolae and wouldn't hold back. Lionel couldn't wait to tell the others what he had learned.

"One more thing," Pavel said. "My father had a talk with a man in Carpathia's communications department yesterday. He told him there are missiles pointing into outer space."

"Missiles?" Lionel said.

"The potentate is afraid of meteors sent by God."

———

Conrad winced when Melinda slapped Darrion across the face. Darrion didn't answer her questions. She only looked at the girls and said, "Water. I need water."

Felicia took her turn hitting Darrion and yelling at her. Conrad knew they expected the same from him.

He kicked Darrion's chair out from under her and shoved her under the table. Out of sight he winked. "You're doing great," he whispered. "Keep it up."

———

Judd knew if anyone could calm Shelly, it was Vicki. Shelly kept saying she had to get out. Judd and Mark stayed back.

"She's losing it," Mark whispered.

"I can't blame her," Judd said. "I should have stayed awake."

"We'll get Lionel back in a few hours," Mark said. "A fire and some food will change things."

Judd nodded. He wanted to believe Mark was right, but he wasn't sure.

Lionel heard more movement upstairs and crept near the GC officers. One was talking on the radio.

"Go ahead, Commander," the man said.

Lionel felt a chill when he heard his boss's voice.

"Ferguson, you and Wilcox stay there until nightfall," the commander said. "We'll send a chopper for you."

"What if they come back, sir?" the man said.

"I think they've moved on," the commander said. "No use wasting manpower."

When the commander was through, Ferguson said to Wilcox, "Awful lot of trouble to go through for a bunch of kids."

"He wants to make a lesson of this one," Wilcox said as he rattled a piece of paper. "Washington. Kid made him look bad."

"He's not gonna exactly throw a party for the other two, Byrne and Thompson."

"Cute girl," Wilcox said. "Wonder what they did?"

"Get your stuff together," Ferguson said. "We'll catch 'em. And when we do, the commander will make sure none of these little Morale Monitors ever cross him again."

28

THE COMMANDER'S conversation had left Lionel uneasy. He should have been happy the GC were pulling out. That would make things easier. They wouldn't have to stay in the cave. But the way the commander talked troubled Lionel. Something didn't seem right.

Lionel took the three packs of provisions and put the most important stuff into one blanket. Food, water, matches, and the laptop. All the batteries were charged, so the kids would have enough power for hours of computer use.

Lionel dug his way through the mound of dirt that covered the secret entrance. When he was nearly through, he pulled out the GC officer's phone and scrolled through the list of names and landed on *Comm. B.* Lionel punched the Send button and listened.

"Ferguson?" an aide to the commander said.

"Yeah," Lionel said, trying to sound like Ferguson.

"Glad you called. Commander wanted me to give you a message. You found your cell phone?"

"Yeah, it was under the chair," Lionel said.

"Too bad," the aide said.

"What do you mean?"

"You know, we hoped whoever was in the house had taken it."

"Right," Lionel said. *They know I'm in the house!*

"Here's the plan," the aide said. "You and Wilcox make a big deal about getting out of there. Slam the door, whatever you have to do. Flank the house on both sides until your backup comes. They'll be there within the hour."

"How many are you sending?" Lionel said.

"We went over this," the aide barked. "We'll have a chopper and ten men. Now the kids may try to come back in, or the one inside will go to the others. It's important we get them all."

"I got it," Lionel said. He hung up the phone and gave a low whistle. He only had one chance, and he had to act fast.

Vicki stayed with Shelly the whole day. Staying at the top of the cave had calmed Shelly. Vicki left her only once to get her a drink of water, but Judd stopped her.

"This stuff needs to be boiled before we drink it," Judd said.

"She needs something," Vicki pleaded. "Let me just give her a little."

278

"It'll make her sick," Judd said.

Vicki stomped off and climbed the rope again. She put her feet on the side of the cave to balance herself. The more she did it, the better she got at climbing.

"Just a few more hours," Vicki said. "We'll get a fire going, get some food and water—"

"I don't have the strength to help tonight," Shelly said.

"It's OK," Vicki said. "You rest, and we'll take care of getting Lionel."

Vicki watched Mark and Judd gather the remaining sticks and wood from the cave. She was so hungry. Her mouth was dry and her lips cracked. The only good news was that the snakes were gone. But Vicki wondered if they would return if it started raining again.

Lionel shoved the blanket filled with provisions through the hole until it almost fell out the other side. He didn't hear a chopper or any GC troops. He crawled on hands and knees to the middle of the opening and pulled the cell phone from his pocket. He found the number listed for Larry Wilcox and pushed Send.

The guard with the deep voice answered. "Wilcox."

"Ferguson still hasn't found his phone?" Lionel said angrily.

"No, sir," Wilcox said. "We think—"

"Never mind what you think," Lionel interrupted. "The commander wants you inside until the chopper gets there with the others."

"All right," Wilcox said.

"Where are the dogs?" Lionel said.

"Outside, on either side of the house, like we were told," Wilcox said.

"Bring them in," Lionel said.

"But, sir—"

"Do you want me to get the commander on the line?" Lionel said.

"No, sir," Wilcox said. "We'll bring them in right away."

Lionel waited a few minutes, then pushed the pack of provisions the rest of the way out with his feet. He wiped the dirt from his face and looked around. Light was fading. No one was in sight. He grabbed the heavy pack, slung it onto his back, and took off for the meadow.

He heard a faint rumbling in the distance. On the horizon he spotted a helicopter. It was still at least a mile away. Lionel ran as fast as he could toward the cave.

Judd went over the plan once again. He and Mark would go for Lionel while Vicki and Shelly stayed behind. Vicki seemed miffed that she didn't get to go, but Judd wasn't going to worry about that now.

"Somebody's coming!" Shelly said from the top of the cave.

"Quick," Judd said, "get down!"

Judd pulled out his gun and aimed it at the opening. Dirt fell as someone tried to get in.

"Lionel!" Vicki shouted.

280

"Somebody give me a hand with this stuff," Lionel said as he replaced the door. Judd climbed up to help. Shelly and Vicki tore into the blanket and found the water.

"Why didn't you wait for us?" Judd said.

Lionel told him what he'd discovered. In the middle of his story he stopped. "Chopper's landing," he said. "If I'd have stayed, they'd have caught you guys for sure."

Judd lit a match, but Lionel blew it out. "The GC might see the smoke," he said.

The five ate and drank until they were full. Lionel spread the supplies out and showed them the phone and laptop. "We'll have to conserve the food," he said.

"How long are we gonna be here?" Shelly said.

"The GC won't give up looking for us," Lionel said. "I think we have to wait here until we find a better place."

"No way," Shelly said.

"What about Conrad and Darrion?" Vicki said.

"Conrad's message said for us to stay where we are," Lionel said. "Until we run out of supplies, I think that's exactly what we should do."

"Anything has to be better than this," Shelly said. She told Lionel about the snakes.

"I don't like snakes any more than you," Lionel said, "but—"

"I'm telling you, I can't stand another night in here," Shelly said.

Lionel nodded. "I know you're scared, but there are a dozen GC troops out there right now looking for us. If they find one of us, they'll find the rest. You might get off with a reeducation camp. But they'll court-martial me, and who knows what they'll do to Judd and Vicki."

Shelly looked away.

"We'll keep you safe," Judd said.

Shelly stood. "That's what you said last night. I just can't handle another night in here, OK?"

Shelly walked away.

Lionel told the others about his conversations with Pavel and Mr. Stein. When Vicki heard the news about Mr. Stein and his belief in Christ, tears welled up in her eyes. "I wish Chaya were here," she said.

"There's something else," Lionel said. "Chloe's going to have a baby."

Vicki's mouth dropped open and she cried harder.

Judd grabbed the cell phone. Lionel showed him the number. Mr. Stein answered.

"Are you all right?" Mr. Stein said. "I was so worried after talking with Lionel this morning."

"We're OK," Judd said. "Lionel told us about you."

Mr. Stein chuckled. "Do you know that I am probably one of the 144,000 witnesses?"

"I imagine so," Judd said.

"There is so much to learn. I need to meet with you and Vicki. I want to become strong and tell others about God. Just like the apostle Paul."

"Keep reading Tsion's Web site," Judd said.

"I am. But I've also written Nicolae Carpathia."

"You what?" Judd said.

"There were so many messages pleading with the potentate to provide safety for the rabbi. I wrote Nicolae himself and said surely a lover of peace, who helped the rabbi escape his homeland, has the power to return him safely to Israel."

"Carpathia took the credit for getting Ben-Judah out of Israel?" Judd said. "Buck said—"

"Of course he took credit," Mr. Stein said. "He wanted to look good in the eyes of the world."

"Did you get a reply?"

"Not with words," Mr. Stein said. "This afternoon, Global Community officers appeared and took my computer away. I have others, of course. They asked again about my involvement with Vicki."

"What did you say?" Judd said.

"I told them the truth. I don't know where she is."

Judd heard a click on the line.

"I have withdrawn all my money from—"

"Mr. Stein," Judd said, "hang up and get to a safe place."

"What's wrong?"

"I think someone's listening."

"But Dr. Ben-Judah believes each of the witnesses is protected by God. Not everyone who has the mark on their forehead is protected. Only the 144,000 evangelists."

"Then be safe and get out of there."

"All right," Mr. Stein said. "But how will I reach you?"

"Use my E-mail address and tell me where to call you," Judd said. "Hurry."

Lionel and the others prayed that Mr. Stein would get to a safe place. Though their gathering wasn't the church setting Lionel had longed for, just being with other believers made him feel better. He prayed for Shelly and asked that her fear of the cave be taken away.

When they were through, Lionel hooked up the laptop. Just like the food, they would need to ration the use of the computer.

"If the batteries last as long as they say," Lionel said, "we could go forty minutes a day for more than three weeks."

"You think we could be in here that long?" Vicki said.

"I think we have to prepare for the worst," Lionel said.

Lionel logged on to the site where Eli and Moishe were shown live each day. The camera at the Wailing Wall carried live audio as well. Lionel knew these were the two preachers predicted in the book of Revelation. Judd pointed out their smoky burlap robes. They wore no shoes and had dark, bony feet and knuckled hands.

"They look like they're a thousand years old," Vicki said.

Their beards and hair were long, and they had dark, piercing eyes. They screamed out warnings to those who continued to reject Jesus as Messiah. As some in the crowd protested, Eli said, "Do not mock the Holy One of Israel! He came that you might have life, and have it to the full.

"Woe to you who reject the Son of God," he said. The camera showed a close-up of Eli's face. It was leathery and sunbaked. "And woe to those who fall prey to the one who sits on the throne of this earth."

"Who's he talking about?" Vicki said.

"The only person I can think of is Nicolae Carpathia," Lionel said.

Conrad rushed to the commander's tent with Melinda and Felicia. The commander smiled and came out to meet them.

"We've just heard a conversation between Stein and Thompson," the commander said. "This guy fooled us. He is in contact with them, and he's one of the fanatics. Told Thompson he was part of their elite group of 144,000, whatever that means."

The commander answered a phone call. When he was finished, he slammed the phone to the ground.

"The computer they took from his home came up empty," the commander said. "But we have enough on him now."

"What will you do, sir?" Conrad said.

"Question him and see if he'll talk now that we have him on tape," the commander said. "If he doesn't tell us what we want, we'll execute him."

"And if he does tell you?" Conrad said.

The commander smiled. "We'll execute him anyway."

29

FOR the next three weeks, Judd tried to make contact with his friend Pete. Pete had access to motorcycles, but he hadn't returned Judd's calls. The kids all agreed they would be safer away from the Mount Prospect area, but none of them wanted to leave without Conrad or Darrion.

Judd and the others coaxed Shelly into staying. She slept in the highest spot in the cave each night and kept an eye out for snakes. Vicki still talked about finding Phoenix. Judd tried not to discourage her, but he didn't hold out much hope.

"Maybe that biker group got Pete," Vicki said. "After what happened at that gas station, they sounded pretty upset."

"That's it," Judd said. He phoned the gas station and left a message.

Their food was running low, but Judd knew if they

were careful, they could last a few more days. Judd and Mark had made two midnight attempts to retrieve more supplies. Each time, they had to turn back. The GC still had guards posted at the house.

Though there was enough room in the cave, the kids quickly got restless. Each time they accessed the Internet, Mark searched for his cousin John. After two weeks he still had no word.

Judd and the others limited their computer time to twenty minutes each morning and twenty minutes each night. It was their only contact with the outside world.

One evening they gathered around the computer, and Judd read aloud an E-mail from Tsion Ben-Judah.

If you see media reports about a shooting in Denver, it is true that Buck was there, Tsion wrote. *Don't believe anything else about the reports.*

Judd clicked on a news flash and saw a video of the shooting in Colorado. The reporter said, "Two men, one claiming to be Nicolae Carpathia's pilot, broke into this clinic and killed a receptionist and a guard."

Footage from security cameras showed blurry video footage of three men.

"Isn't that Buck in the middle?" Vicki said.

Judd nodded. "Tsion said something about a friend of Chloe's being in trouble," he said.

The video showed a picture of a woman embracing Nicolae Carpathia. "That's Hattie Durham!" Vicki said.

"The two killers reportedly abducted the fiancée of Potentate Nicolae Carpathia," the reporter said. "The public is asked to provide any information about the identities of these men, or the whereabouts of Ms. Hattie Durham."

The news channel showed an enhanced photo of Buck and another man, along with Hattie Durham. Judd shook his head. "I want to hear Buck's version of what happened," he said.

With their water running low and no word from Pete, Judd had to make a decision. They hadn't heard from Mr. Stein, and Judd feared the man had been caught. His fears were confirmed the next morning when Conrad sent an urgent message.

We brought Mr. Stein in late last night, Conrad wrote. He stayed hidden as long as he could, but we got a call from one of the shelters. He went for food, and someone recognized him from a photo the GC had passed around.

I was with Melinda and Felicia when we found him. He's lost a lot of weight. He saw me and almost said something. I felt so bad taking him in. The commander's questioning him now. He's threatening to execute him if he doesn't give you guys up. Behind closed doors the commander says he'll execute him by noon, no matter what.

"That's in a few hours!" Vicki said.

Judd kept reading the message. *I don't know what to do. The commander is talking about shipping Darrion away by the end of the week. If we're going to do anything, now's the time.*

Judd turned off the computer and hung his head. "We're going to get him out of there," he said. "Darrion too."

"How?" Mark said.

Judd's phone rang.

"Hey, pal, what's up?" Pete said.

Judd told Pete their situation.

"I want to help," Pete said, "but there's no way I can make it by noon. Need time to get other riders together."

"What about tomorrow?" Judd said. "If we can stall them long enough, we have a chance of getting our people out."

"Sounds good," Pete said. "I can meet you at eight tonight, then have my other people there in the morning."

Judd gave Pete directions and thanked him.

"Hey, you saved my life," Pete said. "Plus, I've been wanting to see you. I have a surprise."

———————————

Every day Conrad felt more confident about his standing with Commander Blancka, Melinda, and Felicia. The girls no longer whispered when he was around. Together, Conrad and the girls followed leads and looked for Lionel and the others.

Commander Blancka was astounded that Darrion could last so long without food or water. Conrad knew he was taking a great risk slipping Darrion her provisions. He had now come up with a different plan. During one of their meetings he spied a letter in Commander Blancka's trash sent by an upper-level GC officer. He stuffed it in his pocket while no one was looking, then photocopied the insignia onto another sheet. He wrote a brief note that said, *A starving girl in a GC prison would not reflect well on the potentate or his friends.*

Conrad found a plain brown envelope and scribbled

T. B., the commander's initials, on the outside. When Melinda and Felicia were on an assignment, Conrad rushed to the commander's tent.

"I was told to give this to you, sir," Conrad said.

Conrad turned to leave as the commander opened the envelope.

"Hold on," the commander said. "Who gave you this?"

"I'm not sure, sir," Conrad said. "I've never seen him before. He headed back toward the airfield."

"Did you read this?"

"Should I have, sir?" Conrad said.

The commander scratched his chin. "No, I just wish I knew who was behind it."

The next day Darrion received three meals.

Conrad had very little contact with Darrion after that. Only a wink or a nod in the interview room when no one was looking. Conrad listened closely and tried to pick up information.

A chill ran through Conrad as he heard the commander talk about Mr. Stein. "After tomorrow there'll be one less fanatic in the world," the commander said.

Judd talked over the plan with the others, and they agreed it was their best shot to save Mr. Stein's life. Judd dialed the number. Commander Blancka's aide answered gruffly.

"This is Judd Thompson. I want to speak with the commander."

Conrad watched as the aide rushed in and handed the commander the phone. "It's Thompson," the aide said.

"Are Washington and Byrne with you?" the commander said.

Conrad's plan to save Mr. Stein was to try and whisk the man from the back of the jail. But Conrad knew that would endanger his rescue of Darrion, who was now being held in a different area.

"What do you propose?" the commander said.

"First of all, if you harm Mr. Stein in any way, or if the girl is harmed, the deal's off."

"You're making a deal with *me?*" the commander said. "You're not in that kind of position."

"I'm one of three people you want in custody," Judd said. "From the way you guarded that house, you want us bad."

"And I'm still going to get you."

"I'm offering an even trade," Judd said. "I'll come in if you let them go."

The commander laughed. "No deal. I want Washington and that Byrne girl too."

"Three for two?" Judd said. "Doesn't sound fair to me."

The commander lowered his voice. "Thompson, I can make it easy for you. Are the other two right there?"

"I can talk."

"We have to make you pay for what you did to GC property," the commander said. "Honestly, you'll be in and out in a couple months max. I'll put in a good word for you."

"I thought you were the one making the decisions," Judd said. "If I need to talk with someone else—"

"You're right," the commander interrupted. "I do make the decisions, but those are always reviewed. Now, I'm willing to work with you, and I assume that by your call you're willing to work with me."

"What about Vicki and Lionel?"

"Now's not the time to concern yourself with them. Byrne has a murder rap and an escape on her head. Washington . . . we have to make an example of him. But I'll do what I can. You just come in—"

"You have to assure me that Mr. Stein and Darrion won't be hurt," Judd said.

"We can hold off on our plans for him if you come in today," the commander said.

"Tomorrow," Judd said. "Five o'clock at New Hope Village Church."

Judd hung up.

Conrad studied the commander's face as he told them what Judd had said.

"Couldn't we trace the call?" Melinda said.

"Not with a GC phone," the commander said. "Unfortunately, they have one."

"What are you going to do?" Felicia said.

"We're going to give them the girl and Stein," the commander said. Conrad began to protest. The commander held up a hand. "They're going to walk to a trap, and you three are going to be there to watch it."

293

Judd volunteered to meet Pete at the bridge. The others had questions about how they were going to overpower the commander and get away.

"You know they'll be waiting for us," Mark said.

"That's where Conrad comes in," Judd said. "He'll be working from the inside."

Vicki shook her head. "If Mr. Stein is right and he's one of the 144,000 witnesses, he's going to come through this. But we don't have that kind of guarantee."

"You're not actually planning on having us all there, are you?" Shelly said.

"That's the plan right now," Judd said. "We'll talk with Pete—"

"I don't need to talk with anybody," Shelly said. "You've kept me cooped up here for weeks and for what? You want me to surrender to this commander guy? No way."

Judd held up a hand. "We want to get Darrion and Mr. Stein out of the GC hands, right? If somebody has a better plan than this, I'm open to it. Let me go get Pete, and we'll see how he can help us."

Judd plastered mud on his face and tunneled through the wall of mud and rocks in the drainpipe. He listened carefully when he came to the mouth of the pipe and didn't hear anything.

The sky was cloudy and made traveling difficult. He didn't want to use Lionel's flashlight until he had to. It had been weeks since Judd was outside. The smell of the earth and the fresh air made Judd feel alive.

He climbed over fallen trees and up steep hillsides along the riverbank. Judd saw the lights of the bridge in the distance. He moved cautiously toward it.

The bridge was complete, though it looked nothing like it once did. Pieces of plywood covered the holes. At the other side sat two GC guards.

Judd crawled beneath the bridge and waited. With his back against a pylon, he nearly fell asleep. In the distance he heard a rumbling and saw two headlights approach.

The guards looked over some papers and waved the two ahead. When the cycles neared the end, Judd signaled the lead driver with Lionel's flashlight.

Pete parked his cycle and ran down the embankment toward Judd. The two embraced. Judd had to catch his breath after Pete's hug. He was as big and burly as ever.

"Good to see you," Pete whispered. "Been praying for you."

"We've got a big job ahead of us tomorrow," Judd said. "I'm not sure we're up to it."

"God is," Pete said. "I've seen him do some amazing things the past few weeks."

The other rider parked his motorcycle and walked with a limp toward Judd and Pete. He was tall and thin.

"I almost forgot," Pete said. "You're gonna love this."

Judd stared at the man. Bruises and scratches covered his face.

"Don't you recognize him?" Pete said.

Judd fell back against the bridge and gasped. "It can't be," he said.

30

JUDD blinked. "Is it really you?" he said.

Taylor Graham dropped his helmet and goggles and put out his hand. Judd noticed a huge bruise on the side of his head.

"Didn't think you'd ever see me again, huh?" Taylor said.

"I saw you go over the cliff," Judd said. "I looked for your body."

"The log hit me in the head," Taylor said. "I stayed conscious until I went over. When I woke up, I was on a ledge next to the water. Bodies were floating everywhere."

"I hate to break up this reunion," Pete said, "but those guards are gonna get suspicious."

Judd helped Pete and Taylor hide their motorcycles under the bridge. The three ran toward the meadow. Taylor asked about the Stahley hangar, and Judd briefly told him their story.

"How's Ryan?" Taylor said.

Judd took a deep breath and told him about Ryan's death.

Taylor shook his head. "He was a good kid," he said.

The three slipped through the top of the cave. Judd introduced Pete and Taylor to the others.

"Finish your story," Judd said. "How'd you get out of that lake and hook up with Pete?"

"Hank and Judy," Taylor said. "I couldn't climb out myself, so I just waited to die. I don't know how long it was, but this farmer and his wife spotted me and got a rope long enough to reach."

"The same couple who helped me," Judd said.

"After I told them about the quake and the van, they said you had been there and left. I wasn't in any shape to travel, so they let me have their son's room."

Judd explained that the couple were also tribulation saints and had a son who had died in the earthquake.

"A couple of days later GC guards came by," Taylor continued. "A few people from the reeducation camp had escaped. Hank and Judy covered for me. They told me their story. Tried to get me to believe like them."

Judd looked closely at Taylor's forehead. There was no mark. "They're really good people," Judd said.

"They *were* good people," Pete said. "I went to see 'em a few days after I met this guy. The GC had come back and found out they'd been hiding people."

"What happened to them?" Vicki said.

"They were executed on the spot," Pete said.

Vicki gasped.

"This guy almost got himself killed too," Taylor said, pointing to Pete.

Pete shook his head. "Wasn't like that," he said. "I was just giving some friends the gospel."

"Your former biker group?" Judd said.

"We had a score to settle at that gas station," Pete said. "I found the owner and told him about Jesus. Said he wasn't into religion, but he was impressed with the way I'd helped a stranger. So he prayed with me like I did with you.

"Next thing I know, the gang is back. That's when Taylor comes walking into the middle of our fight. Only it turns out not to be a fight."

Taylor laughed. "This big monster was preaching to the rest of them. Couldn't believe it."

"It was the second time I'd told them," Pete said. "Not everybody responded the way I wanted, but most of them believed. They're coming to help tomorrow."

Lionel listened to the stories and held back as long as he could. He could see the resemblance of Conrad in Taylor's face.

When there was a lull, Lionel said, "I know your brother. He's been worried about you."

"Conrad?" Taylor said. "How do you know him?"

Lionel explained how the two had met. "Conrad's working on the inside trying to get our friends out," he said.

"Sounds like something Conny would do."

"He's changed since you last saw him," Lionel said. "He believes in God. He has the mark."

Taylor shook his head. "Not that again."

"God's after you, man," Pete said. "Your brother's no dummy. Why can't you see—"

"I don't argue that you people have something," Taylor interrupted. "I just don't think it's for me. At least not yet."

"None of us knows how long we have left," Pete said.

"Before I turn to religion, I've got a few scores to settle," Taylor said. "And the first thing I want to do is get Conrad away from the GC."

Judd told Pete and Taylor what they would do the next day.

"Doesn't sound like much of a plan," Taylor said.

"Exactly," Mark said. "We need guns, grenades, and a few snipers in position."

Judd looked at Mark. "I thought you learned your lesson with the militia," he said.

"We're not going to kill anybody. We just want to get our own people out."

Pete yawned. "We're all tired," he said. "Let's get some sleep and talk in the morning."

Judd made sure everyone had a place to sleep. As he lay down he noticed Taylor and Mark whispering.

Conrad couldn't sleep. He kept going over the plan in his head. There were things Judd didn't know, things Conrad didn't have time to explain.

Melinda and Felicia were almost bursting with glee

about the prospect of getting Lionel, Vicki, and Judd. They had talked about it on the way to their tent that night.

"The commander told me they're all gonna get it tomorrow," Felicia had said. "There's no way they're going to let that Stahley girl go. And Stein is toast."

Conrad had also overheard the commander talking with another officer about the operation. The GC would have men in position overnight with the latest high-powered rifles. The commander didn't want any surprises.

Conrad needed to talk with Darrion and Mr. Stein about the plan, but he couldn't get to them. He would have to wait and hope they followed his lead the next day.

Conrad sat up and checked his gun again. He could think of only one way to get Darrion and Mr. Stein out. And he knew his plan could get him killed.

Judd awoke from a deep sleep. Pete was shaking his shoulders.

"Do you know where Taylor is?" Pete said.

Judd saw the empty spot on the ground. "Could he have gone for some firewood?"

"Not likely," Pete said. "He was pretty fired up last night once he found out where his little brother was."

Judd woke Mark up. "What were you guys talking about last night?" Judd said.

Mark looked sheepish. "How wimpy your plan is," he said. "Taylor said there's no chance of any of us getting out of there the way things stand."

"Do you know where he went?" Judd said.

Mark shook his head. "He said he might leave early. I asked to go with him. He said he'd think about it."

Judd checked both entrances but found no sign of Taylor. He pulled out the computer and figured there was only enough battery power for one more session.

Conrad's last message gave Judd the location of the GC snipers. *I'll be right next to the commander, he wrote. Be warned. They're not taking prisoners.*

"We're walking into a trap," Mark said.

"We have to chance it," Judd said.

Vicki spoke up. "Maybe God wants us to stop running. Maybe he wants us in one of those reeducation camps."

"Don't you understand?" Mark said. "Conrad said they're not taking prisoners. They're going to make an example of you." He turned to Judd. "If I can get a rifle, I could pick off—"

"No!" Judd said.

Mark walked away. Judd looked at Shelly and Vicki. "You guys don't have to go," he said. "I could have Pete take you somewhere."

"I don't know what'll happen," Vicki said, "but I'm not leaving Darrion and Mr. Stein alone. I'm in."

Shelly hesitated. "I can't take it anymore," she said. "I'll take a ride."

Before they left the cave, Judd pulled a piece of paper from Ryan's packet he had found. "I found this last night," he said. "It's in Ryan's handwriting."

Judd spread the verse out on a rock. It said: *Zechariah*

4:6, *"It is not by force nor by strength, but by my Spirit, says the Lord Almighty."*

Mark said, "I want to do things in God's strength too, but this is like putting David in front of Goliath without a slingshot."

"You don't have to go," Judd said.

"You know I don't mean that," Mark said.

Pete stood, and the kids grew silent. "I haven't been at this long, but I know if somebody's in trouble and I can do something, I'm going. I think we should pray."

Vicki's hand was dwarfed by Pete's. One by one the others joined hands.

"God, you showed me the truth about you, and I thank you," Pete prayed. "I thank you for these brave kids who want to help their friends. Show us what to do and when to do it. Amen."

Conrad stayed close to Commander Blancka throughout the morning. Melinda and Felicia went to the church to view the progress. Reports from the site didn't sound good for the kids.

"The snipers have been in place since early this morning," Melinda radioed back. "They're hidden so well I had to have them pointed out."

A few minutes later Felicia made contact with the commander. "We've found that weird kid, Charlie," she said. "He was staying down here with a dog. What do you want us to do?"

"Get him to one of the shelters," the commander said, "and keep everyone else away from the area."

The commander rubbed his hands together and talked to his aide. "We'll let them come to us," he said. "I want no choppers, no observation of any kind. We want them to think everything's just like I said."

———————

Vicki squinted at the sky as she climbed out of the metal pipe. Her skin had grown pale inside the cave, and it felt good to be out. The sun was blocked by dark clouds, but the natural light felt good. The kids followed Pete to the bridge and found only one motorcycle.

"Where do you think Taylor went?" Judd said.

Pete shook his head. "Can't worry about it now," he said. "Duck under here."

The kids watched the patrols on the other side. "How are we gonna get across?" Vicki said.

"Watch," Pete said.

Vicki saw a cloud of dust about a mile away. When the cloud moved closer, the roar of motorcycles echoed across the water.

"We go now," Pete said, starting his motorcycle and heading for the other side.

"Stay close to me," Judd said as he trotted across the bridge.

The patrols stopped the gang. The motorcycles revved their engines and drowned out the noise made by Pete. As he rode past, he snatched the gun out of one guard's hands and knocked the other to the ground. One bearded man picked up the gun and motioned for both guards to get on the ground.

"What are they doing?" Vicki said.

"They won't hurt them," Judd said. "They'll lock them in the guard building and take their radios until this is over."

Vicki and the others walked past the guards. Vicki counted fifteen motorcycles, each with a single rider. Most were men, but there were also three women. They were dressed in leather and wore helmets or bandannas.

"I was hoping Red would be here," Judd said.

Pete shook his head. "Still workin' on Red," he said.

Shelly climbed on a motorcycle.

"Take her to the place," Pete said.

The female rider nodded. As the two sped off, a woman stretched a gloved hand out to Vicki. "Sally," she said.

"Pleased to meet you," Vicki said.

The group roared off. Vicki felt queasy.

Conrad looked at his watch. It was a few minutes before 5:00 P.M. His hands were sweating. Thick blue-and-black clouds rolled into the area.

The commander sat on his jeep, looking through binoculars. A cloud of dust appeared on the horizon. Conrad noticed a faint rumbling.

"What in the world?" the commander said. He looked to his aide. "Find out what that is."

"Sir," the aide said, "you said no one was to—"

"Just get somebody up there!"

"Yes, sir," the aide said.

Conrad unsnapped his holster and waited. A lone figure appeared on a small hill above the church. Conrad looked at the snipers hidden behind trees and in the church rubble. They were poised to fire.

Two other figures appeared on the hill.

"There they are," Commander Blancka said. He clicked his radio. "They look unarmed, but be careful. No one fires unless I give the order. We've got them now."

31

CONRAD watched the scene closely, wondering when to make his move. The commander lowered his binoculars and said, "Bring those two up here."

Two guards kept watch over Darrion and Mr. Stein. Conrad hurried to them and gruffly led them away by handcuffs. When they had gone a few steps, Conrad slipped a key to Mr. Stein. "Unlock them, but keep them on," Conrad whispered.

"Are we going now?" Darrion whispered.

"Not yet," Conrad said. "If you try to run, they'll be all over you."

"I don't believe they'll let us out of here alive," Mr. Stein said.

"Don't worry," Conrad said. "I still have to get you to the Meeting of the Witnesses in a couple of days."

Mr. Stein sighed. Darrion shook with fear.

"We're gonna make it, I promise," Conrad said.

The three were nearly back to the commander's position when Conrad whispered, "When I make my move, you two stay as close to me as you possibly can. Right next to me, OK?"

Darrion and Mr. Stein nodded.

Judd pointed toward the jeep. "That has to be the commander," he said.

"Where're Darrion and Mr. Stein?" Vicki said.

"There," Lionel said, as Conrad led the two into view.

The kids stood on a knoll that overlooked the church property. A black cloud hovered over them.

"If I'm right," Lionel said, "they'll have snipers around the church and—look there, behind the tree."

"Let's just hope Conrad can come through for us," Judd said.

A squeal from a loudspeaker split the air. The commander blew into the microphone and said, "Put your hands in the air and come down the hill! Nothing will happen to you."

Conrad watched Judd turn to confer with Lionel and Vicki. *Don't do it*, Conrad thought.

"Send Darrion and Mr. Stein halfway, then we'll come down," Judd said.

The commander cursed, then clicked the microphone and spoke calmly. "Now, Judd, I gave you my word nothing would happen. We're here waiting, like we said. We didn't try to find you or follow you."

"What are the snipers doing at the church and along the tree line?" Judd yelled.

The commander radioed the snipers and told them to get ready. "Fire on my command," he said.

Conrad reached for his gun. Suddenly, the sound of engines roared in the distance. Motorcycle riders encircled the three on the hill.

"I count ten cycles," someone said on the radio.

"They're not armed, sir," another said.

Conrad saw a huge man get off his cycle and say something to Judd. The engines revved, then shut off.

Judd yelled, "You said no one would try to stop us! What are your troops doing moving around behind us?"

Commander Blancka fumed. He meant to key his microphone but spoke over the loudspeaker instead. "I told you people to stay out of sight—" When he heard his voice echo, he clicked on the microphone. "Pull back! Pull back!"

"Commander, we have clear shots on all of them," a sniper said.

Conrad studied the commander's face. If the snipers started shooting it would be all over in seconds.

———————————

Lionel heard movement behind them. Mark crawled up the hill. "Cycles are ready," Mark said. "Enough for us and the three of them."

"Start them now," Judd said.

A wind kicked up and blew dirt and sand in their faces.

"Assuming we get all three," Vicki said, "where are we going?"

"Leave that to me," Pete said. "I got it covered."

Conrad reached for his gun again. The commander bit his lip. "I wanted to bring them in without this," the commander said.

"Targets are clear, sir," a sniper radioed.

"This is probably as good a time as any," the commander said. He keyed his microphone.

"No!" Conrad yelled, pulling his gun and holding it against the commander. The man was so stunned he kept the microphone on and shouted, "Graham, what is this?"

Darrion and Mr. Stein closed in on them.

"I've got a gun on the commander," Conrad said. The commander looked down and let go of the microphone. Mr. Stein slipped his handcuffs on the man.

"Hold your fire," Conrad heard a sniper say. "One of the Morale Monitors has a gun on the commander."

Vicki shielded her eyes from the wind. "What's he doing?" she said.

"It's part of the plan," Judd said. "He doesn't want to hurt him—his gun's not even loaded—but the GC don't know that."

"Bring 'em out, Conrad," Lionel coaxed.

"Everybody down," Judd said.

310

From the ground, Vicki saw a comical sight. Mr. Stein and Darrion held hands around Conrad and the commander. The group turned in circles as they moved toward the hill.

"Why's he doing that?" Vicki said.

"The snipers," Lionel said. "They won't want to hurt the commander, and it's harder to hit a moving target."

Conrad ripped the radio from the commander's shoulder. It was just after 5:00 P.M. but it looked like night.

"You'll pay for this, Graham," the commander said.

"We don't want to hurt you," Conrad said. "Keep moving."

Conrad heard someone running. Darrion screamed. Melinda ran at them with her gun outstretched. When she saw Conrad she yelled, "You traitor!"

A deafening roar split the sky as a helicopter rose up behind Melinda. The pilot trained his spotlight on her. The wind blew the chopper. The pilot couldn't keep it steady. Melinda fell to the ground in terror.

"We got you now!" the commander shouted. "You might get to your group, but you'll never escape the Global Community!"

The chopper, only a few feet off the ground, turned and faced the rubble of New Hope Village Church. "Stand clear of the building," the pilot said on a loudspeaker. A missile shot from the side of the helicopter. Snipers scattered from the building as the bomb exploded, sending a plume of smoke and debris into the air.

"What in the world—?" the commander said.

The pilot turned the chopper and faced the small group. The blades beat the air above their heads. Conrad peered into the cockpit and saw the pilot give a thumbs-up and smile.

"Taylor?" Conrad said. "It's my brother!"

Taylor motioned for them to get in. With the commander still in the middle of the group, Darrion, Mr. Stein, and Conrad stepped onto the struts.

Conrad was inches from the commander's face. "You'll never get away," the commander said.

Conrad opened his gun to show it had no bullets. "We might not, but you can't say we didn't give it a good try," he said. He handed the gun to the man as the helicopter lifted off.

"Fire, fire!" the commander shouted as the door closed.

Bullets pinged off the bulletproof glass.

Judd and the others rolled away from the hilltop as bullets aimed at the helicopter whizzed past them.

"What's happening?" Vicki said.

"New plan," Judd said. "Just get ready!"

The helicopter landed just over the hill. Darrion, Mr. Stein, and Conrad scampered out.

"I'll hold them off," Taylor yelled. "Get out of here!"

Taylor lifted straight up. The wind swirled and lightning flashed above the kids.

"Here they come!" Vicki yelled.

Judd peeked over the hill and saw a wave of GC soldiers. Commander Blancka ran with handcuffs still on.

Another helicopter appeared from behind the GC troops. Taylor shot a missile into the ground before the oncoming soldiers, and they fell back. The other helicopter bore down on Taylor with its guns blazing.

Lionel tugged on Judd's arm. The two ran down the hill as an explosion rocked the earth. One of the helicopters had crashed. Judd hopped on the back of Pete's motorcycle, and they sped away.

Judd turned and saw a group of snipers topping the hill. They knelt and aimed their rifles at the kids.

Judd gulped. *And we were almost out of here*, he thought.

But the snipers didn't fire. Instead, they ducked, put hands in the air, and fell to the ground. Judd felt something on his head, like someone was throwing gravel. Pete and the others stopped and tried to cover themselves with their motorcycles. Judd felt sharp stings on his arms, his neck, his back.

"It's hail!" Pete said.

Then the sky opened up. The hailstones grew bigger and pelted the motorcycles. They were almost the size of golf balls, falling around them and piling up like snow. Judd watched from ground level, protected by the motorcycle. The hail clanged off the gas tank and cracked the speedometer.

An orange glow encircled them. Judd thought it was lightning at first, flashing across the sky, but it wasn't. The hailstones, at least half of them, were in flames!

"What's happening?" Pete yelled.

"One of God's judgments!" Judd screamed. "I read something by Dr. Ben-Judah about an angel throwing hail and fire to the earth."

Judd saw Vicki a few yards away, huddled under a motorcycle. Mr. Stein had pulled his shirt over his head for protection. When the flaming hail hit the ice, it sizzled, and smoke curled from the ground.

Some of the fiery hail hit trees. They burst into flames, their branches sending fire and smoke into the air. Grass caught on fire and scorched the hillside. Judd was mixed with fear and wonder. God had promised this thousands of years ago. Now it was coming true before his eyes.

Judd saw more ice fall on the blackened ground. It piled up white, then in sections began to turn red. The drops looked like paint balls exploding on the ground and spreading in all directions.

"Blood!" Judd said.

It poured from the sky. The melted hail mixed with the blood, sending rivers of red around them. Judd put a hand into the stream of red. It was thick, oozing through his fingers. He held it to his face. It even smelled like blood.

Lightning flashed and thunder shook the ground. The hail started again, this time bigger. Some were as big as softballs. The trees that had burst into flames now sizzled as the hail put out the fire.

Judd could only cover his head and pray. It was like being in a video game with thousands of fireworks falling around him. Only this wasn't a game.

The black cloud rolled on. As the last of the hail fell, the sun peeked out. Judd saw the results of the angel's judgment. The trees had turned black as ash. Bushes and shrubs were burned to a crisp. The blood and water seeped into the ground. Charred grass broke through the white and red.

Pete pushed the bike upright. Red blotches marked his face where he had driven into the first volley of hail. Judd jumped on the back of the cycle, and Pete kicked the machine to life.

They slid through the slush and blood. Mr. Stein's motorcycle wiped out. The man came up with blood dripping from his shirt.

Judd had heard the screams of the Global Community soldiers who lay unprotected as the hailstorm began. He didn't want to think about what the softball-sized hail could do to a person without any protection. He wondered if Taylor Graham had been in the helicopter that crashed.

Judd counted heads as they made their way over the wet earth. The Young Trib Force was alive, at least for the moment.

Judd glanced back to see if Commander Blancka and the others would give chase. The motorcycles topped a hill and looked down on the scene. Several soldiers lay lifeless in the red earth. The charred remains of a GC copter lay smoldering nearby.

Pete gunned the engine and raced away. Moments later Judd heard the roar of rotor blades. He held on to the motorcycle and prayed.

315

32

JUDD held on as Pete drove recklessly through the blood and slush. A few minutes after the sun came out, most of the hail and blood had dissolved into the ground. A helicopter passed nearby. Judd guessed the pilot had lost the bikers in the woods. He glanced at Conrad. The boy looked grim.

Pete found a main road and picked up speed. They passed abandoned cars with broken windshields. A crater had opened in the middle of the road. The remains of an exploded fuel truck lay in the bottom of the hole.

They drove through the crater and on the other side saw a helicopter coming right for them. Pete stopped. The aircraft was pocked with dents from the hail.

To Judd's surprise, the helicopter landed and Taylor Graham stepped out. He gave a thumbs-up to the group. "Almost out of fuel," he said. "Think you could give me a ride?"

Pete motioned for one of the single riders to come forward. As he did, Taylor fired up the chopper and perched it on the side of an embankment by the road. Taylor left the rotors going and stepped out. The rotors slowed, and then the black craft tipped forward and fell into the ravine. A fiery explosion shook the earth.

"Better leave before they see that smoke," Taylor said.

————————————————————

Vicki was glad Conrad's brother was safe. She didn't like it that he had tried to kill the commander and the others, but he had gotten Darrion, Mr. Stein, and Conrad out alive.

Vicki held tight to the motorcycle driver. She kept looking over her shoulder, thinking the GC would be right behind them.

They drove without resting, the wind in their faces. When night fell, the motorcycles looked eerie with their headlights piercing the darkness. Vicki was exhausted when they finally reached a gas station. The manager came outside with a gun, then grinned at Pete.

"Don't park out here, bring them on in," the man said.

The kids and Mr. Stein went inside while the others pulled their motorcycles into the garage. Shelly had prepared hot chocolate and sandwiches. The kids ate hungrily.

"Boyd Walker," the man said, extending a hand to each of the kids. He pointed at Judd. "This young fellow and Pete helped me out in more ways than one."

Along with grease stains, Vicki saw that the man had the mark of a true believer on his forehead.

Boyd told the story again of how Pete had saved his station from the motorcycle gang. Then Pete had returned and told him the truth about Christ's return. "I been readin' that rabbi on the Internet," Boyd said. "Got a computer in the back."

Vicki noticed that Conrad and Taylor Graham were in a heated discussion outside.

"That's not how we do things," Conrad said. "How many did you kill to get that bird from the GC?"

"I saved your tail back there," Taylor said. "A simple thank-you would be nice. Besides, I gave those guys warning before I shot."

Conrad shook his head. "I'm glad you're alive. But you have to stop trying to get revenge against the GC and start listening to what I'm saying."

"Like I told the others, I don't have time for religion right now."

Boyd had given Mr. Stein a T-shirt to replace the blood-stained one. Mr. Stein embraced Vicki. "I didn't think I would ever see you again," he said. "I still have so many questions, but Rabbi Ben-Judah is answering them now."

"Chaya would be so happy," Vicki said.

Mr. Stein blinked tears away. "I can only tell you how sorry I am," he said. "God has forgiven me for my hard heart. I know one day I will see Chaya and Judith again."

"Conrad said you're pretty set on going to Israel," Vicki said.

"The meeting is this weekend," Mr. Stein said. "I'm

afraid I'll have to watch it on the Net like the rest of the world."

Vicki thought about Phoenix. It would have been impossible to bring him with them, even if she had found him. But she still felt guilty not keeping her promise to Ryan.

———————————

Lionel found Boyd's tiny black-and-white television and tuned in a station. Darrion sat beside him with a cold drink. "I can't wait to see what kind of spin Carpathia's newsmen put on what's happened!" she said.

The news anchor looked flustered, as if he had witnessed the hail and didn't believe what he was reading. The anchor gave staggering statistics about the amount of hail the area received in the few minutes the storm raged. "But Illinois was not the only area hit. In fact, this seems to have happened worldwide at the exact same time."

"So how do you explain it?" Lionel said to the TV.

The anchor introduced an expert who said the event was a "one-time occurrence" and was easily explained as an "atmospheric disturbance."

Darrion shook her head. "Yeah, and it definitely did not have anything to do with God or with his judgment of the earth."

"As many of you saw earlier, Potentate Nicolae Carpathia responded to this world crisis with decisive action," the news anchor said. "He held a news conference less than an hour ago in which he outlined the Global Community response."

Nicolae was dressed casually, as if he had strolled in from a dinner party to answer questions. But Lionel could tell the man was concerned. If he had been reading Dr. Ben-Judah's Web site as Pavel said he had, he knew this was no fluke. This was God speaking in a forceful way.

"Because of the momentary disruption in communications, I have called a halt to all travel. This means the meeting scheduled in Israel that I had approved will have to be rescheduled."

"How convenient," Darrion said.

"Citizens of the Global Community should not be alarmed," Carpathia continued. "We have everything under control, and the effects of this storm should not hinder us as we move forward in our quest for a better world."

"So if it's no problem," Lionel said, "why does he have to postpone the Meeting of the Witnesses?"

The news shifted to local effects of the storm. Video showed traffic snarls and streets filled with hail. The anchor referred to the "sticky red substance" but never called it blood. He said a few fires were also reported.

"Look!" Darrion shouted. Bikers gathered from around the station.

A shot of a downed GC helicopter flashed on the screen. Several GC soldiers lay facedown in a field near New Hope Village Church.

"At the time of the storm," the anchor continued, "the Global Community was conducting a training exercise in Mount Prospect."

"Training exercise!" Lionel yelled.

"Seven soldiers were killed by the hailstorm, and a dozen others were treated for fractures and burns at a local shelter. The leader of the exercise, Commander Terrel Blancka, has reportedly been reprimanded and will be given another assignment."

"You know the real reason they're upset with him," Darrion said.

"Yeah," Lionel said. "He let us get away."

Judd found the laptop in the saddlebag of Pete's motorcycle. It had taken a beating from the hail but still worked. He hooked it up beside Boyd's ancient machine and logged on to the Net.

"That thing's got some speed," Boyd said, admiring the laptop.

The list of forwarded E-mails from Tsion was growing. Now that they were away from the GC, Judd thought he might have a chance to answer some of them.

Judd let out a whoop and yelled for Mark.

"What's up?" Mark said.

"It's from John," Judd said.

John's message was short. It read, *If you get this E-mail, please respond. If you've seen any of my friends or family, please report.*

Judd quickly wrote and gave Boyd's phone number. He sent a second E-mail detailing their flight from the Global Community. He sent the second message and logged off. The phone rang a few seconds later.

"Yeah, he's right here," Boyd said, handing the phone to Judd.

It was John. "I've been trying to call since I saw your first E-mail," he said. "Did everybody make it OK?"

"Ryan's gone," Judd said.

John didn't speak.

"And you knew Chaya Stein. She was killed in the quake too."

"What about Mark?" John said.

Judd handed the phone to Mark. The two talked a few minutes and then Judd got back on the line. "Give us the update," he said.

"You won't believe it," John said. "The quake hit in the middle of classes at college. I saw the lights shake and remembered what Tsion said. I made it out the window before the whole building came down.

"Then everything went crazy. I helped pull bodies out of buildings and get help to the injured. The GC showed up a couple days later looking for anyone who could walk. There's a naval base on the coast, and some of their guys didn't make it."

"You volunteered?" Judd said.

"You don't volunteer with the GC," John said. "I said I was a first-year engineering student, and they told me to get in the truck. I didn't have a choice."

"Where are you now?" Judd said.

"I'm finishing up training," John said. "They put me in communications. We're pulling out tomorrow for the Atlantic."

"You're right," Judd said. "I don't believe it."

"The good news is I have access to everything," John said. "We get orders and reports from New Babylon just about every day. Plus, I saw your picture, which was sent from Chicago yesterday."

"A picture?" Judd said.

"More like a wanted poster," John said. "They had mug shots of you, Vicki, and Lionel."

"Have you heard the reports about what happened?" Judd said.

"You mean the training exercise?" John laughed. "The report I get is that the head guy, Blancka, has been demoted from his Morale Monitor position. They don't even know whether they'll continue the program or not."

When he was finished with John, Judd called a meeting of the Young Trib Force. Pete and a few of the other bikers sat in, along with Boyd.

"I have a message from Tsion I want to read," Judd said, "but first, I have to say something. We're wanted by the GC. They know about Darrion, Vicki, Lionel, Mr. Stein, and me. We have to make a choice. Do we stay together? And when the GC school starts, should we attend? Where do we go?"

Mark raised a hand.

"If it's OK," Judd said, "I'd like you all to sleep on it, make some notes, and be ready to talk tomorrow."

Judd opened Tsion's E-mail and read it.

> We serve a great God who delivers his children. I have been praying for you since I heard of your difficulty, and will continue to pray.

I am going to Israel as soon as possible. Eli and Moishe confirmed that the time is right. The other day Eli said, "Woe unto him who sits on the throne of this earth. Should he dare stand in the way of God's sealed and anointed witnesses, twelve thousand from each of the twelve tribes making a pilgrimage here for the purpose of preparation, he shall surely suffer for it."

Then Moishe said, "Yea, any attempt to impede the moving of God among the sealed will cause your plants to wither and die, rain to remain in the clouds, and your water—all of it—to turn to blood! The Lord of hosts hath sworn, saying, 'Surely, as I have thought, so it shall come to pass, and as I have purposed, so it shall stand!' "

This lets me know the time is close. The first of the seven angels have sounded their judgments with fiery hail and blood which burned a third of the trees and all green grass.

Next to come is the second angel, which brings with it a great mountain burning with fire. This will turn a third of the earth's water to blood, kill a third of the living creatures in the sea, and sink a third of the ships.

The third angel's trumpet sound will result in a great star falling from heaven, burning like a torch. It will bring disaster with it, and many will die.

I tell you this not to scare you, but to prepare you for what is ahead. Be bold. You may be asked to give your life. Ryan and Chaya already have.

Judd paused. Mr. Stein wept. Judd felt the emotion well up. He turned to the screen to keep from crying himself, and he read:

> Wherever you are, I encourage you to think of the great soul harvest before us. I wish I had believed before the Rapture, but I rejoice in the opportunity before us. Many will become believers in Jesus in the next few months.
>
> Be careful. The next judgments may come soon. May God help you make right decisions as you seek to lead others to the truth.

33

JOHN Preston sat at the communications center of the United North American States ship *Peacekeeper 1*, wondering if he would ever see his friends again. Less than two years earlier, he and his cousin Mark Eisman had met Judd Thompson Jr. on their first day back at Nicolae High. The kids had seen their share of trouble, and even death. Several times John had begun typing a message but erased it when someone came near. He had to wait for the right moment.

John had hoped the kids could be together at the Meeting of the Witnesses in Jerusalem. Now that seemed out of the question. John had set up a computer in his quarters to record each session and couldn't wait to hear Tsion Ben-Judah teach live.

An alarm sent people scurrying. Officers barked orders. John studied a blip on a radar screen and pointed it out to his friend, Carl.

Carl nodded. "Finally gonna see some action."

After the Wrath of the Lamb earthquake, John had been taken from college and put to work with the Global Community Navy. Carl had taken John under his wing. There didn't seem to be anything about computers or technical equipment Carl didn't understand.

Carl smiled. "Only ships allowed out here now are GC approved," he said.

"Who else would want to be?"

"Drug pushers, weapons dealers, you name it," Carl said. "We consider them modern-day pirates."

"Three miles and closing, sir," an officer shouted.

"Should we be worried, Carl?"

Carl smiled. "Not even God could sink *Peacekeeper 1*. Best communications, most precise weaponry, and amazing speed."

John stared through a scope at what looked like a cargo ship.

"No registry evident, sir," an officer reported.

Carl raised his eyebrows. "Guys on deck," he said.

John saw patrols with high-powered rifles walking back and forth.

"Attention," the captain said over the loudspeaker. "The ship we're intersecting is in violation of Global Community maritime law. We could destroy it from here, but we suspect illegal weapons and hostages."

Carl shook his head. "I don't like their chances."

"We're sending a team into the water before the ship spots us," the captain continued. "We'll give the hostages every chance."

John watched the undersea monitor. *Peacekeeper 1*'s small sub approached the cargo ship, and men in wet suits floated through the hatch. Another monitor displayed a few climbing the side of the ship.

The captain rushed to the communications center and pushed the talk button in front of John. "Stay down! Stay down! Unfriendlies coming your way."

But they had been spotted. The men in wet suits dropped back into the water as men onboard opened fire. John saw blood in the water. One diver made it back to the sub.

The captain ordered pursuit, and the sudden acceleration threw John back in his chair. The cargo ship turned to flee, but it was no match for *Peacekeeper 1*.

"They don't stand a chance," Carl said.

"What about the hostages?" John said.

Carl shook his head.

As they closed in, bullets pinged off the hull, and John saw the frightened faces of the enemy patrols.

"Warning," the captain said over the loudspeaker. "Release your hostages now or we sink your ship."

The patrols fled below deck. John thought they might release hostages, but two masked men returned with bazookas. John felt the explosion, and the captain rattled off a series of orders. The *Peacekeeper 1* turned its guns on the scared crew.

Carl shook his head. "Idiots," he said.

Peacekeeper 1's cannon opened a huge hole in the cargo ship. It tipped one way, then the other. As water filled the hole, the crew leaped overboard. John saw one of the divers from the *Peacekeeper 1* scramble onto the deck of the other ship and disappear into a smoke-filled stairwell.

"Pelton, no!" the captain shouted. "Get him out of there!"

Carl clicked a button and spoke to the diver, but there was no response.

John's heart raced as five civilians appeared through the smoke. As soon as they hit the sloping deck, they slipped and fell over the railing. Within seconds the submarine surfaced and picked two civilians from the water. John watched for any sign of the diver who had performed the rescue. Just as the stairwell sank below the waterline, the diver emerged. The submarine surfaced. John moved closer to the monitors.

Seconds seemed like an eternity. A whoop went up in the ship as the lone diver shot out of the water with the three remaining civilians clinging to him.

Since the judgment of fire, hail, and blood, the kids had hidden at the gas station. Judd was surprised by the anger of the Young Trib Force.

Shelly began, "We've been—"

"I don't want to hear her," Mark said. "She turned and ran."

"What are you talking about?" Shelly said.

"You took the easy way out and got a ride without facing Blancka," Mark said.

Vicki's face flushed. "You have no right to judge," she said. "You don't know what she's been through."

"We've all been through a lot," Mark said. "Let's not decide stuff on emotion."

Shelly's lip trembled. Judd cut in. "Everybody is equal," he said. "We'll listen to everybody."

Vicki crossed her arms. "He probably wants to go blow people up, like Taylor Graham."

"If it weren't for Taylor," Mark said, "we'd have never gotten out of there. Judd's plan was wimpy."

"Everybody be quiet!" Judd yelled. Judd saw Taylor storm out the front of the gas station.

Conrad put his face in his hands. "I didn't know it was gonna be like this."

Judd closed the office door. Boyd Walker, manager of the gas station, and Judd's friend Pete stood nearby.

Shelly stood up. "That's it. Either Mark goes or I do."

Mr. Stein stepped forward. "I am new to this," he said. "We have been through a lot. We could have died yesterday."

"Not her," Mark said.

"From what I understand," Mr. Stein said, "this young woman intervened on your behalf at the Stahley mansion."

"Yeah," Vicki said.

Mr. Stein put up a hand and stared at Mark. "Is it not true she put her life on the line and could have been arrested by the Global Community guards, not once, but twice?"

"I'm not saying she can't be part of the group," Mark stammered, "I just—"

"I have read only a little of the Scriptures, but aren't we supposed to love each other?" Mr. Stein sat. Everyone seemed a little calmer. Judd nodded at Lionel.

"Tsion's E-mail got to me," Lionel said. "With all the judgments coming, we don't know how much longer we have left. We have to be smart but bold."

"What does that mean?" Vicki said.

"People need to know the truth," Lionel said. "If we hide, we're wasting a chance to be part of the soul harvest."

Judd said, "The Global Community knows our faces. We're spending our energy running from them."

"Shelly, Mark, and John are the only ones they're not onto," Lionel said.

Darrion spoke up. "My family has a place in Wisconsin," she said. "If it survived the earthquake, we could go there."

"I'm tired of running," Vicki said.

The meeting ended. The kids argued every day. Mr. Stein pestered Judd for Tsion Ben-Judah's private E-mail address, but Judd was reluctant. Tsion was busy and Judd didn't want to bother him. But Judd had finally relented, and Tsion had written to Mr. Stein. The rabbi encouraged him to get to Israel, but recommended against a face-to-face meeting in the States.

Mr. Stein said he had hidden a stash of money before he was arrested by the Global Community. In the wee hours of the morning, Mr. Stein, Taylor Graham, and Judd's friend Pete prepared to retrieve the money. Judd awoke and heard the rumble of motorcycles.

Pete stuck his head in the door. "Looks like we've got company. Hide."

Judd recognized the voice of Red, the big, long-haired biker with an attitude. "Guess you're pretty proud of yourself for breaking up the gang," Red said.

"We didn't have to split," Pete said. "You decided to leave."

Red cursed. "The holy rollers in there?" he said.

"If you mean the rest of the gang, no," Pete said. "They moved on. You want to come inside?"

"Done talkin'," Red said.

Judd saw a light in the window of the gas station. He ducked but it was too late. A bearded man with two gold teeth looked at him. "Gotcha," Gold Tooth said. "Hey, Red," the man shouted as he ran to the front. "Think we got something back there!"

———————————

Before his shift began, John stood on deck and watched the sun rise over the ocean. He had grown up singing about God's love being as wide as the sea, but he had never seen anything so impressive.

Carl approached, clutching a piece of paper.

"I was thinking about those kidnappers," John said. "You think the sharks—"

"Look," Carl interrupted. He handed John a fax. It looked like a drawing of something in space.

John shook his head. "I don't get it."

"You will," Carl said. "It's a new meteor."

John rolled his eyes. "Big deal."

"It *is* a big deal," Carl said. "This thing's headed straight for Earth."

John remembered Tsion Ben-Judah's warning about an object falling from the sky. A judgment from God. He studied the picture closely.

"When's it supposed to hit?" John said.

34

JUDD hurried to the front of the gas station. The guy with the gold teeth ran to Red.

"I thought you were smarter than that," Judd heard Red say. "I know who's back there."

"God's trying to get your attention," Pete said.

Red pulled a crumpled piece of paper from his back pocket. "And the Global Community's gonna get yours," he said. "There's a GC post about a half hour from here."

Pete looked toward the station and frowned. Judd knew what was on the paper.

"Don't do this," Pete said.

"Watch me," Red said as he kicked his motorcycle to a start and sped off. The gold-toothed man followed.

Pete ran a hand through his hair and walked into the station. He handed Judd the paper. Mug shots of Vicki, Lionel, Conrad, Darrion, and Judd. Also a description of

Mr. Stein. "Reward for information leading to an arrest and conviction."

The others slowly filed into the room.

"Think he'll turn us in?" Vicki said.

Pete shook his head. "Can't take the chance," he said. He put on his helmet and started his motorcycle. "If I'm not back in an hour, get out of here."

"You can't go up against all of them," Lionel protested.

"I won't let Red do this to you," Pete said. He throttled and roared off.

Boyd Walker leaned quietly against an old soda machine. "I have an idea if you're interested," he said. "A fellow in Des Plaines owns a gas station a lot like this one. His son has a little business on the side—tattoos. He might help you."

"I don't understand," Judd said.

"Kid's a genius," the man said. "Phony IDs and disguises."

"New identities?" Lionel said.

"I can't see us going anywhere near there," Vicki said.

"Zeke and Zeke Jr.," the manager said, writing it down.

Shelly stepped forward. "We need to do something now." She found a pair of scissors and some hair coloring for sale on a dusty shelf. Vicki's hair went from strawberry red to jet black and shorter than ever. Judd was almost bald when Shelly was through with him. The kids stood in a line.

"Not bad," Mark said. "Now all you guys need are some fake IDs."

The phone rang. The manager handed it to Mark.

"John?" Mark said.

Judd and Vicki gathered around. Mark said a few words, then put the phone down.

"What did he say?" Judd said.

"Told me there wasn't time to talk," Mark said. "Didn't want them catching him making the call. He said to turn on the television and watch. Then he said it was going to be some ride."

Judd flicked on the television. News bulletins interrupted every station.

Newscasters reported that only a few hours ago astronomers had discovered a brand-new comet on a collision course with Earth. The Global Community Aeronautics and Space Administration (GCASA) had probes circling the object. The data they sent back was startling.

"Under normal conditions," a spokesman for GCASA said, "we would have seen this a few months or even a few years ago. But these aren't normal conditions. I can't explain why we just located it today."

"Doctor, this meteor is how far from us right now?" the male anchor said.

"*Meteor* is the wrong term," the scientist said. "You were correct when you called it a comet. The data shows the comet to have a consistency of sandstone. Very brittle. When it enters Earth's atmosphere, it should disintegrate."

"Should?"

"It's impossible that it will miss us, unless it can be destroyed before it enters the atmosphere."

"And when will that happen?" the anchor said.

The scientist squirmed. "I'd rather let our director address that when he gives an update."

Judd moved closer to the television as a picture from the probe flashed on the screen. "Look at the size of that thing."

"What else have you learned?" the anchor said.

"The comet is irregularly shaped, but it's immense. Global Community astronomers estimate it is no less than the mass of the entire Appalachian Mountain range."

"Wow!" Lionel said. "How could they not see that until this morning?"

The anchor furrowed his brow. "And what kind of damage could something that big actually do?"

"The potential is enormous," the scientist said. "On a scale of one to ten, ten being the worst, I'd say this is a . . . ten and a half."

"We're all gonna die!" Shelly said.

Judd turned.

"W-w-we studied this in school," she stammered.

Vicki hugged Shelly. "It's gonna be okay."

"That's not gonna happen," Judd said.

"Let's say it is as hard as granite," the anchor said. "What then?"

"Once the object comes into Earth's gravitational pull, it will accelerate to thirty-two feet per second squared. No matter what it is made of, it will burst into flames. Pieces will fall to Earth."

"Worst case, what could happen?"

The scientist stared at the camera. "Worst case? Earth would be split in two."

The news anchor sat speechless.

The scientist added, "Or our orbit could be altered. Either would be disastrous for the planet."

"We're gonna die," a biker said.

Someone handed the anchor a piece of paper from off camera. "This message from GCASA," he said, stunned. "The . . . uh . . . collision will occur at approximately 6 P.M. New Babylon time, which is midnight in Tokyo, 3 P.M. in London, and 10 A.M. New York time."

"Nine our time," Vicki said.

"It's seven now," Lionel said.

In his quarters, John pulled out his Bible and turned to Revelation. He remembered something Tsion Ben-Judah had said about a meteor.

John found the passage that talked about the hail they had just come through. The next verse said, "Then the second angel blew his trumpet, and a great mountain of fire was thrown into the sea. And one-third of the water in the sea became blood. And one-third of all things living in the sea died. And one-third of all the ships on the sea were destroyed."

The verses sent a chill through him. *The comet is coming from God. It will fall somewhere over the water. But where?*

John pulled up the rabbi's Web site and found a message concerning the disaster.

339

This is the second Trumpet Judgment foretold in Revelation 8:8-9. Will we look like experts when the results are in? Will it shock the powers-that-be to discover that, just as the Bible says, one-third of the fish will die and one-third of the ships at sea will sink, and tidal waves will wreak havoc on the entire world? Or will officials reinterpret the event to make it appear the Bible was wrong? Do not be fooled! Do not delay! Now is the accepted time. Now is the day of salvation. Come to Christ before it is too late. Things will only get worse. We were all left behind the first time. Do not be left wanting when you breathe your last.

John put his head in his hands. He thought of Carl. He hadn't talked with him about God. *Maybe it isn't too late.*

He quickly typed a message to the rest of the Young Trib Force and sent it. He ran to the command center and found Carl amid a whirl of activity.

"I have to talk to you," John said.

"Things are nuts right now," Carl said. "They're talking about shooting the thing down before it hits." Carl handed John a printout. "It's going to hit here in the Atlantic. They say it's the best possible scenario."

"Best for who?" John said. The Global Community predicted tidal waves would engulf coasts on both sides of the Atlantic for up to fifty miles inland. Coastal areas had already begun evacuating.

"If they don't shoot the thing down there's no way we'll survive," Carl said.

John looked at a monitor and saw a simulation of the impact. An incredible wall of water stretched to the sky. Carl was right. No way anyone could survive.

———————————————

Vicki was relieved when the news anchor reported the comet was heading for the Atlantic. She drew close to the screen. The earthquake had killed so many people, but it came without warning. This was worse.

"Those military personnel and passengers and crew members on other oceangoing vessels that can be reached in time are being airlifted to safety."

"John!" Vicki said. "He was headed to the Atlantic, wasn't he?"

Judd nodded and looked around the room for Mark.

"I'll get him," Vicki said.

Vicki found Mark outside, staring at the sky. She explained the situation, and Mark's shoulders slumped.

"We've been through so much," Mark said.

Vicki left Mark. She found Judd intently watching the coverage. An anchorman put a hand to his ear and nodded. "We're being told now that His Excellency, Potentate Nicolae Carpathia, is prepared to address this crisis. We go now to the Global Community Headquarters in New Babylon."

Nicolae spoke from his plush office. "My brothers and sisters in the Global Community, we have weathered many storms together, and it appears there is another on the horizon. Let me first answer a question that has come up, and that is, How could we not have known?

"I assure you, our personnel alerted us to this potential disaster as quickly as possible. We could not have known about this phenomenon any earlier.

"I am also confident, having taken precautions with my military advisors some time ago, that we have the firepower to destroy this object. However, we have been advised that an attempt to destroy the comet would be too great a risk to life on our planet. We cannot predict where the fragments might fall. The risk is simply unacceptable, especially considering that this falling mountain is on course to land in the ocean.

"We will keep you informed of any developments as we know them. Please cooperate with the officials in your area. We will get through this difficult time together, as we build a stronger world."

———————————————

The crew of the *Peacekeeper 1* assembled on deck. They stood at attention as the captain explained the situation. The men looked shell-shocked.

"I had hoped to have better news," the captain said. "Potentate Carpathia has decided not to try and shoot the comet down."

The crew groaned in unison.

The captain held up a hand. "We're heading away from the impact point as fast as we can, but if the scientists are correct, there's no way we'll outrun the thing.

"There is one chance," the captain continued. "We've recovered the submarine. If we get far enough away from impact and the sub goes down far enough, some may be able to survive."

"That thing can hold only a handful of people," John whispered to Carl.

"We'll draw names within the hour," the captain said.

35

JUDD watched for Pete while the kids searched for the latest about the comet. Finally, Pete rolled in. He did a double take at Judd and the others.

"What happened?" Judd said.

Pete shook his head. "Don't want to talk about it. Let's just say you're safe for the time being."

The group gathered around the television. Updated pictures from the probes showed the comet in more detail. It was light in color. The anchorman reported, "Ladies and gentlemen, I urge you to put this in perspective. This object is about to enter Earth's atmosphere. It should burst into flames any second."

Lionel called Judd to the laptop and showed him what Tsion Ben-Judah had written. Judd ran a hand over his head. "I sure hope John's not near that thing."

The coverage switched to a local reporter. The man's voice sounded urgent. "GCASA projects the collision at approximately 9:00 A.M. Chicago time. If the predictions are accurate, the collision will take place in the middle of the Atlantic Ocean. But keep in mind that if the comet splits, fragments could possibly fall in the Midwest."

"Splashdown is less than an hour away," Vicki said.

The reporter continued, "I'm told by one meteorologist that this kind of disruption could cause severe weather around the globe. We won't deal with tidal waves like the coastal areas, but we may see strong winds and possibly tornadoes."

The crew stood silently watching as the captain picked the remaining names to occupy the sub. The rescued hostages were given priority. That left only seven seats for the crew.

John looked at Carl. "I don't like these odds," Carl said.

The sixth name the captain called was John's. Carl patted him on the shoulder. John sighed heavily and nearly fell to his knees. But he couldn't shake the truth. He hadn't given the most important message to his friends.

"You're the lucky one," Carl said, shaking hands.

"I need to talk with you," John said. "Now."

When the last name was called, John took Carl to his room and opened his Bible. "I haven't talked to anybody on the ship about this. I was scared to."

John quickly explained the plan of salvation. He told Carl everyone has sinned. "Everyone is separated from God. Jesus died to bring us back to God. People who ask forgiveness in Jesus' name will spend eternity in heaven."

Carl shook his head. "Staring at death makes you think. I figure God will accept me for the good stuff I've done. If not, saying a prayer won't help."

"It's not like that," John said. "God can't accept anything that's less than perfect. That's why Jesus came. He lived a perfect life—"

"Preston!" the captain shouted. "If you want to get off this ship, you go now."

John looked at Carl. Carl shrugged. "Sorry, I can't buy it."

"Preston, now!" the captain said.

"Sir," John said, "I'd like to give my spot to Carl."

The captain furrowed his brow. "Don't be foolish, son. This is your chance to survive."

John opened his Bible. He scribbled something inside the cover. "Read this later. I want to do this. I have some friends who can help you. If you make it back, look them up and tell them what happened."

Carl staggered. "You can't do this, man. You hardly even know me."

"I know what I'm doing," John said. "Read this stuff. It'll change your life if you let it."

The captain scowled at John and took Carl away. John took a deep breath as Carl squeezed into the sub. The crew stood on deck and watched as the sub slipped beneath the surface and headed to the bottom of the ocean.

"I don't know why you did that," the captain said when he returned to John.

"I'd like to speak with the others," John said, "before splashdown."

347

The captain shook his head. "I'd like to let you, Preston," he said. "After what you did today, you deserve it. But it's against policy."

"Sir, with all due respect, we're gonna die in less than an hour. I have something to say that could change everything. For you and the others."

"Sorry, Preston," the captain said. He walked away.

Vicki felt nervous about the comet. Even though it was supposed to land in the ocean, part of her felt they were still in danger. The way Pete acted when he returned spooked her as well.

As the moments ticked down, the kids watched the updates. A disabled cruise ship was stranded in the Atlantic.

Shelly put a hand to her mouth. "Those poor people," she said.

"Other Global Community vessels are at sea," the reporter continued, "but rescue operations are impossible with the splashdown so close. Efforts to move boats to safety along the Atlantic shoreline have stopped."

There were reports of some who refused to evacuate their homes. "Stayin' right here," a grizzled old man said. "Lived through the disappearances and the earthquake. Don't see any reason why I can't live through a big wave."

Vicki looked at Judd. She had been so angry and hurt by him. But the possibility of losing their lives put things in perspective. Their fights seemed petty compared to the fact that a comet could split the earth in two and send them hurtling into space. She believed that wouldn't happen because of what the Bible said, but the prospect made her shudder.

Vicki thought about Phoenix and her promise to Ryan. She longed to find the dog, not only to keep her word, but also because the dog reminded her of Ryan. Phoenix had helped Ryan move through the pain of losing his parents. Vicki thought the dog could do the same for her.

After the launch of the sub, John and the rest of the crew were in a daze. They were trapped. Moving to any part of the ship was pointless. They were about to see a wave unlike any in the history of the world.

John knew his decision to let Carl have his spot would be considered heroic by some and foolish by others. He didn't feel like a hero. He was sorry that he hadn't told the others about Christ.

John looked at the empty command center and thought, *What have I got to lose?*

He hurried to the command center and punched the controls that sealed both entrances. He flipped the switch that let him speak to the entire ship and pecked on the microphone.

"Test . . . can you hear me?" John said.

The captain and a few officers came running. When they tried to open the door, John put up a hand. He prayed silently, his hands shaking. Then he keyed the microphone.

"My name is John Preston. The captain wouldn't let me talk to you, so I've had to sorta take over. I don't mean any harm by this, and I promise to open the doors in just a minute. First, I want you to hear me out."

The captain beat on the door. John couldn't hear the man's voice, but he could read his lips. "This is mutiny," he said. John turned his back and knelt under a desk.

"My name was chosen to go in the sub, but I let a friend take my place. I couldn't go and not tell you guys about living forever."

John peered through the transparent but bulletproof glass and saw the entire crew standing on deck. Some looked toward the command center. Others turned and walked away. John heard pounding behind him and kept talking.

"When I was a kid, my parents used to take me to church. I sang and did my time in Sunday school. But it didn't sink in. I never really thought what I was singing about was true.

"Then came the disappearances, and most of my family was taken away. I wished I'd listened closer. Maybe some of you lost friends and family too.

"When the captain called my name, I was relieved to have a chance to survive. But the more I thought, the more I knew I had to stay. I want to tell you about the person who can save you."

John didn't hear pounding and wondered whether the captain was listening or figuring out a way to get in.

"The comet is a judgment from God. It's meant to get

your attention. It's predicted in the Bible. Everything the Bible says has come true.

"Unless a miracle happens, we're gonna die. Each one of us will stand before a holy God. If you've done anything wrong, *anything*, God will have to turn you away."

John looked out over the crew. Several stood with their arms crossed, listening intently. Others milled about and laughed nervously. John turned. The captain had a gun. Someone was talking with him. *The diver who had saved the hostages!*

"Everybody's done wrong things," John said. "Everybody deserves to be turned away. But God loved us enough to put himself on the line and give his life. Jesus was God. He lived a perfect life and died in your place, in my place."

A burst of light flashed. John heard a boom that shook the window. The crew hit the deck.

"We don't have much time," John screamed. "If you ask Jesus to forgive you, he will. And when you're in front of God, he won't see the bad things you've done. He'll see the perfect life of Jesus."

Some of the men talked to each other. Several cried and looked toward the sky. The captain stared at John, his hands against the glass.

An eerie silence fell over the gas station as Judd and the others watched. As the news anchor talked, he picked up a pen, then repeatedly pulled off its cap and put it back on.

"The Global Community military has positioned aircraft so we can see the first glimpse of this more than one-thousand-mile-square mountain as it enters our atmosphere," the anchor said.

A spokesman for the Global Community Aeronautics and Space Administration revealed a final report. The object consisted largely of sulfur. When the mountain broke through the atmosphere, Judd and the others heard a terrific boom. Windows in the station shattered.

"The comet has now entered our atmosphere and has burst into flames," the spokesman said. "The trajectory will take it into the Atlantic as expected." He paused. "The next few minutes should be spectacular."

The sky turned black as the comet eclipsed the sun. The burning ball of death was heading straight for them.

John turned on the outside microphone and listened as men cried out, "No! God help us!"

"You can be sure of heaven," John continued, trembling. "Pray with me. God, I'm sorry for the bad things I've done. I believe Jesus died for me. Come into my heart right now and forgive me."

Most of the men were still lying on the deck. A few knelt. John saw several with marks on their foreheads. "I'll meet those who want to talk more at the front of the ship," John said as he opened the doors.

The captain burst through with two guards. "Arrest him!"

The captain grabbed the microphone and yelled, "We're going to die like men! We don't need religion."

The crew panicked. A group rushed John and the guards who were holding him.

"Get him to the brig, now!" the captain yelled.

"What's going to happen to us?" a young man screamed.

Officers whisked John down the stairs before he could answer. They left him in a dank cell.

A few minutes passed. John wondered if he would die in this room. Then keys jangled and John saw the face of the diver who had rescued the hostages. The man turned slightly. In the dim light John saw the outline of the telltale mark on his forehead.

"You're being released into my custody," the man said.

"Why?" John said. "How?"

"Come on. There's not much time." He put out his hand. "I talked with the captain after you were taken away. I convinced him you could calm the crew down."

John followed the man on deck and walked to the front of the ship. The man held up a hand and asked for quiet. Clouds above them scrolled back. The wind picked up and the water became choppy. John held on as the ship bobbed on the surface like a child's toy. The man turned to John and nodded. "Go ahead. Say what you want."

John shouted over the noise, "Those of you who prayed, look at me. This mark on my forehead means I've been sealed by God. I'm his."

"I can see it," one man said.

"What mark are you talking about?" another said.

"If you can't see the mark," John said, "it means you don't believe." John went over the message again. A few prayed. Others had questions.

The sky took on a ghostly appearance. Black clouds rushed over the crew. The force of the comet was creating a weather phenomenon never experienced by anyone. Hurricane-force winds blew between the comet and the surface of the sea.

John looked at the men scurrying across the ship. He called together all who had the mark. "Go to everyone you can and tell them what happened to you. These guys need God. It's their last chance."

The men, shaking, spread out on the deck. Many of the crew ran to their quarters when they saw the darkening sky. One man wrestled a gun from a guard. He ran to the edge and raised the pistol. A shot rang out. His body fell into the surging water.

John bit his lip. *Just a few more minutes before it hits. It's hard to believe this is really happening.*

36

MAYHEM. Confusion.

John had never seen anything like it. The sea churned. Men screamed and grabbed anything to keep from going over the edge.

The wind was furious. It nearly ripped John's clothes from his body. He fell to his hands and knees and crawled to the stairs leading to the command center.

"What are you doing?" the diver yelled behind him.

"I have to get a message to my cousin and his friends," John screamed.

"They'll throw you in the brig!" the diver said.

John turned. Huge waves washed over the bow. "I have to try."

Judd watched as experts paraded through the Global Community broadcasts. "What we're seeing may be a repeat of what happened millions of years ago with the dinosaurs," one scientist said.

"I still don't understand how this could sneak up on us," the anchor said.

"Funding for research has been small until the last few months," the scientist said. "Our best guess is that the comet was somehow thrown off course and came directly toward Earth."

The anchor took a deep breath. "I'm told we're about to see our first glimpse of the comet," he said.

Even on the small screen the sight made the kids gasp. The shot from the airplane showed a huge glowing mass heading for Earth. Gray and black clouds encircled the plane and the cameras lost sight of the comet for a moment.

Judd watched Mark fumble with the computer through tear-drenched eyes. "I just sent John a message," Mark said.

Judd put an arm around Mark.

"Five minutes until impact," the scientist said.

The captain threatened to throw John in the brig again, but the diver was able to talk him out of it. Several officers had been sick in the room. The smell turned John's stomach. As the crew in the command center grew frantic, John strapped himself in behind a computer and began typing.

One man urged the captain to turn the boat around. The captain shook his head. "No way we can outrun this.

They're predicting tidal waves on both sides of the Atlantic. Where do we go?"

"We have to do something," the man said.

The captain looked at John and lowered his voice. "What you said before seemed to calm them. Can you do anything?"

John swiveled his chair toward the frightened men. Again he explained the gospel. The men listened. "God, you give a peace that passes our human understanding," John prayed. "I ask that you would help each of these men to know you now and that you would give them that peace."

"I've got a wife and a baby back at the base," a man interrupted. "What about them?"

John led the man in a prayer and told him to quickly e-mail his wife and give her Tsion Ben-Judah's Web site. "She'll find out what to do by reading that."

Others left the room, but John was glad he had been given another chance. He opened an E-mail from Mark and read the hastily written message.

If you're where we think you are, Mark wrote, *you probably don't have time to read this. We all want you to know we're praying for you. You'll see Bruce and Ryan and Chaya before we will, so tell them we said hello.*

John finished reading through blurry eyes.

I know we've had our disagreements, and I haven't been the best cousin, Mark continued, *but I'm proud of you. I'll miss you.*

John put his head on the console and wept. He would never see Mark in this life again. Never talk with Judd or

Vicki. If he'd gone in the submarine . . . but he couldn't think that way now. He recalled what Jesus said to his disciples: "The greatest love is shown when people lay down their lives for their friends."

"There it comes!" an officer shouted.

The others moved toward the window. John looked up.

Blinding light.

Clouds whirled.

Wave after wave tossed the ship.

John shielded his eyes. His skin, though exposed only a few seconds, turned red. John saw one man on deck put his hands over his eyes. The ship pitched and the man lost his balance, flipped, and tumbled into the railing. Like a rag doll, he went limp and fell over the edge.

John shook his head. The diver who had helped him came close. "Guess this is it," the man said.

"I can't remember your name," John said, extending a hand.

The man shook it firmly. "Jim Pelton."

"We'll have a lotta time to talk once this is over," John said, "when we're finally home."

"I don't like the thought of dying," Jim said. "I wanted to live until the glorious appearing of Christ. But I just realized, today I'll see members of my family who disappeared."

The comet streaked behind a dark cloud. The sky looked golden. The wind blew harder and the ship rocked violently.

"It's funny, the things that go through your mind,"

Jim said. "I remember a preacher at our church talking about the *Titanic*. He said there were only two types of people on that boat: those who were saved and those who were lost at sea."

John nodded.

"The guy asked what we'd do if we only had an hour to live. I went out in the parking lot with my friends. We made fun of him. Now I wish.I'd have listened."

The comet appeared again, a huge, burning ball of smoke and flame. Men on deck shuddered and cried out.

"Let's go down there," John said. He looked at the captain and nodded, but the man didn't return his gaze.

John led the way to the deck, shielding his face and trying to keep his balance. Others who had the mark followed. At the center of the ship, the men joined hands and knelt. The crashing of waves didn't drown out John's voice.

"God, I thank you that you're true to your word, that what you say happens. I pray right now you would give us the strength to go through this and that you would bring others to yourself."

Men prayed. Some yelled, "Help us!"

As the comet neared the surface of the water, the sky peeled back, revealing a smoking trail miles long. The heat from the object singed hair and melted John's watch-band. He peeled it off and threw it over the edge.

The wind died. The comet reached the horizon and fell out of sight. Then the most terrifying sound. An explosion on the surface of the water.

Vicki covered her mouth with a hand as the GC plane transmitted images of the impact. The water boiled from the intense heat and steam rose, along with water spouts and typhoons. The plane broadcasting the event was knocked out of the sky by the force of the impact.

"They're gonna be showing this video for a long time," Lionel said.

John grabbed a metal post and hung on. The sky surged in turmoil. The captain shouted over the loudspeaker for the men to remain calm. Some grabbed extra life preservers and jumped overboard.

John calculated that the ship's position was two hundred miles east of the comet. A few minutes after he lost sight of the comet, the ship was drawn backward toward the splashdown site. Water surged around them. It felt like he was a kid standing at the edge of the beach, the tide rushing around his feet.

Part of him wanted to go below deck and hide, but John couldn't stop watching God's mighty judgment. The ship gathered speed and surged along, powered only by the turbulent ocean. Men were swept overboard as they stood and felt the awesome wind. There was no sound but the howling of the wind and the thundering of water.

Then John saw it. It started on the horizon and slowly rose as the ship rushed toward it. A wave so huge it seemed to scrape the clouds. Blue water rose skyward. John had seen pictures of waves that looked like canyons, with boats nothing but specks. But he had never seen anything like this. The blue turned to red. The bloody water churned all around the ship. It splashed on board. John felt it ooze down his back. He rubbed the liquid between his fingers. It was thick and sticky.

The thought of drowning had terrified John as a child. Now, he felt a sense of peace. *I'm ready for home, God,* he prayed.

The ship sped on, men screaming when they caught sight of the wave. John looked at Jim and nodded. Nothing to say and no one to hear it if you did.

The wave blotted out the sky. The ship rose against it, then turned slightly and rolled. John held on to the metal pipe as the ship plunged into the water. Submerged, the blood stung his eyes. He was in what felt like an underwater typhoon. Bodies and ship and equipment became one with the wave.

In the sea of red, John held his breath. The pressure of the water was unbearable. Seconds later he tried to breathe.

No air. John reached for the surface, but he felt miles away. Panic. Blackness.

Then light. Blessed light.

Judd gasped as newscasters described the devastation. Hovering aircraft showed America's Atlantic coast. Billions of tons of water crashed onto homes and businesses up to fifty miles inland. The remains of shrimp boats were scattered over roadways. An oil freighter, whose crew had been plucked from the deck by a helicopter just in time, lay on a mountainside in Virginia. A plane flew over the area where the old man had refused to leave his house. It was completely underwater.

Judd tried to think of something to say to Mark, but couldn't. Vicki shouted for Mark to come to the computer. "It's from John!"

Judd read over Mark's shoulder.

Incredible opportunity to give the message, John had written. *Nothing like a killer comet to wake you to reality.*

Some day I hope you meet Carl. He can tell you what happened here. No time now. Just enough to say I love you all. Keep fighting the good fight. We'll be cheering you on. Never give up. John.

Judd put his face in his hands.

"He probably died within minutes after sending that," Mark said.

Vicki and Shelly held each other and cried. Lionel put a hand on Mark's shoulder.

"You had a great cousin," Lionel said.

Mark nodded. "I know."

Nicolae Carpathia responded to the crisis with a grim face. In another address to the world he revealed that all travel would be affected by the damage. The meeting of the Jewish witnesses would be postponed another ten weeks.

"The loss of any human life is tragic," Carpathia said. "We grieve with the families whose loved ones perished in this latest catastrophe. However, our experts were correct. Had we attempted to explode the object, many more lives would have been lost.

"But we can do something in memory of those who died. We can rebuild. Travel routes and cities that have been wiped out will be restored. Let this hardship draw us together to create a new world that loves peace."

In response to the potentate, the two witnesses at the Wailing Wall went on the offensive. Judd and the others watched on the Internet as Moishe and Eli boiled in anger.

"Behold, the land of Israel will continue to be dry, as it has been since the signing of the unholy treaty!" Moishe said.

Eli picked up the message. "Any threat to the evangelists who are sealed will be met with rivers of blood!" he said.

To prove their power was from the Almighty, Moishe and Eli called upon God to let it rain only on the Temple Mount for seven minutes. From a clear, blue sky came a sheet of rain. The dust turned to mud. Televised reports showed families running from their homes, laughing and dancing. They believed their crops were saved. But seven minutes later the rain stopped. The mud returned to dust. The people were speechless.

"Woe unto you, mockers of the one true God!" Eli and Moishe shouted. "Until the due time, when God allows us to be felled and later returns us to his side, you shall have no power over us or over those God has called to proclaim his name throughout the earth!"

37

THE COMET affected weather around the globe. Vicki watched thick clouds roll into the Midwest. The news reported a tornado warning.

Vicki knew Mark was grieving John, but she didn't know what to do when he went off by himself. She offered to get him food, but he waved her away.

Judd and Mr. Stein were at the computer.

"People are begging to know God," Judd said. "I don't think Tsion has time to—"

"If he does not have time, he does not have to talk," Mr. Stein said.

"He's already talked to you," Judd said.

"Judd, if I am one of the 144,000 evangelists described in the Bible, I want to know," Mr. Stein said. "And I think Rabbi Ben-Judah will welcome a conversation."

Judd logged on and tried to contact Tsion. Vicki saw hundreds of messages. "Are those all questions for the rabbi?" Vicki said.

"They're waiting to be answered," Judd said. "I did as many as I could last night—"

A beep interrupted Judd. Vicki was excited to see the face of Tsion Ben-Judah on the screen. Judd gave Tsion an update about the kids. Tsion was saddened to hear about John. "He is another of the tribulation martyrs," Tsion said.

Judd introduced Mr. Stein, who leaned toward the camera and waved. Mr. Stein was shaking with excitement.

"I am glad to see you," Tsion said.

"My brother," Mr. Stein said, "I had to get in touch once more. I want to know if I am a Witness and what my assignment will be."

"I'm afraid only God can reveal that," the rabbi said. "I urge you to come to the meeting."

"Perhaps I could go with you," Mr. Stein said.

Judd flinched.

"I'm afraid that would be impossible," Tsion said. "Thousands of people are pleading with me to come to their countries and train them face-to-face. The Meeting of the Witnesses is designed to accomplish this.

"God is working out the details. The first twenty-five thousand to arrive will gather in Teddy Kollek Stadium. The rest will watch on closed-circuit television at sites all over the Holy Land. I will invite Moishe and Eli to join us. It will be a great time of teaching and learning."

Mr. Stein looked dejected. "I had hoped you could help me personally," he said.

"You have me now," Tsion said. "What are you concerned about?"

Mr. Stein glanced at Vicki and Judd. "I have doubts," he said. "I believe that Jesus is God, that he died for me. But I feel so unworthy. At times I think I will somehow go back to my old life. I fear God could not possibly use me."

"You struggle with sin," Tsion said. "You think you should be perfect and you are not."

"Exactly."

Tsion smiled. "The apostle Paul struggled with the same thing. Read Romans, chapter 7. You are not perfect and never will be until you are with God."

"But at times I do not even feel like I am a follower of Christ."

"Your enemy is at work. He does not want you to follow Christ. This struggle shows you are not falling away. Just the opposite. As you grow in your faith, you will see more of your sin. How much you care about yourself. It is happening to me every day.

"But this fight is not a sign of defeat. God is working in you."

Mr. Stein nodded. "But what if I don't feel like—?"

"Feelings are always difficult," Tsion said. "Do not base your faith on your feelings. Instead, read what God says in his Word about you. If you have asked God to forgive you and come into your life, he has.

"Second Corinthians 5:17 says you are a new person. God has begun a new life in you. Romans 15:7 says you have been accepted by Christ. When God looks at you, he no longer sees your sin. He sees the perfection of Jesus.

"In Romans, chapter 8, Paul asks, 'Can anything ever

separate us from Christ's love?' " Tsion paused. "Do you have trouble? Are you in danger from the Global Community? Paul says, 'Despite all these things, overwhelming victory is ours through Christ, who loved us.' "

Mr. Stein rubbed his forehead. "But how could God love that way? I have done terrible things."

Tsion smiled. "We judge people by *our* standard. When you believe in your heart that Jesus died for you and was raised from the dead, God views you no longer as an enemy, but as a son.

"The Scriptures are clear. God is working in you to do the good things he planned for you. You are kept not by your own power to do good things, but by his love and mercy."

Mr. Stein nodded. "I have many more questions."

"I'm sure," Tsion said. "Continue studying. See if what I say is true. It is clear now. The world is taking sides. Many people will follow the Antichrist. But many will believe in God's only Son. It is our job to take that message to everyone."

Vicki felt encouraged by Tsion's talk with Mr. Stein. Before he signed off she asked about Chloe.

"She is making great improvement," Tsion said. "Wait right there."

Vicki watched Chloe hobble to Tsion's computer. She smiled when she saw Vicki. "I want you to know how saddened I was about Ryan," Chloe said.

"What happened to you?" Vicki said.

"Long story," Chloe said. "When the earthquake hit, I ran from Loretta's house. Someone found me and transported me to a Wisconsin hospital. Buck caught up to me in Minneapolis. The GC had some kind of plan, but we were able to escape."

"Is it true about you having a baby?" Vicki said.

Chloe beamed. "It's true," she said. "Buck's acting like a mother hen, but we're both really excited."

Vicki asked about Chloe's father, Captain Rayford Steele.

"Pray for him," Chloe said. "Amanda's body was found in the plane wreckage. He had to dive into the Tigris River. Her death really shook him up."

Chloe said hello to Judd and the others. Judd asked about Buck and what happened in Denver. "Is he really being charged with murder?"

Chloe whispered something to Tsion. The rabbi nodded. Chloe said, "Buck went there to get Hattie Durham. She's pregnant with Nicolae Carpathia's child."

Vicki gasped.

"The Global Community is after Hattie," Chloe said. "Buck went to rescue her. He hit a guard in self-defense after the guard killed a staff worker. The guard died. They blame Buck, but it's not true."

"Is Hattie okay?" Vicki said.

"As well as can be expected," Chloe said. "We've got a new member of the Trib Force. A doctor. He's been helping both of us as we try to recover."

"Is Buck still working for Carpathia?" Judd said.

"He's putting the magazine together on the Internet," Chloe said. "He doesn't know how much longer he can work for such an evil man."

Vicki wanted to talk with Chloe about Judd. Vicki had remained cordial to him, but she felt something brewing under the surface. Chloe asked about the kids' escape from the GC and heard the story of Mr. Stein.

"We really need your help with E-mail," Chloe said. "Some of the messages are people saying they're praying. But many need replies."

"As soon as we figure out our next move," Judd said, "we'll get two or three people on it."

Chloe thanked them. "I miss having you guys around. I wish we could keep you here."

"We understand," Vicki said. "I hope we can talk more sometime."

Chloe gave them her cell phone number for an emergency. Tsion prayed for the kids and closed the connection.

Vicki heard a rumble of engines. Pete, who had been sleeping in the back of the service station, ran to the front. He cursed, then looked at the kids. "Sorry. You guys are going to have to hide again."

"What's going—," Judd said.

"No time to explain," Pete interrupted. "Hide."

———————————————

Judd and the others climbed into the oil-changing bay while Boyd parked a car overhead. The room was dark and smelled like gasoline.

"I wish we could see what's happening," Lionel said. "You think it's Red back with the GC?"

"Pete said Red wouldn't bother us," Judd said. "I don't know who it could be."

Judd whispered to Boyd, but the man said, "Keep quiet. There's a GC guy out front."

A few minutes later someone came inside. Judd heard angry voices. Finally, motorcycles started and drove away. Boyd moved the car, and the kids climbed out.

"What?" Judd said.

The manager bit his lip. "I don't know what to tell you," he said. "Pete said he had to go with the GC."

"I heard what happened," another biker said. It was Sally, who had given Vicki a ride to escape the commander. "I talked with Pete this morning. Had to drag it out of him, but he finally told me.

"Red was going to report you guys. Pete wanted to catch up to him and talk him out of it. When he did, Red freaked. He drove wild and tried to force Pete off the road. Pete yelled at him, but Red wouldn't stop.

"Red and Clyde, the guy with the gold teeth, both forced Pete onto a road that leads to a rock quarry," Sally continued. "Red tried to cut Pete off, but Red lost control of his bike. He hit Clyde, and they both went over the edge. I guess it was hundreds of feet to the bottom and nothing but rock."

"How awful," Vicki said.

"But the GC think Pete killed them?" Judd said.

Sally shrugged. "Pete said he'd show the GC where Red and Clyde fell. I hope they believe his story."

Judd frowned. If the GC suspected Pete, they would return.

"Everybody get ready to move," Judd said. He dialed the number Boyd had given him.

"This is Zeke," an older man said.

"I'm looking for your son," Judd said.

"What for?"

"We were told he could help us," Judd said. "We're in some trouble."

The man yelled, "Z!" and a moment later Zeke Jr. was on the phone. He seemed cautious and asked who had recommended him. Judd told him and Zeke Jr. laughed. "Boyd? That old coot?"

"Can you help us?" Judd said.

"I don't know you from Adam," Zeke Jr. said.

"The Global Community is on our tail," Judd said. "It's only a matter of time until they find us."

Zeke Jr. paused. "I think I can scrounge up some papers for you," he said. "As far as changing your faces, we'll have to see. When?"

"Tonight," Judd said.

"Whoa," Zeke Jr. said. "That's a little fast. There's bad weather between you and me. Tornadoes."

"Any way you can come to us?" Judd said.

"Not a chance," Zeke Jr. said. "You come to me or I pass."

Judd gave him the name and descriptions of each of the members. "When will you be ready for us?" he said.

"Make it before sunup," he said.

38

JUDD gathered what the kids would need for their trip. He asked Taylor Graham to help Mr. Stein locate his hidden money, but Taylor refused.

"I'll go," Mark said.

"If Pete doesn't come back, I'm going for him," Taylor said.

Conrad frowned. "You're gonna get the Global Community any way you can."

"That's right."

"You're gonna get yourself killed," Conrad said. "Pete can take care of himself."

Taylor smirked. "You don't get it. I'm not just going to get the GC back for what they've done; I'm gonna stop them."

"If you really want to do damage," Conrad said sarcastically, "why don't you kill Nicolae Carpathia?" Taylor stared at Conrad. "You wouldn't try anything that stupid, would you?"

Judd couldn't believe what he was hearing. "You don't need revenge."

373

Taylor rolled his eyes. "I know, I need God. Well he's never done anything for me. If you guys want to play your Bible games and try to figure out what's happening next, fine."

Darrion Stahley stepped forward. "I've known you since I was a kid. You're smart. Hasn't any of this sunk in? The disappearances? The earthquake?"

"I know your mom and dad are dead, little lady," Taylor said. "And the Global Community's responsible. I'll stop them if it's the last thing I do."

"God saved your neck for a reason," Conrad said. "Don't waste an opportunity—"

"I saved my own neck," Taylor snapped. "I don't believe you people. If you want to get something done, you do it yourself. You don't wait for some god to do it for you."

"That's enough," Judd said, looking at Conrad and Darrion. "He's free to make his choice." Judd turned to Taylor. "We could use a pilot."

Taylor looked away. "If I can help you, I will. But I don't promise anything."

"Fair enough," Judd said.

The wind howled. Tree branches scraped the windows of the gas station. "We leave at midnight," Judd said. "Hopefully we'll be at Zeke's place by sunup."

Vicki heard voices. Crying. Kids ran through the woods in front of her. Someone waved her forward. A boy. She could only see the back of his head. It looked like Ryan.

Breathing hard, Vicki tried to catch up. The woods

were dense. She could see her breath in the crisp air. She wanted to turn back, find safety, but she couldn't let the kids down. She kept going.

Someone was after the kids, after her. She turned around but no one was there.

Clouds hid the stars. Hard to see. One foot in front of the other. A branch. A fallen tree. She fell and scraped a knee.

Then flickering light in the distance. She stood and limped toward it.

She reached the clearing and saw a few kids bounding across a meadow toward a building. Others gathered on a second-floor balcony.

Vicki heard movement to her left and saw the boy running toward her. Behind him were soldiers. Vicki screamed.

Vicki followed the boy, scared. Kids lined the balcony, waving to her. "Run," they shouted. "Come on!"

The light was coming from the house. Beams shone through windows. "I don't understand!" she shouted at the boy.

"What's to understand?" he said.

It sounded like Ryan. She ran faster.

"What is that place?" Vicki said.

The boy didn't answer but kept running. Vicki glanced behind her. When she turned, the boy was gone.

"Hurry!" someone said from above.

Vicki reached the steps. The soldiers stopped, turned around, and went back into the woods.

"Why did they leave?" Vicki said.

375

"Why did who leave?" Shelly said, shaking Vicki awake. "Come on, time to go."

Vicki rubbed her eyes and followed Shelly outside. Members of Pete's group had loaned their bikes. Darrion rode with Judd. *Good,* Vicki thought. She put on a helmet and sat behind Conrad. Lionel rode alone on the third bike.

"Good luck," Shelly said. "I hope I don't recognize you when you get back."

Conrad followed Judd. Vicki relaxed and thought about the boy in her dream. Did she miss Ryan that badly? Could it be some kind of message?

"Did Mark and Mr. Stein leave?" Vicki yelled to Conrad.

"Half hour ago," Conrad said. "Pete's still not back."

The wind had blown down makeshift power lines. Judd held up a hand, and the kids carefully drove around the dangerous wires.

"What happens if we run into GC?" Vicki said.

"Judd said we'll try to outrun them," Conrad said. "I hope we don't have to."

The kids stayed away from main roads, even going across fields. By early morning Vicki was tired of all the ruts and ridges. She was glad to find paved roads again, even though they still had huge cracks from the earthquake. Dogs barked as they rode through neighborhoods.

Vicki told Conrad her dream. "What do you think it means?" she said.

"Could mean you haven't been getting enough sleep," Conrad said. "Then again, it might be God trying to tell you something."

"What?" Vicki said.

Conrad shrugged.

Judd stopped and turned off his motor. They were on the edge of what had once been downtown Des Plaines. The streets were deserted. A light was on in a broken-down one-pump gas station.

"Let me check it out," Conrad said. "I'll signal if it's okay."

Judd nodded. Conrad crept toward the filling station. A few minutes later Vicki saw a light flash inside.

Zeke Jr. opened the creaky garage door and the kids pushed their cycles inside. Zeke Jr. was in his mid-twenties, had long hair, and was covered with tattoos. He wore black cowboy boots, black jeans, and a black leather vest over bare arms and flabby chest.

"People call me Z," Zeke Jr. said as he looked at each of their foreheads. "I guess 'cause it's easier."

Judd said, "Where's all your equipment for—"

"I know it didn't look like much," Z said. "By the time I'm through, this place'll be a shopping center for believers."

Vicki looked around the station. Dirty rags lay on black oil drums. There were out-of-date calendars with pictures of cars. An oily phone book lay on a counter. Everything looked grimy. Vicki wondered how they could trust someone who kept such a dingy business.

Z seemed to read her mind. He grinned. "Follow me," he said. Z led them to a tiny washroom. The sign said Danger. High Voltage. Do Not Touch.

"Anybody puts a hand on here and they get a little

buzz," Z said. "Not enough to hurt, just make 'em think twice. Come on."

Z knew where to push. The panel opened and Z slid it out of the way. He led the five kids down a wooden staircase to his shelter. It was fashioned out of the earth beneath and behind the station. Deep in the back Vicki saw boxes of food, medicine, bottled water, and assorted supplies.

"If you guys need anything back there, let me know," Z said.

The room had no windows and was cool. *Perfect,* Vicki thought, *to keep the food and medicine fresh.* A TV news broadcast was on low in the background. Beside the TV was a dog-eared spiral notebook and a laptop.

"When I'm done, we'll need to get a picture," Z said. As he set up his camera he told the kids his story.

"Before all this I did a few tattoos, pinstriped cars and trucks, airbrushed some T-shirts, and even painted murals on some 18-wheelers. That business dried up a long time ago."

"What happened to the rest of your family?" Vicki said.

"My dad, Zeke, runs the station," Z said, fiddling with the camera. "My mom and two sisters died in a fire the night of the disappearances. We were tryin' to get over that when this friend of my dad's, a long-haul trucker, comes through. Starts talkin' 'bout God and his plan. I didn't buy it at first. The more he talked, the more it made sense. He gave us a Bible, and we started reading in Revelation, of all places.

"I don't mind tellin' ya, I've done a lot of drugs. When I wasn't smokin' or shootin' up, I was drinkin'. I'd stay high until I needed some more money; then I'd go back to work a few days.

"God got hold of both of us. My dad and I go to an underground church in Arlington Heights now. I want to be a major supplier to Christians. Hopefully, with my contacts with truckers, we'll turn this place into a warehouse for believers."

"You mean you'll ship stuff from here?" Judd said.

"With what's ahead, somebody's gotta do it," Z said. He pointed to the computer. "Rabbi says it's gonna get worse and worse. We have to prepare."

Z tacked a sheet on the wall. "Before I take your pictures," he said, "we gotta figure out what to do with you." He looked at Vicki. "That's not your natural color, is it?"

Vicki shook her head. "Red."

"The hair's okay, then," Z said. He put on plastic gloves and opened a desk drawer. Inside were dental materials. He fitted a device over Vicki's front teeth. They stuck out a little and seemed to change the shape of her face.

"You should be able to leave this on all the time, once you get used to it," Z said.

"Incredible," Lionel said. "What can you do for me?"

"You're a challenge," Z said. "We'll shave your head to start. Then a scar on your face might draw some attention. Sunglasses, maybe."

Z worked on the kids' appearances. He changed hair

color, cut hair, and added scars and tattoos that amazed the kids. When he was finished he took their pictures.

A bell rang above. "Dad's probably still asleep," Z said. "Let me get that and I'll be right back."

Z unlocked the station and helped a customer with fuel. When he returned he squatted behind an old couch and swung open a rickety filing cabinet. He grabbed a cardboard box filled with different types of identification. Some were driver's licenses. Some were student IDs.

"Sorry I'm not too organized yet," Z said.

"Where did you get those?" Vicki said.

Z slammed the filing cabinet shut with his boot. "The earthquake claimed a lotta lives. These weren't doing the dead any good, and they could sure help out our cause in the future."

Vicki looked at the faces and names scattered throughout the box. "All of these people are dead?" she said.

Z nodded. "I get the wallets before the GC gets the body." He dumped the contents onto a table. "Don't go by the faces," he said. "Try to find somebody who's close to your age."

Vicki rummaged through the cards and found a girl a year older than she and about the same height.

"Jackie Browne," Z said. "Looks good. She's an organ donor, too. Good citizen of the Global Community."

"How much can we change on this?" Judd said.

"If you want me to get this done today, you have to take it the way you find it," Z said. "Give me a couple of days and I can make you a member of Enigma Babylon, or even a GC soldier."

"We don't have that kind of time," Judd said.

Lionel found a smaller box on the filing cabinet. "What's this?" he said.

"Those are from this week," Z said. "I don't use ones that fresh."

Lionel rummaged through the box and gave a low whistle. "Look at this."

The kids crowded around. The military ID card showed a stocky man with medals and decorations. Beside his picture it read *Commander Terrell Blancka.*

"I remember that one," Z said. "Strange. Found him in a culvert near a church, or what was left of it. Looked like an execution. Gunshot wound."

"I thought he was being reassigned," Vicki said.

"He was," Lionel said. "Permanently."

Vicki glanced at the stack of cards and gasped. Among them was Joyce's, the girl who had accused Vicki of murdering Mrs. Jenness. "Do you know how she died?" Vicki said.

Z shook his head. "I've got a friend at one of the GC morgues," he said. "A believer. I got that one from him."

Vicki felt a sudden sense of relief. If her accuser was dead, she was off the hook for the murder rap. Then Vicki felt a wave of guilt. Joyce had heard about God but rejected him.

Z gave the kids blankets and showed them an area where they could rest. Vicki was exhausted. She watched Z through the doorway as he turned on his magnifying light and began cutting the pictures. From this day on she would be Jackie Browne.

39

MARK thought about John as he drove beside Mr. Stein. The video of the comet's crash kept flashing in Mark's mind. It was so spectacular that the networks would run the footage for weeks. Reports of lost boats had filled the news. Mark had logged on to the list of crew members on the *Peacekeeper 1* and found John's name.

He was so engrossed in his thoughts that he didn't realize he had lost Mr. Stein. Mark turned the motorcycle around and backtracked. He found the man and his cycle in a ditch.

"I must have hit the accelerator instead of the brake," Mr. Stein said, limping away from the bike.

"Climb on," Mark said.

Mr. Stein hobbled onto the back of Mark's motorcycle.

"Is the money in cash?" Mark said.

"Large bills," Mr. Stein said. "I hope we can take it in one load. . . . Are you thinking about your cousin?"

Mark nodded.

"I am sorry for your pain," Mr. Stein said. "I was just reading the passage where Jesus said those who mourn are blessed."

"If that's so, you've had a double helping," Mark said.

"Tsion teaches about this," Mr. Stein said. "He points those who are struggling with the death of loved ones to the end of Revelation. God says he will remove all sorrows, and there will be no more death or crying or pain."

"Can't wait for that," Mark said. "But I gotta be honest. I don't understand why God would let all this happen."

"You have been a believer longer than I have," Mr. Stein said. "I should be asking you these questions."

The two rode in silence. Mr. Stein pointed the way. When they got close he said, "My office is on the next street. Stop here."

Mark pulled to the curb. Businesses were in shambles. A construction crew had cleared the road of debris, but the sidewalk was twisted.

"The GC might still be guarding your place," Mark said.

Mr. Stein nodded and gestured for Mark to follow him. They squeezed between two buildings and checked for cars near Mr. Stein's office.

"I don't see why we're risking this," Mark said. "If your money's hidden somewhere else, let's go there."

Mr. Stein pointed to a broken window in the bottom floor of his office. "We'll crawl through there," he said.

"But—"

"My money is here," Mr. Stein said, "if the Global Community didn't take it."

Mark followed Mr. Stein and kept watch. They passed a wall safe, its door lying broken on the floor.

"Just as I suspected," Mr. Stein said.

They moved upstairs. Mr. Stein pointed to desks with missing computers. "Either vandals or the GC," he said.

They reached a second-floor office with a couch and desk. The computer tower was gone, but the old monitor was still on the desk.

"Good," Mr. Stein said.

Mark watched in amazement as Mr. Stein unscrewed the back of the monitor.

"I was on the phone with Judd when he alerted me there was a bug," Mr. Stein said. "I had already hidden the money, but I wanted whoever was listening to think otherwise."

Mr. Stein took out the last screw and opened the back of the monitor. The contents of the monitor had been removed, and the space was crammed with bills. The man pulled out wads of hundreds. Mark had never seen so much money in his life.

Glass broke downstairs. Someone cursed. Two voices. One of them said, "Got almost everything last night. There's still some computer stuff upstairs."

Mr. Stein looked wildly at Mark.

Footsteps banged on the stairs.

"Quick, help me put the money in the drawer," Mr. Stein whispered.

They dumped the cash in the drawer and fumbled

with the back of the computer. At the top of the stairs the footsteps stopped. Another man, this one with a squeaky voice, said, "I thought you said this place was deserted."

"Come on," the other said.

Mr. Stein motioned for Mark to get behind the door. When the two came into view, Mark was safely out of sight. Mr. Stein sat in a chair, his feet on the desk.

"Welcome, gentlemen," Mr. Stein said cheerily. "I'm glad to see you're back."

Squeaky Voice was short and walked with a slight limp. The other man was tall and thin. He looked like the picture of Ichabod Crane Mark had seen in his reading book as a kid.

"Who are you?" Squeaky said.

"I'm the proprietor of this establishment," Mr. Stein said. The two stared at him. "The owner," Mr. Stein explained. "This is my office."

Mark noticed Ichabod had a gun. Mr. Stein pointed to it and said, "There's no need for violence. You're welcome to whatever you'd like."

Squeaky squinted and jerked his head sideways. "You *want* us to take stuff?"

Mr. Stein smiled. "When I found the office standing, with all the other buildings on this block in ruins, I was shocked. The insurance won't pay unless there was real damage. But now that you boys have 'cleaned up' for me, I should be paid quite a bit."

Squeaky still didn't understand.

"He's in it for the insurance money," Ichabod explained.

386

"Did you find the safe downstairs?" Mr. Stein said.

"Oh yeah, that was a piece o' cake," Squeaky said.

"How about the telephone equipment in the basement?" Mr. Stein said.

"Didn't know there was a basement," Ichabod said.

Mr. Stein pointed them toward the correct door, and the thieves left. Mr. Stein followed them. Mark opened the drawer and stuffed the money into a black satchel. When Mr. Stein returned he said, "We must hurry. There is no telephone equipment down there."

Mark cleaned out the drawer. The satchel was full and very heavy. Mr. Stein grabbed the satchel and raced down the stairs, Mark right behind him. Mark was almost out the window when he heard Ichabod shout, "Hey, there's two of them!"

The sun was coming up as Mark raced toward the alley. A shot rang out. A bullet pinged against a brick wall nearby. Mark took the satchel from Mr. Stein, who was lagging behind, and ran for the bike. By the time Mr. Stein made it, Mark had the motorcycle roaring. Mr. Stein clutched the satchel tightly to his chest as Mark sped away.

Vicki awoke first and, peeking through the doorway, found Z still at work on the IDs. Judd was now Leland Brayfield. Conrad found the driver's license of James Lindley, two years older. Darrion had become Rosemary Bishop. But it was more difficult for Lionel. Z admitted his stash of African-American IDs was lacking. The closest Lionel could come was a twenty-five-year-old who was at least fifty pounds heavier. Z said making too many changes to "Greg Butler" could tip off whoever scanned Lionel's new ID, but he would do it anyway.

Z was laminating Lionel's card when Vicki shuffled into the room. She yawned and sat by his desk. It was nearly noon.

"You've been at it quite a while," Vicki said.

"Not so bad," Z said, pulling the magnifying light down to inspect the card. He handed "Jackie Browne's" card to her.

Vicki gasped. "This is amazing," she said.

Z blushed. "Where are you guys headed from here?"

Vicki laughed. "Who knows? We've been fighting about our next move since we escaped the GC."

"What kinda choices you got?"

"Darrion's folks have a place in Wisconsin," Vicki said. "It'd be good for us to get away from Chicago, but . . ."

Z nodded and opened a packet of beef jerky. He leaned back in his chair as he chewed. Rolls of fat jiggled under his black vest. "Who says you guys have to stay together?"

Vicki paused. The Young Trib Force had been separated before, but it had never been their choice.

"If you guys are fighting about what to do," Z said, "split up. You may be able to do more good apart."

"What do you mean?" Vicki said.

"I'm helping people get supplies and fuel," Z said, "and keepin' the Global Community out of your hair. If the rabbi's right, pretty soon more and more people are going to need supplies, which means more people will have to help. I could use somebody right here in the office."

Vicki admired Z and his dad, but she couldn't imagine working for them. But something stirred in her as he spoke.

Z picked up a notebook by his laptop and turned to the back. Vicki couldn't read a word of the scratching. "I'll tell you another thing that's gonna happen," he said. "With parents raptured or dead, a lot more young people like you are gonna be on the run. Especially believers."

Vicki looked straight at Z and said, "The dream."

"What's that?" Z said.

"I had this dream," Vicki said. "I was running through woods, following a boy. The GC was chasing us. We ran down by a river and came into a clearing and saw a huge house. There were kids on the balcony, waving and calling. When I made it to the front door, the GC stopped. It was like I disappeared. Then—"

"This is spooky," Z said, sitting forward, the chair legs slamming on the floor. He opened a desk drawer and rummaged through some papers.

"Tell me what the house looked like," Z said.

"I don't remember except that it had a balcony and was really long," Vicki said. "I think there was some kind of pole in front. Like a flagpole."

Z stared at her. "I don't believe it."

He rummaged through another drawer and moved to the filing cabinet.

"What is it?" Vicki said.

Z snapped a piece of paper from a file. "Got it!" he said.

He handed Vicki a ten-year-old real estate listing. Statistics covered the bottom half of the page. Fifty acres, zoned residential, well water, etc. On the top half was a picture that took Vicki's breath away. The photo was fuzzy, but it looked exactly like the house Vicki had seen in her dream, even though the house was blocked by trees.

"It even has the flagpole," Z said, pointing to the right side of the picture.

"What is it?" Vicki said when she caught her breath.

"An old boarding school," Z said. "About forty miles south of here. My grandpa bought it from the state. Hadn't been used in years. He didn't do much with it. Then he died and left it to my dad. Nearly sold it a few times, but the buyers always backed out."

Z pointed to a brown streak behind the house. "And it's in a flood plain," he said. "Right next to a river."

"What are you going to do with it?" Vicki said.

"It's not that far from a major trucking route. Plan is to store supplies there. We already have some meds, food, water—that kind of thing."

"Won't it attract attention?" Vicki said.

Z pulled out another sheet of paper. Along the top was written *Condemned.*

"This document says the place is a hazard and people should stay away. Some of the neighbors think the place is haunted. They don't come around."

Vicki scratched her head. "You're going to think this is stupid," she said.

"Go ahead; I'm listening."

"For a long time I've had this idea of a place where kids can go," Vicki said. She stood. Thoughts swirled in her mind. Ideas came fast. "What if we use this as a training center for the Young Trib Force? What if kids who want to know the truth come there to study? We could make it a distribution center for all your food and medicine, too."

Vicki could see it, a fulfillment of her dream. Z put his hands behind his head and listened.

"It's far enough away that the Global Community wouldn't find us," Vicki continued, "but close enough to help believers who need supplies."

"What would that mean for the rest of the group?" Z said. "If some want to go to Wisconsin or they don't like the school idea, what happens then?"

Vicki turned and saw Judd in the doorway. He looked funny with all his changes. But Vicki didn't smile.

"I guess we'll each have to make our own decision," Vicki said.

JUDD didn't like Vicki's idea. Something about taking over the school bothered him. The others awoke and joined them.

"You're taking for granted that Z is offering," Judd said.

Z handed him some beef jerky. Judd declined.

"This place has been in the family for years," Z said. "I'd have to ask my dad, but I see it as a win-win. You guys get a place to stay, and we get someone to watch the supplies."

"What about Wisconsin?" Darrion said.

"Everybody has to choose," Vicki said. "We can't force people to join us."

"You're talking about splitting up the group," Judd said.

"You don't like it because it wasn't your idea," Vicki said.

"That's not true!" Judd shouted.

Lionel held up a hand. "Hold it! What's important isn't whose idea it is; it's that we respect each other."

Vicki explained the school option to the whole group. Darrion held up a hand. "Wisconsin reminds me of my parents, but Vicki's idea sounds good. If God gave her that dream, maybe we should do it."

Judd looked at Vicki. "I'm not trying to shoot this down. I don't think we can base an important decision like this on a dream."

Vicki squinted. "Remember when you went to Israel to check on Nina and Dan? Wasn't that partly because you'd had a dream about them?"

"That was different," Judd said.

"Forget the dream," Lionel said. "We need a place that's safe, and it sounds like we can help Z and his dad with supplies."

Z nodded. "I can't say when we'll start running. Let me go talk with my dad." Z left.

Lionel looked at Conrad. "What do you think about all this?"

Conrad pursed his lips. "I don't know. I'm mixed up. Makes you wonder if God's really helping us, or if we're trying to do this on our own."

"What do you mean?" Vicki said.

Conrad swatted at a fly. "If we're all on the same team, why do we argue so much?"

"Just because we disagree doesn't mean we're not on the same team," Lionel said.

Vicki scooted closer to Conrad. "Is it deeper than that?"

"What Mr. Stein said to Tsion," Conrad said. "I just don't know if this is real."

"You heard what Tsion said to Mr. Stein, right?" Judd said.

"What if I turn away?" Conrad said. "What if I go with Taylor and try to kill Nicolae, or just turn my back on the whole thing?"

Z came back in the room. "Good news—"

Judd held up a hand and pulled out his pocket Bible. "Let's go over this again. John, chapter 1. Everyone who believes in Jesus and accepts him becomes a child of God. They are reborn."

Conrad nodded.

"John, chapter 3 says everyone who believes in Jesus has eternal life, and chapter 5 says those who believe will never be condemned for their sins, but they have already passed from death to life.

"Romans 10 says if you confess with your mouth that Jesus is Lord and believe in your heart that God raised him from the dead, you will be saved."

Conrad read the verses with Judd.

Vicki spoke up. "I've been reading Revelation to see what's ahead. I love the verses that talk about the Book of Life. When you believed, Conrad, your name was written there. God knows you."

"So I can't un-save myself?" Conrad said.

Judd smiled. "When you asked God into your life, he saved you by his power. And he'll keep you by his power. It doesn't mean you won't have doubts or you won't sin." Judd looked at Vicki. "And it doesn't mean you'll always treat your brothers and sisters the way you should."

Conrad was silent. Finally, Z said, "My dad thinks your idea about the school's great."

Vicki took the key and the directions to the old schoolhouse. "One more thing," she said. "I want to look for Phoenix."

Judd shut his eyes and held his tongue.

"You mean the dog that was with you?" Conrad said. "I might know where he is."

"Can I talk with you for a minute?" Judd said to Vicki. "Alone?"

———————————

Vicki climbed up the narrow staircase and entered the gas station in front of Judd. Z's father was with a customer.

"If you kids only wanted to use the rest room, you have to buy something," Zeke said.

"Yes, sir," Judd said. He picked up a couple of candy bars from a cardboard bin on the counter and left two bills by the cash register.

"Teenagers," the customer said in disgust.

Vicki knew Zeke was covering for them. The customer didn't have the mark of the believer. This is what it would be like. To stay alive, they would have to be careful with everyone without the mark.

Judd handed Vicki the candy bar and they walked outside. Vicki blew dust from the wrapper. Clouds blocked the sun and a hazy gloom hung over the area.

"I didn't want to talk about it in front of the others," Judd said.

"You don't want me going for Phoenix," Vicki said.

"What I want or don't want isn't the point. You saw what Conrad's going through."

"Which is exactly why this school would be such a good idea," Vicki said. "Kids need to understand what the Bible really teaches."

"There's nothing wrong with the idea, but why can't kids get the same thing from Tsion's Web site?"

"They can get information there, but I think they need a person to show them. Flesh and blood." Vicki stopped walking. "Try to picture it. Believers coming together to study, soaking up the teaching, asking questions, figuring out what to do. At the same time, we help set up a supply line so people can survive."

"Would you let anyone in who wasn't a believer?"

Vicki started to answer, but Judd cut her off. "What if some say they really want to know more, but their real intent is to expose us to the Global Community? What if they want to lead them right to us?"

"We have to use caution," Vicki said. "We'd have to discern—"

"Use your power of discernment like you did with that guy Charlie?" Judd said.

Vicki threw the stale candy bar on the ground. "I cared about Charlie. He helped me carry Ryan's body."

Judd walked a few more steps. Vicki stood her ground. "Maybe it's time we split up," she said.

"That's exactly what I'm talking about," Judd said. "You're driving a wedge into the group."

"And you're the only one who can have an idea? You want women to remain silent and be good little girls. If God gives me an idea, I'm not gonna keep quiet."

"You know I've valued your input," Judd said.

Vicki scoffed. "As long as I agreed with you."

Vicki clutched the key and directions in her hand. "I'm going back for Phoenix right now!"

"Vick, that's crazy! In broad daylight?"

"Conrad said they caught Charlie with Phoenix and sent him to a shelter. I'm gonna keep my promise to Ryan, no matter what you say."

"Vick, wait!"

When Vicki reached the station she looked back and saw Judd kneeling on the ground.

Judd and Lionel waited until evening to leave Z's place. Lionel didn't ask about Vicki. Z scribbled another set of directions to the old schoolhouse and gave them to Judd.

"Sounds like you guys have been through a lot," Z said.

Judd nodded. "More than I can tell you."

Z scratched at a few scraggly hairs on his chin. He tipped his chair back. "I ain't an expert on anything but tattoos, but I do know one thing. When you got people you care about, no matter how much you fight, you got somethin'."

Z looked away. His eyes pooled with tears. "I'd give

anything to spend one hour with my mom and sisters. I'ᴄ
give anything to tell them about God."

When they left, Z shook Judd's hand and put an arm
around Lionel. "You need anything, you holler. We could
use a couple guys like you to drive for us, if you decide to
help out with the supplies."

"We'll let you know," Judd said.

Lionel started his motorcycle. "I hope Pete's back
when we get there."

Vicki, Darrion, and Conrad drove near the remains of
New Hope Village Church. They parked their bikes
behind the rubble and looked at the damage. The
downed helicopter had been removed. The grass and
trees were black from the scorching hail.

Vicki found shell casings from rifle fire. The bullets
had been intended for her and her friends.

"From what I remember," Conrad said, "Charlie and
that dog were taken to a shelter near here."

"Should we split up?" Darrion said.

"Let's stay together until we get close," Vicki said.

The three hiked to the nearest shelter. The smell of
campfires and outdoor cooking made Vicki hungry. They
passed tents and people in sleeping bags. Vicki motioned
to Conrad and Darrion to stay back as she entered the
medical tent.

A stout woman with black hair rushed about. Vicki
caught her eye. "I'm looking for a friend. He has a dog
with him."

"This isn't an animal hospital," the woman said.

A younger girl heard Vicki's question. She said she had seen a boy with a dog and described Phoenix perfectly. "Saw them two days ago," the girl said. "The boy seemed a little strange."

"Where'd they go?"

The girl shook her head. "A couple guys took them away in a jeep. Haven't seen them since."

Vicki thanked the girl.

"Doesn't sound good," Conrad said when Vicki returned. "The GC might have taken him in for questioning."

"Where?" Vicki said.

Conrad held up his hands. "No way, you can't—"

"They won't recognize me with the changes Z made," Vicki said. "I have to find Phoenix."

Darrion darted behind a tree. "Get down," she whispered.

Vicki and Conrad crouched low. Melinda and Felicia, the Morale Monitors, crept into the medical tent. "What could they be doing?" Vicki said.

"I don't know," Conrad said, "but if you're gonna look for Phoenix at the GC headquarters, now's the time to do it."

As Judd and Lionel reached Boyd's gas station, Shelly met them. She was frantic. "I thought you guys had left me. Pete still hasn't come back, but Taylor said he was going to find the GC and get him out."

Judd winced. First Vicki and now this. Boyd opened the garage door and let them in.

Judd heard a rumble and saw a motorcycle coming.

"Maybe that's Pete," Shelly said.

"No, it's two people," Judd said.

Mark and Mr. Stein brought the cycle in. Mr. Stein had a satchel with him.

"Did you get the money?" Judd said.

Mr. Stein nodded. Mark briefly told them about their adventure. Judd explained where Vicki and the others had gone. He looked at Boyd. "Can you point me toward the GC headquarters?"

"You can't!" Shelly said.

"I have to try," Judd said.

"Perhaps money would help," Mr. Stein said.

Judd shook his head. "Whatever's happened to Pete, I don't think any amount of money will help him now."

VICKI rode with Darrion. They followed Conrad to the GC headquarters in Des Plaines. Vicki was glad Commander Blancka was out of the picture, but Melinda and Felicia were not far away.

The kids parked their motorcycles two blocks from headquarters. Conrad led them to the side window. Someone was sleeping in a cell, but there was no sign of Phoenix.

Vicki walked around the corner and tripped on something metal. It clanged against the back wall. A dog barked. A door opened and a shaft of light hit the yard. Vicki gasped. Phoenix stood in a pen behind the station.

"Shut your yap!" the man yelled at Phoenix, but the dog kept barking. "This'll shut you up." The man picked up a stone. The rock bounced off the cage and Phoenix cowered.

When the door closed, Vicki rushed to Phoenix. The dog barked, then whimpered when he saw Vicki. A wave of relief spread over her. She had thought about Phoenix every day since the earthquake.

"Hey, boy, how are you?" she said gently.

Phoenix looked like he hadn't eaten in days. He wagged his tail. Vicki tried to get her hand through the fence, but the opening was too small. Phoenix tried to lick Vicki's face but couldn't.

"I'm glad to see you, too."

Conrad inspected the lock on the pen. "No way we're gonna get him out without the key."

"Why would they lock him up here?" Vicki said.

Conrad shrugged. "Maybe they're still using him to look for us."

"Wish we had some wire cutters," Darrion said.

"Let's dig him out," Vicki whispered.

The kids got on their hands and knees and scraped at the dirt. Darrion found the piece of metal Vicki had tripped over and used it to dig faster. When they had dug a few inches, Conrad sat back.

"The fence is deep," Conrad said. "We're never gonna get him out this way."

Vicki pulled at the top of the cage, but it was welded tight. Phoenix whimpered and paced, keeping his eyes on Vicki.

"We're gonna get you out of here, boy," Vicki said.

Suddenly the back door opened. Light shone in the kids' faces.

Judd and Lionel rode nearly past the small, two-story building the Global Community had seized. Lionel stayed with the bike while Judd moved closer. Judd ran toward a lighted window, peeked over the edge, and ducked when he saw someone walking toward him. He looked again. Pete sat patiently in a chair near the window.

Judd ran back to Lionel. "Pete's in there. No hand-cuffs, and it doesn't look like the guy is threatening him."

"Probably only a matter of time," Lionel said.

Lionel touched Judd's arm and nodded toward the building. Someone was inching up the side.

"That's Taylor!" Judd said.

Judd and Lionel rushed to him. Taylor's face was painted black.

Taylor climbed down, and the three moved away from the building.

"What are you doing?" Judd said.

Taylor took a knife from his mouth and put it in its sheath. "Jump a guard and get Pete out of there."

"You were going to kill somebody?" Lionel said.

"If I have to, yeah," Taylor said.

Judd shook his head. "No need to kill anyone. Let me try."

"I'll give you five minutes," Taylor said. "If they take him to a cell, I'm coming after him."

Judd took Lionel aside. "If Taylor leaves, alert the GC. Nobody gets killed over this."

"But—"

"Do it," Judd said.

Judd ran to the window, which was open a few inches.

The GC officer shuffled papers on his desk. "I've already told you, we believe you. The marks on the road are consistent with your story."

"Let me explain it another way," Pete said.

"I have things to do."

"Please," Pete said.

The officer's chair squeaked. "What you're saying could get you in bigger trouble than if you would have killed those guys."

"I think you're ready to hear it. If you weren't, you'd have thrown me out of here a long time ago."

"Maybe I should have," the officer said.

Judd looked through the window. Pete was leaning forward, his hands on the officer's desk.

"I don't care who you work for or what you've done in the past, God loved you enough to die for you. If you ask him to forgive you for the bad things you've done, he'll make you a new person and you can live with him forever."

The officer spoke in a low voice Judd could hardly hear. "Do you realize what my superiors would do? We're talking life and death—"

"Exactly," Pete interrupted. "What I'm talking about is life and death, too. If you reject God's way, it means you're separated from him forever."

Judd knelt. He knew Pete was bold, but he didn't know he would be this bold. He looked for Taylor but didn't see him. Lionel sat with his back to a tree.

"If I believe what you say," the officer said, "and I'm not saying I do, how would I do it?"

As Pete explained what the man should pray, Judd looked closer at Lionel. He was struggling. Judd ran and found Lionel tied and gagged.

"Taylor must have heard us," Lionel said as he gasped for air. "He grabbed me from behind." Lionel pointed to the building. "Look!"

To Judd's horror, Taylor Graham had already climbed to the second floor of the building.

"We've got to stop him!" Judd said.

Vicki rolled to her right and out of the light. Darrion and Conrad went the other way. A thin man closed the door and walked toward Phoenix. She thought they had been seen. Finally, she lifted her head.

The man held something in his hand. He opened the narrow slot and dropped it on the ground inside Phoenix's kennel. Phoenix approached warily and sniffed.

"There you go, boy," he said. "They wouldn't let me feed you. I found some scraps. Hope you like 'em."

The voice sounded familiar but Vicki couldn't place it. When he turned, Vicki whispered, "Charlie!"

Vicki rushed to him. Charlie jumped back. "What do you want? I was just feedin' the dog. I won't do it again."

"It's okay," Vicki said. "I'm not going to hurt you."

Charlie held his arms close to his chest. *He doesn't recognize me*, Vicki thought. *Good.*

Vicki signaled for Conrad and Darrion to stay where they were. "Why do they have the dog in the cage?"

"Those guys in there are using him," Charlie said. "They're trying to find some people."

"Really?" Vicki said. "I've been looking for a dog like this. He seems nice."

"He is," Charlie said. "He's kept me company ever since my friends got killed."

"What friends?" Vicki said.

"A girl and a guy and some others," Charlie said. "They got killed by the commander before he died."

Vicki stepped closer. She wanted to talk with Charlie and tell him the truth, but she was afraid the GC officers would find them any moment.

"I have some good news," Vicki said. "Your friends aren't dead."

Charlie scrunched his face. "What?"

"Your friends are alive, and I know where they are," Vicki said. "I can take you there if you'll help me get the key to this cage."

"The guys in there'll be really mad if I do that," Charlie said. "They're looking for these two girls, and if I run off—"

"What two girls?" Vicki said.

"I can't remember their names," Charlie said. "They were with that commander guy a lot."

"Melinda and Felicia?" Vicki said.

"Yeah, yeah, that's them. They got away."

Vicki thought a moment. Why would the GC want Melinda and Felicia?

And then she knew.

"This is really important," Vicki said. "If you go in and get the key, I'll take you to your friends."

"How do I know you're telling the truth?" Charlie said.

Vicki took him by the shoulders. "Because your name's Charlie. I'm here to help you."

Charlie smiled. "How'd you know my name?"

"Will you get the key?" Vicki said.

Someone yelled for Charlie. His eyes darted to the door. "Okay."

"Don't tell anyone I'm out here," Vicki said.

"I won't," Charlie said. "You just stay here, and I'll see if I can find the key. Stay right here."

Conrad and Darrion approached as Charlie scampered off. Vicki took them to the side of the building.

"I've got a bad feeling," Vicki said. "I think the GC is trying to wipe out all the people who were involved with us."

"You think the GC killed Blancka?" Conrad said.

Vicki nodded. "And now they're after Felicia and Melinda."

"Good," Darrion said. "I hate those two."

"When they find them," Vicki said, "they'll get rid of Charlie, too."

Conrad bit his lip. "Blancka is dead. Joyce, the girl who accused you of murder, is, too. They're looking for Melinda and Felicia, and they have Charlie and Phoenix in custody. Everybody who was connected with us is winding up dead."

"Why?" Darrion said.

"Who knows," Conrad said. "Image and control are everything to the GC. If Blancka messed up, it was easier to get rid of him than give him a second chance."

"And that means they have to get rid of everybody who knew that wasn't a training exercise in that field," Vicki said, "including us."

"Just when you thought it was safe," Darrion said.

Vicki thought about the schoolhouse. They had to get Charlie away from the GC fast.

Judd watched as Taylor Graham disappeared into the second floor of the GC building. Lionel followed Judd to the front door.

"Get by the window," Judd said. "If the officer goes out, tell Pete what's up."

"Got it," Lionel said.

Judd rushed up the steps and looked inside. A man in a uniform sat at the front desk, talking on the phone. A female officer drank coffee at a desk in the rear.

Judd opened the door and calmly walked in. The man behind the front desk raised his head. Judd didn't make eye contact.

"Can I help you?" the officer said.

Judd didn't answer. He walked straight to the back hallway and closed the door.

"Hey, you can't go in there!" the man shouted. The woman put her coffee down and drew her gun.

Judd shut the door and flipped on the light. He breathed a sigh of relief when he saw the fire alarm. He pulled it. A piercing buzz filled the headquarters. Judd found a back door and rushed outside. He darted to the front and found Lionel, and the two raced to their motor-cycle.

"I figured the alarm would clear the building," Judd said. "Did you talk with Pete?"

"Yeah," Lionel said. "He wants us to go on without him. I told him about Taylor. He said he'd handle it. Pete seemed to think the guy he was talking with was really close to making a decision about God."

"Let's just pray they both get out of there alive," Judd said.

42

VICKI waited outside GC headquarters, peeking in the window every few seconds. Conrad and Darrion walked the motorcycles closer. Charlie finally returned with a key.

"Gotta get to my friends," Charlie said, handing the key to Vicki. "Gotta get that thing on my head. They promised me."

Conrad rolled his eyes. Vicki tried the key. It didn't work. Phoenix whined.

"I'll go back and get another one," Charlie said.

Conrad put up a hand. "We can't let him go back in there," he said.

"How are we going to get Phoenix out?" Vicki said.

Conrad ran around the building and disappeared into the darkness. A few minutes later he returned with a tire iron. "Found it in the jeep out front."

413

Conrad placed the tire iron at the top of the kennel door and pushed until the door bent slightly outward.

"Gonna take more than that," Darrion said.

Charlie helped. Their combined weight opened the door a few more inches. "See if you can get him," Conrad said to Vicki.

Phoenix whimpered and backed away.

"Come on," Vicki coaxed. Finally she grabbed his front paws.

Footsteps behind them.

Vicki let go of Phoenix. "You have to cover for us," she said to Charlie. Vicki and the kids scattered. Charlie stood by the door of the cage. "Cover for you," he said.

"What are you doing out here?" a man shouted.

Charlie stuttered, "Just feedin' the dog, sir."

"I thought I told you to stay inside!"

"Yes, sir," Charlie said, "but the dog was whining and hungry and I didn't think—"

"Do me a favor," the man said. "Don't think. Just do what I tell you. Come inside."

The man left. Vicki heard a voice inside the building say, "He's more trouble than he's worth. We oughta get rid of him tonight."

Vicki hurried to the cage. She took Phoenix by the paws and tried to lift him out.

"Hurry," Conrad said.

Phoenix yelped in pain as Vicki pulled his head through the small opening. Darrion tried to calm him.

"Get Charlie out of here," Vicki said.

"We're not leaving without you," Conrad said.

414

"They're gonna off him," Vicki said. "At least get him on a cycle so we can bolt when I get Phoenix."

Conrad led Charlie to a motorcycle, and they both climbed on.

Darrion put her arms through the cage opening and pulled at the dog's body. Phoenix yelped.

"Hey!" a man shouted. "They're stealing the dog!"

Conrad started the motorcycle. Phoenix slipped through the opening, sending Vicki and Darrion to the ground. Phoenix growled and ran toward the building. The man retreated.

Darrion and Vicki ran to the motorcycle. She tried to start it, but the engine sputtered.

Phoenix stood at the open doorway and barked.

"Go!" Vicki yelled at Conrad.

Conrad shook his head. A shot rang out.

"Phoenix!" Vicki yelled.

The motorcycle roared to life. Conrad sped off.

"Wait!" Vicki shouted. She called for Phoenix. Two men exited the doorway with guns drawn. Phoenix jumped, grabbing one man by the arm. The other man turned to get a shot at the dog, but couldn't. Phoenix bit hard and the man dropped his gun. Vicki screamed again, and this time Phoenix bounded away from the man on the ground and jumped into Vicki's lap.

Darrion gunned the engine. Vicki held on tight to Phoenix and kept her head down. When they turned into an alley, Phoenix yelped in pain and squirmed in her arms.

"It's okay, boy," she said. "You're safe now."

Darrion caught up to Conrad and Charlie. They rode without headlights through the moonlit streets. Vicki knew they had to get to the schoolhouse.

Judd and Lionel raced to Boyd's gas station. Some of Pete's gang waited for news. Judd explained what happened. Shelly said she would keep watch so Judd and Lionel could get some sleep.

Early the next morning, Judd was awakened from a deep sleep. Taylor Graham stood over him. He grabbed Judd by the collar and picked him up.

"Why did you do that?" Taylor screamed.

"Let go," Judd said.

Taylor did and Judd fell hard to the floor.

"That's enough," Pete said, grabbing Taylor by the arm.

"The GC almost caught me because of him," Taylor said.

"I told you to wait," Judd said. "Pete wasn't in any danger."

"He's right," Pete said. "Pulling that alarm kept you from doing something stupid."

"Killing people isn't the answer," Judd said.

"And talking about God is?" Taylor said. "I'm through with you people."

Taylor knocked shoulders with Pete and stalked outside. A moment later, an engine revved.

"He's got your bike!" someone said.

Pete waved a hand. "Let him go."

Mr. Stein looked at the floor as Taylor roared off. "How will I get to the Meeting of the Witnesses?"

"You'll find a way," Lionel said.

The kids moved to the office. "Where's Vicki?" Shelly said.

Judd told them about Vicki's decision to try to find Phoenix and the idea about the old schoolhouse. "She might not be coming back."

Shelly stared at him. "You're not breaking up the group, are you?"

Judd thought a moment. "We all have to make our choices," he said. "I can't stop Vicki any more than I can stop Taylor."

"But it's such a good idea," Shelly said. "We should be at the school right now."

Lionel spoke up. "Did Z give you directions?"

Judd nodded. He pulled a scrap of paper from his pocket and looked at Lionel. Something was happening. Judd felt he was losing control. Would the kids leave him behind to follow Vicki?

He handed the paper to Lionel and turned to Pete. "What about the Global Community officer?"

"Talked with him more after the fire alarm," Pete said. "He didn't pray with me, but I could tell he was close. He knows how to do it if he wants to."

Judd bit his lip. "It was pretty risky talking with him that way."

Pete sat and put his feet on Boyd's desk. "I'm not into risk. I didn't tell that guy the truth because I want to get in trouble. I could tell he was lookin'."

Judd stared at the floor.

"We've been left here for a reason," Pete said. "If people are interested, I tell them. It's as simple as that. If I read it right, the GC police have just the same chance as the rest of us."

"I'm just saying it might not be smart—"

"This isn't about smart," Pete said. "If I didn't tell that guy about God, who was going to?"

Judd looked away.

"Havin' said that," Pete continued, "I can't be sure he won't come after us. And it's a possibility Red's gang will come for revenge."

"I'm going to find Vicki," Shelly said.

"Me, too," Lionel said.

Vicki hung on tight to Phoenix as Darrion and Conrad zigzagged through the torn-up streets of Des Plaines and headed south. When they made it to what used to be I-55, she felt safer. Several times she had the feeling someone was following, but when she looked back there was no one.

Vicki gave Darrion directions as she strained to see the map Z had given. The kids rode past farmhouses and sloping fields.

"Turn here," Vicki said, seeing a dirt road leading up a hill.

Conrad and Darrion rode back and forth along the road an hour before they gave up and pulled to the side.

"Let's get some sleep," Conrad said. "We'll find it in the morning."

The kids found a grassy area a few yards off the dirt road and went to sleep. Phoenix curled up next to Vicki. When Vicki awoke, Conrad was studying the map.

"If the map is right, we gotta be really close," Conrad said.

"When do I get to see my friends?" Charlie said.

"Soon," Vicki said. "Real soon."

"What's that?" Charlie said, pointing to a brown spot on Vicki's shirt.

"It almost looks like blood."

"Phoenix!" Conrad yelled.

The dog lay still on the ground. His fur was matted with dried blood along one side. Vicki held her breath. Conrad leaned over Phoenix and inspected the wound.

Vicki couldn't look. "Is he dead?" she said.

Phoenix whimpered.

"Looks like a bullet grazed his back," Conrad said.

Vicki cradled the dog's head in her lap. Phoenix licked her hand as she petted him.

"He didn't lose that much blood," Conrad said, "but we'd better find something to disinfect the wound."

"Z said they have medicine stored at the schoolhouse," Vicki said.

While Charlie stayed with Phoenix, the kids searched for the road. A few minutes later, Darrion shouted. Vicki found her near some downed trees.

"This is why we couldn't find it last night," Darrion said, pointing to the logs. "It's blocked."

"If this is the right road, it's perfect," Conrad said. "Nobody'll find us unless they know what to look for."

Charlie carried Phoenix, and the kids walked the motorcycles around the logs. The road had shifted and would need some repair if they expected to bring truck-loads of supplies to the hideout. Around a bend they found a small pond; then the road opened to a meadow. On the hillside stood the old schoolhouse. Shutters dangled, a screen door hung at a crazy angle, and the paint was peeling.

"Incredible," Vicki said.

Vicki opened the door with the key Z had given her. A long staircase leading to the second floor was just inside the door. Straight ahead was the kitchen area with a table and a few chairs. To the left and right on the first floor were classrooms.

"This is almost as big as my house!" Darrion said.

"It'd take a year just to find all the rooms," Conrad said. "There's even a bell tower upstairs." He opened a door under the stairs. His voice echoed. "There's a huge basement, too."

"Z said the bedrooms are upstairs," Vicki said.

Charlie carried Phoenix inside and put him on the floor in the kitchen. Vicki and the others searched for the supply room and found it at the north end of the house.

"What do you put on a dog who's been injured?" Vicki said, looking at the boxes of medicine. "Their skin is different from ours, isn't it?"

Vicki found a bottle of antiseptic used in hospitals. She blotted the brown liquid on Phoenix's back. The dog yelped and scampered away.

"Maybe that stuff doesn't work on an open wound," Darrion said. "Maybe some soap and water?"

Conrad held Phoenix as Vicki and Darrion washed the wound. Vicki tried putting on a bandage, but Phoenix chewed it off.

"You told me I could see my friends," Charlie said.

Vicki pulled out a chair and asked Charlie to sit down. "Do you notice anything familiar about me?" Vicki said.

"Your voice," Charlie said.

"Who do I sound like?"

Charlie shrugged.

Vicki took the dental device off her front teeth. Charlie's eyes opened wide. "How about now?"

Charlie squinted. "I still don't know what—"

"Picture me with red hair."

Charlie screamed, "Vicki!"

43

JUDD walked Lionel and Shelly outside. "If I don't hear anything from you, I'll assume you made it."

Lionel shook hands with Judd. Shelly had tears in her eyes. "Why don't you come with us?"

Judd looked at the ground. "Maybe later. I'll stay with Mr. Stein. Get in touch if you need me."

When they were gone, Judd logged onto the Internet and found several messages from Pavel, his friend from New Babylon. A few minutes later he was talking with Pavel live.

"The satellite schools were set to open," Pavel said, "but the comet set them back. I'm amazed at the rebuilding, though. Carpathia has troops opening roads, airstrips, cities, trade routes, everything. And he's using each disaster for his own good."

"What do you mean?" Judd said.

"New Babylon is the capital of the world!" Pavel said. "The worse things get, the more people feel like they have to depend on the Global Community."

Judd nodded. "And you can bet Carpathia will use the next judgment for his own good if he can."

Pavel rolled his wheelchair closer to the monitor. "My father has been able to observe the potentate through his position with the Global Community. Carpathia is furious with Tsion Ben-Judah, the two witnesses, and the upcoming conference."

"From the loads of E-mails Tsion has sent me," Judd said, "Carpathia can't be too happy about the people who want to know more about Christ."

"Have you seen the exchange between Carpathia and the rabbi?"

"What exchange?"

Pavel took out a disk and sent the data to Judd. While Judd opened it, Pavel said, "My father says Nicolae has always been an intense man. Very disciplined. But now he works like a madman. He gets up early, before everyone else, and he works late into the night."

Judd read the document. It was Nicolae Carpathia's attempt to compete with Tsion Ben-Judah. His messages were short. One read, *Today I give honor to those involved in the rebuilding effort around the world. The Global Community owes a debt of gratitude for the sacrifices and tireless efforts of those who are making our world a better place.*

Another brief message encouraged readers to give their devotion to the Enigma Babylon faith. Carpathia also repeated his pledge to protect Rabbi Ben-Judah. *Those who are sincere in their beliefs should know they have the full protection of the Global Community,* Carpathia wrote. *Should Dr. Ben-Judah choose to return to his home-*

*land, I pledge protection from the religious fanatics or others
who wish to harm him.*

"Now look at how Ben-Judah responded," Pavel
said.

Judd scrolled down and read the rabbi's words aloud.
"Potentate Carpathia: I gratefully accept your offer of
personal protection and congratulate you that this makes
you an instrument of the one true, living God. He has
promised to seal and protect his own during this season
when we are commissioned to preach his gospel to the
world. We are grateful that he has apparently chosen you
as our protector and wonder how you feel about it. In the
name of Jesus Christ, the Messiah and our Lord and
Savior, Rabbi Tsion Ben-Judah, in exile."

"Did your dad say anything about how Carpathia
reacted?" Judd said.

Pavel smiled. "The Potentate went into a frenzy. He
didn't even respond to Ben-Judah's message."

Judd signed off and asked Mr. Stein to join him.
"Boyd said we could fix up a little hideout in the oil bay.
One of the best ways to learn about the Bible is to help
me answer people's questions."

Mr. Stein put his hands in his pockets. "My heart is in
Israel with the upcoming conference," he said, "but I
suppose I should learn as much as I can."

Vicki heard the sound of the engine first. She was working on a railing of the balcony when she saw two people
on a motorcycle coming through the trees. She whistled

the danger signal and everyone met in the kitchen. The kids had planned a strategy in case they had visitors.

When Vicki realized it was Lionel and Shelly, she let out a whoop. She ran and embraced the two.

Lionel said they had arrived late the previous night, but couldn't find the road to the school.

"Same thing happened to us," Vicki said. She gave them a tour. Lionel looked shocked when he saw the supply room. The kids had reorganized it since moving in.

"We've got a lot of ideas," Darrion said. "I want to dig an underground tunnel in case the GC ever find us." She pointed to the hillside. "It'd come out somewhere near the river."

Lionel nodded. "We need to hide a boat down there."

"The big drawback is that we don't have electricity or phone," Vicki said. "There's a fuel tank buried in the back and Conrad found a gas-powered generator, but we haven't been able to get it to work."

"Give me a shot at it," Lionel said.

When they were alone, Vicki asked Shelly about Judd.

Shelly shook her head. "He's so stubborn. I begged him to come with us, but he wouldn't."

Judd and Mr. Stein answered E-mails that poured in. People begged to know God. Mr. Stein observed how Judd answered questions and gave advice to young people who didn't know how to begin a relationship with God.

Mr. Stein learned quickly. He kept a list of verses and passages of Scripture they used frequently. Judd checked his answers to make sure they were accurate. Soon, Mr. Stein and Judd took shifts. While one person answered E-mail, the other slept or got exercise.

Several weeks later, Pete returned. Judd and Mr. Stein were thrilled. Pete told them about finding his former gang and their reaction to Red's death.

"Some of them wanted to kill me," Pete said, "but most of them knew how quick-tempered Red was. I tried to talk with them about God again, but they wouldn't listen."

Pete turned on the television and switched to a news channel. "You see this?"

The reporter talked about a Global Community base that had been bombed. "I saw something about it on the Internet," Judd said. "You think there are still militia members alive?"

"The base had planes," Pete said. "They were all destroyed. All except one. It was a fancy six-seater the commanding officer used to get back and forth to New Babylon."

Judd gasped. "Taylor Graham."

Pete nodded. "They're not telling everything in the report. Gotta be Graham's work."

"Can you stay with us?" Judd said.

Pete smiled. "Wish I could. Truth is, I'm not the sit-still type. A few of us are headed down south. There are a lot of people who need to know the truth."

Pete said he would leave one motorcycle for Judd and Mr. Stein to use. Judd told Pete about the boarding school and the possibility of transporting supplies to believers. Pete scribbled something on a piece of paper. "This is a truck stop where I'm headed. I know some long-haul truckers who might be interested."

"They're believers?" Judd said.

Pete smiled. "Not yet. But then, I haven't talked to 'em yet, have I?"

Pete hugged Judd and Mr. Stein. Boyd smiled at Pete. "Don't know what I'd have done if you hadn't come along."

"I can't guarantee the gang won't be back," Pete said. "I'll have a couple people check on you."

The manager thanked him. "Next time you get back here, I hope this place'll look like Zeke's station, complete with a shelter underground."

Pete had been gone an hour when the phone rang. It was Lionel.

"This is the first call we've made since we've been here," Lionel said. "Took me an hour to find a pay phone."

"How's the school?" Judd said.

"You gotta see it," Lionel said. "Z's got enough supplies for an army. It's hidden, and there are a bunch of logs across the road that leads here, so we don't have to worry about the GC. And we could sure use a computer. There's no electricity or phone, but we've been trying to fix up an old generator. No luck yet."

"How's Vick doing?" Judd said.

"Okay," Lionel said. "Darrion too. We get up in the morning and start fixing the place up. We work till sundown. Vick's started a Bible study. We take turns leading it. Wish you were here."

"Yeah," Judd said.

"How about Stein?"

Judd cupped his hand around the phone. "He's learned a lot in the past few weeks, but he's driving me crazy about going to Israel."

"Bring him here."

"I'll talk to him," Judd said. "I don't think he'll settle for less than being at Teddy Kollek Stadium. And if you guys don't have electricity, I know he won't come. He'll miss watching the meeting."

Vicki couldn't believe the feeling of freedom. In the time since she had become a follower of Christ, she seemed to always be looking over her shoulder. At Nicolae High it had been Mrs. Jenness. At the detention center, she had watched her back constantly. Since the earthquake, the Global Community was her main threat.

Now, in the peaceful setting of the boarding school, she looked forward to getting up and going to work. The jobs were ordinary. The kids had to take turns preparing food. Everyone worked cleaning up the place. Darrion's tunnel idea was put on hold. There was simply too much essential work to be done first.

Other than Judd, Vicki's biggest frustration was Charlie. He pestered the kids constantly about getting the mark on his forehead. Vicki would explain the gospel again, but something was holding Charlie back from understanding or accepting the message.

Phoenix improved. His wound healed into a scab, and

429

a few weeks later Vicki could hardly tell he had been hurt. She wondered if Phoenix missed Ryan as much as she did.

Each night Phoenix would make his rounds. He would visit each room where the kids were sleeping. Finally, he would push the door of Vicki's room open and nuzzle against her.

If only Judd were here, Vicki thought.

———————————

Judd was working on E-mails late one night, a few days before the start of the rescheduled Meeting of the Witnesses. Mr. Stein had gone to bed dejected.

Boyd burst into their downstairs hideout. "You gotta come see this!"

Judd ran to the office and saw a frantic-looking spokesman for the Global Community Aeronautics and Space Administration trying to explain yet another threat in the heavens. The news anchor asked how another comet could get by the watchful eyes of the Global Community scientists.

"I do not have an answer for that," the spokesman said, "except to say we have been on constant alert."

"Can you give us an estimate on the size and potential damage?" the spokesman said.

As the man talked, the network ran footage of the splashdown of the previous comet.

"This object is similar in size to the previous burning mountain," the spokesman said, "but it has a different makeup. This one seems to have the consistency of rotting wood."

"Wormwood!" Judd shouted.

"What?" Boyd said.

Judd grabbed a Bible and flipped to the book of Revelation. He found the reference in chapter 8.

"What does *wormwood* mean?" Boyd said.

"It's Greek," Judd said. "Tsion says it means 'bitterness.'"

The news anchor asked the GCASA spokesman, "Sir, we know now that the last comet killed a tremendous amount of fish and devastated ships on the Atlantic. What damage would this do?"

"I am told that Potentate Carpathia, along with his military and science advisors, have come up with a plan," the spokesman said. He held up an enlarged photo of a ground-to-air missile.

"They're gonna blast it from the sky," Judd said.

"If it's made of rotting wood," Boyd said, "it'll go into a million pieces."

"That's what I'm afraid of. The Bible says Wormwood will fall on a third of the rivers and on the springs of water. It'll basically poison the water supply. A lot of people are going to die because of it."

"When is the missile set to launch?" the news anchor said.

"The comet will be in range about midmorning tomorrow," the spokesman said.

"Vicki!" Judd shouted.

"What about her?" Boyd said.

"She and the others don't know about this," Judd said.

"Does this water affect believers too?" Boyd said.

"I don't know," Judd said, "but I can't take that chance. They might be drinking from a well. They have to be warned."

Mr. Stein agreed to go with Judd. After he was packed, Judd realized he didn't have directions to the boarding school. He dialed Z's place, but a message said there was trouble with the phone lines.

"We have to find Z," Judd said.

44

JUDD raced toward Chicago. He was mad at himself for not making a copy of the map. The sky was black. Mr. Stein pointed to an orange glow overhead. "There it is," he said. Throughout the drive the glow got gradually brighter.

Judd found a phone and called Z, but still couldn't get through. Near daybreak he and Mr. Stein pulled up to the station. The place looked deserted. Judd banged on doors and went to the back. Finally, Z's father, Zeke, let them in.

"Where's Z?"

"Couple suspicious people been hangin' around the last few days," Zeke said. "He's lyin' low."

Zeke scribbled directions on a scrap of paper. "I can't say what kind of shape the access road will be in."

"How long will it take us?" Judd said.

"A few hours."

Judd thanked him and told him about Wormwood. "I

433

been watchin' it on TV," Zeke said, pointing to an ancient black-and-white set.

Nicolae Carpathia's face flashed on the screen, and Zeke turned up the volume.

"And I commend the members of the scientific community for coming up with this brilliant plan," Nicolae said. "Ever since the last threat from the skies, our team has been working around the clock. Their hard work has paid off.

"In less than an hour, we will launch this marvel of technology. I assure you, this burning mass of solar driftwood will be vaporized as soon as our missile reaches it. We should see little or no effect on the earth's surface."

Judd shook his head. "Don't bet on it."

Zeke handed Judd and Mr. Stein a few bottles of water. "Be prepared."

Judd and Mr. Stein roared off, going as fast as they could toward the boarding school. Judd wished he could see the launch of the missile. He was sure Carpathia would try to make as much out of it as possible. Not only could he use this to impress the world and gain followers, but the launch would also take attention away from Tsion Ben-Judah.

Judd had pulled onto I-55 when he saw a flash of light. He pulled to the side of the road and unsnapped his laptop. "I have to see this!" he said.

Moments later, Judd and Mr. Stein watched live Internet coverage of the missile's launch. As Carpathia beamed, a team of scientists showed charts and simulations of what would happen when the missile hit its target.

To everyone's amazement, the missile didn't strike Wormwood. Instead, the flaming meteor split itself into billions of pieces. The missile passed through the dust without exploding, as pieces of Wormwood wafted toward the atmosphere.

Judd shut his computer and drove on. By late morning they were dodging bits of fiery wood that landed everywhere, including waterways and reservoirs.

"Surely they will see this and know not to drink from contaminated waters," Mr. Stein said.

"I hope so."

Judd followed Zeke's directions until he came to a road blocked by logs. "This has to be it."

When he and Mr. Stein drove up, the members of the Young Trib Force welcomed them.

Vicki was the last to emerge, her hands dirty from working on the generator. Mr. Stein hugged her. She put out a hand to Judd, then realized it was black with grease.

"It's okay," Judd said, taking her hand. "We were worried since you guys didn't have—"

"Wormwood," Vicki said. "We've been studying. Didn't you think we could handle it?"

"It's not that," Judd said.

Vicki walked away.

Judd put his computer on the kitchen table and pulled up the coverage. Video reports showed fragments of burning wood falling on Paris, London, New Babylon, Seattle, and Bangkok. Reports filtered in about those who drank the contaminated water. A reporter in South America stood near a small village. The camera panned away from him, showing scattered bodies of men and women in the road.

A panic for clean water sent people scurrying to stores. Shocked owners were dazed as hundreds of people emptied the shelves in minutes.

A grim Nicolae Carpathia faced the camera once again. This time he did not praise the work of his scientists, but called the Global Community to order.

"We must work together to overcome this terrible tragedy," Carpathia said. "I am asking the cooperation of individuals and groups. I once again must ask those who have been waiting for the conference in Israel to postpone your meeting."

"What?" Mr. Stein said.

"For the safety of attendees," Carpathia continued, "I believe it is best for all concerned to delay this important conference."

"I'd like to know what Tsion thinks about that," Vicki said.

The kids didn't have to wait long. Judd accessed the rabbi's bulletin board and within minutes saw a message. The first half spoke to Jewish believers. The other half was aimed at Carpathia himself.

The time has come, Ben-Judah wrote. *We must not waste another moment. I urge as many of the 144,000 witnesses as possible to come together in Israel next week. This will be a time of teaching, training, and encouragement we will never forget.*

Tsion then referred to Nicolae as simply *Mr. Carpathia.*

"With all the titles that guy keeps getting," Lionel said, "that has to get to him."

We will be in Jerusalem as scheduled, with or without your approval, permission, or promised protection, Tsion wrote. *The glory of the Lord will be our rear guard.*

Before dinner, Vicki approached what the kids called the reading room. Lionel had asked her to meet him there. She walked in and was surprised to see Judd.

"What are you—?" Judd said.

"Lionel asked me to come here," Vicki said.

"He asked me the same thing," Judd said.

Lionel came up behind Vicki and closed the doors. "Okay," he said, "now that I finally have you two together I wanna get a few things straight."

Vicki folded her arms. Judd leaned against a window that overlooked the balcony.

"I've taken an informal poll," Lionel said.

Judd scowled. "About what?"

"About you and Vicki," Lionel said.

Vicki said, "What happens between us—"

"Is my business," Lionel interrupted. "And it's the business of every member of this group. We're supposed to be part of the same body. We're supposed to support each other. We look to you two as our leaders."

There was a long silence. Finally, Judd said, "What did you ask the group?"

"If there was one thing you could change about the group, what would it be?"

"And?" Vicki said.

Lionel looked at the ground. "Other than getting Ryan back, we all agreed. It was to have you two working together instead of apart."

Vicki scratched her nose. Judd looked out the window.

Vicki started to speak but Judd interrupted. "That Charlie kid is on the ground out there."

"Haven't you been listening to anything Lionel said?"

"No, I mean, I think something's wrong with him," Judd said.

Phoenix barked. "What's Phoenix doing outside?" Vicki said. "We locked him up so he wouldn't drink any of the bad water."

"Well, he's out there on the ground with Charlie," Judd said.

Vicki rushed downstairs with Judd and Lionel right behind her. Charlie coughed and sputtered as he lay on the ground. He grabbed his neck.

"What happened?" Vicki said. "Did you drink from the well?"

"Only a little," Charlie said.

"I told you to leave it alone," Vicki said.

"I know," Charlie said, "I saw those girls and they asked for a drink."

"What girls?" Judd said, out of breath.

"I don't know their names," Charlie said. "I just remember 'em from back home."

"What'd they look like?" Lionel said.

"I don't know," Charlie said, coughing and sputtering harder.

"He's hallucinating," Judd said. "Get him a drink of good water."

Vicki rushed to find a bottle. Phoenix followed. Vicki locked the dog safely away. When she returned, Judd and Lionel had Charlie sitting up on the porch. Charlie drank deeply, but still seemed queasy from the well water.

"It was so sour," Charlie said. "I can't get the taste out of my mouth."

"It's lucky you didn't drink more," Judd said.

"One of the girls did," Charlie said.

Judd rolled his eyes.

Vicki kept a close eye on Charlie as they ate dinner. His face was drained of color and he said he was tired. Vicki made a bed for Charlie downstairs and Darrion volunteered to watch him.

Judd got Vicki's attention, and the two went to the balcony.

"I think Lionel's right," Judd said.

"About what?" Vicki said.

Judd sighed. "I know I've come across too strong at times. I admit that. And I've made you feel like your ideas aren't as good as mine."

"Right," Vicki said.

"I want to be mature about this and stop fighting," Judd said. "Maybe if we got back to being friends . . . "

Vicki put her hands in her hip pockets. "I can work on that. But you can't ask me to stop coming up with ideas. God worked it out. There's somebody out there right now who needs our help. I want to be here when he or she walks through our door."

Judd nodded. "I was wrong. This place is just what we're looking for."

Vicki closed her eyes. *If he'd only said that a couple months ago we wouldn't have had to go through this.*

When she opened them again, Judd was standing over the railing, peering into the woods. "What is it?" Vicki said.

"I thought I saw somebody at the side of the house."

Judd called a meeting of the Young Trib Force that evening. Charlie wasn't much better, but at least he wasn't getting worse. Judd wondered if it had been a good idea to bring Charlie to their new safe house, but he didn't dare bring that up with Vicki and the others now. The ice was just beginning to thaw.

Judd wondered whether he could lead the kids. Would they listen to him without thinking he would boss them around?

Mr. Stein asked to say something before the meeting began. "I appreciate all you've done for me. I have been insistent on going to Israel. It has been my main goal since becoming a follower of Jesus. But it looks as if the meeting will begin next week, and I still have no way to get there."

"What about a commercial flight?" Lionel said.

"If I were able to change my identity like you have," Mr. Stein said, "I would do it. But I'm afraid it's too risky.

I have enough money to buy my own plane, but I have no access to a pilot. I can only assume it is not God's will that I should go."

The kids groaned. Mr. Stein stood with his head down.

The door burst open. Judd whirled. Two girls. One had her arm over the other one's shoulder and looked pale. The other held a gun.

"Stay where you are, Stein!" the girl with the gun yelled.

Lionel glanced at Judd.

"Nobody moves," the girl screamed.

Vicki whispered something to Darrion.

The girls' clothes were in tatters, their hair out of place. They looked hungry and exhausted. But there was no mistake. These were the two surviving Morale Monitors of the Global Community, Melinda and Felicia.

"Everybody on the ground!" Melinda shouted.

ABOUT THE AUTHORS

Jerry B. Jenkins (www.jerryjenkins.com) is the writer of the Left Behind series. He owns the Jerry B. Jenkins Christian Writers Guild, an organization dedicated to mentoring aspiring authors. Former vice president for publishing for the Moody Bible Institute of Chicago, he also served many years as editor of *Moody* magazine and is now Moody's writer-at-large.

His writing has appeared in publications as varied as *Reader's Digest, Parade, Guideposts*, in-flight magazines, and dozens of other periodicals. Jenkins's biographies include books with Billy Graham, Hank Aaron, Bill Gaither, Luis Palau, Walter Payton, Orel Hershiser, and Nolan Ryan, among many others. His books appear regularly on the *New York Times, USA Today, Wall Street Journal*, and *Publishers Weekly* best-seller lists.

Jerry is also the writer of the nationally syndicated sports story comic strip *Gil Thorp*, distributed to newspapers across the United States by Tribune Media Services.

Jerry and his wife, Dianna, live in Colorado and have three grown sons.

Dr. Tim LaHaye (www.timlahaye.com), who conceived the idea of fictionalizing an account of the Rapture and the Tribulation, is a noted author, minister, and nationally recognized speaker on Bible prophecy. He is the founder of both Tim LaHaye Ministries and The PreTrib Research Center. He also recently cofounded the Tim LaHaye School of Prophecy at Liberty University. Presently Dr. LaHaye speaks at many of the major Bible prophecy conferences in the U.S. and Canada, where his current prophecy books are very popular.

Dr. LaHaye holds a doctor of ministry degree from Western Theological Seminary and a doctor of literature degree from Liberty University. For twenty-five years he pastored one of the nation's outstanding churches in San Diego, which grew to three locations. It was during that time that he founded two accredited Christian high schools, a Christian school system of ten schools, and Christian Heritage College.

Dr. LaHaye has written over forty books that have been published in more than thirty languages. He has written books on a wide variety of subjects, such as family life, temperaments, and Bible prophecy. His current fiction works, the Left Behind series, written with Jerry B. Jenkins, continue to appear on the best-seller lists of the Christian Booksellers Association, *Publishers Weekly*, *Wall Street Journal*, *USA Today*, and the *New York Times*.

He is the father of four grown children and grandfather of nine. Snow skiing, waterskiing, motorcycling, golfing, vacationing with family, and jogging are among his leisure activities.

COMING SOON!

Look for the next two books in the Young Trib Force Series!

www.areUthirsty.com

well . . . are you?